The Year the Horses Came

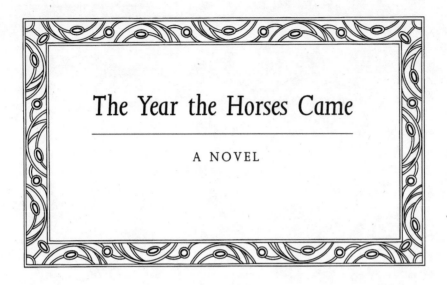

# The Year the Horses Came

A NOVEL

## Mary Mackey

HarperSanFrancisco
*A Division of* HarperCollins*Publishers*

FIRST EDITION

*Library of Congress Cataloging-in-Publication Data*
Mackey, Mary.
The year the horses came : a novel / Mary Mackey.
—1st ed.
p.  cm.
ISBN 0–06–250735–4
1. Women, Prehistoric—Europe—Fiction  I. Title.
PS3563.A3165Y43 1993          92–56119
813'.54—dc20                 CIP

93 94 95 96 97 ❖ HAD 10 9 8 7 6 5 4 3 2 1

This edition is printed on acid-free paper that meets the American National Standards Institute Z39.48 Standard.

For A.W.

Xori

Sea of
Gray Waves

Gurasoak

Lezentka

Caves of Nar

Itesh

Gira

*N*

Sea of Grass

River
of Smoke

Shambah

Shara

Sweetwater Sea

Blue Sea

## ACKNOWLEDGMENTS

As always, I owe a special debt of gratitude to novelist Sheldon Greene, who with his usual unfailing patience read every version of this novel in manuscript. His suggestions and criticisms were invaluable. Special thanks also to Angus Wright, Joan Marler, Janine Canan, Vicki Noble, and Martha Wood and to Keith Alger and Cristina Alves, who loaned me their computer while I was in Brazil.

I was originally inspired to write a novel about Old Europe after reading *The Language of the Goddess* and *The Civilization of the Goddess* by archaeologist Marija Gimbutas. These ground-breaking works turn back time and give substance to an entire world of goddess-worshiping people whose civilizations have been almost entirely ignored or misinterpreted. As I began my research, Professor Gimbutas was kind enough to meet with me and answer many questions. Although I subsequently consulted numerous sources on the European Neolithic, the encouragement she gave me and the information she so generously shared were priceless.

*A Note on the Ecology of Old Europe*

In the Fifth Millennium B.C., Europe was warmer and wetter than it is today. Human beings had only begun to clear the great forests that stretched from the Atlantic to the Black Sea, and even the hills of Greece were covered with broad-leafed evergreens. In some regions, Brittany, for example, sea level may have been as much as thirty-five feet lower than it is at present, which means that many of the places where Marrah and her people lived can no longer be found on our maps. Lions ranged over much of the continent until well into the early part of the Middle Ages, but horses, which had died out during the drastic changes in climate that followed the last glacial period, were unknown until they were reintroduced from southern Russia and eastern Ukraine at about the time this story begins.

# PROLOGUE

*Pieces of a Broken Vase*

There was a time out of memory when the Goddess Earth lay sleeping under a shining blanket of ice. In those times human beings fled south to find shelter from the wind, and many lands were hidden. One day the Goddess began to wake. Her glaciers melted, and bright streams of clear water ran everywhere. Flowers bloomed on slopes where no flowers had bloomed for countless generations, and the world was dizzy with the scent of the Great Spring. But human beings were frightened. They had grown used to their frozen world, and the melting was a terror in their hearts. "How shall we live now that the great beasts we have always hunted are disappearing?" they cried. Hearing their prayers, the Goddess Earth took pity on them and sent three of Her daughters to teach them new ways. To some, the Divine Sisters taught the art of fishing, to others the arts of weaving and pottery making, and to others the magic of taming animals and planting grain. So for over two hundred generations human children lived in peace and prosperity, praising the Goddess Earth and calling Her by many names.

A TEACHING STORY OF THE SHARATANI PEOPLE
BLACK SEA COAST, FIFTH MILLENNIUM, B.C.

1. Live together in love and harmony.
2. Cherish children.
3. Honor women.
4. Respect old people.
5. Remember that the earth and everything on it is part of the living body of your Divine Mother.
6. Enjoy yourselves, for your joy is pleasing to Her.

THE SIX COMMANDMENTS OF THE DIVINE SISTERS


Lift Her up!
Lift the Great Owl
who blesses us all.
Lift Her up
so the dead can rest
under Her wings.
Lift Her up!
Worship Her with your strength.

SONG FOR RAISING A GODDESS STONE
SUNG BY THE SHORE PEOPLE AT THE FEAST OF THE DEAD
BRITTANY, FIFTH MILLENNIUM B.C.

The Year the Horses Came

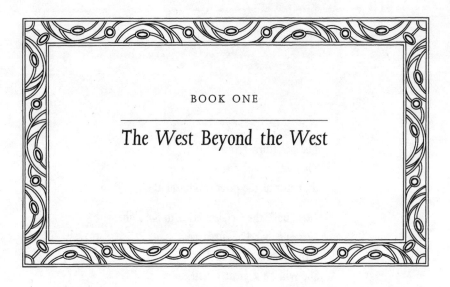

BOOK ONE

The West Beyond the West

The beastmen breathed fire.
They ate whole cities;
they turned the green womb of the world to ash.

"Rise up!" the Goddess cried to Sabalah.
"Rise up, for I've given you
a thrice-blessed child.
She will be a great priestess.
She will travel far.
She will heal her people
like a warm spring rain.
Her name is Marrah,
the Seagull of Shara,
Marrah of dark eyes
and wind-tossed hair.

"The beastmen are coming to steal your daughter.
Rise up and save her before it's too late."


FROM "SABALAH'S DREAM"
A MEMORY SONG: CITY OF SHARA
BLACK SEA COAST, FIFTH MILLENNIUM B.C.

# CHAPTER ONE

The Coast of Brittany: 4372 B.C.

On the day she was to become a woman, Marrah opened her eyes just as the first pale fingers of light were coming in through the smoke holes of her great-grandmother's longhouse. For a moment she experienced a sensation of swimming up from a great depth as if her soul were pursuing her body back to the waking world, but then she remembered what day it was, and suddenly she was wide awake.

She wondered anxiously if it was still raining. Yesterday, just before dark, a big storm had blown in from the north. All evening the rain had fallen in torrents and huge gray breakers had crashed against the beach, shaking the earth with such a deafening roar that people had to yell to make themselves heard. Amonah, Goddess of the Sea, had sent the white foam of Her hair blowing on the wind until you couldn't tell the water from the land, and there had been a scramble to pull the fishing boats up beyond the reach of the waves and fill them with stones before She claimed them as Her own.

Marrah held her breath and listened for the telltale sound of rain in the thatch. If the weather had not cleared overnight, her coming-of-age ceremony would have to be postponed for a whole month until the moon was full again. No doubt this would be just the lesson in patience that Great-Grandmother Ama was always suggesting she needed, but hardly the sort of thing a girl who was about to become a woman could be expected to look forward to. There were only two times in your life when everyone in the community got together to dance and feast in your honor. One was the day you became an adult and the other the day your bones were laid to rest with the bones of your ancestors. Given a choice, Marrah would have much rather had it rain on her funeral.

The thatch above her head seemed to be rustling softly. Was it rain or wind? Wind, she decided, and her heart leapt with joy. Wind, not rain at all! And no great breakers crashing against the shore either; only the gentle sound of the surf, so constant, so much a part of her life that she would have been lost without it. The Goddess Amonah had heard her prayer, all praise to Her!

She stretched, sat up cautiously, and looked around the sleeping compartment. To her right, her eight-year-old brother, Arang, was sleeping soundly, curled carefully around his straw bird mask. Arang was going to be a water rail in the bird dance the Society of Children was putting on this evening, and he had spent the past month standing on one foot, practicing his dips and bobs while his best friend, Kopeta, beat out the rhythms for him on a toy drum. He was a small child with soft dark hair, long eyelashes, and rosy cheeks, and he always looked sweet when he was asleep, but if she woke him up, he'd follow her and probably tease her and she wasn't in the mood for teasing this morning.

On the other side of Arang, Sabalah lay on a pile of sheepskins, her head resting on the shoulder of her partner, Mehe, who was snoring softly, his beard rising and falling with every breath. Marrah inspected Sabalah's face to make sure she was really asleep. It was a face very much like her own, and she had often thought with pride that anyone looking at the two of them would have known at once they were mother and daughter. There were lines around Sabalah's eyes and mouth, like tiny cracks in a fine glaze, but except for these marks of age, both she and Marrah had the same delicate features: long slender noses, high cheekbones, full lips, and heavy black hair, although Marrah's hair was more curly than her mother's. Instead of resting in a neat coil on the nape of her neck the way Sabalah's did, Marrah's hair hung down her back in a thick mane. She looked like someone who traveled quickly, a girl who "rode the back of the wind," as the Shore People put it: courageous, perhaps a little rash, but young yet and untested. There were hints in the firmness of her jaw and the directness of her gaze that in time, perhaps, she might settle down and become as powerful and respected a priestess as her mother, but at thirteen she was hungry for adventure and not too particular how she got it.

Reassured that no one else would wake up for some time yet, she rose to her feet and retrieved her dress from a wooden peg. The dress was the only piece of clothing she owned, a simple long-sleeved shift of soft deerskin that hung from her shoulders to mid calf. Later in the day she would wear a fine ceremonial skirt of imported linen that belonged to the temple, but leather was the stuff of everyday wear, sometimes embroidered with beads and shells but more often plain.

Barefoot, she tiptoed across the sleeping compartment and stepped out into the main part of the house. It was not the largest in the village, no more than seventy by twenty paces and home to only seven families, but it was comfortable and well built, timbered with oak, thickly thatched, and walled with tightly woven hazel rods packed with hardened clay. Roughly rectangular in shape, the long-house had doorways at either end, both closed at the moment by leather curtains battened down with wooden poles. When the wind blew hard, as it had last night, the curtain battens were reinforced with stones. Marrah checked and noted with relief that all the stones were still in place. All seven of the central hearths were blessedly un-occupied, without so much as a sign that anyone had gotten up yet to throw fresh wood on the fires. Not even baby Seshi was awake. Izirda must have already nursed him and gone back to sleep.

The coast was clear. Tiptoeing to the western door, she picked up the stones, laid them carefully to one side, pulled back the curtain, and stepped outside onto a broad path of finely crushed white shells. Zakur and Laino, two of the village dogs, rose to meet her, but since they had known her since they were puppies, they did so quietly. They were large and shaggy with a lot of wolf blood in their veins; if she had been a stranger they would have sounded an alarm that would have awakened everyone.

She stood for a moment, scratching the dogs behind their ears and looking at the sleeping village. There were few prettier sights in the world than Xori just before sunrise. Its six longhouses had been built in a bend in the shoreline, partially sheltered from the worst of the sea winds. They lay in two rows of three each, with a small temple at one end, a wooden platform at the other, and a large space in the middle for ceremonies and festivals. It was a rare month when a feast wasn't cooked in the big stone-lined fire pit, a rare week when the feet of dancers weren't stamping on the seashell pavement, a rare night when the drums and pipes weren't playing. Life in the village was religious and ceremonial. The Shore People praised the Goddess Earth by eating well, singing beautifully, enjoying themselves, and making love, and if Marrah had been told that people existed who worshiped their gods by suffering she would have found it unbelievable.

Behind the village lay the fields, surrounded by living fences of plaited thornbushes reinforced in places with mud and wattle. They were not large, for although the people of Xori ate grain, they lived for the most part on the bounty of the sea. Still, they worked their fields carefully, putting seaweed on the land to keep it fertile, and the land, although rather stony, rewarded them. Marrah could see the first green haze of new growth: the delicate sprouts of wheat and chick-peas and lentils and, behind them, apple trees in full blossom. Beyond the orchard were the corrals. The cows and goats were already up and about, ready to be milked and led to the tide flats to graze on salt grass, but the pigs were nowhere in sight. She wondered if the pigs were sleeping late this morning.

Behind the fields was the forest, looking blue and mysterious in the early morning light. Here the wilderness began, for although there were many settlements along the coast, the interior was mostly a dense mix of oak, pine, and hazel, crisscrossed by wild animal tracks and a few trails that led north to the place where stone for axes was quarried. There was something brooding and animal-like about the forest that always made Marrah feel there were great adventures to be had in it. The hunters of the village stalked and killed red deer there, but they never went too far from the sea. She had often thought that someday, when she was older, she would go right through the center and find out what lay on the other side.

A fine mist was streaming off the trees and freshly planted fields, making the earth seem smoky and insubstantial, but the day was unusually fresh and brightening without a cloud in the sky. She finished petting the dogs, put her hands on her hips, and smiled. She felt as if the world were hers, as if the village and all its people and the day itself had been given to her as a present. There was no sign of the storm. To her left, she could see small waves running gently up the white sand like polite guests coming to wish her good luck. It was an auspicious day, the perfect sort of day to become a woman.

At the far end of the settlement, the Goddess Stone was just catching the first watery-pink rays of the sun, but the small, round wooden temple at the base was still in the shadows, like a black egg at the feet of a giant owl. Twenty hands high and more or less wedge-shaped, the Goddess Stone had been hewn out of gray-white granite so long ago that no one living could remember the day She was raised. At the top, Her large round owl eyes looked in both directions. There was not a village of the Shore People that did not have a similar stone, and She was not big compared to the greater Goddesses who stood in rows at the City of the Dead in Hoza, but Marrah never saw Her without a feeling of kinship. Her name was Xori, like the village itself. Xori meant "bird," and since Marrah's name meant "seagull," she had always imagined that she and the Goddess Stone were linked by a special bond.

"Give me a good flight," she said, kissing the first two fingers of her right hand and throwing the kiss to the Goddess. That was the bargain she had struck last night when the rain was pouring down and it looked as if her ceremony might have to be postponed: if Xori would stop the rain, she would soar through the air like a seagull. She would thank the Goddess by jumping off one of the sea cliffs— not too high a cliff but one worthy of the jump. The jump would be a symbol of trust, a sign she knew the fair weather was a present, not something to be haggled over like trading beads.

"And please make the water deep," she added, throwing Xori another kiss, for although she knew perfectly well that the tides around the village could vary a great deal, she hadn't taken that into account last night. She quickly inspected the sea again and was relieved to see that she was in luck. The tide was coming in, but how high would it get? Half a dozen hands of water could make a real difference when you were jumping from five times your own height. Well, there was no time left to stand around figuring it out. If the water level was dangerously low, she'd have to ask the Goddess for a postponement. Otherwise, she'd take what came.

Commanding the dogs to stay behind, she ran down the beach. When she reached the overturned fishing boats, she skidded to a stop and looked at them longingly. The boats were dugout canoes, about fifteen hands long, their sides carved with scenes from the lives of Amonah and Xori. Marrah knew she could easily turn one over and drag it out into the surf, and even put up the mast and leather sail if the wind wasn't too strong, but although the idea of a swift ride down to the cliffs was tempting, she'd be in big trouble if her aunts and uncles discovered she'd taken a boat again without permission. She'd tried that on her thirteenth birthday, some five months ago, and for weeks afterward she had been forced to listen to tedious stories about children who had taken out boats, flipped over, and drowned. When she was a woman she could sail wherever she pleased, but even though her coming-of-age ceremony was going to take place this very morning, she was still a child. "I'll be back for you later," she promised the boats, and with one more longing glance, she broke into a run—and just in time too: she had hardly put the last of the dugouts behind her when she heard baby Seshi's hungry wail break the morning silence.

She rounded the point, and soon she was standing on one of the sea cliffs looking down at the sea, which was surging against the rocks like a great cauldron of boiling water. At the sight of the surf, her courage almost left her, but then she saw that the tide was nearly at full flood. Stripping off her dress, she threw it to the ground and stood naked in the wind wearing nothing but a small shell necklace. She was a slender girl, with strong arms and legs, tiny breasts, large hips, and a narrow waist, but she was as unconscious of her body as the bird she was named after. She had never been forced to compare herself to a single standard of perfection. Her people admired all forms and shapes and ages of women, believing that human beauty, like the beauty of flowers, was infinitely varied. This confidence that they were perfect was part of what gave girls like Marrah such grace and self-assurance. In the language of the Shore People, the word "ugly" only meant ill-tempered and selfish, and Marrah knew she was neither.

Carefully she counted the pulse of the waves, trying to get their rhythm as they struck the base of the cliff. It seemed as if the water might be getting deeper. If I don't do this now, she thought, I never will. She counted one last time to make sure she had the jump timed right, then closed her eyes, ran forward, and plunged off feet first.

The fall through the air was terrifying, but she had no time to think about it. She heard the sound of a wave slam against the rocks under her, and then she hit the water so hard that the breath went out of her body. Down and down she plunged through the cold salty sea toward the rocks, and then, just as she thought she would surely

be dashed against them, she stopped and her bare feet struck something hard, throwing her forward toward the base of the cliff. She had
a quick glimpse of a dark, jagged shadow rushing toward her. She
reached out instinctively to protect her face, touched something, and
her hand closed around it. Out of breath, she fought her way to the
surface and discovered she was clutching a piece of gray sea flint.
There were no land deposits of flint within a week's walk of Xori, only
bits like this that occasionally washed up from the sea. The sensible
thing to do would have been to drop it back into the water, but flint
was precious, and this was such a large piece that she kept it in her
hand as she struck out for the small sandy beach to the left of the cliff.

By the time she had pulled herself out of the waves, she was exhausted. Panting and shivering, she lay on her back looking up at the
sky, too cold and stunned to think. Gradually the sky grew brighter,
the sun rose over the forest, and the sand began to glitter. Warmed
by the sun's rays, she came back to her senses, sat up, and wrung the
salt water out of her hair. I did it! she thought. She picked up the
flint and examined it closely, pleased with what she saw. Once it had
been properly shaped, it would make a good knife or scraper. She
would give it to her mother. She decided the flint must be a gift
from Amonah. Perhaps it was even a sign that the rest of the day
would go well.

She got to her feet and climbed to the top of the cliffs with the
agility of a goat. Soon she was back at the village, which had become
a hive of activity in her absence. Small children were running off
into the woods and fields and returning with their arms full of roses,
bluebells, violets, yellow trefoil, marigolds, buttercups, and dozens
of other flowers that the older children were weaving into long gar-
lands destined to be hung around the Goddess Stone. Begi and Alaba,
Great-Grandmother Ama's oldest daughters, were digging a pit and
preparing to line it with hot rocks and seaweed so they could steam
two large baskets of mussels, shrimps, and crabs. Goats and pigs
were roasting on spits over the central fire pit, and the communal
oven near the temple was giving off the scent of baking honey cakes,
bread, and a special festival pudding made of acorn meal, dried cherries, dried apples, and goat's milk.

As Marrah made her way through the village, she saw that most
of her friends and neighbors were now awake. Some were standing
outside the doors of their longhouses pouring water over themselves
or scrubbing one another's backs with a harsh brown soap made out

of fat and ashes. Others were combing and braiding their hair or painting family signs on their faces, while others were putting on their best clothes. At the far end of the village the Young Men's Society was drumming and dancing in a frantic last-minute practice session, out of sight but not out of earshot of the Young Women's Society, which had gathered outside the temple to sing. The whole village seemed to be moving to the sound of the drums, and as Marrah stopped to listen, the first of the guests from two neighboring villages began to arrive, calling out greetings and running forward to give the kiss of peace to relatives they had not seen since the Swallow Moon Festival two months ago. Although the three villages were not far from one another, most people tended to stay close to home except for days like this when they would feast together, sing, and catch up on gossip.

Marrah stopped, overwhelmed by the sight. Even though she had seen other girls and boys come of age, she still had trouble believing that whole families had risen before dawn and traveled to Xori just to see her give her child necklace back to the sea. She touched the strand of shells that she had worn for as long as she could remember. Soon she would toss it back to the Goddess Amonah, who had made the shells in Her watery womb. All at once this seemed more exciting than any number of leaps off sea cliffs.

"Marrah," people called to her as she walked through the village, "come over here and touch our children to give them luck."

"Marrah, may Xori and Amonah bless you today."

"Marrah, may you walk with Their blessing."

Some of the men even called to her—"Marrah, we're waiting for you!"—which made her blush with embarrassment, which was ridiculous because she had known them all her life.

The greetings and good wishes went on, until by the time she arrived at her own house she was on the verge of tears. Love enveloped her at every step. Not once did anyone give the slightest sign that they knew she and her mother were adopted members of Great-Grandmother Ama's family. Not once was she made to feel that she had been born far away or that she looked different from the Shore People, who were heavier boned, broader chested, and somewhat lighter skinned than she was. In their eyes she was a beloved daughter of Xori as surely as if she had been born in the temple by the Goddess Stone.

Both doors to the longhouse were wide open. As she entered, she found the place in an uproar. All seven fires were lit now, with tasty things cooking in clay pots or being turned on spits, supervised by

Hatz and his sister, Lepa, who were acknowledged to be the best cooks in the family. Esku, Lepa's current lover, kept appearing and reappearing with great armfuls of wood. Zuriska, having run out of flour, was grinding wheat with a stone pestle, thumping it against the sides of the mortar, while a few steps away her Aunt Hanka was ladling fermented fruit juice from the big vat into small clay jugs. The only person who seemed calm was fourteen-year-old Izirda, who sat with Seshi at her breast and a dreamy look on her face. Having given birth only six weeks ago, Izirda was still excused from all labor, even cooking her own meals, which the others did for her.

Sabalah was seated by three large baskets of strawberries, sorting out the ones that looked overripe. As Marrah approached, she could see that her mother was already wearing the ceremonial earrings, blue stone necklace, and linen skirt she had brought all the way from the city of Shara. She had covered the skirt with a clean straw mat to keep it from getting stained.

"Good morning, Mama," Marrah said, not in the language of the Shore People but in the language of Shara, which Sabalah had taught her when she was a small child and which she insisted that her children speak when the three of them talked among themselves. Marrah lifted one bare foot and scratched the back of her leg with her big toe. It was a nervous gesture that, considering that she had disappeared on the morning of her own coming-of-age ceremony, was completely appropriate. Sabalah was going to be furious.

Sabalah started at the sound of Marrah's voice, but instead of demanding to know where she had been, she went on sorting strawberries. "Ah, here you are at last." She paused, inspected the berries she held in her hand, and threw them on the discard pile. "It's a good thing the rain stopped, or all the fine young men who've come so far to impress you would be dancing in the mud like a flock of wet ducks."

Marrah was surprised by Sabalah's reaction. She had expected to be scolded. She shifted her weight awkwardly from one foot to the other, at a loss for words. Then she remembered the flint. "I brought you a present," she said, handing her mother the lump of grayish white stone. "It's a big piece, even bigger than the one Arang found last fall."

Sabalah took the flint and weighed it in the palm of her hand. Although she appeared calm, she had been very worried when she woke to find Marrah gone. She knew it would be just like the girl to commit some dangerous act to mark her coming-of-age, and she had been tormenting herself with visions of Marrah wandering off in the forest and being torn apart by wolves or swimming out to sea and drowning. All foolish worries, of course, but Sabalah's one flaw was overprotectiveness. She loved her two children so much she couldn't imagine life without them, and whenever Marrah went off without telling her where she was going, she would be seized by a terrible fear that the beastmen had come for her and taken her away. What she was feeling as she looked at the flint was a sense of relief that made her almost ill, but she had no intention of letting Marrah know this, not today at any rate.

"Hmmm," she said, pretending to examine the flint, "not bad. You're right; it is bigger than the piece Arang found. In fact, it's been some time since anyone's come up with a flint this size. This must be your lucky day." She paused and looked Marrah straight in the eyes. "Where did you get it?"

"On the beach." Marrah turned slightly red and looked down as if she had suddenly discovered something interesting on the floor. Technically she was telling the truth, if you were willing to call land under water "the beach."

Sabalah was no fool. She inspected Marrah from head to toe and her eyes narrowed, but she held her tongue. She knew the flint could have only come from the base of the sea cliffs. Given the girl's damp hair, it was all too clear what she had been up to. As recently as yesterday she would have scolded her and then given her all manner of advice on the best way to live a long, happy, safe life—none of which would have included the option of a leap from the cliffs—but she had promised herself that as of today she was going to stop treating Marrah like a child. It was time she got used to the idea that her daughter was a woman.

She put the flint down and went on sorting strawberries. "How about a nice cup of fresh milk?" she asked, as if appearing soaking wet with a large sea flint in your hand were the most natural thing in the world. "Arang just finished the milking, and this morning, by some miracle, he didn't spill it on the way back from the corral." Marrah nodded, amazed that there were to be no questions. She sat down and waited while her mother dipped a cup of fresh goat's milk out of one of the communal jars and handed it to her. The milk was warm and she drank it quickly; she remembered suddenly that she'd had no breakfast. Sabalah watched her for a moment and then reached into the basket of strawberries, took out a handful, and offered them to her.

"May Amonah and Xori bless you on this day," she said.

"And bless the mother who bore me," Marrah said. It was a traditional response, but she meant it with all her heart. As she ate the berries, she was filled with love for Sabalah. The berries were perfectly ripe, firm in her hand, sweet in her mouth. She reached into the basket for more. Not a word had been said about her absence. Amazing, truly amazing. For the first time she began to feel what it might be like to be a woman, but she had no leisure to savor the sensation because almost immediately the first of the ceremonies to mark her coming-of-age began.

"Marrah! Marrah!" a chorus of shrill voices cried. "Come out!"

"That must be the Society of Children come to sing farewell to you," Sabalah said. Taking the empty cup from Marrah's hand, she kissed her on the forehead. "Go to them, and Her grace go with you."

Marrah hurried out of the longhouse to find the entire Society of Children gathered in a ragged semicircle like a flock of little birds about to take flight. They were a pretty, healthy bunch, so excited they could hardly stand still. The eldest was a girl just a little younger than Marrah, and the youngest a boy barely old enough to walk. Arang was with them, of course, looking terribly proud for it was his sister who was about to become a woman today, and he felt he was sharing in her glory. Garlanded with flowers, they all had the rosy complexions of children who had been scrubbed within an inch of their lives with cold water only minutes ago, and as Marrah looked at them, she could almost feel the scrub cloth on her own cheeks. Until today, she had always stood with them. Now, for the first time, she stood apart.

Goodbye, Marrah,

they sang.

Goodbye, goodbye.
Your childhood is over
and you are leaving us.
You are flying away
like the wild geese.
You are leaving
your old playmates
to become a woman.
Goodbye, goodbye.
We will miss you.

"And I am going to miss you," Arang said when the song was over. Running to Marrah, he threw his arms around her waist and gave her a hug. He stood for a moment, clinging to his sister, thinking of all the good times they'd had together: the trees they had climbed, the wild berries they had gorged on, the wonderful stories she had told about bears that talked and deer that danced like people. He couldn't think of a thing to be gained by having her turn into a woman. "I wish you could stay a child forever. I hate the idea of you growing up."

Marrah was touched. She hadn't known she would feel any regret about leaving her childhood behind. She hugged Arang and then lifted him off his feet and gave him a kiss. "Stay a child forever? No, thanks, little brother. I'm looking forward to being a woman." This was silly; if she kept on this way, she was going to cry. She put Arang back on his feet and chucked him under the chin in her most big-sisterly way. "Do you realize, my boy, that as of tomorrow I can eat my whole year's share of honey in one day if I want to?"

"And that's not all," nine-year-old Majina said, winking at the other children, who broke into helpless giggles, for now that Marrah was a woman she would be expected to go off in the woods tonight with some young man of her choosing, and the children who lived in close quarters with adults knew exactly what the two of them would be doing.

"It's going to be Bere," six-year-old Egin predicted, and the rest of the children took up the name as if it were a song. "Bere, Bere," they chanted. "Marrah is going to spend tonight with Bere." Bere was the son of Hostra, one of best hunters in the village. Like his mother, he was quiet and lean, moving like a shadow through the forest, able sometimes to catch rabbits with his bare hands. Also thirteen, he had his coming-of-age ceremony only six months ago. Now that he was a man, he and Marrah had to keep their distance from each other until she became a woman, a prohibition that had made Bere walk around the village with a miserable look on his face that everyone, including the children, found hilarious.

Marrah laughed at the knowing nudges they were exchanging. She knew she was going to be in for a lot of sexual teasing today, all good-humored but bound to grow increasingly explicit as the day wore on. Tradition required that girls becoming women and boys becoming men be welcomed into the adult community with all sorts of sly references to intercourse, as if they might not know what to do without prompting—which was ridiculous, of course, since every child knew how babies were started or, for that matter, prevented. "How do you know it's going to be Bere?" she yelled over the din.

"Because," one of the children taunted, "everyone in the village knows you've been playing sex games with him ever since you were old enough to walk. And everyone in the village knows you were sneaking out in the woods with him for over a year before he became a man."

Dissolving in helpless laughter, Marrah began to pelt them with strawberries, and they scattered in all directions. So much for privacy.

The rest of the morning was considerably more decorous. About five minutes after the children left, the chorus of the Young Women's Society appeared, bare-breasted and dressed in fringed leather skirts and shell waist belts. Crowning Marrah with flowers and kisses, they led her around the village and then escorted her to the temple, singing songs in praise of Amonah, Xori, and the Goddess Earth. Inside, Marrah was stripped and washed with holy water, her body anointed with oil, her hair curled and braided and plaited with feathers and flowers. Then Sabalah, Great-Grandmother Ama, and four other priestesses carefully painted her breasts with the sacred circles and triangles, dusted her nipples with powdered mica, colored her belly and hips black for fertility, and drew nine lines on her cheeks with red ocher to symbolize the nine months of gestation.

When they were finished, Sabalah knelt at Marrah's feet and spread out five shells containing various pigments. Starting at Marrah's left knee, Sabalah drew a snake that wound its way around her daughter's body in life-giving coils.

Although every house in the village had its lucky snake, the symbol was not traditional in Xori, and as Sabalah painted it she could not help thinking of the city of Shara and how different this day would have been if Marrah had been coming of age there. She remembered her mother, Lalah, and Uncle Bindar, and all the other relatives she had left behind, and for a moment tears blinded her and she could no longer see the tip of her brush. The snake wavered, and she had to rub part of it out and do it over again. Turning away, she hid her grief from Marrah. Marrah knew Shara only from stories. There was no reason for her to see her mother grieve, especially today of all days when her heart should be filled with rejoicing.

Marrah stood patiently, letting them adorn her. Closing her eyes, she felt her body changing under their hands. She was only human, but today they were making her into a goddess. By the time she stepped out of the temple, she would be a symbol of everything fertile and life-giving, and a symbol of death too, for the eternal cycle was never left incomplete. She yielded to the touch of the brushes and the soft sweep of their fingers applying the pigments. When she finally opened her eyes and looked down to see what they had done, her body seemed magic and unfamiliar, and she felt a strange mixture of pride, nervous excitement, and even a little fear that perhaps they had gone too far.

Great-Grandmother Ama stepped back, inspected Marrah from head to toe, and declared herself satisfied. Ama was over sixty, which made her the oldest and most respected woman in the village, and no ceremony, however trivial, began or ended without her approval. A large woman with heavy breasts and generous hips, she had a face like a full moon framed by clouds of white hair, but although her face was old, her eyes were bright and full of lusty mischief. Ama had had many lovers since the day she became a woman, but she still remembered what it felt like to be a girl about to come of age. "You'll do," she said to Marrah.

Relieved, Marrah smiled and lifted her leg to inspect the snake. She wanted to say something memorable, but she was overcome with shyness.

"Next," Ama declared, "we put on your clothes." Picking up a large, elaborately beaded leather bag, she untied the drawstrings, reached inside, and drew out a linen skirt and then a feathered cape that made Marrah gasp with wonder. The cape was the most beautiful thing she had ever seen, worked with the golden feathers of partridges and bordered with the bluish green sheen of capercaillies and dazzling blue-greens of kingfishers. It was a cape fit for the Bird Goddess Xori herself, as light as a breath, and as soon as Marrah saw it she knew that Sabalah must have woven it. No one could weave like her mother, who had been trained in the temples of Shara.

"Is that for me?" she cried.

Ama made a pretense of looking around. "I don't know. I don't see any other girls about to come of age in here, do you?" She peered into the shadows and chuckled. "No, I guess you're the only one, so we'll have to give it to you."

Grasping Sabalah's hand, Marrah drew her close and kissed her. "Thank you, Mother," she said, and again she wanted to say more, but she was so happy her voice failed her.

It took only a moment to gird the skirt around Marrah's waist and tie the feathered cape around her shoulders. When they were finished, the older women led her outside and escorted her through the cheering crowd over a path of rose petals to the wooden platform at the far end of the village. The walk seemed to take no time at all. Marrah was so excited she could hardly recognize the faces of people she had known her entire life, but somehow she managed to make it to the platform without stumbling.

"Good luck," her friends and relatives called to her. "May Xori protect you! May Amonah protect you! May you have children when you want them! Goodbye, little girl! Hello, new woman!"

With trembling hands, Marrah allowed herself to be lifted up on the platform by her Uncle Seme. Uncle Seme was her *aita*, which made him the most important man in her life. Roughly translated, *aita* meant "father," but it was not a biological relationship. The Shore People knew very well how children were conceived, having bred domestic animals for generations, but the fact that a particular man had supplied part of the means to start a child meant virtually nothing to them. True fatherhood was won by a lifelong commitment to nurturing and raising a child. When a baby was born the mother would ask a man—usually an uncle or a great-uncle—to be the *aita*. Sometimes, if she had a permanent partner, she might give him that honor. The duties of an *aita* were sacred and were taken very seriously indeed; a man was not thought to have really become a man until he had taken responsibility for a child.

Uncle Seme was Great-Grandmother Ama's youngest son, and Sabalah had chosen him a few months after she arrived in the village with baby Marrah in her arms. He was a fisherman, big and barrel-chested with a bushy beard and ropelike muscles, but she had been impressed with his even disposition and kindness. Now, although he was only in his early thirties, his face was as weathered as a piece of worn leather and he had a permanent squint from looking too long at the sun on the water, but despite his formidable appearance, he had a sentimental streak. As he helped Marrah up on the platform, his eyes filled with tears, although if anyone had asked him he couldn't have said exactly why. Partly it was pride, for who ever had a finer child? And partly it was nostalgia, because when the girl you had sworn to care for became a woman you knew that your own strength was waning.

"May She bless you," he whispered hoarsely to Marrah, and then he handed her over to Sabalah and Ama.

The actual ceremony took only a few minutes. Drawing a small double-headed jadeite ax out of her medicine bag, Ama cut the leather thong of Marrah's child necklace and handed it to her. Then Sabalah knelt before her and offered her a clay bowl of bitter herb tea sweetened with honey. The herbs were the same as those she would drink every month from now on, for although girls officially became women at thirteen they usually did not bear children until they were at least sixteen, although there were exceptions.

Marrah accepted the tea and drank deeply. When she lifted her head, Sabalah took the bowl from her hands, and together they broke it on a large, flat stone. The crowd cheered, and the drums and pipes began to play.

"Behold a new woman!" Ama cried to the people of Xori, and Marrah, daughter of Sabalah, was a child no more.

## CHAPTER TWO

M arrah walked toward the sea with her child necklace in her hands. Behind her came the drummers and flute players, the dancers and singers, the young men and women bearing baskets of white flowers, the crowds of friends and relations, and the children, tumbling over each other for a better view. There was nothing organized about this walk to the sea, nothing solemn, although coming-of-age was the most important moment in a girl's life. Like almost all religious events in Xori, this one was noisy and chaotic, a ragged procession of barking dogs, mothers with babies on their hips, old men dancing the dances of their youth, and young people laughing and talking.

As Marrah's bare feet touched the stones of the beach, the noise stopped and a sudden hush descended, for this was the moment when she was passing from the Bird Goddess's keeping into that of the Sea Goddess. The silence was so deep she could hear the sound of the waves striking the far side of the small rocky island that lay some distance offshore. It was not a loud sound, more like someone breathing and exhaling softly, but when she heard it she felt as if the Goddess Amonah Herself were calling to her. The island was only a large boulder of ragged white granite, but everyone in the village regarded

19

it as an especially lucky place. Gray seals sometimes came to sun themselves on its rocks, the best fish were caught in its waters, and precious bits of flint were often found washed up on its beaches. For these reasons, and perhaps others, the island was especially sacred to the Sea Goddess, and every girl who came of age went out to it alone to toss her child necklace back into the water and then sit a while praying and meditating. But first, Marrah thought, the birds must come and give me leave, for the birds are signs of the Goddess Xori's grace, and without them no one can prosper.

The silence lasted for a long time as everyone stood quietly, waiting for a sign. At last it came: the gruff kow-kow-kow of a seagull, Marrah's namesake, the best possible omen. Then, like an added benediction, a cormorant flew by. At the sight of its long bill and metallic-brown wings, a murmur of satisfaction rose from the crowd. Cormorants could use their wings underwater; what better sign could there be of harmony between Xori and Amonah?

The music and noise took up where they had left off. As the drummers called to each other and slapped out new rhythms, Great-Grandmother Ama's three youngest grandchildren came forward: Hatz, a round, comfortable-looking man in his early twenties who was one of the best cooks in the village, and the twins, Belaun and Hanka, who fished with Uncle Seme. The three of them carried Hanka and Belaun's boat, a sturdy dugout with an image of Amonah carved on the bow. The Goddess had the body of a fish and the face of a woman, and no sailor would have thought of setting out to sea without Her.

"Climb in," Hanka said as she handed Marrah one of the wooden paddles. "I think you know how to steer one of these things by now." At that everyone laughed, for when Marrah was only a child of five she had climbed into this very boat, paddled away from shore, and nearly drifted out of sight before Sabalah had spotted her and raised the alarm.

Marrah got into the dugout and made herself comfortable. As Hanka and Belaun pushed her into the water, the crowd pelted her with white flowers until she was floating on a sea of blossoms.

"Come back as quick as you can," the children called after her.

"Why? Will you miss me?"

The children laughed and threw more flowers. "Hurry," they insisted.

"It's the food," Hanka said. "They can't touch it until you get back."

"That's right," Arang yelled, "it's the pudding and the honey cakes. Can't you smell them, sister?"

Marrah could smell them; in fact the scent of the honey cakes was making her stomach rumble, but her newfound dignity required that she paddle slowly toward the island as if feasting were the last thing on her mind.

It was a short trip, but an exciting one. Almost all the excitement was in Marrah's mind. The sea was unusually calm, the sky clear, the water as blue as a necklace of callais, but with every stroke of her paddle she felt as if she was becoming more of a woman. Never again would her mother or Uncle Seme stand on shore and call her back. This was her sea, her boat, her sky, and she could go wherever she wished, even paddle over the rim of the horizon to the very edge of the world if she felt like it.

When she reached the island, she tied the dugout to a rock with a piece of woven cord, knotted her child necklace into a corner of her skirt so her hands would be free, and waded ashore. She looked around hoping to see some seals, but there were none in sight. Feeling mildly disappointed, she began to climb cautiously up the slippery rocks. On the seaward side there was a level area—not a beach, really, for sand had no chance of staying on the island during the winter storms, but more of a ledge that projected into the water. There, alone and facing the sea, she would say a prayer and throw her necklace to Amonah.

The climb was steep, and the narrow linen skirt was no help. Soon she stopped and tucked the hem into her belt. She was so preoccupied with placing her feet securely on the wet stones that she didn't bother to look at the view, which she had seen many times. After she had passed the roughest part of the seaward slope, she turned and saw something that brought her to a stop again. She shaded her eyes with her hand, looked down at the beach, and gave a low whistle of alarm. There seemed to be something—no, someone—lying on the rocks: a dead someone by the look of it, face down and surely drowned.

What kind of disaster was this? Breaking into a run, she stumbled the rest of the way down the slope. When she reached the body she stood over it, gasping for breath. The dead man—for the body was too large to be that of a woman—lay sprawled and limp among bits of seaweed and wreckage washed up by last night's storm. He was tall, perhaps the tallest man she had ever seen, and he was dressed in a hooded capelike garment made out of a strange material that looked like matted brown fur. The cape covered his entire body except for his hands, which were pale and waterlogged.

She stared at his hands in horrified fascination. On every finger he was wearing a ring of some sort, most carved from bone but two of copper. Copper was the yellow color of bones and death, sacred to the Bird Goddess in her most terrible form. In the land of the Shore People it was only worn for religious ceremonies. She shuddered. A dead man in copper rings lying on her beach! No girl's coming-of-age ever had a worse omen than this. It was as if the Goddess Xori were cursing her, as if She were saying, Throw Amonah your childhood, Marrah, and I'll throw a dead man back at you.

But that didn't make any sense. Why should Xori curse her for no reason? They were both bird women, she and the Goddess. Xori loved her like a mother. Only a little while ago She had sent a cormorant as a sign that She had given Marrah into Amonah's keeping. Xori would never turn against her unless she did something wicked, and she'd done nothing wicked, only paddled out to the island as all girls did on their coming-of-age days. Marrah clenched her fists, fought down her fear, and tried to think like Sabalah. "Marrah," she could hear her mother saying, "we aren't always the center of the world. Things happen that have nothing to do with us. You mustn't go around seeing omens everywhere. A priestess who tries to predict the future from every flight of birds does more harm than good. There are true voices and false ones."

She unclenched her fists and forced herself to confront the dead man for what he was: he'd simply drowned. She remembered the big storm last night, the howling wind. He must have been in a boat that had broken up on the rocks. With that in mind, she inspected the beach, but there was nothing to be seen but some gnats buzzing over a pile of seaweed and half a dozen long-legged avocets hunting

through the tide pools for brine shrimp. Still, that meant nothing. When the rocks ate boats, they often ate them whole.

She knelt down and touched the wet cape gingerly. It was clammy and sticky with salt. The next thing she had to do was turn him over and make sure he was really dead—not that she had any doubt; he must have been in the water a long time to have hands that pale. What if she found a familiar face? Well, there was no help for it. She couldn't just run away from him. Hadn't Great-Grandmother Ama just told the whole village she was a woman?

She mustered all her courage, grabbed the dead man's shoulder, and heaved him over on his back. As he turned, his hood fell back, exposing his face. With relief she saw he was no one she knew. But how strange he looked! He was old, so old that his hair and beard had turned a strange yellow-white, and yet there wasn't a line on his face. It was a thin face, lean and strong-jawed, with skin so pale she could see the veins in his eyelids. In his ears he wore more copper rings: five or six at least, plus two small gold ones. Around his throat hung a necklace of fierce-looking teeth from some animal she didn't recognize, a copper pendant shaped like the sun, and another shaped something like a deer, only more stocky, with thick legs and hair on its head and neck instead of horns.

Marrah sat back on her heels and stared. She had never in her life seen anyone, man or woman, so loaded down with ornaments. No wonder he hadn't been able to swim to safety. What was he doing with so many rings and necklaces? And look at his arms: seven or eight bracelets around each wrist, and a big belt all decorated with shells and copper studs. Why, there was even copper in the hilt of his knife, and what a knife! So long you'd have trouble using it for anything practical and tucked away at his side in a scabbard as if he never went anywhere without it.

With a silent apology to the dead man, who was clearly beyond caring, she reached over and pulled the knife from the scabbard. What a wicked-looking thing it was, made of bone with sharp flint blades set in either side. On the other side of his belt there was another scabbard—no, a quiver—full of arrows with sharp tips, feathered with the plumage of strange birds. She tested one of the slender shafts and found it was perfectly balanced. There was no one in her village who could make arrows like that, or a knife like that either.

She ran her finger cautiously along the edge of the knife, marveling at its sharpness. The old man must be a hunter, but if that was the case, why was he dressed like someone who had been conducting a religious ceremony? Was he a priest? There were men who served the Goddess—not many, because women were thought to hear Her voice most clearly, but sometimes men also heard Her and came to temples to be trained and afterward were admitted to the Society of Priestesses. But priests rarely carried knives unless they were going out in the forest to cut herbs, and what use would a priest have for arrows? And who would go hunting in a copper necklace? It was all very confusing.

She examined him more closely, trying to see something that would resolve the mystery, but everywhere she looked there was only more confusion. His tunic was made of the same strange matted brown fur as his cape, and even though it was late spring he had on leggings and thick boots. Pulling back the cape, she found that the tunic was fastened at his left shoulder with leather thongs. The leather looked tougher than deerskin but not so rough as pigskin, and there were tassels at one end made from coarse white and black and brown hair all woven together in an intricate pattern. The patches of bare skin that showed between the laces were painted with suns, more strange animals, and other symbols she had never seen before, including something that appeared to be a lightning bolt. How could all those designs have stayed on in the water? The sea should have washed him clean. She gritted her teeth, reached out and touched the lightning bolt, and discovered to her astonishment that it wasn't paint but some kind of blue stain that seemed to be part of his skin. The designs had apparently been cut into his flesh, but why would anyone do such a thing? It must have been terribly painful.

She stood up, looked down at him, and tried to figure out what she should do next. Poor thing. Drowned without a sister or brother to carry him to the Tower of Silence, gone back to the Mother with no kin to bid him goodbye. She decided she would have to take him back to the village, where he could be given a proper funeral. There, his body would be washed and blessed and anointed, and when the ceremony was over they would carry him to a tower bed deep in the forest so the birds could gather him back to the Mother. After the birds had stripped the flesh from his body, they would collect his bones, take them down to Hoza, and lay them in the Womb of Rest with the bones of the ancestors. The old man would not have to sleep alone. He would rest under protection of the owl-eyed goddesses until his soul was clean and ready to start over again in the body of a small bird, or a tree, or perhaps even the body of a human child.

She said a short prayer for him and then turned to more practical matters. Should she bring the boat around through the rough water on the seaward side of the island and try to haul the old man's body into it, or should she go back to the village for help? She was just weighing the advantages and disadvantages of trying to negotiate the currents when she saw something that made her drop to her knees, bend over, and scrutinize him intently. Had his eyelids flickered, or was it just her imagination?

She waited, but there was no further sign of life. Ah, well, that was what came of hoping too much. You saw things that weren't there. She was about to rise to her feet when she saw it again: a movement so quick and faint she would have missed it if she hadn't been staring directly at his face. He *was* alive! His left eyelid had fluttered, and even as she watched, it fluttered again!

Excited, she impulsively reached out and touched his eyelid, and as she did so, both eyes opened, startling her so much she sat back with a cry. The old man gazed blankly up at the sky for a few seconds, but there was no sign that he had seen her or anything else. Marrah felt relief, and then pity. He was alive but he was blind, poor thing. His eyes were two colorless blanks that looked like stones under sunlit water. Perhaps colorless wasn't quite the right word. They were blue, not the dark blue of the ocean but the very pale blue of an early morning sky. She had never seen such strange eyes. But what was she doing sitting here, wondering about the color of his eyes, when she should be getting the salt water out of him! Had she lost what little sense the Goddesses had given her?

She grabbed the stranger, turned him on his side, and pounded him on the back as hard as she could until he began to spit up seawater. Wiping his lips with the hem of her skirt, she pinched closed his nose and began to breathe into his mouth, watching his chest rise and fall. It wasn't pleasant, but Sabalah had trained her well and she wasn't squeamish. When she saw color coming back to his cheeks and felt his chest begin to rise and fall of its own accord, she stopped breathing into him and began to slap and chafe his wrists. Straddling him, she bent his arms and used them to pump more air into his lungs. If she'd had a flint and some dry wood, she would have made a fire to warm him, but she had nothing except a feathered cape and a thin linen skirt, so she concentrated on getting the water out of him.

By the time she was done, she was shaking and covered with sweat, but the old man, although still unconscious, was alive and breathing normally. She rose to her feet, walked unsteadily to the edge of the beach, knelt, and splashed cold seawater on her face. Then she sat down on the pebbles, put her hands over her face, and tried to understand what she had done. Everything had happened so fast. She felt drained and odd, as if she'd eaten something that didn't agree with her. Her stomach was upset, and every time she tried to take a breath it caught in her throat. Somewhere, not far away, a seagull barked and the waves went on slapping the shore. Bit by bit, the numbness passed and she began to understand that she had fought death and won, but instead of making her feel triumphant the knowledge sent her into a fit of tears. She'd been so scared, so sure she was going to lose him. Now what was she supposed to do, all by herself out here without any help? If this was what it meant to be a woman, she'd just as soon have stayed a girl.

After a while, she calmed down and her crying degenerated into a few self-pitying sniffles. As she wiped her eyes on her bare arms, she saw that all her beautiful paintings were now a big smear. She felt a moment of childlike regret for the snake Sabalah had painted on her leg, and then she came back to reality and the old man who was lying on the beach behind her: the old man who was her responsibility, whom she was going to have to get back to the village all by herself because it was clear she couldn't take the chance of leaving him on his own long enough to go for help.

She walked over to him and reassured herself that he was still breathing normally. He looked a little better now—clammy and pale but not dead. She didn't want to leave him in this condition, but she didn't have any choice. Someone had to go around to the other side of the island and get the dugout, and it certainly wasn't going to be him. She looked down at the remains of her finery and sighed. Her linen skirt was stained with green bits of seaweed, and the feathers of her beautiful cape were muddy and bedraggled. She must look like a big wet bird. She took off the cape, folded it carefully, and placed it under his head. It wasn't much, but perhaps it would make him more comfortable. Grabbing the soiled hem of her skirt, she tucked it into her belt and began the climb back to the other side of the island.

She found the dugout where she had left it, rocking peacefully in a back eddy. Before she untied it, she faced the shore and waved and called for help, even though she knew there was almost no chance anyone would hear her over the sound of the drums. In the village, smoke from the central fire pit was rising into the air in a calm, steady stream, and people—looking like ants from this distance— were gathered around it dancing or sitting in small groups gossiping or perhaps gambling with carved knucklebones, always a favorite pastime at festivals.

"Help!" Marrah yelled. "Look over here! Mama, Ama, Uncle Seme, help me! I need help!" Finally, exhausted and hoarse, she gave up trying to attract their attention. She untied the cord that held the boat and launched it angrily. She couldn't help feeling her relatives were to blame for not noticing her, but why should they? They weren't expecting her to come back for a long time.

She dug the blade of her paddle into the water and tried to recall how the currents ran around the island. The leeward route was longer, but if she went the short way round, she would risk being blown up against the rocks. There were always unpredictable gusts of wind this time of year, so leeward it was, like it or not.

At first the going was fairly easy and she made good time, but once she passed around the point, the currents were strong. Crouched in the bottom of the dugout, she paddled vigorously, dipping the blade into the water and pulling it back so hard the muscles in her arms knotted and she felt the breath burn in her chest. On the seaward side she had to fight not to get washed into the rocks, but she hung on and kept paddling. Finally, after what seemed like forever, she came in sight of the beach, and with ten more long hard strokes she was in, the dugout bottom grating against the ledge.

She leapt out of the boat and pulled it to safety. The old man was lying where she had left him, still breathing, but blue-lipped and much too cold. She put her arms around him and tried to lift him, but he was too heavy. She struggled, panted, and wrestled, but he hardly budged. Frustrated, she sat down and tried to figure out how to get him down to the boat. That wet cloak of his must weigh as much as a small dog, not to mention all the other things he had on. One thing was certain: he wasn't from any of the shore villages. No one born near the Sea of Gray Waves would climb into a boat wearing such an outfit. Given the way he was dressed, it was a miracle he hadn't drowned. She'd have to make him lighter.

She untied his belt, took off his knife and quiver, pulled off his boots, and untied his cape. Then, putting her arms under his, she wrestled him into an upright position and dragged him over the rocks toward the boat, apologizing silently every time she stopped to get her breath. Fortunately his heavy tunic and leggings kept him from being cut by the rocks, but by the time she got him to the edge of the water the strange material they were made of was torn.

Draping the upper part of his body over the edge of the boat, she put her head and hands against his butt and heaved him in unceremoniously. He fell to the bottom with a thump and a moan. She climbed in after him and turned him on his side in case he had to spit up any more seawater. The moan had been encouraging. It was the first sound he had made.

"I'm sorry about this," she said, after she had gone back for his things. She laid his wet cloak under his head and put the rest in the boat. "I don't normally go around throwing sick people around like baskets of fish, but you can see I don't have any choice. No, you can't see, can you. But maybe you can hear me. If you can, blink or move your hand, or do something to tell me you can hear." The old man didn't move. He only lay in the bottom of the boat, taking up most of the room.

She shoved him toward the bow, knelt down behind him, and began to paddle back around the island, talking to him as she went. She didn't care that he couldn't hear her. It was a comfort to talk to someone. "I'm taking you back to my village. Its name is Xori. Have you ever heard of it? It isn't very big, but we have a Goddess Stone and a good well and we're protected from the wind. The longhouses are warm. My brother, Arang, and I helped Aunt Zuriska rethatch our roof just last fall. You'll sleep in a dry bed tonight and have hot food. I don't cook much myself because I have a tendency to burn things. My *aita* says this is because I'm too impatient. My *aita*—that's Uncle Seme—cooks a limpet broth that would be just the thing for you. Only please don't die. If you die before I get you back, I'm going to be very, very upset."

He never said a word in return or gave any sign that he heard her, but he was still breathing as she rounded the island and headed for the mainland. As she drew closer to the beach, some of the children spotted her and began to wave. Soon the whole shore was lined with people dancing and singing songs of praise to Amonah. They couldn't see the cargo she carried. They only knew she was coming home quickly, with strong, firm strokes.

"Marrah has left her child necklace behind her," they sang. "She has given it to Amonah."

Her necklace! Blessed Goddess, she had forgotten to throw her child necklace into the sea! Marrah shipped her paddle and tugged the hem of her skirt out of her belt. There, knotted in one corner, was the strand of white shells that had been the whole point of this trip. Had any girl in the whole history of the Shore People ever forgotten to give her necklace to Amonah? She untied the knots with shaking hands, dumped the necklace into her lap, and sat for a moment looking at it, wondering what she should do. She certainly couldn't go back to the beach on the other side of the island. Not with a sick old man in the boat, likely to die any minute.

Impulsively, she picked up the necklace, whirled it over her head, and tossed it out of the boat. It flew in a white arc, struck the surface, and disappeared with a splash. "Sweet Goddess," she said, "take my childhood and bless me." It was a short prayer, many words shorter than the one she should have said, but she knew Amonah would understand. A human life always came first with the Goddess. Besides, if she wasn't a woman by now, she never would be.

She seized the paddle and began to pull furiously toward the shore. Her friends and relatives had no idea what a surprise she was bringing them.

# CHAPTER THREE

"**W**ho is he?"
"Where did you find him?"
"How did you get him in the boat all
by yourself?"

"Is he dead?"

Marrah looked from one face to another, not knowing which question to answer first. The whole village—men, women, children, babies, and dogs—were standing in a semicircle around the dugout, looking in amazement at the old man she had brought from the island. The dogs barked and the babies cried.

"Is this a sign from Amonah?"

"Did he drown?"

"Is he a sailor?"

"A priest?"

Marrah put up her hands, begging them to give her a chance to say something. "The old man's not dead," she cried. "I saved him by sitting on him and pushing the water out of him."

"When you save a man's life, he belongs to you," Belaun said. Belaun, nineteen and a man for some six years now, was the sort of person who liked to keep his fishing nets well mended and his relationships with others correct. "You'll have to take him in."

"Well, I don't want him," Marrah snapped. "I have no use for him at all. I'm sorry for him and I hope he lives, but I certainly don't want him in my sleeping compartment."

That brought a laugh from the crowd. Marrah glared at them and then glared at the stranger in the bottom of the boat. Having got the old man to shore, she was feeling considerably less charitable toward him. He clearly wasn't going to die, and meanwhile he was spoiling her coming-of-age day. That was probably the most selfish thought anyone had ever had, but she couldn't help it.

Sabalah saw the look in her eyes and sympathized. She had been thirteen once herself and knew how much this day meant. "Come now," she said, stepping forward, "they didn't mean to make fun of you, dear. They're just startled. We all are."

People were now nodding, sober-faced, ashamed of themselves for having laughed. Belaun came up to Marrah, bent forward, and touched the sand by her feet. It was a very formal gesture, a way of saying that the person performing it was swearing by Goddess Earth Herself.

"I'm sorry; I didn't mean to laugh at you, Marrah, daughter of Sabalah. I honor you. We all honor you for saving this stranger's life."

There was a murmur of assent from the crowd. Several more people made the same gesture. Now, instead of feeling teased, Marrah felt embarrassed. "I only did what I had to do," she protested. "I only did what any of you would have done."

"And that," Ama interrupted, "is just the point." She walked forward slowly, and people drew aside to let her pass. The sight of her gray hair brought instant silence. She turned and faced the crowd. "Listen to me, all of you. Sabalah has trained Marrah well. Marrah instinctively helps those who need help, and she's so modest she thinks her efforts are nothing special. This right action, this is what the Goddess Earth requires from us." She gestured at Marrah, whose face was red with embarrassment. "Today this girl not only became a woman, she performed the most sacred duty of a priestess. As you know, I don't usually give orders, but I'm giving one now: we aren't going to let this ruin Marrah's coming-of-age day. Instead we'll honor her twice as much as we would have honored her before. It's sad to see this stranger so near death, but Sabalah and I will take care of him. The rest of you must feast and sing and dance in honor of Marrah. Today she's not only a woman, she's a hero, and we'll give her a hero's celebration."

Softly and then with more force, the drummers began to pound out the rhythm of the song they had been playing when Marrah arrived. Someone joined in on the pipes.

"Sing," Ama commanded.

> Marrah has left her child necklace behind her.
> She has given it to Amonah.
> She has thrown her shells back to the womb of water
> where all shells are made.

Soon they were all singing. Arang and the other children came forward and scattered flower petals at Marrah's feet, making a path for her as she walked from the boat to the central fire pit.

> Welcome back, Marrah.
> Welcome back, dearest sister.

Ama took Marrah's hand. "Now go," she said, "and enjoy your day."

Marrah felt a bit dazed by this sudden turn of events. She stepped onto the carpet of petals and began to walk toward the center of the village. About halfway there, as the crowd sang to her and cheered her and threw more flowers at her feet, she felt an overpowering sense of relief and happiness. "Thank you," she whispered, partly to Ama, partly to her friends and relatives, but most of all to Amonah and Xori, who had given her such a strange and wonderful day.

When she was sure there would be no more interruptions in Marrah's coming-of-age, Ama ordered the sick man to be carried into her longhouse and settled on a pallet in front of one of the central hearths. Building a big fire in the stone pit, she and Sabalah began the task of stripping off his wet clothes so they could wrap him in sheepskins and put hot stones at his feet. Although they had no word for what was wrong with him, they had both seen people so cold that there was no way to warm them again, so they worked quickly and a little roughly, although not without sympathy.

The first thing to come off was his tunic, damp and stiff with salt. Ama grabbed it with both hands, pulled it over his head, and tossed it in a sodden heap on the floor. Bare-chested, the stranger now lay revealed as something quite different than what they had first taken him for.

"Why, he's not old!" Sabalah exclaimed.

Ama pinched a bit of the man's skin between her thumb and index finger. "You're right," she agreed. "We don't have an old man here; we have a bleached-out young one. You don't find skin like this on people over twenty." She stood back, put her hands on her hips, and clicked her tongue against her teeth to express surprise laced with disapproval. "But it's no wonder Marrah was confused. With all those wet clothes on and that old-man-colored hair, he was doing a passable imitation of an elder. How do you suppose his hair ever got that strange yellow color, Sabalah? It's the ugliest I've ever seen on a young man. If I had hair like that, I'd dye it with walnut juice."

"His hair doesn't look so bad to me." Sabalah bent over the stranger's leggings and began to pull at the wet leather laces, but the knots had shrunk tight. Picking up the end of one lace, she began to force it back through, hoping to loosen it. "The poor thing can't help that he was born looking strange. Now that we know he's not old, I'll try to think of his hair and beard as the color of sunlight."

"Heh." Ama snorted. "The color of dead bone is more like it. But the rest of him is in fine shape. Look at that chest." The stranger had a strong chest, broad muscular shoulders, a slender waist, and well-proportioned limbs, and there was not an ounce of fat on him. Although Ama preferred age and experience in men, she still appreciated the sight of a body in such excellent physical condition. For one thing, it meant she was less likely to have to conduct a funeral ceremony in the near future. With a body like that, a man could survive a lot, even a night on a cold beach. Now that she had a better look at him she could tell that he couldn't be more than eighteen at most—more likely somewhere around seventeen. Of course he was so unnaturally tall you couldn't help but feel he'd spent years growing, but his skin was definitely the skin of a young man.

"He may not be old," Sabalah said, "but he's blind." She slipped a fingernail into one of the knots and began working it back and forth until it gave. "At least that's what Marrah thinks. While you were out getting the firewood, she sent Arang back to tell us that the stranger had opened his eyes while she was working over him. It seems she got a good look at them. They were colorless, she said."

"Do tell." Ama frowned. "This gets stranger and stranger." She reached out and lifted the man's eyelid. A sightless blue eye stared up at them.

"What do you think?" Sabalah bent closer. "Is he blind or isn't he?"

Ama shrugged. "I have no idea. I've never seen anything like it. Maybe he's an albino. I suppose we won't know until he wakes up, if he ever does."

Sabalah nodded absently, preoccupied with her own thoughts. She wanted the stranger to live, of course, otherwise she wouldn't have been doing her best to warm him up, but she was worried about more than keeping him alive. The sight of him was bringing up disturbing feelings—half memories she couldn't quite put her finger on. She felt as if she'd seen tall men with yellow hair and beards before, but she couldn't remember where. And blue eyes— they too seemed familiar. Something told her that when he woke he was going to be able to see as well as anyone, but how did she know that? Where had the knowledge come from, and why did it make her so uncomfortable?

She suddenly had a horrible thought. Maybe he was one of the beastmen who were coming from the east to steal Marrah. But that didn't make sense. The Goddess Batal had given her a good look at the beastmen. It had been a terrible vision, the most terrible of her entire life, and even after fourteen years she hadn't forgotten a moment of it. The beastmen had traveled as fast as the wind, destroying everything in their path. They were monsters with six legs and two heads—one human and one a giant animal with wild eyes, foaming lips, and a short bristling mane. This man certainly didn't have six legs or two heads. He was just a strange-looking person who'd nearly drowned.

"What I don't understand is where he got all those scars."

"What?" Sabalah blinked and came back to the task at hand. "I'm sorry, I wasn't paying attention."

"Those scars," Ama repeated. "I was wondering what he'd done to get so many at his age, especially that one—which makes him look as if something tried to rip his guts out." She pointed to the ugly red scar that ran all the way across the upper part of the man's stomach. There were more scars on his chest and shoulders, not quite as bad, old and white with time, but still puckered at the edges as if the cuts had been deep. "Now the only thing I can think of that could scar a man like that would be a she bear defending her cubs, but if those scars had been made by a bear there would be several tracks where she raked him with her claws, not one long line like this one."

Sabalah looked at the scars, and suddenly a feeling of foreboding came over her. "I think he's been cut with a knife," she said.

Ama nodded. "My thoughts exactly. You remember that strange long knife he was carrying in his scabbard, the one with the sharp flint edges? Its blade would make just that kind of scar on a man. Now that's possible to imagine; I heard once of a woman who lived in a village near Hoza who slashed her lover with a hunting knife. They were fighting over something incredibly stupid—whether there was enough venison in the stew, I think—and she picked the knife up in a rage and went for him. He lived, but she was exiled. Her people cut off her left earlobe to show she was no longer human and cast her out of the village, and no one would take her in. And once, a very long time ago when I was a girl, a man actually killed another man on purpose when they were hunting together—put an arrow straight through his neck and claimed he thought he was a deer. Later he confessed to the dead man's clan mother, and she had him buried alive, which is the most horrible thing that has ever happened in my lifetime. But look at the scars on this stranger." Ama pointed again to the angry red lines.

"I can imagine someone attacking him once, but it looks as if he's been wounded dozens of times. These scars aren't all the same age. What kind of world does he come from where people use knives against each other this way? Do you know? You've come farther and seen more different kinds of people than anyone I've ever known. Does this sort of violence make any sense to you?"

Sabalah shook her head. "No, I've never heard of people who use knives against each other." Even as she spoke the words, she sensed they weren't true. She was lying to Ama. But how could she be lying? She had traveled all the way from Shara to Xori and never heard of people attacking each other with knives. There had been a few villages, far up the River of Smoke, where feuds had existed for generations, and people spat when they saw their enemies and sometimes even hit each other, but knives were another matter. You could kill someone with a knife. Murder was sacrilege against the Goddess Earth Herself. No sane person would even think of it.

The two of them worked in silence for a while, taking off the stranger's leather leggings, drying him, and wrapping him in sheepskins. Each was lost in her own thoughts.

"And another thing," Ama said, when they had the last of the well-wrapped hot stones tucked in at his feet and he seemed to be resting as comfortably as possible. "Those designs on his shoulder bother me. In the first place, they're cut into his skin, which seems like a terrible thing to do to a person; in the second place, they aren't like any marks I've ever seen before."

She pulled back the corner of the blanket, exposing one of the stranger's shoulders.

"These aren't the signs of the Goddess. There aren't any triangles, or circles of fertility, or snakes, or any of the other designs you'd expect to find on him if he were a priest. Look at this. What is it, a sun? And this one. Like Marrah said, it appears to be a lightning bolt, but why would he want to put a lightning bolt on his shoulder? And this strange animal. What do you make of it? It isn't a deer, that's certain, but what is it? Whatever it is, it must be important to him, because he had another one made out of copper hanging from his necklace. I suppose he might come from very, very far away, from somewhere so distant they don't know how to paint proper symbols on a man without hurting him, but frankly I don't like it. The whole thing makes my skin crawl."

"Mine too." Sabalah was getting more uncomfortable by the minute. Ama was right, there was something disturbing about the blue designs. That animal especially—the one with all the hair on the back of its neck—it wasn't ugly, but just the sight of it repelled her. Once again, she had the odd feeling she'd seen it before.

Ama replaced the blanket, tucking it in tightly around the man's shoulders. "If he lives," she announced, "I'm taking him to Hoza. We have to go there anyway to celebrate the raising of the new Goddess Stone; our young men are supposed to share the honor of lifting Her into place." She pressed her lips together and gave Sabalah a worried look. "I think the arrival of this stranger on our beach is something too important for the village council to deal with. Of course it's possible that he'll wake up and explain himself, but I suspect, when he opens his mouth, we aren't going to understand a word he says."

That night the young men of Xori and the surrounding villages danced for Marrah. They had braided heron feathers into their hair, put on leather loincloths, oiled their bodies, and painted gray herons on their backs so when they moved they seemed to be taking flight. Stamping their feet and moving their hips suggestively to the rhythm of the drums, they imitated the courtship of birds, singing to Marrah and asking her to honor them, for the man a woman took to bed on her coming-of-age night was considered blessed by the Goddess Earth Herself. The dance went on for a long time, growing faster and wilder until the ground itself seemed to be vibrating to the rhythm of the drums; the men stamped and leapt and whirled until they became a haze of half-naked bodies turning in an endless coil. It was a complicated dance, one that demanded endurance and skill, but there was a kind of innocence to it too, a wild tenderness. "I will use my strength to give you pleasure," the young men sang. "Come, Marrah, stretch out your hands to me; take me to your bed."

At the end, a few of the strongest dancers made spectacular leaps over the fire, turning in midair and coming down as lightly and gracefully as wildcats. Then, as quickly as they had started, the drums fell silent, and the young men stood waiting for Marrah to make her choice.

The full moon drifted slowly across the sky. Beneath it, the forest came alive. Shadows of limbs and trunks and leaves reached out to embrace one another; frogs called to their mates; a tawny owl, hunting through the darkness, sent out a trembling *eo-oo-oo*, and small animals scurried to safety. Beyond the forest, the sea stirred against the shore, leaving a long thin curl of foam, white as a necklace of shells.

Beneath an oak tree, pillowed on a bank of soft moss, two lovers lay under a warm cloak lined with rabbit fur. Around them the sounds of other lovers drifted up toward the moon like thin fingers of mist: whispers and laughter, the rustle of leaves, a soft moan of pleasure. The festival was over. Marrah was a woman now, enjoying a woman's happiness.

Bere drew Marrah to him and kissed her lips for a long time, so long that their breath was like a soft rush of wings swelling in the darkness. Naked and curled into each other, they thought of nothing but pleasure. Their lovemaking was so slow that the moon moved and the shadows shifted before they did anything more. Finally Marrah sighed and touched her breasts and, understanding, Bere moved slowly from her lips to her nipples, kissing them until they were hard and sweet, like cherries in his mouth. He was in love with her, and he wanted to kiss and possess her whole body, but he would only move as she indicated. Nothing would be done that she did not invite. This was the way of the Shore People, and their men were trained to it from an early age.

More time passed. At last Marrah touched Bere's cheek and he moved away from her breasts. Now it was his turn. Starting with his lips, Marrah kissed her way down his body until he was twisting in a fever of excitement. For a long time she held him there, on the edge of pleasure, making it last. Then, just when he thought he could bear it no longer, she drifted slowly back up his body, finishing with his lips. Again and again, this sequence was repeated. Sometimes, it was Bere who did the long, slow body kiss, burying his head between Marrah's legs until she arched her back and bit her lips; sometimes it was Marrah who led Bere to the place where time ceased to exist. Finally they came, each in turn, clutching each other tightly, digging their nails into each other's shoulders. They cried out and laughed and cried out again as the final eddies of pleasure swept them up.

Afterward, they lay in each other's arms, relaxed and happy, talking about nothing in particular. Finally they made various arrangements: they turned, rearranged arms that were about to go to sleep, tucked in the cloak to keep out the cold, exchanged one more kiss, and fell asleep, their lips barely touching.

Marrah's coming-of-age night was over. It had been an important event, but—as was customary—mostly symbolic. Tonight, for the first time, she and Bere had been two adults making love instead of two children playing in the bushes, but they had done nothing they hadn't done together many times before. The Shore People did not think of the loss of virginity as a single traumatic event; in fact, they did not even have a word for "virgin." You could call a young woman *ezhhaur*, which meant "she-who-has-not-borne-a-child," or even *bihotz*, which meant "happy-by-herself" (that is to say, without a partner), but there was no word for a woman who had not yet had full intercourse. The Shore People delighted in sex and were experts at exploring ingenious ways to please each other, but it was not uncommon for a woman to pass the years between thirteen and sixteen enjoying herself in ways that would not produce children. Indeed, the Shore People were such a mixture of abandoned licentiousness and abstinence that it was hard to say if they were one of the most permissive people on earth or one of the most restrained.

Bere slept well, without regrets. He had expected that this night would be no different than any other, for although Marrah could choose to try to start a child now that she was a woman, he had hardly expected her to do so. True, he had allowed himself to hope that she might tap the inside of his thigh to signal that she was willing to have him enter her—what man wouldn't hope such a thing?—but the tap had never come, and he was not really disappointed. She had often told him she wanted to wait until she was at least sixteen to become a mother, and despite the herbs she had drunk to prevent conception, there was no surer way than the one she had chosen, so he felt neither surprised nor rejected. He was honored that she had picked him to spend her coming-of-age night with. So many young men had danced for her, yet when the dance was over, she had risen to her feet and held out her hands to him.

Marrah turned in her sleep. Without waking, Bere curled around her body and cupped her bare breast in the palm of his hand. The two lovers slept without moving again until the light turned purple and the first white-winged gulls circled in the cool salt air above the Goddess Stone.

In Ama's longhouse, the stranger turned restlessly under the sheepskin blankets. He was dreaming: not the calm dreams of Marrah and Bere but confused, fevered dreams. Sometimes he dreamed he was in the dugout again, yelling to the traders that they were sailing too close to the rocks; in this dream the small sail would grow larger and larger until it became a tremendous brown wave. The wave would descend on them, roaring like an animal, and he would be thrown out of the boat, which would break into pieces. He would fight to keep his head above water, but the currents would suck him down and his lungs would fill and he would taste the fear of death. But mostly there was nothing in his dreams but fever and more fever and a burning feeling in his chest, and faces that came and went, women's faces mostly: his mother, long dead, and the brown faces of the savage women, and once the face of Jallate, Vlahan's first wife, who had died years ago when he was only a boy.

His lips moved but no sounds came out. He tried to pull in air, but it was liquid fire. Violent coughs shook his body. His lungs were filling with liquid; he was strangling. All night he coughed and burned and dreamed feverish dreams of fighting the sea.

"I think we may lose him," Sabalah told Marrah when she returned to the longhouse after her night with Bere. "His skin is as hot as a fire rock, and the worst of it is, he hasn't made a sound except that terrible coughing. He opens his eyes but we can't tell if he's conscious. As you said, he may be blind. But blind or not, he's not doing well."

Marrah, who had almost forgotten about the stranger, felt guilty that she had spent the night lying happily in Bere's arms while he suffered. "Poor old man," she murmured.

Sabalah remembered that of course Marrah didn't know. "Not old," she corrected, "young. About seventeen, Ama thinks, maybe younger. That's why he's lasted this long."

Marrah was surprised. She was about to ask how such a young man came to have white hair, when the stranger began to cough again: wet, racking sounds as if he were trying to spit up his lungs. "Come help me." Sabalah rushed over to the pallet by the fire where he lay shaking and drenched in sweat. "We can't stand here talking; we have to try to stop that cough and bring his fever down, or the only place we'll be taking him is back to the Mother."


For the next five days the three of them nursed the stranger, trying to pull him back from the edge of death. It was hard, exhausting work, made all the harder by the fact that they seemed to be failing, but they went on even when it seemed foolish to hope. Often people stopped by to sit outside Ama's longhouse for a while, chanting and praying as was customary when someone was very ill inside, and the news quickly spread that it would soon be time to build a new Tower of Silence in the forest.

But the women never gave up. First they tried to sweat the fever out of the sick man by wrapping him in a deerskin dipped in hot water, putting extra stones at his feet, bundling him in furs, and forcing oyster shells full of steaming willow-bark tea between his lips. When that didn't work, when he only began to rave and push them away, they tried alternating hot and cold. First they would bundle him in furs until he broke out in a sweat, and then, pulling off the blankets, they would douse him in cold well water. Sometimes this would appear to work; the fever would break, and he would stop shaking and rest for a few hours. But always, as the day darkened toward nightfall, his fever would rise with the moon, and by early morning he would be coughing and shaking again, speaking wildly in a strange language no one recognized. The only good thing that came out of all this was that they discovered that he was not blind. In his lucid moments, it was clear that he not only could see them but recognized that they were trying to help him, and sometimes he would submit to the shock of the cold water with such a desperate, hopeful look that they turned away to hide their own tears of frustration.

On the afternoon of the fourth day, Sabalah called Marrah outside the longhouse. "There's a plant that grows in boggy places. It has a small, tough root that's covered with little red hairs. The flowers are very small too, white and only open in the sunshine, so you may not see them, but you won't have any trouble spotting the leaves." She knelt, picked up a stick, and began to draw an outline of the plant in the dirt. "The leaves lie flat, like this, and they have more red hairs on them. The hairs curve inward, like this, and each one has a drop of liquid on it that looks like a drop of dew." She stood up and brushed off her hands. "Bring back as many as you can find—remembering, of course, to leave at least two so more will grow." She looked back at the door of the longhouse and shook her head. "Ama and I are going to make a special drink for him. Some of the ingredients are dangerous and I hate to use them, but I don't think we have any choice."

Marrah hurried into the forest and spent most of what remained of the day searching unsuccessfully for the plant. Although Sabalah had trained her to be a priestess and a healer from the day she could walk, she had always taken this training casually. It had been her birthright, something she was expected to do, and she had often been restless and impatient when her mother stopped to spin out an endless tale of the curative powers of some drab little flower or fistful of moss. Now, with a human life at stake, she wished she'd listened more closely. Frustrated, she went from one boggy place to another, finding only mud, pondweed, and water lilies. Finally, when it was almost too dark to see, she spotted three flat-leaved, scraggly plants

growing halfheartedly in the mud.

Only three! And she would have to leave two so the plant could continue to grow in that place. She knelt and picked one plant; the rule of two was hard to follow when someone was very sick, but breaking it would be a sin against the Goddess Earth. She held the plant in her hand and apologized to it for taking it from its home.

"Thank you for giving yourself to me," she said to the flat, dew-tipped leaves. If she had killed an animal, she would have thanked it too. Nothing was ever taken from the forest or the sea without honor and thanks. She stowed the plant carefully in her gathering basket and hurried back to the village, where she found Ama and Sabalah waiting for her.

Sabalah shook her head when she saw the single plant at the bottom of Marrah's basket. "It's not enough, but it will have to do." She took it inside and dropped it into a small pot of water that sat steaming on the coals. The pot had already been filled with other things: poppy syrup, barks, mosses, and seeds. When the tea was properly steeped, Ama removed the clay pot from the coals and began to cool it, dipping it first into warm water, then into cold, until the potion inside was lukewarm. The final ingredients were dirt and moldy bread pounded into a paste.

Arang, who had been tending the fire, wrinkled up his nose and turned away.

"You're going to make him drink that?" Marrah exclaimed. The mixture looked foul and smelled worse.

Ama nodded. "Yes, every drop if I can get it down him." She motioned to her youngest grandson, Belaun, who had watched the mixing of the medicine with fascination and disgust. "Do you think you can hold him still while we pry his mouth open?"

Belaun shook his head. "No, even though he's sick, he's too big and he'll probably fight. I know I would if you brought that stuff to me and I didn't know it was for my own good. It smells like poison, Grandmother."

"Never mind what it smells like," Ama snapped. "Go get some help."

A few minutes later, Belaun was back with Hiru and Urte, two strong young men who lived in the next longhouse. Ama looked at the two men and then at the stranger, who was sleeping fitfully on his pile of sheepskins with no suspicion of what was about to happen. "Good." She turned to Sabalah. "Why don't we let Marrah try to give it to him first? He might take it from a pretty girl—woman, I mean. Sorry, Marrah. I know you came of age a few days ago, but I really haven't had time to think about it." She poured a small amount of the potion into a clay bowl, handed it to Marrah, and then turned to Belaun, Hiru, and Urte. "You three stand behind him out of sight. If he spits this out, I want you to come up suddenly and hold him down before he knows what's going on. If he doesn't drink enough of it, he's going to die." She shook her head. "Of course he may die from it, but that's a chance we have to take, and may the Goddess forgive us all if he does."

Marrah picked up the bowl with a steady hand, but inside she was trembling. She had saved this man once, pushed the salt water out of his lungs and carried him to safety, but now, perhaps, she was going to poison him. She had never before felt what a terrible responsibility it was to be a healer. Kneeling beside the sick man, she touched him gently on the shoulder. He started and opened his eyes.

"Hello," she said. "Don't be afraid. I know you can't understand me, but I want to help you. You're a dear, ugly thing and we've all gotten very attached to you, but, you see, you aren't getting well and we have to do something."

"That's right," Sabalah whispered. "Talk to him."

Encouraged, Marrah continued. "I want you to drink something. It smells terrible and it probably tastes worse, but it will bring down your fever and stop your cough—that is, if we're lucky." She put her arm under the stranger's head and lifted him up a little so he could swallow. He was looking at her in the strangest way, as if he understood every word she was saying, although that was obviously impossible. She put down the bowl for a moment and touched his lips with her fingers.

"Open," she commanded. The stranger opened his lips. She lifted the bowl and quickly poured some of the potion into his mouth. The stranger gasped, screwed up his face, and made a terrible gagging sound. Then he yelled out a string of angry words and struck her arm, knocking the bowl out of her hand.

Although the words were in no known human language, there was little doubt what they meant. A few moments later Belaun, Hiru, and Urte were holding him down while Sabalah, Ama, and Marrah poured the rest of the medicine through his clenched teeth. He fought them as if he thought they were trying to kill him, which perhaps he did. It was lucky, they later agreed, that he was so weak. As it was, most of the medicine spilled down his chin, but he must have swallowed enough because after a while the poppy syrup took effect, and he stopped struggling.

"The man's like a wolf," Ama muttered as she wrapped Marrah's bruised wrist in crushed comfrey leaves and a clean leather bandage.

"Maybe he didn't know you were trying to save his life," Arang suggested. He had watched the whole scene with great interest, made himself useful by keeping the fire fed with dry wood, and kept quiet so the grown-ups wouldn't notice him and send him outside to play. What a tale this would be to tell the other children! The stranger had no more sense than a three-year-old, and he might even be danger-ous. Arang picked up the bowl and sniffed at the remains of the po-tion. Belaun was right; it stunk. "Maybe you scared him."

"It doesn't matter how frightened he was," Sabalah said. "There's no excuse for what he did. He didn't just knock the bowl away. He struck out at your sister as if he intended to hurt her."

"Lucky we took that knife away from him," Ama said as she tied up the ends of the bandage. "Suppose he had used it on Marrah?"

Marrah was shocked. "You don't mean you think he'd try to kill me just for giving him a cup of tea?"

Ama thought it over. "No, I suppose I don't. But he troubles me. He's not like our men. I'm not exactly sure how to describe the dif-ference, except to say he uses his strength irresponsibly."

Sabalah said nothing. She was thinking a terrible thought, one that she intended to share with no one: perhaps it's a mistake to save this stranger's life. Perhaps we should just let him die.


But the stranger did not die. That evening his fever broke and never returned. Thin and pale and still given to fits of violent coughing, he lay in front of the fire, staring at everyone with hollow, questioning eyes. At first he was so weak they had to tend him in shifts, washing and feeding him like a baby. Sometimes when Marrah or Sabalah knelt beside him to spoon shells full of warm broth between his lips, he would touch their hands gently as if trying to thank them. If one of the men was taking care of him—Esku or Belaun or especially Seme—the stranger's face would brighten, and he would try to talk to them in his incomprehensible language, making complicated ges-tures that no one understood.

Sometimes, however, he managed to communicate simple things. One morning, for example, he indicated to Belaun that he wanted to be taken outside. Sweeping the sick man up in his arms, Belaun car-ried him into the sunshine and placed him gently down on the shell path with his back resting against the longhouse.

"Poor man," Belaun said to Marrah. "He's as light as an armful of kindling." Marrah, who was busy weaving a basket, nodded absently and went back to her work. After a time, she became so absorbed in plaiting the reeds she forgot the stranger was sitting near her. When she finally looked up again, she saw that Zakur and Laino had am-bled over to sniff at him. Satisfied that he was no threat, the dogs had laid their woolly heads in the stranger's lap, and he was petting them and staring out to sea with such a lonely look in his eyes that Marrah would have traded her basket and whole morning's work for the ability to say one friendly word to him that he could understand.

He was not always so pleasant to have around. Although he now took the medicine they offered him without protest, he could be suddenly and unpredictably rude: pushing the women away abruptly when he had eaten his fill, throwing things carelessly to the floor, resisting them when they tried to wash him even if they warmed the water first. He was particularly rude to Ama, as if her gray hair made her hardly worth noticing—a serious mistake on his part, Marrah thought, since Ama could have turned him out to die in the forest with a word—but Ama was too busy running the family and the village to pay much attention to his lack of manners, and after a few minor incidents she simply ignored him.

As the days passed, Marrah was not sure if she liked the stranger or disliked him, and her ambivalence was shared by Arang, Sabalah, and everyone else who came in contact with him. For a while they all wavered back and forth, feeling sorry for him one minute and annoyed with him the next, until the afternoon he did something so outrageous it brought the wrath of the whole village down on him.

It happened about three weeks after he arrived. Once again he was sitting outside, looking at the sea. By this time he was walking, and he had made himself comfortable on a folded sheepskin, crossing his long legs and leaning back against the side of the longhouse. Marrah, several women including Lepa, and four men were standing a few paces away, talking about the Feast of the Dead scheduled to take place in Hoza.

"I hear the new Goddess Stone is going to be the biggest we've ever tried to raise," Gorriska was saying. He was a barrel-chested young man with reddish tints in his hair and hands as broad as ax blades. Ama had given him the honor of leading the group of lifters from Xori, which meant he was both proud and worried because, although it was a fine thing to sing the first lines of the work song, there was always a chance that the leader might sing off-key or get the rhythm wrong, and the workers might falter, and the Goddess Stone slip from Her ropes, fall, and shame them all.

"How many villages are going to send men to help lift Her?" Marrah asked.

"Twenty," Gorriska said, and he was just about to elaborate when he was interrupted by a bellow of anger and a wail of pain. Spinning around, Marrah saw nine-year-old Majina sobbing and running for safety as the stranger tried to box her on the ears a second time. For a moment everyone was too dumbfounded to do anything but stare in disbelief.

"He hit Majina," Gorriska gasped.

"My daughter!" Lepa screamed, running for Majina and taking her in her arms. "The savage slapped my daughter!" Burying her face in her mother's bosom, Majina cried hysterically. She was terrified. In her whole life no adult had ever struck her. She had been reprimanded, even yelled at, but the Shore People treasured their children as sacred gifts from the Goddess and would no more lift a hand against them than burn the temple and overturn the Goddess Stone.

Marrah knelt beside Majina. "Did you do anything? Did you hurt him in any way, dear? Try to stop crying long enough to tell us. It's not your fault, darling. When he's hurt, he's like a sick dog who bites without warning. Majina, please; calm down and tell us what happened."

"I only . . ." Majina wailed.

"Only what, dear?"

"Only pulled his beard a little, Aunt Marrah." She wiped her nose on the back of her hand and choked off a sob. "It's such a funny color and I just wanted to know it if felt like Uncle Seme's beard or if . . ." She began to cry again. "I suppose maybe I pulled it too hard, but I didn't mean to. I didn't mean to wake him up, but he jumped like he was startled and then he . . . he slapped me!" Breaking down, Majina went off into another round of tears.

"Slapped her, did he?" Lepa glared at the stranger. "Well, he's not going to slap her or any other child ever again, or I'll personally see to it that he's carried out in the woods and left for the wolves." It was an extravagant threat, one they'd never dream of carrying out, but everyone sympathized. Swooping Majina up in her arms, Lepa stormed over to the stranger, who was still sitting with his back against the longhouse looking puzzled. Lepa planted her hands on her hips and confronted him. She was a strong woman, a sailor who spent her days hauling in fish baskets, crab traps, and nets. In her late twenties and mother of two children, she ran her family with a tight hand. Like her mother and grandmother, she was slow to anger but fierce when roused.

"You did a bad thing." She stamped her feet and shook her finger at the stranger as if she were correcting a dog. "Bad, bad, bad! You must never hit a child." The stranger looked faintly amused.

"He doesn't understand," Marrah said.

"Then I'll make him understand," Lepa said grimly. "Come," she turned to the others. "Help me. Let's beat the ground around him with sticks to frighten him and let him know how angry we are." In a moment everyone had some kind of stick: lengths of firewood, hoes, poles, ax handles. Surrounding the stranger in a noisy semicircle, they lifted the sticks over their heads and brought them down on the path with a thump that raised clouds of dust.

"Bad!" Lepa yelled. "Bad man." She pantomimed hitting Majina and pantomimed Majina crying. "You must never hit a child again, never, never, never!"

The stranger struggled to his feet and then shrank back, clearly alarmed by the circle of angry villagers. Too weak to escape, he was forced to stand in one place as the sticks crashed down around him, barely missing him. "That's enough." Lepa lifted her hand and signaled for them to stop. "I think he understands now."

"I don't think we should leave it at this," Marrah protested. "Even if he does understand, we have to teach him that it's not good enough not to hit children; you must also love them."

"Yes," everyone agreed. "We have to teach him love."

Lepa drew Majina to her and embraced her warmly. "You see," she told the stranger, "you see how we love our children." She passed Majina to Marrah, who hugged the child, stroked her hair, and passed her on to the next person. One by one, the villagers hugged the little girl, calling out to the stranger to witness their affection for her. As the child passed from one set of loving arms to another, the expression on his face changed from fear, to puzzlement, to understanding, and then something close to shame.

"*Bnoah doni,*" he said softly.

Lepa put her face close to his. "Does that mean you're sorry?" she asked. "Does that mean you understand?"

"*De,*" the stranger whispered, stretching out his arms to Majina.

"I think he wants to hug her too," Marrah suggested.

Lepa looked at the stranger uncertainly. "I don't know if I like the idea. What if he slaps her again?"

"If he does, we'll do more than beat the ground around him," Gorriska promised.

Lepa turned to her daughter. "Majina, if you want to let this strange man hug you, you may, but if you're afraid to go to him, we'll all understand."

Majina looked at the stranger, who still stood with his arms outstretched. "I'm not sure." She frowned. "I feel sorry for him, but that slap hurt." She folded her small arms across her chest and stood with her feet apart just like her mother. "Arang told me baby Erori knows more about people than this man does, and now I think Arang's right. Still, I do feel sorry for him." She unfolded her arms, walked up to the stranger, and stood for a moment, just out of reach. "Be good," she commanded, and then she stepped forward, threw her arms around him, and hugged him. A look of surprise crossed his face. Bending down, he folded the child in his arms and stood for a moment, holding her, his face buried in her hair. When he finally released Majina, they saw tears in his eyes.

"He's human, after all," Gorriska said.

"And he *is* sorry," Marrah said.

It was Majina who had the last word. Kissing the stranger lightly on the forehead, she walked back to her mother. "He's not so bad," she said.

But when Ama heard of the incident, she was not so sure. The stranger might regret slapping Majina, but there was no way to tell what he would do next. Summoning Egura, the village carpenter, she told her to put together some sort of litter so they could carry him to Hoza, since he was obviously still too weak to walk. Perhaps the Mother-of-All-Families would know what to do with him. Mother Asha was an old woman, well over ninety, and she had seen many strange things in her time.

Sabalah was even less optimistic. Although the stranger seemed gentler now, she couldn't shake the feeling of foreboding that came over her as she watched him gaining back his strength. When she sat down next to him to eat from the communal pot, the food stuck in her throat.

"Don't speak the language of Shara where he can hear you," she cautioned Marrah and Arang.

"Why not?" Arang was surprised to hear his mother speak with such suspicion of a man who was obviously too weakened by his illness to do anyone much harm. Ever since the incident with Majina, the stranger had been making a real effort to be friendly to the children of the village, and Arang was beginning to like him a lot. He was fascinated by his gold earrings and long knife and the idea that he had come from somewhere no one had ever been before, not even Sabalah. Only yesterday the stranger had spent the whole morning

carving a toy animal modeled after the one that hung from his necklace. When he had finished, he had picked up the animal and pranced
it around on the floor, snorting and making high-pitched cries. Then
he had laughed, tossed the toy to Arang, and said something that
Arang would have given anything to understand.

Instead of answering Arang's question, Sabalah merely repeated
that he and Marrah were only to speak the language of Shara in the
privacy of their own sleeping compartment. "I have a feeling that if
he heard us talking, it could bring bad luck," she said. It was a feeble
explanation, but all she had to go on was an ache in the pit of her
stomach and the uncomfortable sensation that something was going
wrong. Whatever it is, it's coming this way and I'm powerless to stop
it, she thought, as she lay awake at night listening to the wind in the
thatch. But perhaps I'm mistaken; perhaps it's nothing; perhaps this
feeling will pass.

But instead of passing, the feeling grew worse. Gradually, Sabalah
felt the world around her grow more menacing. Things that had for-
merly given her pleasure were no comfort, and although she could
see that the sun was shining and her children were in good health
and all was well, she couldn't feel the joy such sights should have
brought her. A few days before they were supposed to leave for
Hoza, she asked her partner, Mehe, to move back to his mother's
longhouse for a while. Mehe was Arang's *aita*, a large man with a
bushy beard as dark as winter honey. He was sharp-eyed, intelligent,
and kind and had a fine sense of humor, but although he had been
her partner for three years and she loved him, her heart was no
longer in their lovemaking.

The morning after he left, Ama appeared with a bowl of tea containing powdered barberry bark, ground flaxseed, and dried mint.
"Drink this," she ordered sternly.

Sabalah drank, but the problem was not her stomach. By now she
was convinced that as long as the stranger sat by her fire no purge,
however strong, could restore her peace of mind. Soon, she thought,
we'll take him to Hoza, and perhaps Mother Asha will let us give him
to another village. But she knew this was unlikely.

Then, on the morning of the day before they were to leave, when
the litter was already prepared and the bones of the dead lovingly
collected, something happened that flung Sabalah out of her black
mood. She was working barefoot in a field of wheat, digging out the
weeds with a wooden hoe. The hoe was merely a long stick, notched

at one end so that each stubborn shoot could be grubbed out of the rocky soil quickly, but it was so well balanced that the shaft seemed to move back and forth in her hands with almost no effort. Sabalah loved working the soil; it was peaceful to stand in the fields and see the ocean on one hand and the forest on the other, to hear the bleat of the goats, the drumming of the surf, the distant laughter of children. The smell of fresh earth was soothing, and often, if she was lucky, she would see something particularly beautiful: a small butterfly with delicate purple-blue wings or, if she was very lucky, the bright black eyes and flat gray head of a grass snake.

Yet on this particular morning, the work was giving her no joy. She labored thoughtlessly, bending and reaching, bending and reaching, her mind lost in a bank of fog. She was so absorbed in her own misery that several times she dug up wheat instead of weeds and had to stoop down and replant the shoots as best she could. At one of these moments, just as she was taking a step forward to survey the damage she had done, she felt something sharp and painful enter the sole of her left foot. With a yelp of pain, she dropped her hoe, sat down on the ground, turned her foot over, and discovered that she had stepped on a long sharp thorn. She gritted her teeth and tugged at it, but it wouldn't come out. Curses and double curses! she thought. She dug her nails into the surrounding flesh, pulled harder, and the spine came out.

She sat for a moment examining the thorn, wondering what kind of plant it came from. She had never seen one like it. It was about two inches long, dark brown, slender as a needle at one end and broad at the place it had broken off from a bush or tree. There was a sheen to it, as if the thorn had been smoothed by something, and it occurred to her that perhaps it had come from far away, floating on the currents. If that were true, it must have been tossed up on land a long time ago, because she had never heard of a storm wild enough to run waves all the way up to the fields, but she had seen shells everywhere, even in the forest, so it was possible that the thorn had come to Xori by way of the sea.

As she had this thought, a realization suddenly came over her: this thorn was the disaster she had been fearing! She scrambled to her feet and tried to walk and found, sure enough, that a small bit of the thorn was still in her foot. The splinter wasn't terribly painful, but it made her limp. She felt so relieved she had to sit down again. This was it, then, only this and nothing more: she had sickened at the sight of the stranger, feared a catastrophe of the worst sort, but in the end it had only come down to a thorn. Like the stranger, the thorn had come from the sea, but it was the thorn, not the stranger, that brought sudden unexpected pain. The warning had been clear and simple, but she had misinterpreted it. Her life wasn't going to fall apart after all. She was only in for a few days of inconvenience while the puncture healed—perhaps a week at most.

As she limped back to the village to clean the wound and spread the sore with a salve made of lavender and black currant leaves, she rejoiced every step of the way. That evening she went over to Mehe's mother's longhouse and asked him to come back and share her bed again, and as she sat by the fire with Mehe on one side of her and Arang and Marrah on the other, she found herself smiling at the stranger, who no longer seemed dangerous.

"I won't be able to walk to Hoza," she called out to Ama, who was busy packing the last of the supplies. "I've hurt my foot, and it takes a good four days to get there and four more to get back."

"Are you badly hurt?" Ama straightened up from the packs and looked at Sabalah with concern.

"No"—Sabalah smiled—"not badly at all. In fact you might say I'm hurt in a good way." This of course made no sense to anyone but Sabalah, who laughed as she said it from sheer relief, but seeing she was in a good mood again, Ama, Marrah, and Arang laughed with her, and for the first time in weeks the whole family was happy.

# CHAPTER FOUR

Every three years the Feast of the Dead brought all the villages of the Shore People together in a great communal celebration. From all up and down the coast, representatives of the village funeral societies traveled to Hoza, bringing the bones of those who had died since the last feast. The bones, which had been picked clean by the birds, were carried in embroidered leather bags, and when each new village arrived they lifted the bags over their heads and sang out the names of the dead and their exploits.

> In this bag we carry Osaba,
> son of Tasa,
> a great trader
> who braved many storms

one village would sing, and another would reply:

> In this bag we carry Bilera,
> daughter of Goiza.
> She was a good hunter
> who brought us many deer.

*Men went crazy for her*
*and slept outside her door*
*but she was very picky.*

The songs of the funeral societies were raucous, sometimes obscene, often funny, for the Owl Goddess who governed death also governed life and regeneration, and how could you be expected to put on a long face and mourn when those you had loved were being taken back to the Mother to be reborn? Bones were only the cast-off shells of the dead. Their souls were safe in the care of the Goddess Earth, so it was best to celebrate, laugh, get drunk on fermented honey and fruit wine, and tell stories of how good (and bad) these same white bones had been when they walked the earth covered in flesh.

The result was a party that went on for three days. A new Goddess Stone was always raised, and there was nonstop feasting and singing that ended with a dance around a tall wooden pole erected in the central plaza. If a woman was having trouble getting pregnant, she might anoint one of the Goddess Stones with honey and oil and rub her naked body against it for luck, or, more to the point, she might invite some young man from another village to go off into the woods with her. Love was easy to come by at Hoza, and there were always many babies born the following spring.

The last time a Goddess Stone was raised, Marrah had been too young to attend the ceremony. Now she was a woman, but so new a woman that she was awed by the spectacle. Sabalah had entrusted the stranger to her care, but as she stood beside his litter on the first morning of the feast, she all but forgot he was there. All she could think about was the new Goddess Stone. She was a huge thing almost three times as tall as a grown man, and one false move could send Her crashing down. Perhaps that would happen and perhaps it wouldn't, but only the Stone Herself knew if She wanted to live upright among the other Goddesses of Hoza, and She seemed indecisive, tilting first one way and then the other, as if She might decide at any minute to fall and crush the men who were trying to lift Her.

If She toppled, it would be a disaster. It had taken nearly three years to get Her ready for this day. First She had to be delivered from the earth like a baby from its mother's womb. Crews of young men had spent months quarrying Her and shaping Her, using only fire, water, and stone mauls. They had drawn the shape of Her great body on the granite in charcoal, laid twigs soaked in animal fat along the lines, set them on fire, and doused them with cold water so the stone would split. They had pounded Her loose, loaded Her on a sledge of square-cut timbers, lashed Her down with vegetable-fiber ropes, and dragged Her to Hoza on a series of oak rollers carved from tree trunks. It had taken a thousand men to move Her and twenty more to carry the rollers from back to front, but what did it matter how much time and sweat and pain it cost? She was their Goddess, their mother, their darling, and they had sung and prayed as they tugged Her up hills and lowered Her down toward the sea.

When they got Her to Hoza, the young men had chipped Her bottom to a blunt point, strewed her with flowers, and left Her to get acquainted with the other Goddesses. For almost two years She rested, waiting for the next Feast of the Dead. Then, about a month ago, more young men had arrived to dig a deep rectangular pit for Her to stand in. The pit had three straight sides and one that sloped. When they finished, the men slowly maneuvered Her down the slide into the hole, raised Her head with wooden levers, and put logs under Her. The logs were called "the Goddess's pillows," and what pillows they were, growing steadily, log by log, until She almost stood upright.

Once again they left Her to rest, and once again they waited. Today they had returned to lift Her to Her feet and pull Her toward the sky, to love Her and sing to Her and beg Her to stand alone and bless them, but no Goddess was easy to persuade and no lifting was a success until it was over. As Marrah stood watching the young men strain and sweat and sing, the suspense was so unbearable she sometimes forgot to breathe. Most of the time, though, she cheered and clapped her hands like a child at a party. Once she made a belated attempt to be dignified, but before she realized it, she was standing on tiptoe again, bobbing up and down to get a better view as she called out words of encouragement along with everyone else.

It was no wonder she yelled herself nearly hoarse. Who wouldn't be excited? This was not only her first feast, it was the first year her own village had been entrusted to lead the lifting. She had friends out there pulling on the ropes—cousins and uncles and neighbors—and no matter how loud she cheered, she could always hear Gorriska's voice booming out above the roar as he urged them and the other men on.

> Lift the Great Owl
> who blesses us all;
> lift Her up,

Gorriska sang. Inspired by his voice, the young men pulled harder on the ropes, straining with all their might. All night they had chanted and danced themselves into a hypnotic state until their separate minds and wills had become one. Now as they tugged the stone skyward, lifting their beloved to Her resting place, their hearts rose with Her. On the far side of the stone other men strained on ropes attached to long levers, while still others piled more tree trunks under the Goddess until Her pillow became a tower. In a moment, the crucial point would be reached: She would rise and stand unsupported, perhaps forever, perhaps only for an instant.

Suddenly the stone wavered and turned slightly in the mouth of the foundation hole, bringing a gasp from the crowd. May She not fall, Marrah prayed, clutching for Ama's hand. This was too much; she couldn't bear it. She looked away, jammed her fingers in her ears so she wouldn't hear the stone crash to the ground, and tried to think of other things.

There behind her, dominating Hoza, was the Womb of Rest, which she had seen for the first time yesterday after years of hearing about it. Placed on the summit of a small hill covered with purple and gold heather, the Womb was a large circular mound of stone with eleven passages cut in the southeast side, aligned so they would catch the light of the rising moon. The doors of the passages were open and ready to receive the bones of the dead, and ceremonial fires were already smoking in front of them, sending the sweet smell of pine and herbs into the clear summer air.

There were no other buildings because Hoza wasn't a city in the ordinary sense; it was a ceremonial center built on a windswept bit of shoreline where nothing grew except heather and stunted bushes. The only houses were temporary shelters warmed by campfires that would be doused with seawater at the end of the festival. But long after the crowds had returned to their villages, everything in sight would vibrate with spiritual energy. The energy would come not only from the Womb of Rest but from the long rows of Goddess Stones that marched down toward the sea, some only a few feet high, some giants. Each column was a sacred owl who would look after the dead when Marrah and the others were gone, but none was as tall as the new Goddess they were raising today.

She took her fingers out of her ears and heard Ama catch her breath and mutter something in a low, anxious voice. Not a good sign. Still convinced that the new stone was about to fall and break into a hundred pieces, she began to distract herself by counting the old ones: ten, twenty . . . nearly seventy Goddesses in all.

Suddenly there was a deafening cheer from the crowd. Unable to resist any longer, Marrah looked back toward the plaza and saw the new Goddess tilt dangerously to the left and then slip quickly into place. Leaping out of the way, the young men quickly secured their ropes to dozens of wooden pegs that had been pounded deep into the stony soil, fanning the lines out so the column was held upright like the center post of a tent.

"Praise to you!" the crowd yelled. "Well done!"

The lifters fell back sweating and exhausted. Some turned and smiled at the crowd in a dazed way as if they had just noticed the thousands of anxious faces surrounding them. They reached for jugs of water, drank deeply, and poured the rest over their heads and shoulders, tossing it off like seals. Although the lifting had been a success, their job was not over yet. Rocks and earth still had to be piled at the base of the Goddess to brace Her, but the most dangerous moment had passed. She had not fallen, and unless Amonah herself sent a great wind to break the ropes, She would stand for many generations.

There was a saying among the Shore People that the two most dangerous things to leave unattended were fire and the strength of young men. Both were precious, but both had to be put to good use and well cared for or they might explode and cause great destruction.

"You have worshiped Her with your strength," the crowd called to the lifters. "We love you; we honor you; only you could have done this!"

The young men smiled, feeling proud and satisfied. A new Goddess had been raised to guard the dead, all the villages of the Shore People had been united again, and for another three years there would be peace.

Marrah found herself crying with joy and relief. The stranger who had sat beside her all morning noticed her tears and was puzzled. He had watched the whole ceremony without understanding a bit of it. What makes these savages work so hard? he wondered. What do they get out of it?

Mother Asha, the Mother-of-All-Families, had also watched the young men raise the new Goddess Stone. She had sat on a wooden platform on a comfortable pile of sheepskins, shaded from the summer sun by a tightly woven straw canopy. Around her stood half a dozen village mothers, ready to bring her a drink of cool water or fan her or do anything else she asked, even though most of them were grandmothers many times over. Even so, Mother Asha thought, none of them is as old as I am. I've already outlived my youngest child and the grayest head of my council by more than twenty years, and, who knows, I may live twenty more.

At the age of ninety-eight, she needed all the small comforts they could give her, for although her eyes were bright and her mind as sharp as ever, her skin was so old it looked like worn leather, and all of her teeth except three back molars were the subject of fond memories. How I used to tear into a piece of venison! she thought absently as the lifters bowed to the cheering crowd. She was cheering too, of course, because the young men would have been mortally disappointed if she had failed to show enthusiasm, but she had seen this same ceremony many times before, so it no longer moved her the way it once had. As she called out words of approval and pounded her walking stick against the platform, she found herself remembering exactly how her mother's venison stew had looked and tasted ninety years ago. She could see the dark brown clay pot, simple and round-bottomed, sitting on a stand over hot coals, see it right down to the double row of dots and bands incised on the sides, even see the hunks of venison floating in rich gravy, flavored with herbs only her mother seemed to know how to find.

Mother Asha nodded, pleased with herself. Lately she had begun to fear she was forgetting things. Take the words to songs, for example. The entire history of the Shore People was memorized; to forget the words to even one song was to forget some essential piece of the past. Lately she had caught herself unable to remember a few of the ones that were rarely sung. Of course she still knew thousands of verses, but in the past year or so there had been several little unnerving gaps, so it was a relief to discover her memory was still sharp enough to bring back the smell of a stew that had been eaten generations ago.

Tired of cheering, she put down her walking stick, placed her hands on her knees, and looked out at the crowd. These were her children, her responsibility, and now that the Goddess Stone had been successfully raised she soon would have to begin doing what only she could do. It often struck her as strange that she should have so many thousands of children in her old age when the four children she had given birth to in her youth were dead, but a Mother-of-All-Families did not actually have to have living children. Nor was it enough for her simply to be the oldest woman alive, although that was frequently the case. The position was not hereditary; if she had been quarrelsome or dull-witted or unsuitable in any way, the village mothers would have met in council and given another woman the honor. In fact the only qualification for the job of Mother-of-All-Families was that you couldn't want it; it had to be thrust on you.

Well, thrust on her it had been, Mother Asha thought, as she motioned to two of the younger women to help her rise to her feet. The younger women, one of whom was fifty-three and the other nearly sixty, caught her briskly under the arms and lifted her gently to a standing position. When they saw their Mother rise, the crowd fell silent and turned toward her, their faces lifted like the faces of eager children.

Mother Asha cleared her throat. When she spoke, her voice was clear and strong, wavering only a little in the higher ranges. "My dear children," she said, "we will now begin taking the bones of those we have loved back to the Womb of Rest." She looked from one village group to another, wondering where to begin. There had not been many deaths this year, but even one was too many.

"Bring your dear ones to me," she called out, motioning to the people of the village of Shiba, the smallest of the villages and the farthest away. "Let me give them Her blessing one last time." As the villagers from Shiba came forward carrying two bags of bones, a change came over Mother Asha. She might watch the lifting of a new Goddess Stone with mild boredom after seeing it for the twenty-eighth time, but the blessing of the dead was another matter. As the villagers knelt in front of her, untied the bags, and spread the bones out in the sunlight for the last time, she felt the spirit of the Goddess Earth pour up through the souls of her feet. Like lightning, the divine power coursed through her body, filling her with grace until she was no longer an old woman trapped in an old woman's skin but the very messenger of the Goddess herself.

"Sleep in peace," she called to the spirits of the dead, waving her hands over the bones. "Sleep as you slept as children, in the womb of a Mother who loves you."

She blessed the dead, village by village. After she had said the sacred words and passed her hands over the bones, the villagers gathered them up again and carried them into the Womb of Rest through one of the eleven stone passages, called *alus*. As a rule, only women could pass through the *alus*. The Shore People believed that since

The
Year
the
Horses
Came

59

women brought people into the world they should take them out of it, but if a man had become a priest, he too could enter, and there were several men who helped lay their friends and relatives to rest that afternoon.

The walls of the *alus* were decorated with sacred carvings that seemed to dance in the torchlight: triangles; snakes; axes of fertility to remind the mourners that life always existed in the midst of death; shepherd's crooks, because She tended Her flock well; and always the Goddess Herself, sometimes rendered with Her breasts and necklace, sometimes reduced simply to Her all-seeing eyes.

Each of the *alus* ended in a circular womb-shaped room, leveled and paved with white stones. No two of the rooms were exactly alike: some had corbelled ceilings, some were supported by large granite slabs, and still others were subdivided into smaller compartments, but all had three things in common: darkness, silence, and peace.

Yet despite the silence and the peace, Marrah was so startled when she first entered that she came to a full stop, very nearly tripping Ama, who was following close behind. The room was cool and smelled of incense and damp earth. The bones of the dead were everywhere—she had expected that—but she had not expected them to be so lovingly arranged. The skeletons lay next to each other, laboriously put back together like pieces of a puzzle. The finger bones of one often touched the finger bones of the next, as if members of the same mother family were holding hands even in death. There were no babies, because when infants less than six months old died, they were buried under the floors of the longhouses, but there were skeletons of young children, curled up front to back as if they were sleeping in the same bed.

Only three people had died in Xori since the last feast: an old man named Bizkar who had sat on the village council; a woman named Koskor who died in childbirth; and Pentsatu, a nine-year-old girl who had caught the summer sickness last year. Silently, Marrah helped Ama and the other women unpack the bags and reassemble the three skeletons. When they were finished, the women scattered finely powdered red ocher over the bones to symbolize the fertile blood of life, knelt for a few moments, touched the earth, and prayed. Then Ama rose to her feet, reached into her leather pouch, and drew out three objects small enough to hold in the palm of her hand. By Bizkar she placed a stone arrowhead, for he had been a good hunter in his youth; by Koskor she placed a single blue bead, because Koskor had always loved the sky and the sea; Pentsatu got a few brightly colored feathers of the sort that would have been woven into her hair if she had lived long enough to become a woman.

It was a moving ceremony, but after it was over, Marrah was glad to be back outside in the sunshine. As she stepped out of the *alu*, she took a deep breath and filled her lungs with fresh air. The Womb of Rest might be the most holy place in Hoza, but she was relieved that it would be at least three years before she saw the inside of it again. I may not be cut out to be a priestess, she thought, as she and the other women walked silently past the sacred fires, down the aisle of Goddess Stones, to cleanse their hands in the sea. She splashed cold seawater on her face and licked the salt from her lips. She liked living things: the feel of the wind in her hair, the smell of the seaweed, the rough scrape of gravel beneath her feet. How good it is to be alive! she thought.

The blessing of the dead took a long time. When it was finally over and all the bones had been carried into the Womb of Rest, Mother Asha withdrew to her tent, ate a small meal, took a long nap, and then limped back to the platform to listen to complaints. By the time Ama of Xori appeared to discuss the stranger who had washed up on her beach, the Mother-of-All-Families had been dispensing advice and justice most of the afternoon and was weary, but it was her duty to solve the problems of her children, so she sat and listened attentively, drinking water flavored with fruit juice to keep her head clear.

Ama spoke for some time. "And so," she concluded, "that's the story of how Marrah found the stranger. Now what we need to know is what to do next. As I said, he doesn't exactly fit into my family, or into anyone's family for that matter. On the other hand, it's hard to dislike him altogether. He has his good points." She opened her hand and held out the toy animal the stranger had carved for Arang. "He made this for my great-grandson. He's handy with a knife." She refrained from saying that some of her people were afraid he might be *too* handy with one when he got his strength back. She motioned to the stranger, who was standing a few feet away, looking from her to Mother Asha as if he expected some flash of magic might make their conversation intelligible. "I have to confess I'd like some other village to adopt him, but he does have a bad temper, so perhaps Xori is stuck with him. You may remember what a bad temper old Bizkar had. Well, *his* temper is worse by far."

Mother Asha chuckled. "I've seen you take care of plenty of difficult young men in your time, Ama."

"Well, this one's different. He comes from who knows where? The end of the earth, perhaps. We know he's human, and that's about it."

Mother Asha inspected the stranger from head to foot, and he returned her stare, not arrogantly but as if he found the idea of two women talking about him mildly amusing. "Does he understand us?"

Ama shrugged. "I think he's picked up the words for 'yes' and 'no,' but even a dog will do that if you keep it by your side long enough." She sighed. "Mother Asha, what shall we do with him?"

Mother Asha frowned. "I'll have to think it over. We certainly can't send him out into the wilderness like an outlaw, and in light of what you've told me, I don't know if I can ask another village to adopt him. I'll give you my decision at the end of the feast."

"At the end of the feast!" Ama had hoped to get the matter settled before village groups started drifting away from Hoza. There were always some who couldn't stay for the whole three days.

Mother Asha clicked her tongue and shook her head. "That's the matter with you young people: you're too impatient."

Young! Ama thought. Did she just call me *young?* Stifling her annoyance, she bowed respectfully, took the stranger by the arm, and went off to inform everyone that they'd have to wait.

But as it turned out, the wait was a short one. Ama hardly had time to sit in the shade of her own shelter and drink a cup of water before Mother Asha sent a messenger to call her back.

"She says you're to bring the stranger with you," the messenger said. He was a young man who had obviously come in haste, since he was red-faced and out of breath. "Also, she told me to tell you to bring Sabalah's daughter, Marrah."

Ama was perplexed. "What could the Mother-of-All-Families possibly want with us again so soon?"

"Another village has arrived, and they brought more with them than the bones of their dead." The messenger pointed to the stranger, who was sitting by the campfire combing out his beard with a bit of driftwood. "They brought another like him."

Although the stranger was weak, he insisted on walking, so it took them some time to cover a distance that would have taken a well man no time at all. Every step of the way, Marrah and Ama were consumed by impatience, but there was no way to make him hurry even though they tried by waving their arms and making the sounds herders made when they were trying to get the goats into the corral. At last they arrived, to find Mother Asha sitting on her platform like a grim old owl. At her feet stood a group of people Marrah had never seen before. There were five in all, dusty, travel-worn, and bewildered-looking, two men and three women, one by her age clearly a village mother. At their feet lay a litter much like the one the stranger had been carried on from Xori, and on the litter lay a human form covered by a deerskin blanket. At the sight of the blanket, Marrah felt her throat go tight. Whoever lay under it was obviously dead.

Mother Asha motioned to the oldest of the women. "This is Hega of Zizare," she said. Marrah recognized the name of the village, which was well north of her own. Zizare was famous for its ceremonial jadeite axes, which were traded all up and down the coast. "Hega and her people have come bearing a strange burden." Mother Asha gestured toward Marrah and Alma. "Hega, here are two daughters of Xori, and with them, as you see, is the stranger they found on their beach."

Hega looked at the stranger and shook her head. "I can't believe it," she said. "May the Goddess Earth take me to Her womb if I have ever seen anything so remarkable in all my life." She was a heavy woman with pendulous breasts, a round face, and sharp eyes, the kind who looked like she could tend a brood of grandchildren, run a village council, and keep her family supplied with fresh venison without even feeling the strain, but as she spoke the color drained from her face. "The likeness is unbelievable!"

Ama bowed respectfully to Mother Asha and then to Hega of Zizare, but her eyes betrayed impatience. "Could someone please tell me what's going on here? The messenger told us another stranger's been found." She pointed to the form on the litter. "Is that him?"

"Yes," Hega said, "or rather what's left of him." She turned to Mother Asha. "If I may have your permission to speak, dear Mother, I'll tell this sister what I told you."

"Speak." Mother Asha pounded her walking stick on the floor of the platform. "Speak and forget the formalities. This is no time to stand on ceremony."

Hega cleared her throat and folded her arms across her chest. "The long and the short of it is that there's a dead man under that blanket. He looks like your stranger: same ugly yellow hair and beard, same sky-colored eyes, same fish-belly skin. He's even bigger, though, so big we nicknamed him 'the giant,' and I'd say he was quite a bit older when he still walked the earth."

"Where did you find him?" Ama asked.

"Same place you did, on the beach." Having been ordered to dispense with formalities, Hega was clearly in no mood to waste words. "He washed up after the last big storm, but he only died the day before yesterday. That's why we're late. We weren't planning to come to Hoza at all. We had no dead to bring—or at least we thought we didn't—and the giant was obviously too sick to make the trip, but when he started to die we decided that instead of waiting to lay him out on a Tower of Silence we'd better hurry down here and let Mother Asha have a look at him. We hoped there'd still be some life in him when we arrived, but it's a five-day walk and the Goddess willed otherwise. He was so strange-looking and he was wearing so many ceremonial adornments that frankly we thought he might be some special kind of priest. Of course we had no idea there were any others like him, so imagine our surprise when we got here and were told the village of Xori had pulled its own giant out of the ocean and that giant was alive and sitting in a shelter on the other side of the camp."

Everyone looked at the stranger, who was standing in a patch of sunlight, scratching his head, clearly unaware they were talking about him. There was an awkward pause.

"Perhaps they were traveling together," Ama suggested.

"My thoughts exactly," Hega agreed.

"Of course they were," Mother Asha exclaimed, pounding her walking stick impatiently. "How else could two such ugly men come to be on the same stretch of beach?"

"A good day's walk apart," Ama reminded her.

"A day!" Mother Asha snorted. "What does a day of walking mean to the Sea Goddess? Amonah's reach is infinite and Her waves carry all things. In my time I have seen seedpods from the ends of the earth wash up on our beaches; I have seen Her give back bits of boats lost for generations; I have seen the dead rise from the very pit of Her fertile darkness and travel faster than any trader. She is no respecter of distances, and She strews her gifts where She wills." She lifted her walking stick and gestured toward the litter. "Heave off that blanket and let the stranger from Xori look on the face of the dead giant from Zizare. Perhaps we'll be able to tell by his reaction if he recognizes him, and if he does, I think we will be able to conclude they were in the same boat, lost in the same storm." She lowered her stick. "Although frankly I fail to see what use such information will be to us.

Mary
Mackey

We'll still have the problem of laying the bones of one to rest and finding a permanent home for the other. Still, heave and be done with it."

"Marrah," Ama commanded, "take the stranger by the hand and lead him over to the litter."

Marrah did as she was told. Her hand was cold with excitement; as she touched the stranger, he flinched slightly with surprise and turned to her with a questioning look in his eyes. "Come this way," she said softly, and as if for once he understood, he came without protest. Soon he was standing in front of the litter, looking down at the shrouded form with mild curiosity.

"Ready?" Hega asked, and without waiting for a reply, she seized the edge of the deerskin and drew it back with a quick motion. There was a sudden glint of gold and copper and flesh so white it looked like bone. The dead giant of Zizare lay before them, a huge lean man with a face shaped like an ax blade. He had a wedge-shaped chin under a yellow beard, deeply sunken eye sockets, lips blue with the eternal winter of death. Although his hair was thinner and his face more weathered, he looked so much like an older version of the stranger that Marrah's first impression was that she was seeing ahead in time. Like the stranger, the dead man wore clothes made of matted brown fur; his left shoulder was marked with blue suns and lightning bolts, and he too had rings in his ears and necklaces around his neck. But what rings and what necklaces! There was no copper on him, only animal teeth and gold, so much gold that Marrah could hardly believe her eyes: gold earrings, gold studs in his belt, gold worked into the handle of his long knife, even gold threads woven into the tassels of his boots. The largest piece of gold lay directly over the giant's heart, a pendant the size of a thumb, worked into what by now was a familiar shape: a four-legged deer-not-deer, with hair instead of horns. Beside him lay a strangely shaped bow, bent in the middle like two waves lapping together.

"Great Goddess!" Ama said. "He looks as if he's wearing all the gold in—" But she never got to finish her sentence. The stranger suddenly gave a horrible high-pitched wail of such grief and horror that all of them froze.

"Ai!" he cried. "Ai, ai!" Throwing himself on the body, he gathered the dead man into his arms and pressed him to his breast. "*achan, doboi dan!*" He kissed the dead man's eyes and lips fervently.

"What's he saying?" Mother Asha demanded. "Does anyone know what he's saying?"

No one knew. The stranger lifted the dead man and cradled him in his arms, wailing and crying as if he had suddenly gone mad. Everyone was stunned. They had never seen such grief before. Of course you mourned when someone died, but at the same time you knew that the one you loved was going back to the Mother, so although you wept you didn't entirely despair. But the stranger seemed half out of his mind. Laying the dead man back on the litter, he began to tear his own hair and rip his clothing. He picked up a handful of earth, scattered some of it over his head, ate the rest, and then, before anyone realized what was happening, he pulled the dead man's knife from its scabbard and began to slash at his own flesh.

"Stop him!" Mother Asha screamed, trying to rise to her feet.

The younger people, including Marrah, fell on the stranger and struggled to take the knife from him, but weak as he was, he fought them off. He crouched over the body like a wild animal at bay, screaming at them in his incomprehensible tongue. Blood dripped from his arms, and his eyes rode high in their sockets as if he were about to have a fit. Marrah shrank back, truly afraid. She had never seen anyone so out of control. Suddenly a change came over him. He looked down at the dead man's face and began to tremble. "*Achan, Achan!*" he cried. Letting the knife slip from his hand, he fell on the body and lay there weeping and shaking.

"Get that knife out of his reach," Mother Asha commanded. She lowered herself back down on her sheepskins, trembling and shaken. I'm far too old for this sort of thing, she thought, and she felt her ancient heart flutter in her breast.

Marrah ran forward, picked up the knife, and offered it to Ama, handle first. "Well done." Ama too was shaken. They all were. A crowd was beginning to gather, attracted by the noise. Soon there was a ring of sober brown faces around the litter. People spoke in hushed whispers, unnerved by the sound of the stranger's grief. There was probably something that should be done next, but no one knew quite what it was, not even Mother Asha.

Hega was the first to speak. "Poor man," she said softly. "Poor lost soul."

At the sound of her voice, or perhaps its tone, the stranger lifted his head. His face was pale and tear-streaked, and he looked young— so young Marrah thought that if she were seeing him for the first time she might think him no older than Bere. It was a vulnerable, pleading face, and it brought a murmur of sympathy from the crowd.

"See how he cries."

"See how he mourns."

"Perhaps he's afraid we won't bless the bones of his friend."

"But of course Mother Asha will bless them."

"How can he know that? The poor man doesn't understand a word we're saying."

As if sensing their concern, the stranger lifted his hands, made a gesture toward the dead man, and said something. He repeated the phrase as if frustrated with their inability to understand, but his plea, whatever it was, made no sense to anyone. He clenched his fist and pounded on his chest. "*Xuxu hztu!*" he cried. "*Xuxu hztu!*"

Great Goddess! Marrah thought. She stared at him in amazement. Either she was dreaming or she'd just understood what he'd said! Hurrying over to him, she fell to her knees and put her face close to his. He smelled of sweat and woodsmoke and something else she couldn't quite identify. "*Xuxu?*" she said.

"Marrah," Ama cried, "what are you doing? Come away from there. The man's dangerous."

For once Marrah heard but didn't obey. "*Xuxu?*" she repeated.

"*Xuxu, chau!*" The stranger reached out and caught her by the shoulders. "*Xuxu, vh hztu xuxu ch tzxha achan!*"

"Marrah of Xori, stand up this instant!" Mother Asha commanded.

Disengaging herself from the stranger's embrace with some difficulty, Marrah rose to her feet and turned to face the Mother-of-All-Families. "I understand him!" she cried. "I know what he's saying. The dead man"—she pointed to the body on the litter—"is his brother, Achan." Behind her the stranger was speaking in quick, excited sentences. "He's saying they were wrecked in a great storm and separated by the sea. He's saying that his brother's death is . . . a something for him; I can't quite catch the word, but I think he means it's a terrible thing, like the loss of an arm or leg. That's it. Achan was like his right arm, and he says that without him he's crippled."

Everyone stared at her dumbfounded. "How do you know all this?" Mother Asha whispered. "How can a girl of your age know what no one else knows? Is the Goddess Herself giving you second sight?"

"No, dear Mother." Marrah finally found the presence of mind to bow respectfully. "The stranger is speaking a language that's a lot like one my mother taught me."

"Amazing." Mother Asha looked as if she still didn't quite believe her. "Are you telling me he speaks Sharan?"

"Not exactly, but close enough. I think maybe he's speaking Shambah. The villagers who live on the Sweetwater Sea north of Shara speak it, but he must not really be from there because he has a strange accent. I think his mother tongue must be the one he was speaking earlier, but I believe I can make him understand me if the Mother wants me to translate for her."

"This is a miracle." Mother Asha lifted her hands in the direction of the new Goddess Stone. "All praise to Her who can make even the rocks speak." Having waxed poetic, she turned to practical matters. "Ask him his name, child. Ask him where he comes from."

Marrah spoke to the stranger in Sharan, and once again he embraced her. Pushing him away gently, she decided that from now on she was going to stand well out of reach. He had a grasp that could crush the lungs of a bear. "He says his name is Stavan and he comes from the Sea of Grass."

"A sea of grass? Are you sure you got that right? It makes no sense."

"Yes, dear Mother, I'm sure. He said it twice just as clearly as I'm saying it to you now. And he said something else, something that makes me wonder if perhaps he is not quite in his right mind. He says"—Marrah paused, embarrassed to spout such nonsense before the Mother-of-All-Families—"he says he left this Sea of Grass with his brother Achan about four years ago, and all that time they've been wandering together looking for gold."

"For gold?" Mother Asha lifted her eyebrows. "Do they have so many dead that they need to make funeral necklaces by the dozens?" She turned toward the dead man, who glittered even as he lay motionless on the litter. "From the looks of this brother of his, I should think the two of them had found enough gold for all the temples in their land. Why didn't they turn back long ago? What kind of foolishness is this to waste years of their lives on?"

Marrah shifted her weight nervously from one foot to the other, wishing she had never gotten herself in the position of translator. Not only had she just remembered that Sabalah had forbidden her to speak the language of Shara in the stranger's presence, what she had to say next was so incredible that Mother Asha would probably dismiss her out of sheer disgust. "They were not just searching for gold alone, dear Mother. The stranger—Stavan, that is—says they were searching for a village made of gold that their people believe lies in

Mary
Mackey

the valley of the setting sun." She paused, obliged to speak the truth, yet not wanting to. "Actually he didn't say "village"; he said they were searching for 'a great camp of golden tents.' I asked him if they wanted the gold from the tents to hang around their necks, and he said yes, they did, because their people value gold above all things, but there was more to it than that. He said the search was a sacred obligation, and he and his brother were sent off with great honor to find the place where the sun slept."

"Poor idiot." Mother Asha snorted. "Everyone knows the sun is the Goddess Earth's daughter whom She puts to bed each night at the bottom of the sea."

"The stranger says the sun is no daughter but a great god named Han who rules the sky."

"A sky god." Mother Asha sighed and shook her head. She gestured at the crowd of people who were hanging on every word. "Go back to your camps, all of you. We have a man among us whose whole world is upside down, and it's going to take time to set it straight." She turned to the village mothers, who stood beside the platform. "Go tell your young people to bring us food and drink. This Stavan holds on to his dead brother like a barnacle, and since I can see no prospect of persuading him to move out of the sun, I'll have to sit here and talk to him. This isn't a pleasant task for an old woman to perform, and I have no intention of doing it on an empty stomach."

Mother Asha was right as usual. The conversation with the stranger took a long time, just as she predicted, and although Marrah did her best it didn't go well at all. She translated everything faithfully, and each time she opened her mouth he got more upset. In no time at all he was yelling at her.

"No!" he cried. "No, no, no! why can't you and that old woman understand? I told you before, I don't want Achan's body torn apart by birds. It's a terrible custom; it's disgusting. It's something my people do only to traitors who betray their chiefs."

"It's more disgusting to let him rot in the ground," Marrah yelled back. She had meant to keep her temper, but she hated being screamed at. How dare this big ugly man call one of the most sacred customs of her people "disgusting" when he was asking them to dig a hole and throw his brother's body in like a piece of spoiled meat.

The stranger clenched his fist and began to pound on his chest. "Tear out my heart if you must," he yelled, "but don't let the ravens eat the heart of my brother, who was one of the greatest warriors of my people. Achan was my father's heir, his only legitimate son. He would have been Great Chief of the Twenty Tribes if he'd lived, and I'd rather die myself than let you put him on one of your accursed Towers of Silence. I saw a man disposed of that way once, and it made me vomit!"

"Whatever is he raving about?" Mother Asha interrupted. She hated seeing people get upset, especially when she couldn't understand them. Marrah took a few steps away from the stranger, glared at him, and began to translate, her voice trembling with anger. Stubborn fool, she thought, never suspecting that perhaps he was thinking the same thing about her.

When Marrah had finished translating, Mother Asha sighed and shook her head. "I still don't understand why he feels so strongly about the holy birds who gather the dead back to the Mother, but as long as his wishes do no harm, we'll respect them. Tell him we'll bury his brother in a deep hole. That should satisfy him."

And so it happened that on the morning of the second day of the feast, the Shore People were treated to the unheard-of sight of a dead man being laid in the ground with his flesh still on his bones. Except for his bow, a bracelet, and two small gold rings Stavan took from his ears, Achan was buried with his sword at his side and his necklaces around his neck, and that too seemed strange to the spectators, for why throw away perfectly good ceremonial adornments?

By Mother Asha's orders, the burial took place as far away from the Womb of Rest as possible because it was an unclean thing, made even more unclean by the ceremony the stranger performed once the earth had been piled over his brother. As the villagers looked on, he took a young she-goat, slit her throat, and bled her on his brother's grave. Even Marrah, who had known about the goat in advance, flinched and dug her nails into the palms of her hands as the animal staggered and fell.

"Why did the yellow-bearded stranger kill a goat?" the villagers whispered. "Does he plan to cook the funeral feast on top of his brother's body?" They themselves killed animals, but only to eat, never as part of religious rituals. The only sacrifices they knew were sacrifices of fruit and flowers: grain scattered for the birds, petals tossed into the waves to honor Amonah.

Mother Asha, who only had consented to the killing of the goat after the stranger had pleaded with her for a long time, closed her eyes and passed her hand over her face, thinking that she had made a mistake. True, they would eat the animal, but now that she actually saw it being slaughtered, she felt she should have stood firm and refused. No living thing should be slain to honor the dead, she thought. This is too much.

This is not nearly enough, Stavan was thinking at the same moment. Achan should have had twenty horses killed over his grave.

The blood of the goat soaked into the ground, leaving dark stains on the chalky soil. For a moment he almost persuaded himself that he heard the high-pitched gabbling of ghosts coming to drink. He shuddered, wondering if the spirits of the Underworld would be satisfied with something as paltry as the blood of a she-goat.

Marrah slept badly that night. Her dreams were confused, and once she woke to find herself sitting upright with her hands clenched by her sides. By dawn she was worn out and only too ready to pull the covers back over her head and spend some time catching up, but before she could retreat into the darkness beneath the sheepskins, a message arrived from Mother Asha asking her and Ama to come to the central plaza before the ceremonies began. The stranger, Stavan, was to be left behind.

Mother Asha was very particular about this last bit and ordered the messenger to repeat it twice so there would be no possibility of misunderstanding.

"I've come to a decision," Mother Asha announced. She looked out beyond Marrah and Ama toward the new Goddess Stone, which was being decked with flowers in preparation for the final night of dancing, but she saw the she-goat instead—the one that had died for nothing, poor animal. Silly, perhaps, to make so much of the death of a goat, but she was an old woman whose instinct for trouble had only grown sharper with time, and this morning she could feel an ominous undercurrent in the air, as if a cold wind had swept through Hoza, bringing an early winter. Was the Goddess Xori angry because one of Her beasts had been killed at the wrong time in the wrong place? Mother Asha wasn't sure. She only had a sense that something ugly had taken place and she had unwittingly been a party to it.

She cleared her throat and looked down at Marrah and Ama, who were still waiting respectfully for her to continue.

"I've decided that no other village can be asked to take the stranger off your hands." There, it was out: simple, plain, blunt, and no way for them to mistake her meaning. Before they could object, she went on. "He angers too easily, he grieves too wildly, he's too stubborn, too disrespectful of others, and some of his customs are repugnant." She lifted her hand, taking in the Womb of Rest, the Goddess Stones, the shelters and campfires, and her children, all three thousand of them. "The Shore People have always been a single family, bound together by love and duty." She pointed to herself. "I don't exist outside of this family." She pointed to Marrah and Ama. "And you don't exist outside of this family. But he"—she pointed in the direction of the shelter, where the stranger still lay sleeping—"he does."

"Are we supposed to turn him out to starve in the forest?" Marrah said. She might have a quick temper, but she forgave easily. Last night, before they went to sleep, she had talked to the stranger again, guardedly at first, then with growing pity. She had learned things about him that she didn't entirely understand but that moved her just the same. It seemed he had spent years wandering with only his brother and a few friends for companions, and now they were all dead and he was completely alone. "He's still weak; he has a bad cough that could go to his lungs. Put him out in the wind and damp, and he won't last until the next full moon." Realizing she had just spoken disrespectfully to the Mother-of-All-Families, she put her hand over her mouth and stared at the platform, horrified by her own rudeness.

Mother Asha was amused. "Ah," she said, "I'm glad to hear you take such an interest in his health, Marrah. It shows you have the instincts of a healer and does the mother who taught you credit. No, I'm not suggesting Ama send the stranger into the forest while he's still recovering from his sickness." She paused and looked at Hoza again, at the purple and yellow heather, the bright sunlight shining off the great stones. "The summer has begun, and with it the trading season. This early, only the traders bringing axes from the interior have arrived, but during the long days to come we'll have visitors from as far away as the Blue Sea, and by the time they leave, the stranger should be strong enough to leave with them."

"And if he doesn't want to?"

"Then," Mother Asha said briskly, "we turn him out in the forest to fend for himself. There's no place in our longhouses for such a man. But I don't think you need to worry about his staying. I think he longs to go back to his own people as much as we long to get rid of him." With a wave of her hand, she indicated the audience was over.

Once again Mother Asha was right. When Marrah told Stavan he was to leave with the traders at the end of the summer, he thanked her eagerly. She was surprised by his enthusiasm and even a little annoyed that he seemed so eager to get away. How could she know that ever since he had awakened to find himself in a savage longhouse, he had expected to be sacrificed to one of her gods or hobbled and made into a slave?

As he thanked Marrah, he felt not only relief but cautious admiration for people who could take in a sick stranger, nurse him back to health, and send him on his way without asking anything in return. Achan had always despised the savages, calling them weak and woman-ridden, but during the time he had spent in their care, Stavan had warmed to them. At times he'd feared his friendly feelings might be ignoble and not fit for a warrior, but now that he saw the savages were going to let him go, he knew he'd been right to trust them. He had to take the news of Achan's death back to his father as soon as possible, and he only hoped the other tribes he encountered along the way would be as easy to deal with.

That afternoon a tall tree was felled, stripped of its branches, and dragged to the central plaza of Hoza. Although teams of young men and women lifted the tree as if it were a Goddess Stone, it went up easily, amid much laughter and joking. When the pole had been raised and its base securely anchored, the young people seized the ends of the ropes and began to dance, women moving one way, men the other. The dance was full of sexual energy yet ecstatically religious, and as the dancers wove up, under, over, and around, beating their feet on the earth and singing songs in praise of the Owl Goddess, a change came over them. One by one, they stopped feeling that they were separate individuals and lost themselves in the group until there were no more men or women, only a great circle that turned and turned, sweeping everything along with it. The circle was the Circle of Life, the circle of the Earth Herself, moving from spring to winter to spring, from birth to death to birth, and all Feasts of the Dead ended with it.

Marrah was part of the circle, and as she danced she too felt herself disappearing into the group. Like people reaching out to take each other's hands, the minds of the Shore People reached out to touch one another, and at the moment of contact they became a single Over-mind, greater than any of Its parts. At the instant Marrah became one with the Over-mind, she felt a rushing sensation that seemed to lift her off her feet, and she remembered things she had no way of knowing. The memories of the Over-mind were not intellectual or even intelligent; they were deeper and much more powerful, like dreams boiled down to their essence.

As the Over-mind danced It remembered thousands of dances, all going on at the same time like circles within circles with no end and no beginning. Beside each human danced the spirit of all the ancestors who had ever lived, and beside each ancestor the spirit of every animal, and beside the humans and the animals the forest danced, and the sun and moon danced, and even the stars danced around the tree.

As Marrah moved in the circle, the part of her that was the Over-mind felt the presence of something at the center that was neither god nor goddess, something that stayed perfectly still while everything else whirled around it. *Love,* the stillness whispered to the Over-mind. *Everything is love.* And as the center spoke, the Over-mind was suddenly filled with a love so complete that everything was erased by a blinding joy.

The dance went on and on, and with every step the dancers took, the ropes twisted more tightly around the pole and the circle grew smaller. Finally thirty pairs of women and men stood face to face, unable to move another step. The drums fell silent, and Mother Asha rose to her feet. "All praise to Xori!" she cried in a loud, clear voice, clapping her hands.

At the sound of the Bird Goddess's name and Mother Asha's hands clapping together, the Over-mind broke back into Its component parts. Suddenly Marrah woke from trance to find herself standing in front of a dark-eyed young man from Shiba.

"Praise to Xori!" Marrah, the young man, and the other dancers cried. "All praise to the Great Bird who brings love on Her holy wings!" And dropping the ends of the ropes, they fell into each other's arms and kissed as the pipes and drums played and the crowd applauded.

That evening Marrah went off into the forest with the young man from Shiba whom the Goddess had given her, and as they lay at peace after satisfying each other, she thought how beautiful and mysterious the world was, and how it contained far more things than could be seen with the eyes alone.

CHAPTER FIVE

S tavan broke off a piece of goat cheese, wrapped it in an acorn cake, and ate it thoughtfully. He and Marrah were sitting on a rock, away from the others, eating their midday meal and dangling their feet in a tide pool. It was a fair day, sunny and cool, good weather for walking back to Xori, but they had been moving slowly because Stavan had refused to ride in the litter. To everyone's surprise, he had made it through the morning, but now, white-lipped and exhausted, he was taking a rest and talking to Marrah in Shambah while he ate his cheese and shared a handful of blackberries she had picked along the trail.

Now that Marrah knew he would be leaving at the end of the summer, she wanted to find out as much about him as she could. Except for Sabalah, she had never known anyone who had been more than a five-day walk from the Sea of Gray Waves—except traders, of course, but traders didn't count since travel was their profession and they always earned their supper and a warm place by the fire by telling fantastic tales no one with any sense believed. Marrah had heard them describe distant lands where people flew on golden wings, and villages rose out of the waves at dawn and sank at night, and monsters breathed fire and spit stones, and all sorts of other nonsense, but she wanted to know what the rest of the world was really like.

Stavan seemed willing to oblige her. He spoke slowly, as if conjuring up his people from a great distance, looking at her with steady, cool blue eyes that never wavered, but there was something about his voice that made her suspect he was lonely.

"My people are of the tribe of the Hansi," he began. "Han is God of the Shining Sky and si is our word for wolf, so we're 'the wolves of God,' put on the earth to rule over all living things as the wolf pack rules. Zuhan, my father, is the Great Chief, which means he has the power to call all the Twenty Tribes together and lead them into battle. We live far to the east of here on a great plain we call the Sea of Grass, and we've lived there since the beginning of time. We're famous warriors; we own more horses and cattle and long-haired sheep than any of our neighbors, and so we move often to keep them fed, and when we move the steppes tremble under the hooves of our herds and our enemies scatter out of our way like rabbits. Our strength comes from the rich milk we drink and the blood we stir into our porridge, and we've never been without meat, not even in the lean season of my great-great-grandfather's time when the rains failed to come and lesser tribes starved."

He paused and finished off his acorn cake. Then he licked his fingers and took up where he'd left off. "The first thing I can remember is the grass, higher than my head, green and tasseled against the sky. I must have been about two years old, and I'd wandered away from my father's tent to chase a butterfly." He smiled and his blue eyes suddenly glittered with amusement. Marrah found the effect slightly startling, like sunlight hitting open water. "All at once, I realized my mother was nowhere to be seen, and I began to cry for her. The next thing I knew she was there, bending down to sweep me up in her arms."

The light went out of his eyes as quickly as it had come, and he picked up another piece of cheese and went back to eating in a sturdy, efficient way as if the memory no longer held any great charm for him. "That's the only memory I have of my mother. She died a few weeks later. All I can remember is that she had a soft voice and light brown hair that smelled like flowers and dust. Her name was Nona. She was my father's favorite concubine, but she had been born the daughter of a powerful chief, taken from her people when she was only six and raised to dance for the warriors."

He helped himself to the blackberries and began to eat them, licking the juice from his fingers. "When she found me out there on the steppes bawling my eyes out, she laughed and held me over her head and cried, 'Look at the horses, my little chief!' and I looked and saw the waves of grass"—he waved his hands expansively—"spreading out forever to the horizon, and my father's herd of fine horses, galloping across the plain, running like the gods themselves, and my bastard half brother Vlahan mounted on a roan gelding, driving them toward the warriors who were going to catch them and ride them off to battle."

He finished the blackberries and wiped his hands on his tunic. "Which war they were fighting that year, I don't know. There were always so many. With the Tcvali, perhaps. The Tcvali have never acknowledged my father as Great Chief. They're a pack of thieves, always stealing our horses because all they can breed are swayback nags not fit for a man to mount."

He paused, as if waiting for Marrah to react, but she had so many questions she didn't know where to begin. Whenever he was at a loss for a word, he lapsed back into his own language, which made it hard for her to follow what he was saying. What was a "concubine," a "horse," a "roan gelding," a "bastard," a "chief," a "warrior," and a "battle"? What had he meant when he said his mother had been "taken from her people"? And if it meant what she thought it meant, why wasn't he more upset about it? She felt confused and slightly embarrassed. She had thought she spoke Sharan better than this. Still, Sharan and Shambah weren't exactly the same language; perhaps that was why she was having so much trouble keeping up.

She decided not to ask for explanations. If she tried to get him to explain all the words she didn't understand, he might get impatient and stop talking, and his story was too fascinating. Better to let him think she was following him. There would be plenty of time later to admit he'd used words she didn't know. Maybe when they got back to the village, Sabalah could supply the meaning of expressions like "swayback nags not fit for a man to mount."

"Who became your stepmother after your mother died?" she asked. Now that was a simple question, straightforward and practical.

He stared at her blankly. "Stepmother?"

So she wasn't the only one who was having trouble. Relieved, she explained.

"Oh, I understand. You're asking who adopted me." He shrugged. "No one did."

"No one?" This time Marrah understood the words but had trouble believing them. How could a small child not be adopted instantly? In

Xori there would have been half a dozen women begging to be honored with the stepmothering of a little boy whose mother had died.

Stavan looked puzzled by her reaction. "It isn't too surprising, really. Even though I was my father's favorite son next to Achan, I was only the offspring of one of his concubines, so I wasn't important enough for Zulike, his old peaceweaving wife, to take into her tent. Zulike was terribly jealous of my mother, and I think she would have left me behind for the wolves if I'd been a girl child, but since I was a boy she gave me to Tzinta to nurse. Tzinta was the slave girl who taught me how to speak Shambah. By the way, it was only by chance that I cried out in Shambah when you showed me Achan's body. I'd decided weeks ago that you people didn't speak any tongue I could understand, but I was upset, and sometimes when I get upset, I return to the language of my childhood." He smiled. "I have Tzinta to thank for that. I was very fond of her. She was my half brother Vlahan's mother, and she had been taken from the savages when she was nearly a grown woman, so it took a lot of beatings to keep her in line. Vlahan was always ashamed of his mother, but I admired her spirit." He chuckled. "When old Zulike came at Tzinta with a horsewhip, Tzinta would call her 'goat face' and 'cow shit' in Shambah so Zulike wouldn't understand. The rest of the time she called Zulike the 'old hag,' which for years I thought was the word for 'chief's wife.'"

"Stop!" Marrah cried, putting her finger over his lips to silence him. "How can you laugh when you're saying such horrible things? How could one woman beat another and not be cast out of your tribe? Why, my people would cut off this Zulike's earlobe and drive her into the forest."

Stavan looked at her as if he couldn't imagine why she was getting so upset. "I don't think you understood what I just said," he announced stiffly, and the guarded look came back into his eyes. "No one would dare cut off Zulike's earlobe. She's the wife of my father, the Great Chief, and Tzinta—who died years ago—was only a slave. If a chief's wife wants to beat a slave, she has every right to. My people say that Han created the powerful to rule the weak and the weak to submit to the strong."

"This god of yours sounds cruel." She was too upset to be diplomatic. "If that's an example of one of his commandments, then I think you should . . ." She sputtered to a halt, not sure what she thought Stavan should do, and then it came to her. "You should worship the Goddess Earth instead of Han. Her first commandment is that we should all live together in love and harmony."

Stavan turned pale and made a strange sign with his hands, extending his index and little finger. "Don't say that. You'll bring Han's curse down on us. Say you didn't mean it, please."

He looked so genuinely upset that she relented and said she didn't mean it even though she did, but the conversation didn't get any better. By the time they finished the acorn cakes and cheese, Stavan had explained to her what a "slave," a "concubine," and a "warrior" were, and she left the tide pool so upset by the violent world he had described that she avoided him for the rest of the afternoon.

Stavan realized that something had gone wrong with the conversation, and as he labored to keep up with the others, he wondered what he might do to wipe the disgust out of her eyes. It was not so much that he was attracted to her as a woman—although she was unusually pretty for a savage—but rather that he never liked having anyone think badly of him. He had come in for a lot of mocking and cruel teasing and even sharp reprimands from his father for caring about such things, but he couldn't help himself. If she had thrust burning sticks against his flesh, he would have endured the torture without a cry, defied her, and sung his war songs. He was no coward, but the look she had given him as she walked away from the tide pool made him flinch the way no blade could have and he felt—although he couldn't say exactly why—that he'd done something dishonorable.

The truth was that his ways and the ways of his people weren't one and the same. He had never fit particularly well into the tribe, and his relatives, in turn, had always found him slightly peculiar. Vlahan, his half brother, who hated him and would be glad to see him dead, liked to call him "woman-spoiled," but the other men were less sure that was the problem, for besides being one of the Great Chief's sons, he was big, with plenty of courage, a good eye, and a throwing arm that could fling a spear with the speed of a descending hawk. Even as a child, he had ridden the wildest horses as if he and they were made of a single piece of flesh, and no one could follow animal tracks better or endure hunger, icy cold, and broiling heat with fewer complaints.

As for his loyalty, it was unquestioned. Many younger sons of chiefs spent their lives plotting ways to kill their older brothers and seize power, but Stavan had never once wavered in his fidelity to Achan. Once you were Stavan's friend, you were his friend for life, and this had been true even when he was a child.

Then there was the matter of the Tcvali raid. When he was thirteen he had been guarding the horses and cattle with five other boys when a band of Tcvali warriors took them by surprise and fell on them, killing everyone but Stavan, who was left for dead. It was winter and the steppes were covered with snow, but instead of giving up and freezing to death, he had survived and staggered back to camp to sound the alarm.

No one had expected him to live through the night, although Changar, the diviner, was called in, and Zuhan ordered a horse sacrificed—which was remarkable considering that the boy was only the son of a concubine. But live Stavan did, and the raw courage of his journey through the snow to warn his people was repeated so often and so widely through the Twenty Tribes that no one could ever again reasonably ask if the youngest son of the Great Chief had what it took to be a man—no one, that is, except Stavan, who secretly asked himself that question more often than was good for his peace of mind. He knew what no one else could: under his brave exterior was a person not really born to be a warrior.

He first discovered this weakness in his character on the retaliatory raid that took place soon after he recovered his health. Sometime during the season of snows when the Warrior Stars rode high in the sky and the days were short, Zuhan had called Stavan into his tent to tell him that he was going to be allowed to ride with the men to avenge his slain companions, and for the first and last time in his life Stavan felt the hot, excited thrill of that moment when a warrior knows he will soon be shedding the blood of his enemies.

"We'll wipe out the Tcvali and take back our horses and cattle," Zuhan promised, looking at Stavan through narrowed eyes and liking what he saw, for the boy was big for thirteen, and he had the arms and legs of a man born to ride. "And if you kill one of their warriors—not one of their women, for that would be too easy—I will order Changar to cut the marks of manhood into your flesh even though you're still a year too young for the ceremony."

No one was ever prouder than Stavan at the moment he heard his father promise to make him a man, and as he bowed and kissed the ground at Zuhan's feet, he promised himself he would be the fiercest warrior the Hansi had ever known. The next morning he rode out armed with a spear and a battle-ax, knowing nothing about war except the games boys played and the stories men told as they sat around the campfires at night.

His education was quick and brutal. So much snow had fallen since the raid that it should have been impossible for the Hansi to track the Tcvali across the steppes, but they had Chinzu, the best tracker in the Sea of Grass, and he followed every hump in the snow, every grain of dust, until they saw the smoke of the enemy fires drifting across the horizon. Knowing the Tcvali thought they were safe, they waited until just before dawn and then fell on the camp, taking the enemy by surprise and slaughtering every man, woman, and child, except for a few girls who were spared to become slaves and concubines.

When the tents of the Tcvali were nothing but charred rings of burned hides and the blood of the dead had soaked into the snow, they divided the surviving women among themselves and rode back to camp singing songs of victory. It had been a brilliantly successful raid, all the more so because the Tcvali had not expected to be attacked so late in the season, when fierce storms blew down from the north and a war party could be lost before it ever had a chance to strike.

"Hail to Zuhan!" the warriors sang as they threw skins of fermented mare's milk to one another and drank until they were drunk. "Hail to the greatest of Great Chiefs!"

Only Stavan was not singing. White-lipped and silent, he sat on his horse, sick at heart that he had ever come on the raid. The wholesale slaughter had turned his stomach. He had not been in battle more than five minutes before he realized that no power on earth could make him kill women and children, and more than once he had turned away instead of striking, an act that would have brought eternal shame on his father if anyone had noticed. Fortunately for his reputation, no one had. The smoke from the burning tents had hidden his cowardly acts of mercy—which had done the women and children no good since they were slaughtered anyway. Meanwhile, there had been plenty of Tcvali warriors to fight, and he had stabbed and slashed until he was dizzy with exhaustion, fending off armed men who did their best to beat him to the ground. By the time it was all over, he was covered with blood like everyone else, most of it from his own wounds, which by some miracle were not too serious, but the victory had given him no pleasure.

"Stavan has killed his man," the warriors sang. Chinzu, his oldest cousin, had grinned and thrown him a skin of fermented mare's milk, and Stavan had drunk deeply, wondering if drunkenness could erase the memory of the man he had supposedly killed. The Tcvali warrior had been wounded and dying before Stavan ever came near him. He had charged wildly, and Stavan had done no more than strike at him once with his spear, knocking him off balance, but the other men were determined to give him the glory of the kill so he could be initiated into manhood, and as they rode back to camp, they sang his praises and invented deeds of courage he had never so much as thought of.

They were proud of him, his father was proud of him, but Stavan was not proud of himself. He knew there was something wrong with him, something that made him unlike other warriors, and that night as Changar cut the ceremonial scars into his shoulders and the palms of his hands, he prayed to Han that he would never have to fight again. Yet what other life was there for a man? He had a fine singing voice, but singing and dancing were something warriors only did when they ate the sacred mushrooms and prepared for battle. Men did not cook, or make pottery, or gather wild roots, or sew clothing, or milk cows, or cure hides, or tend children, or do any of the things he really enjoyed doing. Once in a great while, a man might be chosen by the gods to become a diviner as Changar had been when lightning struck him and he lived, but the only life for most men was the warrior's life, and if this was true for most, it was especially true for the youngest son of a Great Chief.

Still, even as Changar made the marks that would tell anyone who saw Stavan that he was forever a warrior of the Hansi, Stavan prayed never to ride into battle again, and to his astonishment, Han heard his prayers and gave him his wish, for not long afterward Achan came back from the west, lay down in his father's tent, and dreamed of the golden tents of Han. Soon after, he became obsessed with the idea of going west again to find them, and impressed by Stavan's courage and the fact that he spoke Shambah, he persuaded Zuhan to let Stavan go with him. So for four years Stavan had wandered with his brother through strange lands without ever having to admit that he preferred peace to war, took no joy in battle, and wasn't like other men.

That evening, after they had made camp, Stavan walked over to where Marrah was sitting and sat down beside her. He had noticed she had been avoiding him all day, and he was afraid if he didn't set things right with her now, he might not have another chance.

"I'm sorry I upset you this afternoon," he said. The words didn't come easily: a warrior rarely apologized to anyone, particularly not to a young woman, but he had enough sense to see that he was moving in a different world where the old rules no longer applied.

"You should be sorry." Instead of bowing her head when she spoke to him, she looked him straight in the eyes, a habit he found disconcerting. "I've been thinking all day about the things you told me, and the more I think the more upset I get. Slaves, wars, concubines! I've never heard of such things. I don't think you're so bad, at least not as far as I can tell on such a short acquaintance, but your people sound horrible."

Stavan was annoyed. He'd come to make peace, not be attacked by a savage who didn't know what she was talking about. "They have their good qualities."

She gave a snort of disbelief that reminded him of a bad-tempered mare. "Well, if they do, you haven't told me what they are. From what I've heard, they should all have their left earlobes cut off." She made a slashing motion as if she were perfectly willing to do the cutting herself and then glared at him.

He stood perfectly still for a moment, and then he began to laugh—not just a polite laugh but a long, deep-bellied, red-faced laugh that left him half choked. He knew she'd be insulted but he couldn't help himself.

"What's so funny?"

"You!" he gasped. "The thought of you cutting off the earlobes of the Hansi warriors is funny. Great Han, is it funny! And I bet you could do it too. That look on your face would turn the bravest man to stone."

She rose to her feet. "Eat goat dung," she spat. "And when you want someone to translate for you, don't come to me."

He grabbed her arm. "Wait, please, I didn't mean to make you mad again. I seem to be doing everything wrong. I apologize for laughing at you. It was a stupid thing to do. I sat down here hoping we could be friends."

"Why?" She set her chin stubbornly. "I know I'm the only one who can understand you, but when we get back to the village, my mother and Arang will be able to translate for you, so you won't need my friendship."

"I want to be your friend because I think you're . . . interesting."

"Interesting?" Some of the anger went out of her chin. No one had ever called her "interesting" before, and she liked the sound of it.

"Yes. The way you think is different from the way I think, and I find that interesting. When I tell you something about my people, I can never predict how you're going to react. Tzinta—the woman who taught me Shambah—was like that, completely unpredictable. You and Tzinta both"—once again he groped for words—"you both act like horses that have never been broken." He grinned. "And I've always liked a wild ride."

The sexual implications of the expression "wild ride" were lost on Marrah, but she could tell he was trying his best to be pleasant. Somewhat but not entirely appeased, she sat down beside him again. There was a small, slightly awkward silence.

"I want to tell you some good things about my people and the land I come from," he said. "There *are* good things, you know. For one thing, the Sea of Grass is incredibly beautiful." He held up his hand. "I'm not saying that it's more beautiful than your land, but I think if you saw it, you'd agree that there are few finer sights. In the spring it turns into a blanket of flowers that stretches as far as you can see. There's one flower in particular, a white one we call 'Han's Bride,' that grows as big as your fist, and others so small and delicate you could hold a dozen in the palm of your hand."

He went on to describe the Sea of Grass as it looked in winter with snow stretching from horizon to horizon, spoke of rivers frozen hard enough to camp on and a black sky filled with thousands of sharp white stars, and as he talked Marrah forgot she had been angry. Sometimes when he couldn't find the right word he stumbled and she had to help him, but except for such minor lapses, he spoke with eloquence and power, bringing the world of the steppes to life.

She was captivated. She had always wanted to travel and now, in a sense, she was traveling. He made her smell the scent of spring calving, the heat of midsummer, the dust that rose in clouds when the Hansi drove their herds to new pastures. Through his eyes she saw cattle standing patiently, their backs covered with the first snows of winter; leather tents pitched along clear rivers; the slowly spiraling smoke of cooking fires. She heard the laughter of the children as they played in the tall grass, the moan of the wind, the quail calling to each other at dusk. "Why, you're a natural poet!" she exclaimed.

He looked mildly embarrassed. "I've talked too much. I'm boring you."

"No, not at all. Tell me more."

"Really?"

"Yes, please."

"Then I'll tell you about my people themselves." He paused. "I realize you already know a lot about them that you don't like, but as

I said, there are good things to know too. They're a brave people, the bravest in the whole Sea of Grass. Even the women of the Hansi are brave."

"Of course the women are brave." She looked puzzled.

Realizing he was once again treading on dangerous ground, he hurried on. "I told you the men of my people were warriors, and you were offended, but you see, we don't have any choice. We're forced to fight. We're surrounded by enemies, and if we didn't defend ourselves we'd be slaughtered. But we don't just fight like animals. We have a code of honor. When we go out in a war party, we go as a band of brothers, and even though we may quarrel back in camp, out on the steppes we love each other. My brother Vlahan may hate me when we sit around my father's campfire, but if I'm being attacked by a Tcvali warrior, he'll defend me even if it means the Tcvali puts an arrow through his heart. We're absolutely loyal to each other, perhaps the most loyal people in the world, and we never fail to repay a debt of honor.

"For example"—he pointed at Marrah—"if you saved my life, I'd be bound to serve you and do whatever you wished until I saved your life and won mine back again. If you asked for my favorite concubine, or even my wife, I'd have to give her to you. You could even demand my firstborn son, unless he was the heir to the chiefdom. The heir is sacred to Han, and so—"

"What did you say?" she interrupted.

"I said 'the heir is sacred to Han.'"

"No, before that."

"You mean about saving my life?"

"Yes, that part."

He smiled. "I said that if you saved my life, I'd owe you mine, but that isn't very likely, of course, since you're a woman and not—"

"But I did."

"Did what?"

"I saved your life." And as he stared at her in open-mouthed amazement, she explained.

"You mean *you're* the one who pulled me from the sea? I'd always assumed it was one of your men. You mean to tell me it was *you?*"

"Of course," she said briskly, hoping they could move on to other topics. Now it was her turn to be embarrassed. She hadn't meant to make so much of the rescue, and given the rough way she'd dumped him into the boat, she was glad he couldn't remember the details.

"But then"—he rose to his feet—"I owe you my life."

"No, you don't." She realized she'd made a mistake. "It was nothing; it . . . well, it was the sort of thing anyone would do, and—"

He suddenly knelt at her feet, startling her so much she nearly fell over backward.

"Get up," she begged. "What are you doing?"

"Marrah of Xori," he said solemnly, "I don't know if a warrior has ever pledged his loyalty to a woman before, but I pledge mine to you. Before Han and all the gods, I swear—"

"Don't swear anything. Just get up. Please. Everyone's looking at us."

"—to defend you against all enemies—" he continued.

"I don't want you to defend me." She was touched by his sincerity, but it was embarrassing to have him kneeling at her feet promising to protect her when all she had done was take him back to the village so Ama and Sabalah could look after him. "I'm flattered that you think I did so much for you, but it was really my mother and my great-grandmother who—"

"—to give my life for you." He was unstoppable. "My bow will be your bow and my spear your spear." He was reciting the oldest, most sacred vow of the Hansi people, but to her it sounded like the ravings of someone with a high fever.

"Be sensible!" she cried, frustrated past all endurance. "I'm not a hunter. What would I do with a spear? Oh, please, I don't want to hurt your feelings, but you must see that this promise of yours doesn't make sense—"

"As long as I have a tent, you and your family will have a place to sleep; as long as I have food, you and your family will have food to eat, and from this moment until the moment I win back my life from you, I will obey you in all things." He grabbed her hands and kissed them ceremoniously. "I seal this vow with a kiss, and if I fail to keep it, may Han strike me dead."

She jerked back her hands and stared at him dumbfounded. She was flattered, impressed, annoyed, and more than a little awestruck by the seriousness of the vow he had just taken, and she couldn't help wondering if he was likely to keep it. "You're a madman," she said, not knowing whether to laugh or cry or do both simultaneously. "Why can't you ever act like a normal person?" To her surprise, he immediately got to his feet, sat down beside her, apologized once again, and after a few awkward moments started talking in a reasonable way. The rest of the evening he conducted himself like a man of the Shore People, or at least as much like one as he could, behaving so well that she began to wonder if she'd imagined him kneeling at her feet, and it was not until she had gone to bed—puzzled and more than a little mystified—that she realized he had acted normally only because she'd ordered him to.

They got back to Xori several days later, just before noon. When Arang caught sight of Marrah, he ran to greet her, followed by a crowd of relatives and a stream of whooping children. "Welcome home!" he cried, hurling himself against her and giving her a hug that nearly knocked her off her feet. "We've been watching for you forever. What took you so long? Did you like Hoza? Is it as grand as they say?"

"How many men did it take to lift the new Goddess?" Majina begged, pulling at her sleeve.

"Did you get to dance around the Tree of Life, Marrah?"

"Did you go off into the forest with anyone, because Bere has been worrying that you did, and—"

"Slow down," she pleaded, laughing so hard she could hardly speak. Zakur and Laino were licking her hands and sniffing at her feet, and every time she tried to take a step, one of the dogs moved in front of her to keep her from getting away. "I can't answer more than one question at a time." She pushed the dogs aside, gave Arang a kiss on the forehead, and folded her arms across her chest to indicate that she wasn't to be rushed, but the children kept asking more questions, hopping first on one foot and then on the other just the way she had three years ago. "I'll tell you about Hoza as soon as I've washed up and had something to eat."

"You've turned into a grown-up." Arang groaned. "I knew I wasn't going to like you being a woman. How can you even think of washing up before you tell us about the food and the dancing? By the time you've finished dragging a rag over your face, I'll be an old man."

"And I'll be an even older one," Bere interrupted. He stepped forward and gave Marrah so long a welcoming kiss that it brought cheers and laughter from the crowd.

"He can't live without you, Marrah," Izirda called, holding up baby Seshi so she could see how much he'd grown in the past two weeks.

"Bere's been pining," Belaun agreed.

"He's been unbearable."

Bere, who was used to being teased, ignored the jibes. Stepping back, he searched Marrah's face anxiously for some sign that she had changed, but her smile was as welcoming as ever. "I missed you," he murmured.

She leaned forward and put her mouth close to his ear. "Then how about meeting me in the forest tonight?"

Bere nodded, and his face flushed with relief. There were so many young men at Hoza; he hadn't been able to sleep for thinking of Marrah in their arms.

There were more welcomes, more questions, until it seemed as if everyone was talking at the same time. Ama described Mother Asha's health ("excellent for her age"); Gorriska and the young men bragged about how they'd lifted the new Goddess Stone into place; dogs barked; babies cried; and for a moment Marrah, lulled by the noisy chaos, felt there was nothing missing.

"But where's Mother?" she cried, suddenly realizing that Sabalah hadn't come out to welcome her.

"Your mother's foot's still hurting," Bere said.

"I'll go get her," Arang volunteered. A few moments later, Sabalah appeared in the door of Ama's longhouse, leaning on a crutch made from oak and padded with deerskins.

"Marrah!" she cried, and with one hand on Arang's shoulder, she came hobbling forward, dragging her injured foot behind her. Shocked at the sight, Marrah ran to meet her. "Don't look at me like that," Sabalah ordered as she hugged Marrah. "I'm not on my deathbed, you silly girl. It's nothing. The thorn went deeper than I thought, so my foot's taking longer to heal. It's not falling off; it's just sore." She turned toward Stavan, who had been standing behind the others watching the homecoming. "So you brought the stranger back." Sabalah shook her head. "I suppose that means we're stuck with him. Well, at least he's back on his feet, poor ugly thing."

"Mother," Marrah interrupted, "he can—"

Mary
Mackey

"Marrah is about to tell you that I speak Shambah," Stavan interposed.

"Great Goddess!" Sabalah dropped her crutch, sat down on the edge of the fire pit, and stared at Stavan in astonishment. "He talks!"

In the days following Marrah's return from Hoza, two things happened that changed her life forever: Sabalah's foot did not get better, and Stavan carved a new toy for Arang. At the time, only the foot seemed important, for as the skin around the hole left by the thorn festered, Sabalah began to run a high fever.

"I'm worried about her," Ama told Marrah one evening after they had bathed Sabalah's foot in herbal decoctions and wrapped it in a clean bandage. "She won't admit she's in pain, but I've seen wounds like this before." She shook her head. "First the flesh drains and swells, and then it begins to turn black. In a week or ten days the red lines appear, and once that happens you only have a little while to decide whether or not to try to take the foot off."

Marrah frowned and poked at the fire with a stick. She had seen infection sweep up a leg on a path of red lines that ran straight toward the heart. Four years ago, she had held the lamp while Ama and Sabalah pleaded with a young woman named Epela to let them cut off her right leg before she died, but Epela had been stubborn. Sure that the Bird Goddess would hear her prayers and heal her, she had refused to lose her leg. As Marrah and everyone else in the village knew, Epela's bones now lay in the Womb of Rest in Hoza, and her three children were being raised by her sisters.

"You're mother's too proud," Ama continued. "She hides her pain, and that's dangerous. Sabalah herself once told me that the Goddess Earth gave us pain so we'd know when something was wrong."

Marrah tossed the stick into the fire and watched it burn. "Maybe she's telling the truth," she suggested. "Maybe her foot doesn't hurt all that much."

"Marrah, don't fool yourself. It's getting worse."

The next evening, when Marrah changed Sabalah's bandage, she knew Ama was right. The wound on her mother's foot wasn't healing, but at least there was no black flesh or thin red lines running toward her heart.

Over the next few days, Stavan spent a lot of time with Sabalah, and the attention he paid to her made Marrah like him better than she had thought possible. He sat silently beside her bed, always ready to change the cool compress on her head or fetch her a drink of water. Sabalah drank so much that no one could keep her cup full, and the fever never left her for a moment.

"The men of my people never nurse the sick," he told Marrah one afternoon as they sat together, whispering quietly so as not to wake Sabalah, who had fallen into a restless sleep. "But I enjoy it."

"Perhaps you can be a healer when you go back to the Sea of Grass."

He shook his head. "No, I don't think so. In my land only divin-ers are healers, and they don't sit beside sick people. They dance around them, and chant, and burn *wzitza*, and sometimes reach into their bodies and pull out stones, and everyone's afraid of them, be-cause if a diviner gets mad at you he can cast a spell that will make you unhappy for the rest of your life. And when he's done, he goes away and leaves the women to get the drinks and change the com-presses and do the kinds of things I've been doing for Sabalah." He paused suddenly and listened with intense concentration. "I think I hear her waking up." He got to his feet.

"I've been wanting to ask you something." She stood up and looked at Stavan thoughtfully for a moment. "Why do you spend so much time with her?"

"Because she's your mother."

She realized he hadn't forgotten the promise he'd made on the way back from Hoza. "You don't have to sit with her for my sake. I'm perfectly capable of taking care of my own—"

"Also," he interrupted. "I like her. She's like you: interesting."

He was telling the truth. Sabalah did interest him, but having once made the mistake of telling Marrah about battles, slaves, and concubines, he was more careful what he told her mother. For the most part he held his tongue, but when he did speak, he spared Sa-balah accounts of war parties and raids. Instead he told her the stories he had heard as a child. There was the old Hansi tale of the Great Chief's son who got lost in a snowstorm and found his way back to camp by using the stars as snowshoes, the tale of the wise white bull that could talk like a human being, and the tale of the Sun Maiden who danced for Han wearing a red and gold dress. If Sabalah had been well, she would have noticed how strange and unfamiliar these stories were, how all the colors were mixed up, how dark was bad and white was good and women only existed to please men and gods, but they were entertaining and she was too ill to pick them to pieces, so she lay back and let Stavan's voice drift over her, only half hearing what he was saying. It had been a long time since she had heard anyone except her own children speak Sharan—or rather some-thing so close to Sharan as to be almost indistinguishable from it— and as the familiar words fell from his lips she felt soothed. Often, instead of hearing him, she spent the time remembering her youth, her mother, and all the friends she'd left behind.

Then one day, when almost everyone in the longhouse had gone out to help hunt for some missing goats, Arang brought Sabalah the new toy Stavan had carved for him, and as she held it in her hand, inspecting it from all angles, the clouds of fever cleared from her mind, and she saw that the disaster she had fled from fourteen years ago had not only followed her but overtaken her when she least expected it.

"What's this?" she demanded sharply, holding the piece of carved wood out to Arang. Arang looked at his mother's flushed face and her wild hair, and his voice wavered.

"Stavan calls it a horse." He pointed to the four-legged animal with hair on its neck. "You've seen one before, Mother, remember? Ama took it to Hoza to show to the Mother-of-All-Families, but she lost it on the way back, so Stavan made me another one."

"And what's this?" she jabbed her index finger at the two-legged figure seated on the back of the animal.

"Why, that's a person, of course."

"Arang." Sabalah lifted herself up into a sitting position, wincing as her foot touched the sheepskin. "Think very hard now and don't speak before you're sure. Are you telling me that Stavan's people actually *ride* these animals called horses?"

"Oh, yes." He was relieved that she wasn't angry with him. "Stavan says that to get a horse to carry you, you have to climb up on him and let him thrash around until he's tired. Usually the horse will try his best to throw you off, but after a while, he gets to understand that you're his master, and then he'll take you anywhere you want to go. Stavan says that when he came west from the Sea of Grass, he and his brother rode so swiftly that they often traveled five days' walk in a single day, and . . ."

She had stopped hearing him. She was counting something, counting it repeatedly as if she might be able to make the total come out differently: four legs on the horse, two legs on the man, six legs in all. The beastmen with six legs and two heads. Come from the east just as the Snake Goddess Batal had foretold.

"Stavan says—"

"I don't want to hear what Stavan says!" she cried, throwing the horse and rider to the floor. "Get out and leave me in peace!"

Struck dumb by fear, Arang ran from the sleeping compartment, and she fell back on her bed cursing the evil day that had brought Stavan to Xori.

Stavan returned to the longhouse in the late afternoon. When Sabalah heard the sound of his voice, she called him into her sleeping compartment and asked him to sit beside her. Although her face was pale and her chin set grimly, no one would have guessed by looking at her that she had spent the day alternately raging and crying. Being a priestess, she knew you couldn't bargain with Batal or any other goddess, and when the occasion demanded, she had as much self-control as any Hansi warrior. She had rebelled against the fulfillment of the prophesy with every fiber of her being, but after that first passionate outburst, she had come to her senses and realized that she had to find out as much as she could about the disaster that was clearly at hand.

"Tell me about your people," she commanded, and Stavan, seeing that she was no longer to be lulled by children's tales, told her what he had told Marrah, explaining the words that had to be explained and not glossing over things that might upset her. His description of Hansi life took a long time. For the most part, she let him speak without interrupting, but occasionally she asked questions.

"How far away is the Sea of Grass from the River of Smoke? How many warriors ride on these beasts called horses, and how long would it take them to reach the lands of those who worship the Goddess Earth if they traveled west?"

He couldn't give her exact answers, but he did his best. The Sea of Grass was a huge place, he told her, stretching so far that it took many months to cross, even on horseback. It was a world in itself, walled in by deserts to the east and south and endless forests to the north. The only opening was to the west, and although there were several mountain ranges and many rivers, a man on a horse could easily make his way into the valley of the River of Smoke if it lay where she said it did. How long this would take would depend on where the man started. The tribes called no place home; they moved constantly, never camping in one place more than a few weeks. In ancient times they had followed a sacred white stallion, setting it free to choose the path of their migration, but since his great-grandfather's time, there had been too many tribes looking for fresh pastures, and battles over grass and water rights were common.

As for how many warriors there were, that was even more difficult to say. When all the tribes of the Hansi got together, their campfires looked like the stars. And the Hansi were only one tribe. There were others: the Tcvali, the Zikulzu, the Abakaz, and so forth. How many warriors were there on the Sea of Grass? Only Han knew. Go down to the beach, he suggested, and count the grains of sand. Go down to the ocean and count the water drop by drop.

When he had finished speaking, she sat silently for so long that he began to fear he had offended her, but she was not offended; she was frightened. This was worse than she had feared. If Stavan was telling the truth—and she had no reason to think he wasn't—the beastmen weren't coming to steal Marrah; they weren't even coming to conquer Shara. They were riding west to destroy every family that worshiped the Goddess Earth.

That evening Sabalah had Seme and Belaun carry her to the temple. There, alone in the sacred darkness, without a candle or a fire, she opened a small doeskin pouch and spilled a piece of dried fungus into the palm of her hand. Although she couldn't see what she was holding, she knew the fungus was black and shaped like a thorn. The Shore People called it the Bread of Darkness, and it was so potent that those who took it without the proper training sometimes went permanently insane.

"Dearest Batal," she prayed, "I'm so far from your dreaming cave and so far from Shara that perhaps you can't hear me, but if you can, I beg you to give me another vision. Show me what I can do to save my people from the beastmen, because I can see that our world is about to end and this is too much knowledge for me to bear all by myself." When she had finished praying, she turned and kissed the earth; then quickly, before she lost her courage, she put the Bread of Darkness in her mouth, swallowed it, and lay back, trembling with fear but determined to see whatever of the future could be seen.

For a long time nothing happened, but finally, when she was almost ready to give up, Batal heard her prayer. The vision she had asked for came without warning, and this time when it swept over her it was terrible beyond words: time stopped, space stopped, and her heart paused between beats. She knew she was dead and alive at the same time, she was there and not there, and in her agony she cried out for light, and light came, whirling out of the darkness. All colors and no colors, it burned her until she screamed, licking at her lips and eyelids, searing her flesh. When at last she was completely consumed and nothing was left of her but darkness and cinders, a voice spoke.

*Who seeks to know My mysteries?* the voice demanded.

"I do," she cried courageously. "I, Sabalah, daughter of Lalah."

*Then send to Shara the two things you love the most.*

"What things, Batal? What do you mean? Do you mean my children? Am I to send Marrah and Arang back to Shara with a warning?"

*Don't ask me. Ask your heart.*

"Spare me this!" she cried. "Dear blessed Goddess, don't make me send my children away." But the voice was silent and spoke no more.

She waited for three days after her vision, trying to convince herself that she had misunderstood Batal's message, but on the third day when she looked at her foot and saw the black flesh beginning to form around the wound, she called Marrah to her. "Hold out your hand," she commanded, and when Marrah stretched out her palm, she placed Arang's toy on it—such a little thing, light as a stick, cunningly carved, pretty to look at, but such a grim omen that it might as well have been made from the bones of the dead. "Count the legs," she ordered. Marrah, who knew the prophecy, didn't have to count. One look at her mother's face told her more than she wanted to know. With a cry, she let the toy fall to the floor.

"The men of your dream," she whispered. "They're Stavan's people." She waited for Sabalah to deny it, waited for her to say no, of course not, but instead Sabalah nodded. Marrah tried to speak, but she couldn't. She sat down next to her mother, picked up the toy, and looked at it again, trying to understand how she could have been so blind. Stavan had told her his people rode horses, but she had never understood that a mounted man would look so much like a part of the beast. For a moment she felt numb, then terrified, then angry.

"I saved his life." She nearly choked on the words. "I hauled him back to the village when I could just as easily have let him die on the beach. You and Ama nursed him back to health. We fed him, gave him a place by our fire, put up with his bad temper, and even took him to Hoza, and this"—she pointed to the toy—"this is our reward? We should have let him die; we should have let the birds have him."

Sabalah put her arm around Marrah's shoulder and drew her close. "Shh," she said, stroking Marrah's hair, "calm down. This isn't your fault. Stavan's not the problem. Of course you saved him. No daughter of mine would let a man die. Stavan isn't a bad man; oh, he had fits of temper when he first arrived, but he's changed. It was almost as if no one had ever taught him that people could get along with each other. He seemed to think he had to fight us for every crust of bread, and he was afraid of us. Ama said he acted like a child who'd never had a mother, and when I asked her if that meant we should cast him out of the village, she shook her head and said no, it only meant we had to give him more love; and you see, it worked. We've loved him as best we could, and now I think he loves us—or at least cares for us." She took the toy from Marrah. "No, Stavan isn't the problem, but his people are." She put the horse and rider down on the ground and looked at them for a moment. "Did he ever tell you how many Hansi warriors there are?"

Marrah shook her head.

"They're like grains of sand, he told me; like the stars. And if they choose to ride west, there's nothing to stop them. And they will ride west; the prophecy tells us they will." Her eyes narrowed. "I've lain here for three days trying to imagine what it will be like when they arrive. I've lain here lost in an old nightmare." She raised Marrah's hand to her lips and kissed it. "At first I was only afraid they were coming for you, but after I talked to Stavan I began to understand they were coming for all of us. It will take them a long time to get to Xori, perhaps so long that by the time they arrive you and I will be dust, but Shara and all the cities of the East are close to the Sea of Grass." She spit on the ground. "May the Goddess send a flood to drown the Hansi; may She send a great wind to blow them away and a fire to burn them and their horses to ashes!"

Marrah was impressed. She'd never seen her mother so angry. "What can we do? How can we warn them?"

"I've asked myself that; I've lain here asking myself the same question, and when I couldn't come up with an answer I went to the temple to beg the Snake Goddess Batal to tell me what to do. I ate the Bread of Darkness and gave my body to the shadow world, and a voice spoke to me telling me something I didn't want to hear. 'Send to Shara the two things you love most,' it said. I cried out against it; I begged to be spared, but the voice wouldn't speak again."

Marrah turned the words over in her mind, trying to make them mean something less terrible, but the message was clear. "I'm supposed to go to Shara; I'm to warn them, and Arang's to go with me. Is that right? Is that what Batal wants?"

"I think so, but I don't want to think so. Arang's so young. And you, my precious daughter, how can I send you so far away? I can't; I won't. At least not until I'm sure. Not until I hear something besides riddles. The Bread of Darkness can lie. It can make the seeker hear false voices. I won't ask you to go to Shara, because I know that if I do, you will. I won't force this decision on you. If the Goddess wants you to be Her messenger, let Her tell you plainly. You're ready; I've taught you everything I know." She picked up the horse and rider, put it in Marrah's hand, and closed her fingers around it. "You're a woman now, and the time has come for you to ask for your own visions."

Between the temple and the communal oven was a small round hut with no windows. The hut, which was only six feet long, looked like a tunnel. On the end closer to the temple, there was a door so small that anyone entering had to crawl; the other end was the back wall of the oven. When water was thrown against the hot stones of the oven wall, the hut filled with steam.

That night Marrah and Sabalah went to the steam hut to purify themselves. Breathing the steam, they rubbed their bodies with mint and scented oils, and as they sweated out the impurities of everyday life, they prayed. "Make us worthy," they chanted. "Make us ready to receive You."

The steam filled their lungs; it grew hotter and hotter in the hut, so hot that Marrah felt as if she might faint, but she went on chanting and praying. At last, Sabalah picked up a large bowl of cold water, poured some over her own head, and dumped the rest on Marrah. Crawling out of the hut, they dried themselves with deerskins and sat for a few minutes in silence. The temple was dark, lit only by a single lamp. Beyond the light, deep in the shadows, Marrah could feel her fear waiting for her, but she had been well taught. She breathed deeply to still her panic and concentrated on the flame.

"Are you ready?" Sabalah whispered. Marrah nodded, never letting go of the light. Sabalah reached into her medicine pouch, drew out a small piece of the Bread of Darkness, and broke it in half. "Take and eat this. Whatever you see will be sacred knowledge that can only be told to another priestess. This is the promise we make when we put Her Bread between our lips." She handed Marrah the Bread, and Marrah put it on her tongue. It tasted slightly sweet. She looked at the flame and swallowed.

Time passed. And then stopped passing. The lamp went out. There was darkness. Marrah stopped being Marrah.

When she woke again, she was flying high above the land of the Shore People. Sabalah was flying next to her, and they were both birds. Marrah saw that her mother had powerful black wings; her own wings were the wings of a seagull. With a cry of delight, she soared upward, riding the wind. Below her, she could see Hoza and, south of Hoza, the village of Gurasoak where Mother Asha lived. Beyond Gurasoak was a great forest and beyond the forest a sea so blue it looked like a morning glory. Deep-keeled boats with white linen sails skimmed across the waves, carrying copper and obsidian, pottery, olive oil, salt, wine, and rare herbs. Along the shores of the sea, there were great cities with temples and public squares, and she could see people going about their daily lives: making pottery, working gold, mining, weaving, worshiping in the temples, planting seeds in the earth, nursing the sick, making love, giving birth, and caring for their children.

She flew higher. Beyond the cities there were more cities and villages, stretching east and north as far as the eye could see, and there were rivers and forests and many peoples, all different yet all worshiping the Goddess Earth. Some raised Goddess Stones to Her; other carved Her image in marble or jadestone; still others took clay and formed it into Her likeness. To some, She appeared as a sacred snake whose coils were the endless energy of life itself; to others, She was the holy bird who brought life and death, or the dog who guarded young life, or the womb-shaped frog. In the north, She was often worshiped as a pregnant bear or doe, while to the south, She often appeared as a bull bearing the horns of the crescent moon, but no matter how She revealed Herself to Her people, Her commandments were the same, and in every city and village and forest, Her children sang of Her love for them and their love for Her.

As Marrah hovered over all this, a voice spoke to her. *Go higher*, it commanded, and so she went higher, and as she rose, the air grew cold, and she saw that beyond the lands of the Goddess there was another land all covered in grass, where men in leather tents prayed to a God of War and killed each other in His name. Their God was a God of Exile who lived in the sky, and the earth was a dead thing to them.

And as Marrah watched, the men mounted their horses and began to ride west, setting fire to the land, killing the animals, destroying the fields and forests, laying waste to the cities, and people fled in terror before them, and a great moaning rose up in the East like a dark cloud, drawing nearer all the time.

*Look*, the voice commanded, *the Time of Destruction is coming, and you, Marrah, are my messenger. Go to Shara and warn my children that the riders are on their way. Take your brother with you, and take the stranger also to prove you speak the truth.*

"Yes," Marrah cried, "I'll go!" and as she spoke, her wings failed, and she began to fall and fall and fall until everything was darkness and falling.

She woke crying in Sabalah's arms.

"The Goddess gave you a vision?" Sabalah whispered.

Marrah nodded.

"You have to go to Shara? And Arang too?"

Marrah nodded again.

"This breaks my heart!" Sabalah cried, and folding Marrah in her arms, she wept with her.

Finally, Sabalah kissed Marrah and released her, and the two sat quietly for a time, each lost in her own sad thoughts. After a while, they began to talk about how Marrah would find her way to Shara.

"When you were a child," Sabalah said, "I came west with you on my back, and as I was crossing from the Blue Sea to the Sea of Gray Waves, I stopped at the Caves of Nar. The caves are the oldest temple on earth." She took Marrah's hands and held them; her fingers trembled slightly, but her voice was steady. "When I left, the priestesses told me that if I ever returned I should stop at Nar again and there would be three gifts waiting for me. Then they took you from me and held you on their laps. The oldest blessed you with a kiss and promised that if you came in my place, the gifts would be yours."

Marrah, who was very surprised at this, asked what kind of gifts the priestesses of Nar were keeping for her, and Sabalah admitted she didn't know. "They wouldn't tell me. All I know is that they come directly from the Goddess Earth, so they must be very powerful. But in the end, it doesn't matter. You have to go to Nar on your way east, because even if the priestesses have changed their minds and given the gifts to someone else, you need to ask their blessing. They're very holy and very powerful. It's said that as long as they tend the caves, the world can never end. They're remarkable women." She paused for a moment as if lost in memories Marrah was too young to share. Then, clearing her throat, she got down to details.

"The forest crossing will be difficult; I won't pretend it's easy to get from one sea to the other, but you should be able to find the caves readily enough if you follow the song-map I made when I came west."

"The one you taught me when I was a child?"

Sabalah smiled. "The very one, and how sweet you looked singing it in perfect Sharan. But, as you probably remember, it was an east-west map. Now we must sing it in reverse, west to east."

"Can that be done?"

Sabalah nodded. "All song maps are reversible. I've sung my song west to east many times in secret over the last three days, getting it ready for you in case . . ." Her voice trailed off, and her smile disappeared. "I'd planned to follow my song back to Shara, but it won't be my song any longer; it will be yours. You'll add verses telling of your adventures, and when you come to Shara you'll sing it to your Grandmother Lalah." She put her arm around Marrah and drew her close again. "Listen. The Goddess has given you a good memory, and except for reversing the direction, I've only made a few changes, most of them at the beginning." She closed her eyes and sat perfectly still for a few seconds. Then, taking a deep breath, she began to sing, not of the Caves of Nar or Shara but of Xori and its longhouses and the Sea of Gray Waves:

> The way to Shara is long,

she sang,

> and the first steps are hardest,
> but Marrah and Arang
> are Sabalah's children.
>
> They watch the Goddess Stone
> grow smaller and smaller
> but they go on bravely;
> they don't turn back.
>
> They follow the whale road
> past the great wombs of Hoza
> to Gurasoak, where the river
> flows out of the forest.
>
> They follow their mother's song to Shara,
> and Sabalah blesses their every step. . . .

Her voice grew sweet and more plaintive. It was hauntingly beautiful, and as Marrah listened, already grieving for all the friends

The
Year
the
Horses
Came

101

she was about to leave behind, her mother's song entered her heart and comforted her.


A few days later, having secured Ama's permission, Marrah, Arang, and Stavan left with two traders from Zizare who were sailing south to Gurasoak with baskets of ceremonial jadeite axes. The last thing Marrah saw as the boat rounded the point was Sabalah standing on the beach, supported by Bere and Uncle Seme.

"The dear Goddess bless you, my children," Sabalah cried, until Marrah could no longer hear her, but she did not break down again and she did not call them back.

When the boat was out of sight, Sabalah turned to Bere and Seme. Seme's face was streaked with tears, and Bere, who had spent the night with Marrah, was crying openly, but Sabalah had no sympathy to spare. Her own tears had dried up days ago, and all that was left was a rasping grief that stuck in the back of her throat. "Carry me back to Ama's longhouse and lay me down beside my own fire," she commanded.

Seme picked Sabalah up in his arms, carried her to the longhouse, and laid her gently on a pile of sheepskins in front of her own fire. Ama was waiting for them, holding a pair of stout wooden tongs.

Sabalah looked at the fire and then at Ama. "Are the stones hot enough yet?" she asked. Ama nodded grimly. "Good," Sabalah cried. "Then take one from the fire and put it against my foot and burn out the corruption. I want to live long enough to see my children again." And shoving the end of her leather belt between her teeth, she lay back, closed her eyes, and let Bere and Seme hold her down as Ama reached into the fire, pulled out a red-hot stone, and thrust it against the circle of black flesh on the sole of her foot, crying, "Sabalah, for-

give me!"

Sabalah took the belt out of her mouth with shaking hands; there were tears in her eyes, and they saw she had bitten through the leather. "There's nothing to forgive," she said. "Do it again if you need to; get it all." And putting the belt back between her teeth, she

gripped Bere and Seme's arms, closed her eyes, and thought of Marrah and Arang waving to her, getting smaller and smaller as they sailed away.

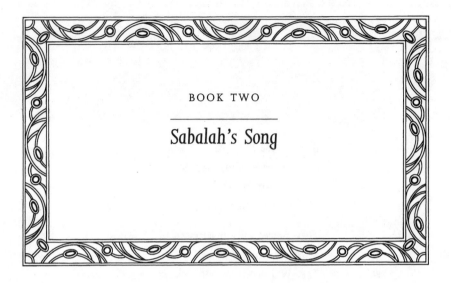

BOOK TWO

Sabalah's Song

Between the Blue Sea
and the Sea of Gray Waves
lie the Caves of Nar
where the animals dance.

They danced for our ancestors
when the world was ice.
They will dance for our children
when our bones are dust.

Walk softly, walk lightly,
the Earth is sleeping.
Walk softly, walk lightly,
She is pregnant with dreams.

SABALAH'S SONG
VERSES 11–13

# CHAPTER SIX

*From Gurasoak to the Caves of Nar*

Mother Asha sat on a litter made of wood and wicker. The litter, which she had designed herself, had a high woven back, armrests, comfortable down-filled pillows, and even a small wooden rail that she could prop her feet on when her ankles began to ache. Big enough to be comfortable but small enough to fit through the doors of the longhouses of Gurasoak, it was the only litter of its kind in the land of the Shore People, and she was secretly vain about having created it. But this particular morning she was hardly aware of the soft pillows, and instead of leaning against the backrest she was leaning forward, her black eyes snapping with excitement as she listened to Marrah of Xori explain why she, her brother, and the stranger called Stavan were headed east.

"So you're following your mother's song. How I envy you." Mother Asha tapped the arm of her litter impatiently, thinking how nice it would be to be able to walk such a long distance without worrying about your knees giving out. "For nearly fifteen years now, ever since I became the Mother-of-All-Families, I've sat here and listened to traders from the Blue Sea tell me about the lands beyond the forest. I was here when your mother first walked out of the wilderness carrying you on her back, and I was the one who adopted the two of you and sent you to Xori to live with Ama." She closed her eyes for a moment, lost in old memories. Just when Marrah thought she'd fallen asleep, she opened them again and sighed.

"I've always wanted to see the temples and great cities your mother sings about, but I never will. I'm far too old, and no doubt before you come back from Shara—if you ever do come back—I'll be dead."

Marrah started to object, but Mother Asha silenced her with a wave of her hand. "No, let's not fool ourselves. I'm not afraid of going back to the Mother. To tell the truth, I sometimes long to shut my eyes and rest forever in Her loving embrace, but you, who are young and strong, probably fear death, which is a good thing. You'll need that fear where you're going. I've seen more young people die from taking foolish risks than from playing it safe, and you're twice as rash as most of them." She extended her hand and placed it lightly on Marrah's head. "So go with my blessing." She paused and noticed Arang standing to one side, looking at her with wide, curious eyes. "Come here, boy, and let me bless you too, for it's a long path for a child to take."

Marrah bowed and nudged Arang forward, feeling relieved. She hadn't been sure how Mother Asha would react to the news that she was about to take her eight-year-old brother all the way to Shara, but as always, Mother had understood without having to be told why the Goddess had commanded Sabalah to send both her children. Arang spoke Sharan. If something happened to Marrah—to put it bluntly, if she died or became too sick to go on—it would be up to him to deliver the warning.

Arang knelt and bowed his head as Mother Asha blessed him. He knew he should thank her, but he was too awed. She must be the

oldest woman on earth. He wondered if it was true that the Mother-of-All-Families could make Goddess Stones rise up just by waving her hands at them.

Mother Asha saw his nervousness and smiled. "Don't be afraid, boy. I don't bite." She laughed such a good-natured laugh that Arang found himself laughing with her. "You look like a brave boy." She had learned long ago that it was better to tell children they *were* good than to command them to *be* good. "You'll be a big help to your sister."

Arang turned red with embarrassment. "I hope so, dear Mother," he managed to stutter, and then, alarmed by his own courage, he backed away from her litter so fast he nearly bumped into Marrah.

Mother Asha smiled, amused by how impressed he was. The little boy obviously thought she was as wise as the Goddess Herself. She wished she still believed there were grown-ups who knew everything. The truth was, she muddled along like everyone else, and some mornings she wondered if she had any more sense than an eight-year-old.

She turned her attention back to Marrah, who was also waiting expectantly for some words of wisdom. "I don't know much about the lands you'll be passing through once you reach the Blue Sea, but I've heard any number of tales about the forest crossing. The country between here and the coast is mostly wilderness. There are a few settlements along the river, but most of the people follow the old ways, only taking what the Goddess gives them in the way of game and wild plants. The traders tell me most of the mother tribes think it's wrong to cut open the body of the Goddess Earth and plant seeds in her, and I've heard that bands of them sometimes come into backcountry settlements to beg the village mothers to stop farming."

"Are they dangerous?" Marrah asked. It was a question that would never have occurred to her before she met Stavan.

Mother Asha shook her head. "No, only the wild animals are dangerous. There are lions in the forest. Two years ago, one killed a trader. He was walking at the end of the line a little behind the others, and a she-lion crept up and took him so fast he didn't even have time to scream. Later, she tried again, but this time the traders were ready for her, and they scared her off. That sort of thing doesn't happen very often, but even so, you should never camp without a fire." She suddenly realized she was probably scaring Marrah, not to mention the boy, who already looked frightened enough to wet his pants. That was the trouble with sitting at home all the time. You forgot that people who were actually going into the forest might not appreciate knowing what dangers lay ahead. It was time to change the subject.

"As for the Forest People, as I said, they're not the least bit dangerous. They disapprove of our ways, but they tolerate them. Like us, they worship the Goddess and respect Her commandments. It's just that sometimes their idea of loving you involves sitting you down and treating you to a long harangue on how you would be happier if you followed the ways of the ancestors. But I'm not sure you'll ever see them. The forest is huge, and they tend to avoid any contact with the outside world. I used to think that was because they were shy, but a trader recently told me it's because they think we smell bad from eating so much milk and cheese."

The
Year
the
Horses
Came

107

Marrah was looking puzzled. "My mother's song doesn't mention any Forest People."

Mother Asha chuckled. "I'm not surprised. Sabalah wouldn't have enjoyed being treated like a jar of sour milk. Maybe she decided not to honor them by including them in her song, or maybe she never met them. As I said, the forest stretches for many weeks in all directions. More than one trading party has disappeared between here and the Blue Sea. Why only five years ago—" She stopped, realizing once again that some things were perhaps best left unsaid.

"But never mind all that. All things considered, the land route is best. It's an easy walk, really, well marked and level most of the way. They say the river forks six times. I don't know which fork takes you to the Caves of Nar but the traders will, even if they haven't been there themselves. The Caves are often visited by pilgrims who come to ask the blessing of the priestesses." She sighed. "I do envy you. Whatever they give you will be priceless."

She suddenly felt weary, as if her duty had been done, but she could not dismiss Sabalah's children until she had given them her final blessing. Reaching into the embroidered leather bag that hung from one of the arms of her litter, she drew out two shell necklaces and sat for a moment holding them in her hands. The necklaces were like the ones children wore except that each was decorated with a small triangular shell pendant.

"Come here and let me put these on you. They're pilgrim necklaces. I don't imagine you've seen them in Xori; it's not a place pilgrims come to. But east of here, people will take one look and know you're traveling under the special protection of the Goddess. If they have food, they'll give it to you even if they don't eat themselves." She paused, suddenly overcome with forebodings. What was she sending Sabalah's children off to? She fastened the necklaces around their necks and placed her hands on their heads one last time. "Remember that wherever you go, you'll always be walking on the body of the Goddess Earth. When you miss your own mother, try to remember that the greatest Mother of all is close enough to touch."

She cleared her throat and motioned for Marrah and Arang to rise. "Enough of this. I'm much too old for goodbyes, so when you leave tomorrow morning, don't bother to drop by my longhouse to say farewell. Just leave quietly and try not to wake the dogs."

Marrah thought perhaps she had misunderstood. "Did you say we're leaving tomorrow, dear Mother?"

"You are unless you want to spend the winter in Gurasoak. Three traders came in from the Blue Sea about two weeks ago. They've been waiting for jadeite axes to come down from Zizare—waiting with far too little patience, I must say. Now that the axes have arrived, they're planning to start back tomorrow at dawn. I've already asked if they'll take the three of you with them, and of course they will although they grumbled about having to guide you to Nar. They seem to be afraid that if they make the detour they may arrive at the Blue Sea too late to catch the last boat going east before the winter rains, but in the end they agreed." She grinned. "After all, how could they refuse? You're pilgrims, and it's their sacred duty to see you safely to Nar, or anywhere else you care to travel, but just to make sure I reminded them—most politely, of course—of two good reasons for giving in gracefully: first, it's bad luck to stand in the way of a priestess who wants to pray at a holy place, and second"—her grin deepened—"I told them there were other traders up the coast who would give anything for two baskets of fine ceremonial axes."

"But dear Mother," Marrah objected, "there aren't any traders north of Gurasoak. We've just come from there, and—" She stopped, suddenly understanding. "Of course, we might not have seen them."

"Yes," Mother Asha said with a perfectly straight face, "it would have been easy for you to miss them, particularly since the weather's been so stormy."

Marrah, who knew for a fact that there had been nothing but a few days of light rain since she left for Gurasoak, nodded solemnly and agreed that the storms had indeed been terrible.

As soon as Mother Asha dismissed her, she found Arang some breakfast and then went in search of the traders. It proved to be a short search, since everyone in Gurasoak seemed to know where everyone else was at all times.

"The southerners are in the guesthouse," a little girl not much older than Arang informed her, pointing in the direction of a small building that sat at the edge of the village. The girl scratched her elbow and eyed Marrah with friendly curiosity. "If you want to talk to them, you'd better do it now. My mama says they're leaving for the Blue Sea tomorrow before sunrise."

Marrah thanked her and hurried to the guesthouse, where she found a man and two women busily packing jadeite axes into wicker

The
Year
the
Horses
Came

109

carrying baskets. The baskets were about three feet long, flat on one side and tightly woven to keep out rain and dust. Each had several leather straps that could be worn across the chest of the person who was carrying it, plus a head strap for balance. There were six, Marrah noticed: five standard-size ones and another about the size a child Arang's age could carry. Evidently the packing was being done in a hurry, since packets of dried fruit and beef jerky lay scattered on the floor, mixed with water skins, flints, extra head straps, and several other tightly wrapped bundles that probably contained trade goods.

"Welcome to the House of Chaos," the man called out cheerfully when he saw Marrah. Letting the basket he had been packing tumble to the floor, he strode across the room, and before she realized what was happening, he knelt, kissed her hand, and rose in a single motion so graceful that it looked like a dance. "I'm Rhom of Lezentka, the most beautiful village on the coast of the Blue Sea, favored by the Goddess and warmed by the sun, where the dolphins dance and the air smells like honey. You must be Marrah of Xori, going south on holy business—Marrah of the dark eyes, who'll capture the heart of every man she meets."

Marrah laughed and turned to the women. "Does he always talk this way?"

"Always," one of them said. She spoke slowly with a heavy accent. "He's full of more hot air and goat dung than anyone else you'll ever meet. Just ignore him, and sooner or later he'll move on to a new victim."

Rhom chuckled. "My dear sisters have no ear for poetry." He waved at them. "Permit me to introduce Zastra and Shema, two of the most practical women ever to walk the forest trail." To Marrah's surprise, the women immediately stopped packing the baskets and hurried across the room to kiss her hand. Hand kissing must be a southern custom, she decided.

"Her peace be with you," Zastra and Shema said politely, rolling the ends of their words in a way she had never heard before. They were clearly sisters, big and broad-shouldered, with stocky arms and legs that looked strong enough to carry baskets twice as heavy as the ones they were packing. Both wore their hair braided up and out of the way, and both had the same flattish noses and clear brown eyes. Except for the fact that Zastra was clearly several years older than Shema, they might have been twins.

Rhom, in contrast, was light-boned and thin, with dark eyes, graceful hands, and small feet. Everything about him seemed exotic to Marrah, from the finely embroidered piece of linen he wore cinched around his waist to the intricate weave of his sandals. If he hadn't had the same flat nose as his sisters, she would have had trouble believing the three were related. She wondered how such a small man had managed to carry a basket filled with trade goods from one sea to the other. Rhom looked as if he'd wilt under a medium-sized load of firewood.

As if reading her thoughts, he walked across the room and picked up one of the baskets. "This one's for you," he said, motioning for her to turn around so he could help her into the straps. Since he was lifting the basket with one hand, she assumed it was almost empty, but when he put it on her it was so heavy she staggered and nearly fell over backward.

Shema caught her and helped her out of the basket. "I told Rhom it would be too heavy for you, but he *never* listens to me." She patted Marrah on the arm sympathetically. "Don't worry, little sister. We'll make you and your brother beginners' baskets. The giant who's traveling with you can pack a full load, but all you'll have to carry are the feather capes and straw bird masks and your own food." Zastra and Rhom nodded in agreement.

Marrah's pride was smarting, but she had enough sense not to argue. She looked at Rhom with new respect. She had always thought of herself as strong for her size, but compared to him and his sisters, she was a weakling.


The next morning the six of them left Gurasoak before the breakfast fires were lit. It was a cool, still time of day, and as Marrah put her back to the Sea of Gray Waves and walked toward the estuary, she felt as if she were entering a new world. The estuary was a large tidal basin, part salt water, part fresh. At dawn and dusk, thousands of frogs ribbeted and droned from invisible hiding places in the reeds. The Shore People called the river that fed the estuary Ibai Nabar, or the River of Many Colors, because its wide, calm surface reflected the sky, changing from dark gray to shell pink as the sun rose. At noon, the estuary shone like a sheet of ice, but in the mornings and late afternoons, on a clear day, it took on a transparent blue tint that reminded her of Stavan's eyes.

Yet as beautiful as the estuary was, it was no pleasure to walk along its banks, especially if you were carrying a basket full of trade goods. Ringed by marshes and bogs, it was treacherous, ankle-spraining

The
Year
the
Horses
Came

country; the mud was waist deep in places, and it wasn't unheard of for trading parties to spend a week or more making their way up to the mouth of the river.

But thanks to Mother Asha, Marrah, Stavan, Arang, and the traders left Gurasoak in style, floating past the muddy shore in two small round *shavas*. Made out of pieces of cowhide stretched on wicker frames and sealed with pitch, the light, watertight boats could be found in every village of the Shore People. Marrah knew them well, having fished from one ever since she was old enough to hold a pole. They were hard to tip over but even harder to steer, and although they could hold their own in calm water and move briskly forward when the tide was with you, they were almost useless against a current.

Since the tide was coming in, they would have presented no problem if Stavan and the traders had known how to steer them, but they didn't. At first they went in circles as Rhom and Stavan cursed and Shema and Zastra floundered on grimly. Finally Marrah took over and showed them all how it was done, and after that they made steady progress, stopping whenever the tide turned and camping on whatever dry land they could find.

On the second night it rained. Turning the *shavas* upside down, they used them as shelters. They had to take turns sleeping since there wasn't enough room under the boats for all six of them plus the trading baskets, but the rain was warm and the traders made it clear that if anything got wet it was not going to be the straw bird masks and feathered capes.

The next morning they set out again, paddling across the estuary under a sun that quickly dried their clothes. It was a lovely, lazy way to travel, and as Marrah dipped her paddle into the great mirror beneath her she felt at peace for the first time since she left Xori. Protected from the strong winds and winter storms of the coast, the estuary was home to thousands of birds of every kind—herons, bitterns, goldeneyes, grebes, kestrels, rails, kingfishers, and black-headed gulls so fat from feasting in the wild grasses they could hardly fly. Sometimes, as the *shavas* passed, huge flocks of mallards would rise into the air uttering cries of alarm. There were so many that the flapping of their wings rippled the surface of the water, and for a moment or two their bodies would blot out the sun. But for the most part, the birds regarded them with indifference, hardly pausing long enough to look at the passing boats before they went back to feeding on the fish and wild grasses. It was clear they had never been hunted and had no fear of human beings; if Marrah had wanted to, she could have reached out and caught one with her bare hands. But there was no need to teach the birds their trust was misplaced. The waters of the estuary were so full of fish that in the mornings they always caught enough to eat well for the rest of the day.

Around noon on the third day, the landscape began to change. First a few trees appeared along the banks, then more. The water became clearer and took on a slightly green tinge, and the tall grasses gave way to islands covered with bushes and saplings. By the time the shadows had begun to lengthen again, the current coming toward them had grown so strong it was impossible to paddle the *shavas*, so they hauled the boats out of the water and carried them like great baskets to the end of the estuary, cursing as they stumbled through the muck. Soon they came to the mouth of the river. Actually it wasn't one river but two, separated by what appeared to be an island. The island was really the northern bank of the Ibai Nabar, and Marrah was amused to learn that the river to the left was called the Ibai Txar, or "Wrong River," named no doubt by some disgruntled trading party that had taken it by mistake.

Hoisting the *shavas* up onto the southern bank of the Ibai Nabar, they washed as much mud off themselves as they could and then set out again, carrying the boats upriver toward the little village of Xemta, which the traders assured them lay nearby. Xemta was either the last settlement of the Shore People or the first of the River People, depending on how you felt about it, but since the entire village only consisted of two longhouses about the size of cow sheds and several garden plots barely large enough to sustain the single mother family that tilled them, it hardly mattered. According to Rhom, the women of Xemta had made children with the men of the Shore and the men of the River as long as anyone could remember, but it was quite a trip in both directions, and they were always happy to extend hospitality to traders, especially *male* traders.

Shema and Zastra shook their heads at this but admitted Rhom was telling the truth. "They're all one mother family," Zastra explained, "so of course they can't share joy with each other. The sons usually leave the village when they get old enough to want a woman, but since the daughters belong to the land, they stay put. Any man who's alive and breathing can always find a warm bed in Xemta—even Rhom."

The
Year
the
Horses
Came

113

Marrah didn't think this was much of a compliment to Rhom, but he seemed to take the teasing with good humor. She was gradually beginning to realize he was harmless. The elaborate flattery he tossed her way was not meant to be taken seriously; it was just his way of amusing himself, and once she had made it clear that she wasn't interested in sharing his bed, he had settled down and become as sensible a traveling companion as anyone could ask for.

Stavan, on the other hand, worried her. He never complained, but he could hardly be described as cheerful. Ever since they left Xori, he had barely spoken to her, and she often caught him looking at her in a way that made her feel uneasy. If he hadn't been so polite and helpful, she would have thought he had somehow guessed he was being taken to Shara as a living example of the beastmen, but he was treating her with so much respect that every time he spoke to her she felt like the Mother-of-All-Families, which might have been pleasant if she had been ninety and toothless, but given that she was young and had all her teeth, she would have preferred he talk to her more like he talked to Arang. Those conversations were mostly about hunting, but they were animated. Stavan had brought his arrows and his brother's strangely shaped bow along, and from what Marrah had overheard, he was planning to show Arang how to hunt once they entered the forest.

Sometimes she wondered if perhaps she was the one who was being unfriendly. She was doing her best to remember that Stavan's people were the problem, not Stavan, but sometimes, when she looked at him, she couldn't help imagining him mounted on one of those beasts he called horses. She would think of burning cities and people fleeing in panic and other things so terrible she tried not to dwell on them. Sometimes she would even find herself blaming him for the fact that she had to leave Xori. She missed her mother and Bere and Ama and Uncle Seme so much she often had to bite her lips to keep from crying in front of Arang, and although she knew it was unfair, she couldn't help feeling that if it weren't for Stavan she would be at home now, eating Uncle Hatz's stew and sleeping in her own bed.

Whenever she fell into one of these moods, she took special pains to be friendly to Stavan, but perhaps he sensed that her friendliness was mixed with resentment. She hoped not, because they were going to be in each other's company for a long time and it was important to get along. Besides, she had grown to like him over the past few weeks, and when she was in a more sensible frame of mind she knew he deserved to be treated as a friend. It was a difficult situation, and that afternoon as they headed upriver she was relieved to find herself sharing a boat with Zastra and Shema.


Marrah might have been even more uneasy if she had known what was going on in Stavan's mind as he, Arang, and Rhom hauled their boat through the brush. Stavan was not unhappy—she was wrong about that—but he was not particularly happy either. Instead, he was caught somewhere in between. He was glad to be leaving the land of the Shore People. He had never liked the cold mists and gray sea, and although he had begun to appreciate some of their customs, he felt trapped between the beach and the forest. He had never stopped longing for the endless horizons of the Sea of Grass, and ever since Achan led him west he had dreamed of going home. Now, at last, he was on his way, moving more or less in the right direction, not mounted on a horse as a man should be, but at least walking on his own two feet instead of tossing around in one of the savages' cursed little boats, the kind that floundered and broke apart like kindling in rough weather.

Yet at the same time he was worried. For one thing, there was no guarantee he would be able to find the tents of the Hansi even if he did manage to get back to the steppes. The tribe moved constantly over an area so large that only Han knew where they were camping at any given moment. Even supposing he picked up their trail before he died of exhaustion or was killed by enemy warriors, what kind of reception would his father give him when he returned on foot to report that Achan was dead and the whole expedition to the Land of the Sun a miserable failure?

All that would have been enough to keep him awake at night, but there was something else bothering him, something he couldn't quite put his finger on. It had something to do with Marrah, but he couldn't say exactly what. Ordinarily when he thought about a woman, he knew exactly how he felt: he either wanted to take her into his bed or he didn't, and that was all there was to it. There were exceptions, of course, women like Tzinta, who had raised him and was practically a mother to him, and who had more spirit and more fine tales to tell than most men, or Zulike, his father's wife, who had enough power to cause a man a lot of trouble if she put her mind to

The
Year
the
Horses
Came

115

it; but for the most part, when he was with a woman he knew what to do with her—or, for that matter, what not to do with her if she belonged to another man.

But with Marrah things had somehow managed to get so snarled up he hardly ever knew from one morning to the next how to treat her. In the Sea of Grass, the problem wouldn't have existed. He could have bought her from her father or brother for a few head of cattle if he'd desired her, and after that she would have been expected to serve him, bear his children, and keep silent when he spoke. She would have been a possession—treasured, perhaps, but always inferior to him the way even the finest mare was inferior to the man who rode her. And if he hadn't desired her, she would have never dared to speak to him. When he passed, she would have cast down her eyes, drawn her shawl across her face, and bowed to him even though he was only the Great Chief's son by a concubine, and he would barely have been aware of her existence except when he summoned her to bring him water or put more wood on the fire.

But Marrah would no more cast down her eyes modestly and bring him a cup of water than a she-wolf. She was not only no man's wife, she didn't even have a father, at least not one she recognized, and as far as he could tell, her idea of treating a man properly was to invite him to sleep with her. He had seen her at Hoza after the pole dance shamelessly embracing a man from some other village, and later, when they'd returned to Xori, he'd gradually become aware that she was going off into the woods with Bere—not that he cared, not that he was jealous—and as far as he could tell, her people thought it was perfectly normal for a young woman to have as many lovers as she wanted. By Han, they not only thought it was normal, they thought it was her religious duty!

He had to admit he liked the idea of sex as a religious duty, but where did that leave him with regard to Marrah? He had better decide, and soon too, because he was going to be traveling with her for the better part of a year, and maybe longer if she and her brother needed him, because when he'd vowed to protect her and her family, he hadn't put any time limit on the promise.

He shook his head and took a quick look over his shoulder at Marrah and the two women traders. Only their feet were visible because they had turned their boat upside down and were walking under it as if it were a giant sunshade, laughing and talking to one another as they picked their way along the riverbank. The situation wouldn't have been so confusing if Marrah hadn't saved his life, but she had, and by doing so she had become the equivalent of his chief. He had pledged his loyalty to her the way he would have pledged it to another warrior, but how did you treat your chief when she also happened to be a pretty, stubborn young woman who did whatever she pleased?

Not that he had any regrets. Under the circumstances, it had been the only honorable thing to do, and he had no intention of breaking his vow; but it was all so . . . confusing. Worse yet, it was making him want her. He didn't want to desire Marrah, and he could see it was going to cause all sorts of complications, but he couldn't seem to put her out of his thoughts. He was starting to feel about her the way he had felt about Jallate, Vlahan's wife, when he was a boy. Maybe he was cursed with a liking for inaccessible women.

Well, he wasn't a boy any longer, and he knew how to keep silent, which was exactly what he was going to do until this un-wanted desire ran its course. He'd treat Marrah as his chief and do his best to forget she was a woman.

He tightened his grip on the rim of the *shava* and looked at the river, trying to calculate how far they had walked. The water rolled by, rippling like the muscles on the back of a mare, so green and clear he could see fish swimming along the bank. Behind him, he heard the sound of Marrah's laughter.


In the early afternoon they reached Xemta, where, as Rhom had promised, they received a warm welcome. Thanks to their pilgrim necklaces, Marrah and Arang were given a whole sleeping compart-ment to themselves; Zastra, Shema, and Stavan made themselves com-fortable under the overhanging eves of the front porch of one of the longhouses, and Rhom disappeared into the forest with the second youngest granddaughter of the village mother, a dark-haired young woman named Koipa who rushed down the trail to greet him, whooping with joy as soon as she saw him step into the clearing. Presumably Koipa had run to be first in line, since there were four other granddaughters who showed similar enthusiasm at the sight of Rhom. Because of his white hair and beard, Stavan was initially mis-taken for a very old man by the lustful women of Xemta, who quickly realized their error. Winking and blowing him kisses, they did their best to entice him, but Stavan ignored them and went down to the river to take a swim. That was too much for the granddaugh-ters, who followed him and sat on the bank, laughing and calling out

The
Year
the
Horses
Came

117

invitations until he waved them away brusquely as if embarrassed. After that, they left him alone, since it would have been inhospitable to go on pestering a man after he'd refused, but there were a lot of long faces at dinner that night, and a good number of longing looks.

The next morning they left the boats behind to be ferried back to Gurasoak, shouldered the carrying baskets, and set off on foot, following the river. At first the path ran close to the water, but soon it turned away and they were forced to struggle up a muddy slope toward the forest, where, Rhom assured them, the going would be easier.

Shema and Zastra agreed. "This is the third time we've made the forest crossing in this direction," Zastra said, "and believe me, it's almost always easier to walk in the forest, not to mention that in a couple of weeks you'll have eaten so much food out of your baskets you'll hardly know they're on your back."

As Marrah struggled to keep from sliding two steps back for every one she took forward, she wondered if Stavan and Arang found the news that it would take at least two weeks to lighten the baskets as discouraging as she did, but she couldn't spare the breath to ask them. Grabbing for a tuft of grass, she slipped, pulled off balance by her load, which felt as if it were made of stones instead of feather capes and food. In front of her, Rhom was leaping lightly from one bit of level ground to another, chatting with Shema about some cousins of theirs who were in the obsidian trade. Marrah grabbed for another tuft of grass, wondering if she would ever be able to leap around like that without noticing the weight on her back. At the moment it seemed unlikely.

They didn't see the river again until evening, when they made camp on a beach that was barely large enough to accommodate six people, six baskets, and a small fire. By that time Marrah was so exhausted she curled up in her cloak immediately after dinner and was asleep almost before her head touched the ground.

Days passed and slowly, step by step, they moved southeast, always following the river. Gradually, as Zastra had promised, Marrah stopped noticing the weight on her back. Her feet grew hard and her legs grew strong, and she began to walk like Rhom and his sisters, not bent under her load but upright and sure-footed. When she looked at Stavan, she saw that his skin had turned an almost normal shade of brown, but his hair was stranger than ever, streaked by the sun and so light that in some places it looked like flax.

Sometimes they came to settlements where the people farmed in a small way, living mostly off fish and wild game. The houses of the River People were built on poles; usually there was a dugout canoe tied up to the front door, and there were always children splashing in the water and old people sitting in the shade mending nets or weaving fish baskets.

Although they had nothing to trade, the River People were hospitable. Often when they saw Marrah and Arang's pilgrim necklaces, they would put the tips of their fingers together or pick up sticks and draw a triangle in the mud.

"They're welcoming us in the name of the Goddess Earth," Marrah explained to Stavan. "The triangle is Her universal sign; it represents the holy triangle of fertility between Her thighs."

When she asked Stavan what the universal sign of his god was, he seemed reluctant to tell her. Finally he admitted that the universal sign of Han was a dagger stuck into the ground point first.

As they moved upstream, the settlements became fewer, and instead of following footpaths they began to follow deer trails. When they could, they walked along the bank of the river, but often the track led into the forest. When this happened, Marrah found herself constantly checking to make sure the Ibai Nabar was still on their left, but the traders never seemed to worry about getting lost. They appeared to know exactly where they were going at all times, even when the trail was so faint Marrah could hardly see it. "This is an old route," Zastra reassured her, "one that's been used by traders for time out of mind." She pointed to a small scar on a nearby tree. "You see that bit of missing bark? It's a blaze. The trail is marked from here all the way to the Blue Sea."

Reassured, Marrah relaxed and began to enjoy the forest. Like a great green ocean it extended north, south, and east, covering the earth. Perhaps if she had walked long enough she might have come to the edge of it, but as the days passed it seemed to go on forever, silent and unbroken as if it had no beginning and no end. It was mostly the size of the trees that created the impression of endlessness. Rising up from ground level like the posts of a great longhouse, they met overhead, spreading their branches to form a leafy canopy. Although there were alders, hazels, elms, lindens, and beeches, almost all the largest were oaks, some so big that two people holding hands couldn't have spanned their trunks. When Marrah stood at the base of

The
Year
the
Horses
Came

119

one of these giants and looked up, she felt like a dwarf, and she could easily imagine that far above her head the trees were talking to one another, whispering secrets no human was allowed to hear.

Everything in the forest made it seem different from the world outside. When they walked along the river, they often had to struggle through brambles, vines, dense brush, and willow thickets, but once they were under the roof of trees they found themselves walking on a soft carpet of ankle-high leaves that muffled their voices and dampened the sound of their footsteps. Every time they took a step their feet disappeared, and when they lifted them they took the leaves along, creating a soft swishing noise that sounded like the murmur of invisible brooks.

The trees themselves gave off a peculiar musty odor that reminded Marrah of mushrooms and decaying leaves and the herbs Sabalah kept in her medicine bag, and sometimes there was another odor, something sweet and voluptuous that must be coming from some invisible flower blooming high above their heads.

But the most remarkable thing about the forest was how quiet it was. Except for the sound of their own voices, the warning cries of the jays, and the chattering of an occasional squirrel, they walked in silence. It was so still that from time to time they found themselves speaking in whispers as if the trees were sleeping giants who shouldn't be disturbed. Whenever this happened, Rhom would break into a song, but no matter how loudly he sang, the forest swallowed up his voice. When he had finished the last chorus, he would pull a small bone flute out of his pouch and play a tune. At this, they would walk more quickly, and sometimes Arang would dance down the trail ahead of them as if he were leading them off to a feast.

Most nights they did feast, for when Stavan shot an arrow it rarely missed its target. Almost every evening after they made camp, he would wander off with his bow, returning with a few fat rabbits or a brace of ducks. Sometimes he even shot fish, bringing them back strung on a sharpened stick. Once, to everyone's distress, he appeared with the tongue and liver of a deer.

"What did you do with the rest of the meat?" Shema cried. Marrah translated and Stavan shrugged and said that of course he had left it behind. "The deer was too heavy for one man to carry, and we don't need it; there are lots of deer in this forest. We could eat venison tongue every night if we wanted to."

When Marrah explained that it was considered an insult to the Goddess not to use every part of the animal, he looked thoughtful.

"Tell Shema I'm sorry I upset her; I won't kill any more deer if you don't want me to."

Marrah still wasn't convinced he understood, so that night she made a special point of sitting down beside him and describing how animals were hunted. "First," she explained, "we ask the animal's pardon. Then we shoot it. After it falls, we thank it for giving up its life so we can eat. For example, if it's a stag we might say, 'Brother stag, thank you for becoming food for my family.' We never kill more than we can eat, and we use everything: hide, flesh, entrails, even the hooves and horns, which we carve into spoons or cups or grind up into a kind of paste. If there's any meat left over, we dry it or give it away even if we have to walk to the next village, but we never cut out the best parts and leave the rest to rot. Animals are sacred; they're children of Earth just like we are."

He listened gravely. "I'll hunt whatever way pleases you," he said, so politely she was sure he still hadn't understood the point she was trying to make. Frustrated, she gave up trying to explain, but the next morning she realized she had underestimated him. He and Arang were standing at the edge of the forest, and Arang was trying, without much success, to draw the string of Stavan's bow back far enough to launch an arrow into the trunk of a large beech tree.

"Remember," Stavan was telling him, "before you shoot an animal, you have to beg its pardon." And stepping behind Arang, he put his arm around him and helped him bend the bow and send the arrow into the tree.

That afternoon, when they stopped for their midday meal, Arang sat down beside Marrah, folded his arms around his knees, and gave her the look he always gave her when he was going to ask for something.

"Well, what is it?" she said, handing him a piece of jerky.

Arang got straight to the point. "I want Stavan for my *aita*."

Marrah reminded him that he already had an *aita*. "Mehe, mother's partner," she said. "Remember him?"

Arang wrinkled up his nose. "I knew you'd say something like that. You haven't been a woman three months yet, Marrah, but you're already talking like you're the mother of a whole family. Of course I remember Mehe, but he's too far away to look after me, and I like Stavan. He knows *everything*."

Marrah, who was not at all convinced that Stavan knew the kinds of things Arang should be taught, promised to think it over. She meant to wait a few days and tell Arang she'd decided it was a bad

The
Year
the
Horses
Came

121

idea, but that same afternoon something happened to make her re-consider. Once again they were taking a short break, eating a few pieces of dried fruit and talking about nothing in particular. Arang was sprawled at her feet, picking his teeth with a twig. "You know," he said, "I've been wondering something. Where are all the animals? Stavan brings back game nearly every evening, but where does he find it? I haven't seen anything larger than a squirrel since we left Gurasoak, and it's so quiet around here I'm starting to think I'm going deaf."

Stavan, who had overheard this, laughed so hard he nearly choked on a piece of dried plum. "You aren't seeing any animals for a very simple reason," he said. "The six of us have been crashing through the underbrush like a herd of cows." He pointed to the ground. "When the leaf-eating animals walk, they don't make a sound. Only a few of the meat-eaters make noise: just bears, who are so big and mean they don't care who knows they're coming, and wild pigs, who'll surround other animals like a wolf pack."

"I thought we *were* walking softly," Arang objected.

Stavan grinned. "Softly for humans, perhaps, but I've hunted in forests like this for almost four years, and I can tell you that we've been making more noise than stags in rut. If you want to see the animals, you have to walk like the she-lion does." He rose to his feet to demonstrate. "You have to lift your legs up high like this instead of shuffling through the leaves, and when you put your feet down you have to pretend you're about to step on duck eggs."

Marrah and the other adults agreed. "Not that I've ever been much of a hunter," Marrah admitted, "but Stavan's right." Soon they put their baskets on their backs and started down the trail again, and it wasn't until some time had passed that Marrah realized what Stavan had done: gently, in the most subtle way possible, he had reminded Arang that there were dangerous animals in the forest.

Perhaps they all needed reminding. The forests along the coasts were tame compared to this one. Except for a few bears, most of the big meat-eating animals had been hunted out generations ago. Marrah had almost forgotten Mother Asha's story of the trader taken off by a she-lion, but Stavan had made her realize it was dangerous to forget. He had traveled through the wild forests of the north, and when he warned that they might run into wolf packs, wild pigs, bears, and—most terrifying of all—lions, she was inclined to believe him. She had never seen anything larger than a wildcat, but she had once seen lion claws on the necklace of a priestess who had gotten them from a trader in exchange for several baskets of rare herbs. They were brutal, as long as a man's finger and as sharp as needles, and she didn't like to think an animal with such claws could hunt without making a sound.

Arang was right. Stavan knew much more than they did about the forest. He might make Arang an excellent *aita*, but she would have to make sure he didn't tell her little brother about things like war and concubines. She walked on, considering the matter, only pausing long enough to look over her shoulder occasionally. The forest no longer seemed quite as peaceful or as safe as it had a short time ago.

Stavan's warning came none too soon. A few nights later, they woke up sure they had heard some large animal, and in the morning Stavan confirmed that a bear had been prowling around the camp. Fortunately, they always hung the food baskets too high for a bear to reach, and after clawing a few times at the trunk of the tree, this one had evidently become discouraged and left without doing any harm.

"We've never had trouble with the big animals," Rhom said as they set out that morning. "It's the little ones you have to worry about. The bears are well fed this time of year, but you have to keep a sharp eye out for squirrels, because those little turds can eat a whole basket of food while your back is turned."

When Marrah saw how unconcerned the traders were, she relaxed. Perhaps the forests along the Ibai Nabar weren't as dangerous as the ones Stavan had traveled through. But just as she was feeling secure again, she woke up suddenly in the middle of the night. This time there was no noise, not a sound, not even the chirping of a cricket. The river flowed noiselessly like a great skirt of soft leather, and even the strip of stars that hung over it seemed unnaturally bright and still.

Looking beyond the dim light of the campfire, she thought she saw a large animal sitting in the bushes watching them as they slept. The animal, whatever it was, was so still that at first she wasn't sure if it was alive or just a tree trunk turned into a lion by her imagination. Then the fire flared up suddenly and she saw two bright yellow eyes, as cold as death, looking straight at her. She rose to her feet with a scream, grabbed a burning stick from the fire, and hurled it into the shadows, but by the time she threw, the beast had disappeared.

In an instant Stavan was beside her, clutching his long knife in one hand and his dagger in the other, but when she pointed to the place where the animal had been, there was no sign of it. After searching the perimeter of the camp as best they could, they spent a bad night huddled around the fire, afraid to go to sleep. The next morning Stavan confirmed that something heavy had been sitting in the reeds, but there were no tracks, not even an overturned stone.

"I can't tell if it was a lion, but it might have been," he warned. "Lions usually hunt by day, but no squirrel crushed those reeds. Whatever it was weighed almost as much as a bear, and bears don't have yellow eyes." He put his hand on Arang's shoulder and was silent for a moment. "I don't want to frighten Arang any more than he's frightened already, but I think he should know—I think all of you should know—that lions particularly like to stalk children. I'm telling you this so you'll understand how important it is to stay together at all times from now on. Arang in particular should never go off by himself. Also, I think that starting tonight we should take turns standing guard. With a little luck, this lion—if it is a lion—will decide we're too much trouble. The beasts tend to hunt in one particular area; in a few days we should have walked out of her territory. There's even a chance she doesn't think of humans as food; we may just be strange, puzzling creatures who may or may not be dangerous, so she's watching us to find out, but I wouldn't like to stake my life on that."

Everyone agreed. The traders were shaken; even Rhom didn't have anything amusing to say about lions.

From that night on, everyone but Arang took a turn at standing watch, and even Stavan stopped going off by himself in the evenings to hunt. Either the precautions worked or there had never been a lion in the first place. Several nights passed without incident. By day they walked steadily, eager to put that part of the forest behind them. The river had been growing gradually narrower ever since they reached the fourth fork and turned west toward the mountains. The smaller it became, the more furiously it flowed; by the time they climbed into the foothills among the pine trees, the great Ibai Nabar was little more than a noisy creek.

As they drew closer to the Caves of Nar, Marrah began to get excited. Would there be gifts as the priestesses had promised Sabalah, or would they have grown tired of waiting for so many years and given them to someone else? She tried not to hope too much, but secretly she longed for some bit of magic or a sacred charm that would take her and Arang safely to Shara.

The night before they reached the caves it was so cold that Marrah and Arang slept rolled up together in their cloaks to keep warm. On the other side of the fire, Zastra and Shema were doing the same thing. Stavan had the first watch that evening, but Rhom suggested he forget about it. "Come share my bed," he offered, eyeing Stavan with a look that said, You may be thin, but you look warm. But Stavan wouldn't hear of it. Not only did he take the first watch, he insisted on standing guard until sunrise, and poor Rhom, who had only a thin cloak, spent the night shivering.

The next morning, just before noon, they came across three rocks with white handprints painted on them. Shortly after that, Arang spotted the entrance to a shallow cave. The cave was sheltered under the overhanging edge of a limestone cliff, and when they explored it they found a small female figure carved on the back wall. The figure clearly represented one of the aspects of the Goddess Earth because Her hips and breasts swelled with fertility and She held the crescent moon in Her left hand, but Marrah had never seen a goddess who looked so much like a real woman. She was only about a foot and a half tall, but the people who had carved Her had used a natural out-cropping in the limestone for Her belly and two smaller ones for Her breasts. The result was a figure that seemed to be stepping out of the wall.

They were all impressed, but Arang was particularly taken by Her. For a long time he stood in silence, looking at the carving. "She's so pretty," he said at last. He reached out and touched Her belly lightly with his fingertips. "Who made Her?"

No one had an answer for that. Rhom said he had once seen a terra-cotta statue from the land of the Hita. The Hita were great sculptors and the figure had all the roundness and grace of a real woman's body, but even that statue wasn't as alive as this little goddess.

Before they left, Arang picked a handful of flowers and placed them at Her feet. They saw nothing else of interest after that, but it was clear they were on the right path and would soon reach the Caves of Nar.

# CHAPTER SEVEN

*From the Caves of Nar to the Blue Sea*

"Hail, Marrah of Xori, Sabalah's daughter," a clear voice said suddenly. Marrah spun around, surprised to hear her name spoken in such a deserted place, but she saw nothing but rocks, brush, and pine trees. The voice echoed off the limestone boulders and repeated itself until it was lost. The travelers stopped and stared at one another.

"Who speaks?" Rhom cried, but there was no answer, only another echo. Shema and Zastra turned in circles just as Marrah had, looking for the source of the invisible voice. Stavan put his hand on the hilt of his dagger and took up a position in the middle of the path. Only Arang did anything practical.

"Come out, come out, wherever you are!" he yelled, as if it were all a game. There was a peal of laughter, bright and quick like a strand of copper bells clinking together.

"Hail, Arang of Xori, Sabalah's son," a chorus of voices replied. "Hail, little boy who has walked so far."

Arang's mouth fell open.

"Mountain spirits," Zastra whispered, biting her lips and peering anxiously at the juniper thickets that lined the trail.

"Nonsense," Shema snapped. "Someone's playing a trick on us." She strode past Stavan, planted herself in the middle of the path, and cupped her hands to her mouth. "Come out where we can see you," she commanded in a thunderous voice. "What do you think you're doing, hiding like that? If you're honest people, come out and show your faces, and if you're spirits, go away and leave us in peace."

"Hail, traders from the south and giant from No-One-Knows-Where," the chorus of voices replied. There was another peal of laughter, and three women stepped out from behind a large bush. One was old, with gray hair that hung down past her waist; one was a dark-eyed woman about Sabalah's age; the third was little more than a child, with newly formed breasts and legs like a young calf. All three were wearing deerskin shifts that had been dyed black, and each had a small crescent moon dangling from a thong around her neck.

"Welcome to the Sacred Caves of Nar," the youngest said, and the three of them broke into fits of helpless giggles.

"They look so surprised," the oldest woman gasped, leaning on the youngest for support.

"Just like a flock of geese that doesn't know whether to fly or stay," the middle one agreed.

"Dear Goddess, they take their lives so seriously!"

"What's going on here?" Stavan demanded. "Who are these women?"

Before Marrah could translate his question, the dark-eyed stranger interrupted. "Tell the giant that we're the priestesses of the Caves of Nar," she gasped. "Tell him we mean no offense, but that it's our duty to laugh at pilgrims to remind them that the Goddess Earth has commanded us to enjoy ourselves because our joy is pleasing to Her."

Marrah was dumbfounded. "You speak Shambah?"

Mary Mackey

128

The oldest shook her head. "No," she said, "but we know what he asked you. All pilgrims ask the same question when they first meet us: Who are these three foolish women, and why do they stand in the trail laughing like children?" She motioned to the younger women, who were still laughing. "Enough," she said. The dark-eyed woman stopped laughing at once, but the youngest had a harder time. Every time she looked at Stavan she had another giggling fit. Marrah had to admit that there really was something funny about the way Stavan was glaring at them. She had never seen less dangerous-looking people in her life. Before the misunderstanding could go any further, she translated.

Stavan took his hand off the hilt of his dagger. "Laughing priest-esses," he said, shaking his head. Marrah could tell he felt foolish, but he took it in stride. "What language are they speaking?"

"The Old Language," Marrah explained. "Only priestesses speak it. And traders," she amended, glancing at Rhom and his sisters. "We'll probably hear nothing else until we get to Shara—at least nothing we'll understand."

Stavan sighed. "Another language—and just when I was starting to understand some of the noises you Shore People make. Well, I suppose there's no help for it."

"Does the giant understand?" the oldest woman interrupted. Marrah assured her that he did. "Good, then it's time for us to intro-duce ourselves. I'm Zahar." She pointed to the dark-eyed woman. "This is Emzate, and"—she indicated the girl who had finally man-aged to conquer her giggles—"this basket of mischief goes by the name of Ume."

"In other words," Rhom interposed, "your names mean Child-hood, Maturity, and Old Age."

"Precisely." Zahar nodded. "The Holy Trinity, the three aspects of She-Who-Is-Everything: Maiden, Matron, Crone."

"I don't call those names," Shema grumbled. "I can't see we're any better off than we were before they introduced themselves."

"Oh, hush," Zastra hissed. "They're the priestesses of Nar, and they can call themselves anything they want."

"How did you know our names?" Arang asked in perfect Old Language.

Ume looked surprised. "He speaks the Holy Tongue?"

"Of course." Zahar smiled. "What else would you expect from Sabalah's son?" She turned to Arang. "I'd like to tell you that we saw you coming in a vision, but the truth is the Forest People have been keeping track of you ever since you left Xemta. The village mother told them that six people were making the forest crossing: three traders from the south, a white-haired giant, and a young woman and a boy who had introduced themselves as the children of Sabalah. I remembered Sabalah well; she came here many years ago when I was the Matron of Nar, Emzate was the Maiden, and the former Crone was in her sixties. Your sister over there was a babe in arms, a fat, laughing bundle. I held her on my lap and sang her to sleep, and now I see she's grown into a fine woman. A few days ago, the Forest People sent a runner to tell us that the six of you had taken the west

The
Year
the
Horses
Came

129

fork of the Ibai Nabar and were heading our way. It didn't take any magic to figure out you'd probably arrive sometime this afternoon, so we sat down beside the trail to welcome you in our customary way."

She turned to Marrah. "But I think we've kept you waiting quite long enough. You must be tired and thirsty after that last climb, and eager to see the caves, and we're not doing our duty by you. Those who wear Her sign must never want for anything we have to offer, little as that may be. So if you'll follow us, we'll lead you to a place where you can eat and rest awhile, and then if you feel up to it we'll take you down into the caves and show you the oldest mystery the earth has to offer."

Having delivered this intriguing invitation, Zahar turned and without another word led them all up the trail, with Emzate and Ume bringing up the rear.

When the Shore People told guests they were welcome to what little the village had to offer, they were merely being modest and polite. It was customary to protest that the food was inferior as you heaped slices of succulent venison onto huge pieces of fresh bread, brought out vats of stewed fruit and cream, filled the guests' cups with fermented honey, and made sure they sampled every delicacy. But when the priestesses of Nar said they had little, they were speaking the truth. It soon became apparent that the three lived like hermits, eating only acorn mush and sleeping outside as often as the weather permitted. When it snowed or rained, they retreated into a small cave and kept one another warm. Unless they were performing a religious ceremony, they were forbidden to use fire after the sun set except when one of them was sick or the ice on the creek was more than a finger thick.

Yet Marrah had rarely seen happier people. The three were like a trio of six-year-olds, constantly talking and laughing and teasing each other, incapable of walking along a path they had walked along hundreds of times before without stopping to point out a butterfly or a pretty rock or a breathtaking view. Of course it was the duty of the priestesses of Nar to remind pilgrims that joy was holy, but as Marrah sat at the entrance to their cave eating cold acorn mush, she got the impression that they would have been happy even if it hadn't been their duty.

"It's like they're drunk," Stavan observed.

Marrah asked Ume if she and the others drank any sacred potions or ate any special herbs. Ume shook her head and laughed. "Nothing but acorns and water," she said. "But wait until you see the caves." And that was all they could get out of her. The priestesses of Nar weren't allowed to describe the caves or even talk about them except in the most general terms when they were above ground.

After they all finished eating, the priestesses rose to their feet, picked up several torches made from pine pitch, and without any further ceremony led the travelers to the entrance of the caves. It was not an impressive opening, only a hole partly covered by bushes, unmarked and easy enough to overlook if you didn't know it was there, but a cool wind blew out of it.

Zahar turned and faced them. "I hope no one is afraid of the dark," she said. And then she proceeded to explain that they would have to crawl for a long time through a narrow tunnel before they came to the first cave. "It's forbidden to light a fire in the tunnel," she warned, "and even if we could, there's not enough room for us and the torches too. It's also forbidden to speak, but don't worry; there's no way you can get lost."

Marrah didn't find that very reassuring, and from the expression on Arang's face, she suspected he was also having second thoughts. Shema and Stavan, on the other hand, looked as if they welcomed the idea of a long crawl through the dark. Rhom and Zastra's faces were hard to read. Both of them were looking at the entrance to the caves, but what they were thinking was anyone's guess. In any event, no one backed out. One by one, they fell to their knees and followed Zahar into the hole.

It was a tight fit. The floor of the tunnel was smooth but slimy. For a few seconds as Marrah crawled in a dim twilight, she could see that the walls and ceiling were limestone. Then Zastra crawled in behind her, and the light went out. She crawled farther, trying not to think about the mountain of rock that lay above her. It was so quiet she could hear her heart beat. The only noise came when someone dislodged a pebble. Gradually, she became aware of Arang's breathing as well as her own. Reaching ahead, she found his leg and gave it a friendly pat. Arang stopped and then started crawling again. She wondered if he wanted to turn back. If he did, it was too late. The tunnel had a slight downward slant; it was too narrow to turn around in and growing narrower all the time. As she inched forward, she found herself wondering if anyone had ever gotten stuck.

The
Year
the
Horses
Came

131

That was not a good thought to entertain, and she put it out of her mind as quickly as she could. The tunnel was drier now, but the roof was so low she had to lie on her stomach and move forward by pushing against the walls. The darkness was beginning to get to her. It wasn't like closing your eyes; it was deeper than that. It had a kind of solidity, as if it were almost alive. When she looked at it (which was a strange thought, because how could you look at darkness?), she saw things swimming in it. She crawled on, determined not to pay any attention to them, but they kept multiplying. I'll just close my eyes, she thought, but when she did, it didn't make the slightest bit of difference. The darkness behind her eyelids and the darkness of the tunnel were all the same.

Time passed. She slid forward on her belly wishing she could have just one breath of fresh air. She was losing all sense of how far she had come, and she was getting scared. I want out of here, she thought. She gritted her teeth and kept on going. More time passed. The swimming things were blue now, the sort of blue you some-times saw at sunset. After a while she forgot why she was crawling. She just did it. It was clear that darkness was never going to end, so she gave herself over to it and let the blue things lead her.

Suddenly she realized her back was no longer scraping the rocks. Raising her hand, she tried to touch the roof of the tunnel. Nothing. Cautiously, she rose to her feet, took a few steps forward, and stum-bled out into a vast black emptiness that smelled of damp earth and mold. A cold breeze was blowing out of the darkness, and some-where close at hand water was running noisily.

"Hello," she called. "Is anyone here?"

". . . here? here? here?" the echo mocked.

"Come over this way," a voice suggested. It was Zahar. Moving toward the sound, she bumped into Arang, who clutched at her hand.

"I'm scared," he whispered.

She wanted to whisper back that she was scared too but that wasn't something an older sister could admit. "Hang on," she urged. She put her arm around his shoulder and drew him closer. "The priestesses will light a torch soon." Behind her, she could hear the others coming out of the tunnel. Ume giggled as she bumped into someone.

Feeling their way to the front of the line, the priestesses of Nar conferred in low voices. There was a scraping sound as one of them struck a flint. Suddenly a spark jumped out of the darkness and Emzate's torch flared, filling the cave with a dull orange light.

Marrah blinked and then gasped. The cave was much larger than she'd realized. Large gray boulders littered the floor, casting strange shadows. Above her a frozen waterfall of white stalactites and glittering crystals was pouring down from the ceiling.

Emzate passed the fire to Ume, and Ume passed it on to Zahar. The light multiplied in flickering orange tongues. When all the torches were lit, the priestesses held them high over their heads and turned to face the pilgrims.

Zahar smiled at them as if she were about to make a speech, but instead she did the sort of simple thing the priestesses of Nar were famous for. "Turn around," she suggested.

They turned, and what they saw made them cry out in wonder and astonishment. Directly above the entrance to the tunnel, seven great stags were swimming through an invisible river, their massive antlers tilted back slightly, their hooves beating the water.

"The stags were painted very long ago," Emzate said softly. "So long ago no one remembers when. The memory songs say our ancestors created them before the Great Spring, when the world was still covered with ice, but perhaps they're even older than that." The priestesses lowered their torches, and the stags disappeared into the shadows. "Come. There are more—three caves in all—and the spirits of the animals dance in all of them."

They followed the priestesses along a wide, well-worn path, past an underground river filled with pale fish that had never seen the light of the sun and white salamanders that scuttled out of their way as they approached. Sometimes a bat twittered or water fell over a precipice and disappeared into the darkness, but otherwise there was no noise, not the song of a bird or the rustling of leaves or even the hum of an insect. The silence was so vast they spoke in low voices, reluctant to disturb it.

The second cave was smaller than the first but even more beautiful: immense bulls, herds of leaping deer, and black stags with spreading antlers galloped around the walls and across the ceiling. There were other animals Marrah didn't recognize, beasts from dreams perhaps: a great cat; a woolly cowlike thing with a massive head; a fat animal with powerful legs, a long canoe-shaped muzzle, and a skinny piglike tail. The animals were painted with quick strokes so that they seemed to move, and as she stood there, enraptured by their beauty, she could easily imagine them charging through the high grass of some long-forgotten meadow.

Once again Zahar, Emzate, and Ume lifted their torches above their heads so the light shone into every cranny. Now Marrah saw that there were other things on the walls: prints of human hands, dots, lines, rectangles, and, scattered among them, half a dozen triangles drawn in red ocher.

"So they worshiped the Goddess also," Rhom whispered.

"Yes." Emzate nodded. "They too knew Her love. Here in Her womb they painted the eternal herds. Perhaps they brought their young people here when they came of age to teach them the sacred art of hunting, and perhaps their priestesses came here just as we do, to sit among the spirits of the beasts. But come along; there's one more cave to see."

"The third cave is the best of all," Ume promised, and, lowering her torch, she led the way.

As soon as Marrah stepped into the final cave, she knew Ume had spoken the truth. One entire wall was a mass of white marble stalactites that dripped toward the floor like giant icicles. The other three walls and the ceiling were so covered with the bodies of animals that they overlapped in one great, dizzy swirl that took her breath away. Here and there, sticklike human figures appeared to be hunting with bows or spears while others danced or lay in trance. Marrah was taking a closer look at a strange animal that looked like a bear with a human face when she heard Stavan inhale sharply.

"Look," he whispered, pointing to the ceiling. She looked up and saw a herd of the beasts called horses. "Perhaps they used to live in these mountains a long time ago," Stavan said softly, and she heard the homesickness in his voice. "Perhaps your ancestors also rode them."

Marrah shook her head. "I don't think so." She was sorry that the sight of the horses made him miss his own people, but as far as she was concerned she would have been just as happy if there'd been some other animals painted on the ceiling. She stared up at the beasts, wanting to dislike them, but she couldn't. They were too beautiful. Ten, twenty, thirty of them galloped across the vault of the cavern, heads raised proudly, manes and tails flowing, embodiments of a wild grace that had vanished so long ago that not even their name had been remembered.

The priestesses let them look as long as they wanted. Then they led the travelers to a natural bench of limestone and told them to sit down with their backs to the wall of stalactites. "Close your eyes,"

Zahar commanded, "take one another's hands, and don't look until you hear the music."

Marrah wondered what music she could possibly be referring to. Perhaps they had brought flutes with them. Certainly not drums or harps, not through that tunnel. Well, no doubt she'd soon find out. Obediently she reached out and clasped Arang's hand. Stavan had sat down to the left of her, so she took his hand too. As she touched him, he flinched slightly, grasped her hand with trembling fingers, and held on. The sight of the horses must have upset him more than she'd realized. She was just wondering if she ought to say something to him when suddenly the cave was filled with a sweet, bell-like sound. As she listened, the sound broke into separate tones, and then more sounds came until the whole cave was vibrating.

Opening her eyes, she looked over her shoulder and saw Ume gently striking the stalactites with a wooden mallet. As she played, Zahar and Emzate began to walk slowly back and forth, holding their torches aloft, and as they moved the shadows moved with them and the animals seemed to spring to life. The overlapping bodies of the bulls merged into a single bull charging forward in time to the music, and as he danced, the horses and stags danced with him.

"This is magic!" Stavan cried, speaking for all of them, and when Marrah looked at him, she saw he was leaning forward, holding his breath as if afraid to break the spell.

The crawl out was not nearly as terrifying as the crawl in. Now that Marrah knew what to expect, she took her time, ignored the blue things that swam in the darkness, and spent an uncomfortable but bearable period thinking about other things. Mostly she thought about the magic of the caves.

When they emerged, it was night. The moon had set, and the sky was strewn with stars that glittered like bits of ice in the thin mountain air. It was cold enough to remind Marrah that winter was on the way, but as she stood shivering outside the entrance waiting for the others, she felt elated. Now she understood why the priestesses of Nar needed no sacred potions to be drunk with happiness.

The next morning the three took her aside and gave her the gifts they had promised to Sabalah so many years ago. It was an oddly unceremonious moment, considering how important the gifts were,

The
Year
the
Horses
Came

135

but the priestesses were vowed to simplicity in all things. Zahar simply reached into a basket and drew out three small leather bags. "This," she said, dropping the first bag into Marrah's hand, "is dried thunder. You throw it on fire and it makes a great noise. Use it well and be careful; it's dangerous."

Marrah opened the drawstrings and found that the bag contained several unremarkable looking balls of clay. She took one of the balls and rolled it between her fingers; it was clearly hollow. Perhaps there was something more inside, but if so, Zahar clearly wasn't interested in telling her what that something might be. Marrah tried to thank her, but the old priestess silenced her with a wave of her hand. "Don't thank me; don't thank any of us. These gifts come from the Goddess Earth, bless Her name. We're only Her messengers."

She held up the second bag. "This is a powder that will make you invisible." She laughed. "Only there's a trick to it: you don't eat it. In fact, I strongly advise you never to let it cross your lips—not that it would kill you. The Goddess isn't all that anxious to have you with Her yet. Still, it packs quite a wallop. You put it in your enemies' food, and poof!"—she waved her hands—"you vanish from their sight. Of course we hope you never have any enemies, but should the occasion arise this may come in handy."

She handed Marrah the bag. Like the clay balls, the powder was unremarkable, the color and texture of dust but smelling slightly sweet as if it might taste better than it looked. Marrah sniffed it cautiously, closed the bag, and put it into the leather pocket she wore tied to her belt.

Zahar paused for a moment and held the third bag by its drawstring, looking at it fondly as if she were reluctant to give it up. "This," she said, "is the most precious gift of all. It's one of the Tears of Compassion shed by the Goddess Earth Herself when She saw Her children crying with fear at the beginning of the Great Spring. Her tears are so rare that, old as I am, I've only seen three of them, and this"—she shook the bag slightly—"is the finest of all. Whoever wears it can never be harmed."

She placed the bag gently in Marrah's hand. It was so light it felt empty. Marrah untied the drawstrings, opened the mouth of the bag, and dumped something into the palm of her hand—something so beautiful she gave a cry of joy when she saw it. It was a stone—or perhaps not a stone; it had no more weight than a breath. Tear-shaped and barely larger than the end of her thumb, it was the color of summer honey. But that wasn't all: at the center of the tear lay a tiny butterfly, wings outspread, as if caught and frozen in flight.

Marrah was speechless. She turned the gift over in her hand, trying to understand how the butterfly came to be inside it. At the place where the stone came to a point, someone had drilled a small hole. She realized it was made to be worn.

As if reading her thoughts, Ume quietly reached out, took the yellow stone, and threaded it on a leather thong. Kissing Marrah formally on both cheeks, she tied the ends around her neck so the tear hung just above her heart.

"Yellow is the color of death," Emzate was saying, as Zahar stood nodding in the background, with an enigmatic smile on her face. "It's the color of bone, the color of going back to the Mother. But the butterfly is life. In winter the caterpillar spins its grave and dies, but in spring it emerges transformed, more beautiful than it could have ever imagined. The Goddess has given the butterfly to us as a sign of Her mercy. It's Her promise that death is only temporary."

Marrah didn't know what to say. Not only had they forbidden her to thank them, no thanks seemed adequate. She touched the stone, awed by its magic. They waited patiently, giving her time to understand how much she'd been honored. Finally Zahar spoke.

"There's one more thing," she said. "Before you go, we want to ask you something." She laughed. "We may be priestesses, but we're just as curious as the next person, and just between you and me, our powers to see into the future are highly overrated. We'd like to ask why you and your brother are traveling east wearing pilgrim necklaces. Emzate and Ume think the Goddess must have commanded you to make the forest crossing, perhaps to deliver a message to one of the villages on the Blue Sea coast; is that true?"

When Marrah told her that she and Arang were not stopping at the Blue Sea but going all the way to Shara, Zahar sucked in her breath and shook her head, and the younger priestesses looked impressed.

"So far," Emzate said. She paused. "And do you carry a message?"

"Yes," Marrah admitted. Since she was allowed to share the prophecy with priestesses, she told them about the vision she had had and the warning she was taking east. As they listened, all the joy went out of their faces, and soon they no longer looked like laughing priestesses. When she finished speaking, Zahar sighed and shook her head.

The
Year
the
Horses
Came

137

"When I heard you were coming, I hoped you'd bring good news. Your mother told us about those beastmen when she came here so many years ago with you in her arms, and I thought, Now Sabalah's daughter, Marrah, is walking east, so perhaps there's been a new prophecy; perhaps the danger is over. But I see the evil days are just beginning."

She turned and stood for a moment looking at the entrance to the caves, lost in thought. Marrah kept silent, not wanting to interrupt her.

At last she spoke again. "We're far away from Shara, and perhaps with the grace of the Goddess we won't ever see these outlaws you speak of, but if they do come, we'll seal up the entrance to the Caves of Nar with stones. Her temple must never be desecrated."

"Where will you go if you have to leave Nar?" Marrah asked.

All three priestesses looked at her as if the question had caught them by surprise. "Go?" Ume said. "Why, we'll go nowhere, of course. We'll be where we belong: inside the caves."

That night Marrah showed her gifts to the others, and they marveled with her, touching the yellow stone reverently, sniffing the powder of invisibility, and balancing the clay balls on the palms of their hands.

"I had no idea you were such a powerful priestess," Rhom said, and when Marrah tried to explain she wasn't powerful at all but merely a young woman who was inheriting something once promised to her mother, he shook his head and remained unconvinced.

They left Nar the next morning, walking back to the main channel of the Ibai Nabar in a day less than it had taken them to follow the western branch into the foothills. This time they took the fork that led southeast, and that night, as they sat around the campfire, Rhom announced that tomorrow they would have to leave the Ibai Nabar altogether and set off overland. "If we keep walking in this direction," he explained, "we'll end up back in the mountains. I don't like going off into the forest with no river to guide us; no one does. Still, the trail runs due east, and it's fairly flat and well marked. With a little luck we shouldn't be out of sight of water for more than two days." He picked up a stick and drew a crude map: two wavy lines connected by a straight one. "We'll be heading for the banks of this river, the one my people call the Orugali. As you see, once we pick it up, we'll be able to follow it all the way to the Blue Sea."

As Rhom had promised, the crossing to the Orugali took two days. Everyone was relieved to see the river, and as they headed east along the northern bank, the traders began to point out familiar landmarks. With every step they took, the forest grew drier and plants appeared that Marrah had never seen before. One in particular, a kind of spiny holly, grew wherever there was an opening in the trees, but for the most part the land was covered with oaks and great pines that sported a purple-brown bark streaked with orange fissures. The soil they walked on was stony in places but fertile, and along creekbeds and the banks of the river it was sometimes blood red and sticky to touch.

The weather turned warmer, and instead of sleeping wrapped in their cloaks they slept uncovered, glad for every breeze. Although they still had several more days to go before they reached the coast, the journey almost seemed over and everyone began to relax. At night they still took turns standing guard, but if there had ever been a lion, they had left her behind on the Ibai Nabar; along the Orugali they saw nothing more fearsome than deer and rabbit prints pressed into the red clay along the riverbank.

Stavan took to going out hunting in the evenings, and they were all glad to have fresh game for dinner again. Sometime during the walk along the Ibai Nabar, he had made Arang a bow and several arrows tipped with tiny pieces of sharp stone. The arrows weren't good for much but stunning small birds, but by now Arang could hit a target with reasonable accuracy and he wanted to hunt too. "Absolutely not," Stavan said. And when Arang began to plead, he picked up his bow and walked into the forest without another word.

"He treats me like a child," Arang grumbled to Marrah. Marrah reminded him that he *was* a child. "I hate it when you talk like a grown-up!" he snapped, and for the rest of the evening he pouted.

At first she was annoyed, but then she remembered how patient he'd been, how he'd always carried his basket without complaint, how he'd helped gather firewood. She knew he missed Sabalah, but he never cried for his mother the way some boys of his age would have. And what other eight-year-old would have had enough courage to crawl through the tunnel that led to the Caves of Nar?

The next evening after Stavan had gone off to hunt, she walked up to Arang, who was sitting with his chin on his hands staring moodily at the forest. "Get your bow and arrows," she suggested, "and I'll take you target shooting near camp."

The
Year
the
Horses
Came

139

"I don't feel like shooting at some dumb old tree," he grumbled, and when Marrah tried to cheer him up by promising that there'd be plenty of real hunting once they reached the coast, he told her to go away and leave him alone.

Well, I tried, she thought, and she went back to her basket to get a line and small wooden bobber. Fishing along the river was a lot easier than fishing in the Sea of Gray Waves, and she had come to enjoy the evenings she spent sitting on the bank, pulling in a few perch or brown trout.

Sometime later she looked up to notice that Arang was no longer sitting where she had left him. Hmmm, she thought, I wonder where he's gone. She pulled her line out of the water and went to look for him, but he was nowhere in sight.

"Have you seen Arang?" she asked Rhom, who was sitting by the fire mending one of the straps on his carrying basket. Rhom shook his head. Shema said she hadn't seen him for a while either, and neither had Zastra.

"He's probably just gone off into the woods to pee," Shema suggested. "He's at that age when children like privacy."

Marrah wasn't convinced. She walked to the edge of the forest and cupped her hands to her mouth. "Arang! Where are you?" she called. There was no reply. "Arang, this isn't funny. I know you can hear me. Answer me." Still nothing.

"Well, he can't have gone far," Rhom said. He wandered over to the bank and looked up and down the river as if expecting to see Arang swimming in the shallows, but there were only the usual snags, reeds, and ducks. "Arang!" he called.

"Arang!" they all cried, but the only answer they got was the quacking of the ducks.

Zastra turned to Marrah with a worried look on her face. "Where did you last see him?"

"Under that tree over there."

"Did he say anything about going swimming?"

"No."

"Thank the Goddess. Then he probably hasn't drowned. But where could he possibly be?"

Marrah stood for a moment looking at the place where she had last seen Arang. It wasn't close to the river at all, but it was very close to the forest.

"I think he's gone off by himself to hunt," she said. Striding over to Arang's basket, she dumped the contents on the ground. The arrows Stavan had made were missing, and Arang's bow was nowhere in sight.

For a few moments they stood staring at the evidence.

"This doesn't look good," Zastra said.

"Surely he'll come back any minute." Shema stirred the contents of the basket with her toe as if the bow and arrows might still turn up. "You can't separate a boy from his dinner, Marrah. He's bound to get hungry." It was a poor choice of words. Marrah was already thinking about hunger—not hungry boys but hungry animals. She was imagining Arang, lost in the forest, confronting a bear or worse.

"The idiot!" she cried. She threw Arang's basket to the ground. "How could he do something so irresponsible?" She was angry and scared, and she wanted Arang back immediately. He was her responsibility, and if he was standing out there pouting, listening to them calling him and stubbornly refusing to answer, she was going to be sure it was a long time before he put another honey cake in his mouth. She looked at the river and tried to calculate how much daylight was left. The water was starting to change from green to a dull gray. There was no time to waste.

"Rhom, go get those long sticks over there, and we'll use them as torches. It may still be light out here, but it's going to be dark in the woods. Zastra, you stay behind in camp, and when Stavan shows up, tell him what's going on. He's a better tracker than any of us and it's a pity he's not here, but I don't think we can afford to wait for him. Shema and Rhom and I will search the woods on this side of the river. I don't think Arang would have been crazy enough to swim across fully dressed, with a bow and a quiver of arrows on his back." She looked out over the water, flowing by quickly like a current of dark soup. She and Arang had both inherited the wild streak that had taken Sabalah all the way from Shara to Xori with a newborn baby on her back. The truth was, he could be anywhere.

Rhom brought over the sticks, and they thrust them into the flames until the ends caught fire. They were poor torches, fast burning and likely to go out, but there was no time to make better ones. Fanning out in three separate directions, they plunged into the forest calling Arang's name.

"Arang!" Marrah cried. "Arang! Arang, where are you? Arang, answer me!" But every time she stopped to listen for an answer, all she heard was the sound of Rhom and Shema calling too. After a while, their voices faded and grew dim. Soon all she could hear was the rustle of the wind in the treetops and the occasional cawing of a

The
Year
the
Horses
Came

141

crow. The torch cast an unsteady flame that prodded the dusky shadows into life; more than once she thought she saw someone moving in them but when she rushed forward, sure she had found Arang at last, it always proved to be nothing more than a pile of brush or a vine swaying in the breeze.

When the torch burned out, she threw it to the ground and went on searching, paying no attention to the twigs that stung her face and the brambles that scratched her bare legs and tore at her dress. The setting sun gave off a pale, watery light that barely filtered through the leaves, but she had sharp eyes and rarely stumbled. Once some big animal moved in a thicket, grunting and cracking sticks, and instead of fleeing as she would have if she had been in her right mind, she hurried toward the sound thinking it might be Arang, but when she got there she found nothing but a trampled place and a pile of fresh bear dung.

"Stay away from my brother!" she yelled, picking up a stick and hurling it at the dung. "Stay away from him, Bear Woman, or I'll make you sorry you ever came into the forest!" It was a crazy threat—even she knew it was crazy—but she no longer cared. A kind of fury possessed her. She picked up another stick and pounded on a hollow log, drumming it into life. The sound was muffled, swallowed by the trees, but still she went on drumming and yelling to Arang. Finally she gave up. Exhausted, she dropped the stick and threw herself to the ground, where she lay panting, trying to catch her breath.

She thought of Stavan and how he could track a deer across stony ground, and she cursed him for being gone when he was needed. Why in the name of that Hansi hell he was always telling her about hadn't he stayed closer to camp? If he hadn't gone off hunting this evening, Arang wouldn't have gone either. But that wasn't fair. How could Stavan have known that Arang would pick tonight to get lost?

She decided she was going about this the wrong way. It was useless to blame Stavan or anyone else. What she needed to do was try to think like Arang. Getting to her feet, she brushed the dirt and leaves off her dress and headed back to the river. When she got to the campsite, she found that Zastra had joined the search. Perhaps that meant Stavan had come back. She threw a log on the fire and stood for a moment listening, but if the four of them were out there calling to Arang she couldn't hear their voices.

She closed her eyes. If I were Arang, she thought, what would I have done? Where would I have gone? I would have been angry at

Stavan and at my sister and hurt at the idea of being treated like a child so I would have moved quickly the way people do when they're angry, and silently too, because I would have been afraid of being caught before I could get away.

She opened her eyes and looked around the clearing. The only quick, silent way to disappear from the camp was to walk behind the large bush on the other side of the campfire and then run into the forest before anyone noticed you were missing. Not only would the bush protect you from prying eyes, it also stood in front of a small rabbit trail, one of the dozens that led down to the water. Arang must have taken that trail!

She hurried over to the bush and looked behind it and was rewarded with the sight of a small muddy footprint. "Stavan! Zastra! Rhom! Shema! Come here!" she cried. "I've found Arang's tracks!" but no one answered. She took her knife from her belt, hacked off another dead stick to use as a torch, lit it, and hurried down the trail looking for more tracks, and soon she found them: not just one, but dozens. There were three kinds: Arang's small bare foot, a larger imprint of a sandal, and a boot. Zastra and Stavan were already on his trail! With a whoop of joy, she ran on, expecting to see Arang at any moment, perched on Stavan's shoulders, looking sheepish and apologetic.

Up ahead a torch shone through the trees. She hurried toward it, calling Arang's name. Soon she found herself face-to-face with Stavan and Zastra. She looked for Arang, but he was nowhere in sight.

"Well, where is he?" she demanded. "Haven't you found him yet?"

"We've found him," Zastra said, and the moment she spoke Marrah knew from the tone of her voice that something very strange and terrible had happened. She came to a full stop and looked from one to the other. Their faces were pale and grim.

"What's happened?" she cried.

"Marrah, come back to camp with us and I'll tell you—"

"Where's my brother, Zastra? Where in the name of a hundred curses is my brother?"

Instead of answering, Zastra put her hands over her face and began to cry. Marrah looked at Stavan. He was holding something out to her. At first she didn't understand what it was, and then she saw it was Arang's tunic, torn and covered with blood.

"No!" she cried.

143

"It was a lion," Zastra sobbed. "Stavan saw the tracks. We ran, Marrah, we ran; we really did. But we were too late; there was nothing left but his tunic. Oh, the poor little boy. I'll never forgive myself. . . ."

But Marrah wasn't hearing her. She had snatched the torn tunic from Stavan and was holding it to her breast, crying that Arang must still be alive and they had to find him before it got any darker.

Somehow they calmed her down enough to lead her back to camp. Somehow she ate the soup they forced down her throat and drank the water they offered her. But she wouldn't give up the tunic. Whenever Zastra tried to take it from her, she yelled at her and clutched it closer.

"Find him!" she screamed at Stavan. "This is your fault. If you hadn't made him that bow, he wouldn't have gone hunting in the woods. He isn't dead! No lion ate him! Find my brother!"

Stavan didn't say anything. He only looked at her with a strange expression on his face, a cold, odd expression that she hated, and then he bowed and turned and went off into the forest.

After that there was only grief and fear and a night so long she knew it would never end. She sat in stony silence, holding Arang's tunic on her lap, never shedding a tear after her first outburst. Sometimes she lifted it to her lips and kissed it, and sometimes she merely caressed it slowly, smoothing out the torn parts and matching them up again. As she touched it, she thought of their childhood together, how she and Arang had run and played and picked berries and dived into the sea.

When she looked up, she saw Shema and Zastra and Rhom, looking at her pityingly.

"She needs to cry," Zastra said, "or her heart will break."

"Cry," Shema commanded, taking Marrah in her arms in a motherly embrace. "Cry, my darling." At Shema's touch, Marrah's heart broke at last. Letting the tunic fall to the ground, she laid her head on Shema's shoulder and sobbed. Seeing her cry, the traders began to cry too, mourning for the little boy.

Marrah never knew how she got through that night. She must have slept, because sometime just after dawn she woke. For a moment it was like any other morning: a dim pink sky, the sound of bird calls, the rush of the river beside her bed. And then she remembered that Arang had been killed by a lion.

"Marrah," a voice said. She turned her head to find Zastra standing over her with a cup of hot broth. It was a special treat, but she had no stomach for it.

"I want to go back to Xori," she told Zastra, waving the cup aside, and when Zastra tried to comfort her she waved that away too, because there was no comfort left for her in the world. Rising to her feet, she walked down to the river to splash cold water on her face, but her feet felt like stone and it seemed to take a long time. Stavan was nowhere in sight, but Rhom was up already, sitting on a rock mending the carrying strap he had left half finished last night, and Shema was eating her breakfast. She looked away and they said nothing, respecting her grief.

She walked into the river and let the cold water swirl around her legs. The ducks were still swimming in the reeds and the current was still circling around the same snags, but nothing was the same. Everything she looked at or touched or thought of reminded her of Arang.

She bent down and splashed some water on her face, and as she rose she heard a peculiar sound. It was high and low at the same time, like a great flock of birds chattering all at once, and it seemed to be coming from the forest. She looked back at the camp and saw that Rhom and his sisters had risen to their feet.

"What is it?" Shema cried.

"I don't know," Rhom said.

The sound grew louder and clearer; it was a song, sung by dozens of people who were coming closer with every passing moment. Now Marrah could hear other sounds: a drum, a kind of clacking like wooden sticks being beaten together, the stamping of many feet. Suddenly an amazing sight burst out of the forest. First came four men carrying a dead lion slung on a pole. They were short, light-skinned, and broad-chested with dark eyes and hair that hung loosely around their shoulders, and at first glance Marrah thought they were naked, but then she saw they were wearing a sort of loincloth made from a leather strap. Behind the men came a line of dancing men, women, and children who stamped their feet and turned and waved their arms, singing at the top of their lungs. Many of the women carried babies on their backs, but all of them— men and women—carried spears that they clacked together as they sang.

"It's the Forest People!" Zastra cried.

And then Marrah gave a cry too and began to run up the river-bank, for there, at the end of the dancing line, coming out of the forest as if he had never been away, was Arang, safe and whole.

"Arang!" she cried, running toward him. They met in an embrace that nearly knocked both of them over. Picking him up, Marrah spun him around laughing and crying and yelling with joy. "You came back! Thank the Goddess! You're alive!" She put him down and tried to look at him sternly, but it was hopeless because she was grinning from ear to ear. "Do you have any idea how much you worried us? We thought you'd been eaten by a lion."

"I almost was," Arang said proudly. "Oh, Marrah, it was so exciting! The she-lion had me treed and she was going to eat me, only they"—he waved at the Forest People—"shot her just in time. You should see how well they shoot. They're the best."

Marrah turned and saw several dozen small half-naked people regarding her with polite curiosity. She wanted to thank them, but for a moment she couldn't speak. Lifting her hands, she somehow managed to put the tips of her fingers together. *I thank you in Her name for saving my brother's life,* she thought, but the words still wouldn't come.

When the people saw her make the sign of the Goddess, they muttered approvingly. The oldest woman and the oldest man stepped forward and returned Marrah's salute. Then they smiled and pointed at Arang and the lion. Slowly, with great emphasis, they began to speak. Their voices were cheerful and pleasant, but Marrah didn't understand a word they were saying. Seeing this, they began to repeat a few simple words over and over. Gradually she realized they were speaking some form of Old Language.

"Boy," they were saying, "lost. Not good, so young. Throw his self-cover to she-lion. Bad idea."

Marrah turned to Arang. "Did you throw your tunic to that beast?"

Arang looked sheepish. "Well, she had me up in a tree," he said. "What else was I supposed to do? I gave her my birds too, all of them, and I even had a pheasant."

"That was bird blood on your tunic?"

Arang looked down at the ground and drew a design with one bare toe. "Mmm, yes. Dumb, huh?"

"Dumb!" she yelled, and she was just about to tell him how very dumb it had been when she realized that the leaders of the Forest People were still waiting for a reply.

"I'm sorry my brother put you to so much trouble," she said slowly, pointing to Arang. "I thank you with all my heart for saving him. The she-lion would have killed him if you hadn't killed her first."

The Forest People nodded and smiled, and the old woman reached out and patted Marrah on the back as if sympathizing with her. "Little brothers big trouble," she said. She pointed to the old man. "He my little brother. Big, big trouble, he." She laughed uproariously, showing a mostly toothless mouth. The rest of the Forest People joined in the laughter as if it were the best joke of the summer. Marrah had the distinct feeling that she had missed something, but she laughed too.

"Follow you long way, Sabalah daughter," the old woman said. "Follow you all the way from Xemta but now got good lion skin, eh?"

Suddenly Marrah understood. These weren't just any Forest People; they were the same ones who had told the priestesses that she and Arang were coming to visit the Caves of Nar. It hadn't just been luck that they'd arrived in time to save Arang from the lion. They'd been watching him for weeks, making sure he didn't get into trouble—and a good thing, too. She wondered where they'd taken him after they killed the lion and why they hadn't brought him straight back to camp, but before she could ask, Stavan abruptly stepped out of the forest holding his knife in one hand and his spear in the other.

"Let the boy and the woman go!" he thundered in Shambah.

The Forest People gave little squeaks of fright and tried to hide behind one another. Babies screamed, and the four men who were carrying the lion dumped it unceremoniously on the ground and began to run toward the forest.

"Put your weapons away!" Marrah yelled. "They're friendly. They saved Arang's life." She turned to the Forest People. "Wait, don't run away. He's harmless."

"Friendly?" Stavan looked unconvinced.

"I mean it, Stavan. Throw that spear down right now. You're scaring everyone half to death."

Stavan threw down his spear, put his knife back in his belt, and ran toward Arang, scattering the Forest People in all directions like frightened mice. Ignoring them, he fell to his knees in front of Arang, took him in his arms, and hugged him. "You're back, you're safe, you're alive! Han be praised! I was sure you were dead. I thought the lion ate you." He stroked Arang's hair, his eyes wet with tears.

The
Year
the
Horses
Came

147

Moved by the sight, Marrah reached out and put her hand on Stavan's shoulder. To her surprise, he seemed to take this as a reprimand. Flinching as though he'd been struck, he rose to his feet, dropped his arms to his sides, stepped back, and stared at her with the same cold, unreadable expression he'd give her last night when she'd screamed at him that Arang's death was his fault.

"I'm sorry I greeted your brother like that," he said stiffly. "No doubt under the circumstances you'd rather I didn't touch him. If you want me to leave, I'll go at once, and you won't ever have to see me again."

Marrah was too surprised to respond. She looked at Stavan and then at the Forest People, who were beginning to emerge cautiously from the forest to reclaim their lion.

Taking her silence as a sign she understood, Stavan continued in the same vein. "I'd ask you to forgive me, but what I did can't be forgiven. In my own country, I'd be sacrificed to Lord Han so that my blood would wash the shame from my father's name, but here I think you're more merciful. I think your Goddess doesn't ask for the blessing of blood."

Whatever was going on in his mind was so foreign he might as well have been speaking Hansi. "What in the name of seven curses are you talking about?" Marrah cried. "First you charge everyone waving your spear, and now you're talking nonsense."

It was Stavan's turn to look bewildered. "Surely you understand that I promised to protect you and your brother with my own life. Well, I wasn't there when Arang needed me. Instead"—he pointed to the Forest People—"they saved him, and I'm"—he paused as if the word were sticking in his throat—"dishonored."

At last Marrah understood. "You think I'm still angry at you?" He nodded. "You think I still blame you for the fact that Arang ran off into the woods and nearly got himself eaten by a lion?" He nodded again. "And you think I don't like you anymore and don't trust you because you couldn't keep your promise?" For a moment he stood like a statue; then slowly he nodded for a third time. Marrah saw shame in his eyes.

Poor Stavan. Since they spoke to each other in a common language, she often forgot how different he was.

"Stavan," she said gently, "I'm not angry with you. I spoke out of turn last night when I said it was all your fault, but I was half crazy with grief. I owe you an apology. And I still trust you."

"You do?"

"Of course. How could you even think for a moment that I really believed it was your fault? If I'd taken your advice and watched Arang more closely, he never would have run off in the first place. As a matter of fact, I've decided that I should ask you to be his *aita*. He's too much for me to handle by myself." She put her arm around Arang. "Of course it would only be a temporary sort of situation. Mehe, Arang's real *aita*, is back in Xori, but you could be a sort of . . . step-*aita* to him. What do you think?"

Stavan looked so surprised she almost laughed, but she had enough sense not to, which was a good thing because he probably would have been mortally offended. "I'd be honored," he stuttered. "Very honored—that is, if you're sure and if Arang likes the idea."

"Like it!" Arang cried. "I've been trying to get her to do this for *weeks*. Take her up on it, Stavan, before she changes her mind."

Stavan did, immediately. "You'll be my son," he said, bending down to give Arang another hug, and when Marrah reminded him that mothers had sons and *aitas* had nephews, he didn't object. "Let him be my nephew, then. We'll mingle our blood as the Hansi do."

Arang wasn't too keen on the idea of mingling his blood with anyone, even Stavan, but he held his tongue. He wanted Stavan for his *aita* no matter what.

That evening, after they had feasted on lion meat and listened to the Forest People sing their lion-hunting songs, Stavan led Arang up to the fire, and there, sitting on the fresh pelt, he cut his finger and Arang's finger and let their blood flow together. Then he pierced Arang's earlobe with a bone needle and put one of Achan's gold earrings in the hole. Arang, who had been warned ahead of time, gritted his teeth, but the finger cutting and ear piercing didn't hurt nearly as much as he'd thought they were going to, and for the rest of the night he sat proudly beside Stavan watching the Forest People dance.

The next morning things returned to normal. Sometime during the night, the Forest People left without making a sound, taking the lion pelt but leaving the claws behind. Gathering the claws, Marrah scrubbed them in the river and wrapped them in a piece of soft deerskin. By the time she was finished, the breakfast fish were cooked and ready to eat. Soon they were back on the trail, following the Orugali once more.

The
Year
the
Horses
Came

149

They walked for two more days. The river widened, and with each step the traders seemed to grow more excited. One morning, Shema and Zastra got up early, washed each other's hair, and wove necklaces of flowers for everyone, including Stavan. On that very afternoon, the thirty-second since they left Gurasoak, they finally came to the place where the waters of the Orugali emptied into the Blue Sea. From there it was only a short walk to the village of Lezentka.

# CHAPTER EIGHT

Rockfish and clams,
dark, sweet figs,
olives and roses,
wines from the east,

deep-keeled boats
with sails so white
they melt on the back
of your tongue like salt—

Lezentka has everything
but not when you want it.
Lezentka's the place
where travelers must wait.

SABALAH'S SONG
VERSES 15–17

Lezentka

The next place they were headed for was the island of Gira, famous for its fine obsidian, great temples, and spectacular religious festivals. It was said that no people worshiped the Goddess with more enthusiasm than the Girans, who were generally acknowledged to be the greatest drummers in the world, and their huge snake dances—some of which involved hundreds of people moving together in perfect rhythm for days at a time—were reputed to bring the Goddess into the heart and mind of anyone who participated.

Marrah had been born in the birth sanctuary of the eastern temple of Gira, when Sabalah had sought refuge there on her way west.

Both of the twin priestess queens of the island had blessed her at birth, rubbing a bit of earth on her forehead and putting a drop of salt water in her mouth to make her part of the Earth and the Sea, and although Marrah couldn't remember the ceremony or anything about Gira itself—having left it when she was only a few months old—she had always longed to visit it.

Knowing how impatient she would be to get to the island, Sabalah had warned her that they might have to wait several weeks before they could catch a boat headed in the right direction. On the way west, she herself had had to wait almost a month in Lezentka before she found a party of traders making the crossing to the Sea of Gray Waves, and although the people had been hospitable, she was the first to admit it had been a boring month. Lezentka, she told Marrah, was not one of the great cities of the earth. Its primary claim to fame was that it lay near the mouth of the Orugali, and although some of the villagers specialized in long-distance trading, it could hardly be called a major port. Its houses were made of wood and mud, just like the longhouses of Xori only smaller, since each only housed a single mother family; the river water had a brackish taste that lingered on the back of the tongue; and there was no Goddess Stone or sweat hut, only a dusty central square and a pretty little temple dedicated to the Earth, whom the villagers worshiped in the form of a pregnant deer.

"Just try to relax and enjoy the wait," Sabalah had advised, but surely she had never in her wildest dreams imagined that the wait in Lezentka would be so long, for as it turned out, the three of them were forced to stay in the traders' village not one month or even two but an entire winter, hoping every day a boat would appear to take them across the sea to Gira and going to bed every night disappointed.

Actually, the problem was not that there were no boats; there were half a dozen small ones right in Lezentka itself, but like the boats of the Shore People, they were made to hug the land, never sailing out of sight of the beach and putting in at the first signs of heavy weather. Gira lay far beyond the range of any of them, many days' journey across open water. Only the most intrepid traders made the trip, trusting in the mercy of the Goddess and guiding themselves by the stars, and their boats were altogether different from the lightweight dugouts that ferried goods locally from one village to another.

Known as *raspas* or "sacred birds" because of their white winglike sails, these long-distance boats were not quite ships in the modern sense; they lacked complicated rigging and were small and hard to steer, but they had deep keels that kept them upright and gaff-rigged linen sails reinforced with battens that allowed them to plow forward when the weather was fair. When the wind failed the *raspas* could be paddled—not an easy task, since the paddler had to stand balanced precariously as the waves slapped against the hull—and although there were no hatches, grass mats and oiled hides could be tied over the cargo if the weather looked threatening.

Still, compared to the winter storms, the *raspas* were fragile, and it was not unheard of for them to disappear without a trace. In Lezentka more than one mother clan threw food and flowers into the sea on the day the dead were honored, and there were more children being raised by aunts and cousins than was usual in such a small village. The men and women of the coast even wove special designs into their clothing so their bodies could be identified if they drowned, and every once in a long while a strange boat would put in and traders from far away would kneel, kiss the earth, and hand a village mother a bag or two of bones that had once set off gaily to the sound of drums and flutes.

Because of the danger, the *raspas* did what their namesakes the birds did: they migrated, which is to say they made open-water crossings from late spring to early fall, lowering their sails as soon as the first hard rains fell and not raising them again until the gray geese flew north and the weather turned fair again. In theory each of the two *raspas* owned by the village of Lezentka made three or four round trips a season, leaving for the last time in the Moon of Dry Grass and returning well before the equinox, but whenever Zastra, Shema, and Rhom made the forest crossing, the boat known as the *Gannet* always waited for them. The fine jadeite axes and soft feathered capes of the Shore People were so valuable that the village council had long ago decided it was worth taking a chance that the crew might have to winter away from home, especially since the worst that could happen was that they would be forced to spend the rainy months on the most beautiful island in the Blue Sea.

This year, however, the side trip to the Caves of Nar had cost the traders more than a week, and when they arrived in Lezentka, the first thing they found out—after being kissed and stuffed with food—was that the *Gannet* had already sailed.

The
Year
the
Horses
Came

153

"Why in the name of twenty curses did they do that?" mild-mannered Shema had yelled, setting her bowl of squid stew down so hard the inky black gravy slopped over the sides and stained the fresh linen skirt she had put on to celebrate her homecoming. She and Rhom and Zastra were sitting beside their mother, Sirshan, surrounded by so many aunts, uncles, cousins, nieces, nephews, and friends that it would have taken days for Marrah to sort them all out, but it was already clear that the Lezentkans had one thing in common: all of them talked, and none of them listened. Rhom and Zastra added their curses to Shema's, the various friends and relatives offered explanations, the dogs barked, the babies cried, and for a few minutes no one could understand anything—especially not Marrah, since the traders had lapsed into their own tongue.

Finally Rhom turned to her and translated. "The boat's gone," he growled. "The one you were supposed to take to Gira. The fools got it into their heads that the rains were going to come early this year, so they left ten days ago. Never mind that they promised to wait, never mind"—he pointed to the bit of sky that was plainly visible through the open door—"that there's not a cloud out there bigger than the ends of my idiot cousins' noses; they threw the divining shells and decided we were in for bad weather, so off they went."

Arang gave a small moan of disappointment. Stavan, as usual, understood nothing and wouldn't until one of them bothered to translate a second time for his benefit.

"Does that mean we're stuck here all winter?" Marrah looked at the unfamiliar faces of Rhom's relatives, the strange tentacled fish in her bowl, the small square house of Rhom's mother that never could have been mistaken for one of the longhouses of Xori. For the first time in many weeks, she felt almost sick with a longing to go back to her own people. Since that was clearly out of the question, they had to keep moving forward. Only the importance of the message she was taking to Shara made up for the pain of missing her mother, not to mention Bere and Ama and Uncle Seme and all her friends. How could she possibly sit in Lezentka for months knowing the beastmen might be riding out of the Sea of Grass at any moment? If she had had wings like the seagull she was named after, she would have flown away with Arang on her back in less time than it took Rhom to answer her question, but instead she felt trapped in this cursedly friendly place like a fly that had stumbled into a pot of honey.

Her impatience must have shown, because Rhom stopped swearing at his irresponsible cousins, grabbed her hand, and patted it soothingly. "Now, now," he clucked, "don't get so upset, pretty dark-eyed Marrah. You've missed your chance to get to Gira on the *Gannet*, but the *Gray Goose* will be back any day now, and maybe if the rains hold off, the village council will let it take you to the island before winter begins." He pointed to her necklace. "After all, you and your brother are wearing Her sign. What sailors wouldn't like to have that kind of luck in their boat, eh?"

Marrah was somewhat reassured, but not completely. As Rhom went back to cursing his cousins in his own language, she put a comforting arm around Arang and drew him close.

"What are we going to do now?" he whispered, resting his head on her shoulder and looking up at her as if she had all the solutions.

"Why, wait for the *Gray Goose* to come back," she told him cheerfully, but from the look Arang gave her, she knew that, as usual, he wasn't deceived.

"What if it doesn't?"

It was a good question, one she had no answer for. What could they do if neither *raspa* showed up before winter? Could they bypass Gira and travel by dugout from one village to another until they got to the next place on Sabalah's song map? Or, if that was impossible, could they walk from Lezentka to Shara the way they'd walked from Gurasoak to Lezentka?

When the welcome-home feast was over, she took Rhom aside and asked him to speak plainly without patting her hand or calling her a dark-eyed beauty. "Because," she told him, "I'm in no mood to wade through your compliments trying to get at the truth." Perhaps she spoke a little harshly, but Rhom didn't seem offended. He might be full of goat dung under ordinary circumstances, but when you really needed advice he could treat you like one of his sisters.

"The local boats aren't a possibility," he said. "They don't have any set schedules, and you might have to wait for months to get from one village to another, especially with winter coming on. As for walking, it takes so much longer to walk around the Blue Sea than to sail across it that no trader I've met has ever tried. Besides, once you left the route your mother sings of, how would you and your brother find your way? You'd be walking into the unknown without her spirit to guide you. No, put it out of your mind. There's only one way you should go: in a good, swift *raspa* straight to Gira."

The
Year
the
Horses
Came

155

He looked toward the sea, which was barely visible in the moon-light. "The *Gray Goose* could be heading straight for us this very minute." He smiled. "Why, I bet you three combs of honey you won't be here more than a few days at most."

Unfortunately, she won the honey. The days turned to weeks, the weeks turned to a month, the rains fell early, as Rhom's unreliable cousins had predicted, and soon it was obvious to everyone that the two *raspas* had decided to winter away from the village.

And so Marrah settled down to wait. Later, she would always say that the months in Lezentka taught her patience, and sometimes, when she was in a particularly nostalgic mood, she would describe the little temple with its whitewashed walls and cobbled floor as one of the most peaceful places on earth. When she was a master potter, she would tell her students that it was in the pottery workshop of the temple of Lezentka that she first came to appreciate clay, and she would describe the simple red and yellow bowls of the village as if they were old friends she had reluctantly left behind.

But at the time she felt more like a goat forced to spend a long winter in a small shed. Still, as she often told Arang, there were worse places they could have been stuck. The people were friendly, the food was good, and whatever beauty the village lacked, nature provided. They had been given a small house to themselves, and they only had to step out the door to see the Blue Sea, bluer even than the morning glory of Marrah's vision. The water was warm and clear, full of strange fish and exotic shells, and the beaches were covered with small white pebbles. When the waves washed over the stones, they made a soft hissing sound that was as sensual as a caress.

If Marrah hadn't been so anxious to get to Shara, she might have even chosen to spend a few months in Lezentka. In many ways, it was more beautiful than Xori. There was something voluptuous about this land, something sweet and mysterious that whispered of the joys of surrendering completely to nature. Golden wheat grew waist-high in the fields, the trees were heavy with fruit, and the sunsets were extravagant spectacles: first a great fiery ball descending behind the western hills, then a crown of light that cast ribbons of pink, vermilion, and purple across a vast, empty sky. Within the first week, Marrah had tasted her first olive, drunk her first cup of wine, pried butter-fried land snails out of their shells, and eaten the first fig she had ever seen, sucking the sweet dried flesh into her mouth and licking the sticky sugar off her fingers.

Although it was soon winter, the weather was mostly mild and sunny. Sometimes a cold, blustery wind would blow down from the north and it would rain for a day or two. When this happened, the villagers would crouch next to their fires and complain, but Marrah and Arang, who remembered the finger-numbing frosts of Xori, went out in all weather. Often they would take a basket with them and dig for the sweet little clams that lay buried under the strip of sand where the river joined the sea, but more often they simply walked for the pleasure of walking. Soon the rain would stop, the clouds would drift out to sea and become no more than a strip of white on the horizon, the birds would begin to sing, the villagers would spread their clothes out on the beach to dry, the air would grow thin, and the golden light would return.

Stavan for some reason rarely walked with them, preferring to go off by himself to fish or hunt. Sometimes he took Arang with him, but he was still cautious. When he went more than a half morning's walk from the village, he left Arang behind, and on those days he made a special effort to spend some extra time with him after the evening meal, telling him stories or teaching him how to string a bow properly or chip a bit of flint into a passable arrowhead.

Marrah was pleased to see him taking his role as *aita* so seriously, but when the two of them went off together, she was left with a lot of time on her hands. The people of the Blue Sea coast spoke a language that sounded like birds twittering; often, as she sat watching them go about their daily business, she wished she could join in the gossip and laughter, but except for the traders and one or two priest-esses who spoke Old Language, no one could understand her. Occa-sionally she managed to have a long conversation with Rhom or his sisters, but having returned to their own families after an absence of many months, they were understandably preoccupied. Shema, who had left her four children with her mother, was trying to make up for lost time; Zastra's partner, Rusha, was pregnant and about to give birth; as for Rhom, it seemed he was *aita* to half the children in the village.

The
Year
the
Horses
Came

157

So one afternoon when Zastra came over of her own accord and settled down to talk, Marrah was both pleased and surprised. For a while they discussed Rusha's pregnancy. Rusha was a strong-willed woman who fished with her brother and uncle in the deep water out beyond the breakers. Zastra had been trying in vain to get her to stay on land now that she was in her seventh month, but Rusha only laughed and told her the more pregnant the woman, the better she floated. Since Zastra and Rusha had gone through six pregnancies together—three each—Zastra should have known there was no persuading her, but she still felt obliged to try.

"I love that woman like my life," Zastra grumbled, "but she has no sense." She sighed and sipped some of the fish broth Marrah had offered her and appeared to settle into her own thoughts. Marrah was reluctant to disturb her. Taking up a net, she began to mend it with a piece of twisted fiber. There was a long silence broken only by the sounds of a baby crying and someone pounding meat with a wooden mallet.

Finally Zastra spoke. "Actually, I didn't come here to talk about myself; I came to talk about Stavan. Shema thinks you know what's going on and so does Rhom, but I don't. 'Leave her alone,' Rhom said, 'it's none of our business.' Shema, as usual, was less diplomatic. She told me she could tell that you weren't interested in Stavan, and if I went poking my nose into other people's love lives I'd probably get it cut off someday, but I'm a matchmaker at heart. I can't help it. I'm not much attracted to men, but I never like to see one going to waste. Did you know that almost every night after you and Arang go to sleep, Stavan goes down to the beach and sits there staring at the sea and brooding like a thirteen-year-old who's never had a lover? Now you and I both know there are any number of unpartnered women in this village who'd be more than happy to take him into their beds even if he is a little strange-looking, so naturally people have started wondering why he's not sharing joy with any of them. 'He probably loves men,' Shema says, 'and there aren't any unpartnered men who love men in Lezentka at the moment,' but I say no, I don't think so. I think he wants Marrah and she doesn't know it."

Marrah had dropped the fish net into her lap and was staring at Zastra with a very odd expression on her face. Suddenly all sorts of things were falling into place: the way Stavan had trembled when he held her hand in the cave, the way he so rarely met her eyes, the look he sometimes gave her when he didn't know she was watching.

"Well?" Zastra took another sip of broth. "Am I right?"

Marrah picked up the net and began to mend it again. Her hand was steady but her mind was racing, trying to put the evidence together, trying to see if it added up to something. "You're right that I didn't suspect Stavan was spending his nights on the beach, but the part about his wanting me . . ." She paused and thought some more. "Maybe you're right about that and maybe not. It's possible, I suppose, but on the other hand, I've been with him night and day for weeks now and he's never once said anything to me that would lead me to think he had the slightest interest in sharing joy. In fact, most of the time he treats me like I'm a village mother." She tossed the net down, folded her arms around her knees, and wrinkled her forehead. "If he wants to share joy with me, why doesn't he just ask?"

Zastra took another sip of fish broth. "Good question. I've been giving it a lot of thought, and I've come to the conclusion that he doesn't ask you because he doesn't know how."

Marrah smiled. "You're saying you think a full-grown man doesn't know how to ask a woman to share joy?"

Zastra nodded. "Right. Any other man would have walked up to you long ago and said something like 'Sweet woman, I'm fond of you and I'd like to share joy with you,' and then you could have said yes or no or told him you were already partnered and not interested, or unpartnered and willing, or whatever in the usual way. Of course it's always possible that in his land the woman always asks the man."

Marrah thought this over. "I doubt that. From what I've heard, Hansi women don't live much better than dogs."

"Well, it's a mystery then. But I can tell you one thing: when Arang was lost, I thought he was going to go crazy. When he saw those lion tracks he gave a scream like a man who had been scalded, and when he saw Arang's tunic lying there on the ground all bloody and ripped to pieces, he took out his long knife and slashed at the trees and cursed. And when you yelled at him that it was all his fault, he cried. You didn't see the tears because he turned his back to you, but the rest of us saw them. There are a lot of things you don't see. When you're not looking at him, he stares at you like he wants to eat you." She finished off the fish soup, put the bowl down on the ground beside her, and wiped her mouth with the back of her hand. "Who knows, maybe I'm way off the mark; maybe I'm just a busybody who sees a reed and thinks it's a basket. But if I were you, I'd at least have a talk with him and find out why he's spending his nights on the beach."

Marrah knew it was good advice, but she was slow in taking it. Despite what Zastra had said, it was hard for her to believe Stavan was suffering because he couldn't tell her he wanted her, and since

The
Year
the
Horses
Came

159

he had taken the trouble to go off by himself after she and Arang were asleep, she was reluctant to invade his privacy. Most likely he was thinking of something else when he stared out to sea—horses, maybe, or who knew what, but certainly not her—and she was going to look pretty foolish when she took him aside and asked him if he was harboring a secret desire to share joy with her. Either he'd be offended by the implication that he didn't know how to ask a woman, or he'd think she was clumsily asking him, which would have been fine if she'd wanted him, but she wasn't sure she did. She missed Bere even though she might not ever see him again, and although she liked Stavan a great deal and had even begun to think that yellow hair and blue eyes weren't so ugly after all, her feelings about him were still complicated and ambivalent. To invite a man to share joy with you and then in the next breath tell him that you didn't mean it was so rude and insulting that she wouldn't blame him if he never spoke to her again, and since she was planning to spend a long time in his company, that wasn't a pleasant prospect.

Over and over she kept coming back to the simple fact that if he wanted her he would have said so. Relationships between the sexes were very direct. You always knew where you stood, and the idea that a grown man might not only keep his feelings to himself but willingly suffer, when all he had to do was ask, was almost incomprehensible.

But the conversation with Zastra made her look at Stavan with new eyes, and the more she looked, the more she became convinced that he was, in fact, unhappy about something. Perhaps it was nothing more than the boredom of waiting for a boat that never came, or perhaps it was homesickness, or perhaps he did indeed have a secret that he didn't feel he could share with anyone, but whatever it was, it made him get up at night to sit by himself on the beach staring at the sea. Even during the day he seemed increasingly withdrawn, only coming to life when Arang ran up to ask him to mend an arrow or take him fishing.

It was clear he needed to confide in someone, and equally clear that, since no one but she and Arang spoke Shambah, it would have to be her. And so it happened that on a mild night a few weeks later she found herself walking on the beach with Stavan, listening to some of the strangest words she had ever heard a man speak.

At first he simply protested there was nothing wrong, but finally he admitted something was bothering him. At least Marrah thought that was what he was admitting. He spoke in riddles like a priestess who had breathed too much sacred smoke, and nothing he told her quite made sense.

"I'm happy," he said, "because you're my chief, and unhappy because you're my chief. The same sense of honor that makes me stay here with you and your brother closes my mouth and stills my tongue. I can't tell you what I'm thinking because what I'm thinking is not what a man should think in the presence of his chief." He turned to her, his face pale and strained. "Don't ask me to tell you why I sit staring at the waves. The temptation's too great. I'm not a strong man; it's hard for me to be silent." He pointed to the sky. "A warrior should be like the stars—fixed, constant, never changing—but I'm more like the moon—inconstant: full one day, shadowed the next."

Marrah found all this very poetic and rather beautiful, but mostly unintelligible. What did you do when you asked a man what was bothering him and he told you he was like the moon? Did you say, "Ah, yes, the moon," and leave it at that, pretending to understand, or did you push on? Once again she felt as if she and Stavan were two tiny figures standing on opposite sides of a wide river trying to talk to each other across the distance that separated them. She took a deep breath, reminded herself that his native language wasn't Shambah, and tried to figure out if there was any part of what he'd just said that made sense. Finally she came up with something.

"You say you're unhappy that I'm your chief and honor keeps you from speaking. Well, what if I weren't your chief? Then could you tell me what's bothering you?"

He nodded reluctantly. "Yes, but then it wouldn't be necessary because—" He closed his mouth abruptly as if he'd said too much, but Marrah finished the sentence for him.

"Because then there'd be no reason for you to be sad, right?" If that was the answer, he wasn't willing to tell her. He stood so still he looked as if he had been transformed into a block of salt.

Well, at last I get it, she thought. Zastra was wrong, he hasn't been thinking about me at all; he's been brooding over that ridiculous promise he made and wishing he'd never made it. I should have known it would have something to do with that thing he calls his "honor." Great Goddess, this man's ways are strange, but at least now that I understand what's bothering him, I can try to do something about it.

The
Year
the
Horses
Came

161

They walked a few more paces in silence. "Listen, Stavan." She decided it was best to be as direct as possible. "I can't think of any particular reason for you to go on keeping that promise you made to me. I appreciate it, of course, and I know how seriously you took it, but now that we're out of lion country, I can't see that Arang and I are going to need you to protect us. What I'm trying to say is that the most dangerous part of the trip is over, so there's really no need for you to go on thinking of me as your chief. To tell the truth, I'm not even sure what a chief is. All I know is that when you think of me as one, it makes you unhappy. So why don't we just forget about it?"

"Are you saying you release me from my vow?"

"Yes, from now on you don't owe me and Arang anything. Frankly, I'd like you to come to Shara with us, but if you don't want to, I'll understand."

"But that's impossible."

Marrah sighed. With Stavan nothing was ever easy. "What's impossible?"

Speaking quickly and with mounting agitation, Stavan explained that no one could release a warrior from his vow but a priest of Lord Han. She was his chief and she would stay his chief until he either won back his life by saving hers or died in the attempt, and there was nothing they could do about it. He was hers to command; he would obey her in everything but this.

"Great Goddess!" Marrah exclaimed. "What a mess!" She sat down on a rock and Stavan sat down beside her and both of them stared glumly at the waves. Suddenly Marrah had a revelation. "You say you'll obey me in everything else?" Stavan nodded. "Well, then, as your chief—a title I'm apparently stuck with—I hereby order you to stop treating me like your chief and start treating me like . . . well, like myself. You can go around protecting me and Arang if you want, provided it ever becomes necessary again, but on a day-to-day basis I want you to act like you never made that promise."

Stavan got very quiet, so quiet she wondered if she had managed to offend him again. "Do you know what you're saying?" he asked at last.

"Probably not, but that's what I'm ordering you to do so you have to do it, correct?" She paused, expecting him to say something, but the only sound was the hiss of the waves hitting the beach. The silence began to get on her nerves. "How does a Hansi warrior treat his ex-chief anyway? Just out of curiosity?"

"If she's a woman," Stavan said, "he treats her like a woman; he treats her like this." Suddenly, before she knew what was happening, he took her in his arms and kissed her. She was so surprised she didn't have the presence of mind to pull away. Kissing him was like being hit by a wave of raw emotions: wild, abrupt, passionate, and a little frightening. He kissed like a man who was used to taking what he wanted, and yet at the same time he held her tenderly as if she might break apart in his hands.

Finally he stopped. Pulling away, Marrah stared at him in disbelief. It wasn't the kiss itself that was such a shock; the conversation with Zastra had prepared her for the possibility that he might want to kiss her. But he hadn't asked! People always asked for permission before they started to share joy. Suppose she hadn't wanted to be kissed, how would he have known? It was rude; it was . . . unthinkable. She should be furious with him. Only maybe he hadn't meant to be rude. Maybe Zastra was right. Maybe he didn't know how you were supposed to ask; maybe this was the way Hansi men always acted around women.

Stavan didn't seem to notice her confusion. Cradling her in his arms, he began to stroke her hair. "I've wanted to kiss you for so long," he said. "Ever since the day we sat together on that rock on the way back from Hoza. I almost did it that very evening, but then you told me that you'd saved my life, and from then on I wouldn't even let myself think of you as a woman. But I couldn't help it. I'd hear you laugh or see you bend down to pick up a stick of firewood, and I'd grow sick with longing."

He took her hand and began to kiss her fingers one at a time. "If I were in my own land, I'd buy you from your father and take you into my tent and never have another wife. I'd pay fifty fine cattle for you and—"

Marrah's anger dissolved at the thought of being bought for fifty head of cattle. Breaking into giggles, she snatched back her hand.

Stavan looked mortally offended. "So you think I'm a fool, do you? You think I'm not worthy of you?" Later, he would laugh with her; later, in the months to come, after they made love, she would put her head on his shoulder and ask him how many cattle he thought she was worth now, and he would say hundreds, thousands, as many as the stars, but that first time he was in dead earnest. Releasing her, he rose to his feet. "I shouldn't have kissed you. No doubt you found it unpleasant."

The
Year
the
Horses
Came

163

Marrah stopped laughing. "No," she said frankly. "I liked it. It was a little wilder than I'm used to, but it was exciting. But you should have—"

Stavan never let her say what she thought he should have done. Swooping down on her again, he took her in his arms and began to kiss her so hard he knocked her over backward. Fortunately they were sitting near the edge of the beach, so she fell on soft ground instead of stones. Clinging to her, he pulled her dress up, nearly ripping it. When he saw her body, he gave a cry of joy and began to touch her breasts and run his hands over her belly.

"Wait!" she tried to say between kisses. Since she had never heard of a man forcing sex on a woman, she wasn't afraid but she was bewildered. "Slow down, we need to talk." But Stavan was lost in his own passion, making love to her and at the same time leaving her behind. In a way it was moving the way being caught in a sudden storm can be moving, but if this was the Hansi way of sharing joy, it left a lot to be desired, and as she tussled with him in the grass, she began to think she'd made a serious mistake. He had enough energy for any two men, but his idea of giving a woman pleasure seemed to involve throwing himself on top of her and knocking the air out of her lungs. She felt him spread her legs, but instead of kissing the insides of her thighs slowly the way Bere or any man of the Shore People would have, he pinned her down and actually tried to enter her.

"Stop that!" she yelled, pushing him away so hard that he fell off her. She sat up, pulled down her dress, and glared at him. "What do you think you were doing just then?"

He looked bewildered. "Making love to you, my darling," he stuttered.

She was not to be placated with pet names. "You never asked if I wanted to share joy with you, and I never gave you the signal," she snapped.

"What signal?"

"The tap." She pointed to his thigh. "I never tapped you. What makes you think I want to start a child? And how dare you assume that you could just pounce on me like that without being invited? Don't you have any self-control? Don't you know how to make love without smashing a person?"

Stavan looked astonished. "You didn't like it?"

She picked the dry grass out of her hair and glared at him some more, wishing he'd just vanish so this whole embarrassing incident would be over. "That's an understatement. I not only didn't enjoy it, I felt like you hardly knew I was there. If that's the way your people share joy, I don't see how you Hansi manage to start children. Why, if I was one of your women, I wouldn't ever let a man near me."

"Marrah," he said softly, "I didn't know. I thought you wanted me; I thought I was making you happy. I love you. I want to touch you the way you want to be touched, but I don't know how to do it." He touched her face delicately with the tips of his fingers, brushing the hair out of her eyes. "Teach me, please."

If he had said anything else, if he had so much as uttered a word to defend himself, she would have walked away without looking back, but he was so clearly upset over offending her that it was impossible to doubt he was telling the truth: he loved her but he had no more idea than a child of how to express that love. No, that wasn't accurate; even a child would have had more sense. Even a six-year-old would have known grown-ups never tried to share joy without asking.

Her anger died out and she felt something close to pity. Poor Stavan. What had it been like to be raised in a world where all the sweetness of love was reduced to a quick struggle that gave men little pleasure and women none at all? He was stroking her hair now, very tenderly, as if afraid he might hurt her, and as he touched her she realized again that he was a good man, decent and loyal, driven to do rude things by customs he had never questioned.

They taught him to be stupid and inconsiderate, she thought, but he could be taught to give women joy as our men do, and as he gave joy, he'd get it back multiplied many times, and then he'd know what love really is. How sad it would be if he went through his whole life not knowing.

She took his hand and held it for a moment and then began to talk to him, explaining the simple things he should have known: that you always asked, that you never imposed yourself on another person, that you followed pleasure slowly until it grew strong enough to sweep both partners away. She didn't consciously decide to become his teacher; she did it instinctively, speaking to him the way she would have spoken to a child, and as she spoke she began to feel warmer toward him. It was flattering to see how attentively he listened.

Stavan was a fast learner. She had only meant to talk to him, but it's dangerous to talk of love on a dark beach when you're young and

The
Year
the
Horses
Came

165

the waves are whispering. Soon he was kissing her again and she was letting him because he had asked like a man of her own people and she had said yes without knowing beforehand that she was going to say any such thing. This time his lips were warm and slow and he held her carefully.

The kiss lasted a long time, much longer than any single kiss in Marrah's memory. He kissed her until she was dizzy. Then slowly—so slowly that she could hardly believe his fingers were moving—he began to touch her breasts, teasing her nipples up through the thin leather of her dress, caressing each one until it came to a point, letting it fall back and then caressing it until it rose again.

Excited, she reached for him, but he pushed her hands away. "No, please," he whispered. "Let me give you pleasure."

Closing her eyes, she dropped her hands to her sides and let him go on arousing her. Everywhere he touched, he lingered until her flesh began to burn under his fingers. She moaned and arched her back and pressed against him, but he went on and on as if the world had disappeared and only his hands and her breasts existed. The tension built, sweet and unbearable, and still his fingers swept over her nipples, teasing and encouraging. Then, all at once, she came, suddenly and violently, throwing her arms around his neck with a loud cry.

He caught her and held her until the spasm was over, pressing his lips against her forehead. She rested for a moment in his arms, then opened her eyes to find him looking at her with a worried expression.

"Did I hurt you?" he whispered anxiously.

She was too content to be surprised even by such an odd question. "Hurt me?" She yawned and stretched, utterly relaxed and comfortable. "Of course not."

"But you yelled."

Marrah suddenly understood. Laughing, she took him in her arms and kissed him tenderly. "Oh, Stavan, you dear silly man," she cried. "Don't you know what happened? Haven't you ever seen a woman come before?"

Lezentka was no longer the dull little town where you sat on a beach waiting for a boat that never came. In the weeks that followed, Stavan began to feel he belonged to the village, and for the first time he understood what Marrah's people meant when they said they loved the land. He had never loved any particular piece of earth. His home had always been a tent, pitched in various places, and there had been no time to love anything but the sky and the great Sea of Grass, which always looked the same no matter how far you wandered. But now when he walked down the beach, he saw the place where he and Marrah had first made love, and when he climbed the hills and gazed down at the village, he saw the small house where they slept together covered by a single blanket, and sometimes, if he let his eyes wander over the fields, he could pick Marrah out from the others, leading the goats down to be milked or hunting for shells at the edge of the waves.

Sometimes after they made love, he would laugh and kiss her and try to tell her how she had given him a home at last. "I used to be a nomad," he would say, tickling her eyelids with his tongue until she laughed and pushed him away, "but you've turned me into a savage. Marrah of Xori, you've converted me with your body."

It was only a joke, but there was a lot of truth in it: he *was* being converted by her, not just by her body—although it was a beautiful body, smooth as a dove's breast, so round and sweet that a man could die of joy just looking at it—but by the things he was learning from her now that they were lovers. Sometimes it was nothing more than a few words of Old Language she insisted on teaching him so he could talk to Rhom, Zastra, and Shema, but coming from her lips the words had a sweetness that made him learn faster than he had ever learned before.

Often it was something more complicated. After they made love, they were sometimes reluctant to go to sleep, and they frequently lay side by side talking to each other until the sky began to lighten. Marrah would tell him how her people saw the world, how when they walked or sat or stood on the Earth they felt as if they were touching the body of a Mother who loved them. Or she would tell him the old story of the Great Spring when the Goddess Earth took pity on her children and sent the Divine Sisters to teach them how to weave and make pottery, tame animals, and plant grain.

Sometimes he would tell stories of his own: how when he traveled with Achan they had been driven west by the little savages of the north country after Achan and two of the other men tried to abduct some of their women, and how the savages—who could have easily killed them—had killed their horses instead and inexplicably spared their lives. Or he would reach into his pouch and take out the strangely shaped white pebble he had found on the shore of the first

The
Year
the
Horses
Came

167

and coldest sea he had ever seen, and while she examined it, he would tell her of the colored lights that danced in the northern skies. In exchange for lessons in Old Language, he taught her a few words of Hansi and told her the legends of his people: of Choatk, who lived underground where the souls of cowards went, and Han, who took the bravest warriors to paradise and gave them stars for horses; and one night, as she sat horrified, staring at him with wide, unbelieving eyes, he even told her how when a warrior dies his wives and slaves are sent after him to keep him company, and horses are slaughtered over his grave, and he is buried with his ornaments around his neck and his spear in his hand.

He knew as he spoke that he risked losing her love, but he told her anyway, wanting to hold nothing back, and when he was done, he took her gently in his arms and asked her to forgive him for having been born among such a people, because he could see now that the ways of the Hansi were brutal and that there was a better way for a man to live his life than wasting it on war and cattle stealing. He was afraid she might condemn him and draw away from him, but instead she threw her arms around his neck and told him that there was nothing to forgive, that he wasn't to blame, that no one chose the place of his birth, and that she loved him, not just because his kisses were the best kisses a man ever offered a woman, but because he had the brains to see that having been born a warrior didn't mean you had to be one forever.

But he didn't risk that kind of revelation too often. Mostly he told her things that made her smile: like how silly a newborn colt looked when it first tried to stand up on its long, spindly legs, or how in the land of the Hansi a girl wasn't considered a woman until a man had put his penis inside her. Once he even tried to explain to her that by the standards of his people she was still a virgin, but the idea that the two of them could make love so wildly without it counting sent her into such a fit of giggles she had to sit up to get her breath. She never let him forget that one, and sometimes when she was doing the most delightful things to him with her hands and mouth, she would whisper, "So I'm a virgin, am I?" and proceed to display a skill that made him utter helpless cries of pleasure that he was afraid might be heard in the neighboring houses.

Fortunately for his pride, everyone was too polite to mention the sighs and groans that came from the little house at the end of the village, but the next morning the women would smile at him when he walked past, and the men would tell him how pleased they were that he was enjoying his stay in Lezentka, and sometimes, if Rhom were in a particularly good mood, he would take out his flute and play a love song or two or appear with a dish of steamed clams, claiming that Stavan was looking tired and everyone knew clams gave a man energy.

Even Arang seemed to approve of the fact that Stavan had become his sister's lover. When it became clear what was going on, he insisted on moving out so the two of them could have more privacy. "It's getting too cold for you to spend the night on the beach," he announced one morning, and, packing up his things, he kissed Marrah, hugged Stavan, and walked across the square to Shema's house. If he was at all jealous of the attention Marrah was giving to Stavan, he never showed it: on the contrary, he seemed relieved.

"I was always afraid you were going to decide to go back to your own people," he told Stavan one afternoon as they sat on the riverbank fishing. "But now that you're my *aita* and sharing joy with Marrah, I think you'll stay."

Stavan assured him he had no plans to leave.

"Good." Arang nodded. He pulled his line out of the water and saw his hook was bare. "Pass the bait, will you?"

Stavan passed him the bait and managed somehow not to laugh. The fact that a boy could chatter about who his sister was in bed with was another example of how differently these Goddess people treated everything that had to do with sex. Back in the Sea of Grass, Arang would have been sharpening his dagger, longing for the day when he was old enough to plunge it into the heart of the bastard who had slept with his sister without paying a proper bride price for her, but all this boy wanted to do with his knife was sharpen hooks and clean fish.

They sat in companionable silence for a few minutes waiting for the fish to bite, but the fish of the Orugali must have been particularly well fed that afternoon because, although they could see several large shadows lazily floating beneath the clear water, neither of the small bladders they were using as bobbers went under. After a while, Arang spoke again.

"You know, I've never understood why you didn't go home before you fell in love with Marrah. Nobody was keeping you. Even the little kids used to whisper that you looked like you missed your mama pretty bad. You can hunt better than anyone, and no one knows more about the forest than you do, so why didn't you just go back to your own people as soon as you could walk?"

Stavan explained the promise he had made. "Since your sister saved my life," he concluded, "I owe her mine. She became my chief, so to speak, so I had to stay with her even when I didn't want to."

Arang looked at him blankly. Obviously he didn't understand, although as far as Stavan could see it was plain enough.

"It was a matter of honor."

"What's honor?"

Stavan sighed and started from scratch. "Honor is what gives a man's life meaning. It's more than loyalty, more even than fidelity, it's . . ." He stopped. There was no way he could put the Hansi concept of honor into words. Honor wasn't something that had to be explained; if you were born into the tribe, you breathed it in like air. But Arang hadn't been born a Hansi. He decided to make it as simple as possible. "It's this way: before I knew Marrah saved my life, I was planning to leave as soon as I could. In those days I was bound by honor to go back to my father and let him know how Achan had died. My father was my chief." Now he was going to have to explain the words "father" and "chief."

Taking a deep breath, he pressed on. "He was sort of the Great Aita of all *aitas*, and I owed him everything: obedience, loyalty, even my life if he wanted it."

"Why?"

The question took Stavan by surprise. "Why? Because he's my father, that's why. And not only that, he's the Great Chief of all the Hansi. So I have to respect him and do as he commands."

"But wouldn't you do what your *aita* wanted you to do just because you loved him? That's how I feel about you and Mama; and Marrah too—most of the time, anyway. I love all of you and I know you're trying to do what's best for me, so when you tell me not to eat green apples or not to—"

"We're getting off the track," Stavan interrupted. "Love has nothing to do with it. You can be bound by honor to obey someone you hate; it makes no difference. As for your mama and Marrah, women's honor and men's honor isn't the same thing at all. A woman's honor is her chastity." He saw Arang looking at him blankly again. "But never mind about that," he said quickly, realizing that he was on the verge of having to explain what a virgin was. "Let's stick to the subject." He held up one finger. "Now, as I was saying: before I knew Marrah saved my life, my duty to my father came first. But after I learned that she pulled me out of the sea and breathed life into me"—he held up a second finger—"my duty was to her. But that doesn't mean I'm released from my duty to my father. If I ever save her life"—he lowered the second finger—"my duty to Marrah will be over, and I'll have to go back to the Sea of Grass and tell my father how Achan died."

Arang's face fell. "I don't understand." His voice was almost a whisper, and the corners of his mouth trembled. "I thought you just said you weren't going to leave us. I thought you loved us. I thought—"

"Arang," Stavan said impatiently, "haven't you understood a word I've said? I don't want to leave you and your sister, but if . . ." Two tears started down Arang's cheeks. "Oh, never mind," Stavan cried. "I'm not going anywhere. Is that simple enough for you?"

Arang brightened. "Then you'll go all the way to Shara with us?"

"To Gira, to Shara, to hell itself if necessary. Now stop crying and concentrate on those fish, or we'll have to go back to the village empty-handed." He paused. "And don't go telling your sister what I said about women's honor being different from men's. She might not like it."

Arang wiped the tears out of his eyes. "Why not? Are you afraid, if I tell her, she might toss you out of her bed?"

Stavan was shocked. "Of course not. What are you talking about? Marrah's the sweetest-tempered woman on the face of the earth, and whether I'm in her bed or out of it is none of your business."

There was another short silence while Arang thought this over. At last he looked up with a face so innocent that Stavan was surprised the birds didn't fly out of the trees and perch on his head. "I was just wondering," he said sweetly.

"Wondering what?"

"Wondering what 'chastity' is."

Stavan had enough sense to know when he was being black-mailed. For a moment he was annoyed and then amused. So Arang's silence was going to have a price. Well, what boy his age wouldn't want to know as much about sex as he could wheedle an adult into telling him? Anchoring his fishing line around a rock, he sat back, folded his arms across his chest, and began to explain, father to son—or, rather, *aita* to nephew—exactly what men and women did in bed together. He was a little awkward, not being used to discussing the subject with children, and some of the words struck him as crude, but he knew no others, so he blundered ahead as best he could, and by the time he finished, he was satisfied Arang understood. "So," he concluded. "Any questions?"

Arang looked thoughtful. "It doesn't sound like much fun." Stavan started to explain gravely that when a boy grew into a man his ideas about fun changed, but Arang interrupted him. "I don't mean that sharing joy isn't fun, Stavan. Everyone knows it's one of the best things there is. What I mean is that your Hansi way of doing it doesn't sound like fun. Are you all really so bad at it?"

Stavan laughed so hard he nearly choked. "Yes," he gasped, "yes. We Hansi evidently have a reputation for being the worst lovers on the face of the earth, as a man of your vast experience can see at a glance. Tell me, in your—what is it now?—nine long years have you ever heard of a people more in need of instruction?"

Arang didn't get the joke. "No," he said, "but don't worry. I'm sure Marrah can teach you how to do it so it's fun."

Stavan could have told him that Marrah had already taught him enough to keep a man happy for the rest of his life, but that also was none of his business. Picking up his line, he cast it out into the water so it fell into a soft loop and floated with the current. "Be quiet, you little brat," he growled, "you're scaring off the fish." It might have sounded harsh except he grinned as he said it.

Time passed, and winter turned to spring. The boat they had been waiting for finally came when the hard rains had been over for several weeks. It was a green, fresh season: lambs and newborn kids romped in lush meadows that would quickly dry to gold under the summer sun, and the houses of Lezentka were covered with roses and honeysuckle whose heady scent perfumed the entire village.

Marrah was sitting in the pottery workshop of the temple trying to shape some damp red clay into a cooking pot when she heard the children crying, "A sail! A sail!" The potmaking had been going a bit better than usual, but she was still awkward, as apt to wreck a pot as make a whole one, and at the sound of the excited voices her fingers trembled, spoiling the rim she had been so patiently shaping. With a cry of frustration, she grabbed the lopsided pot, wadded it into a ball, and tossed it into the corner with the rest of her rejects. Running out of the temple with damp earth smeared up to her elbows, she shaded her eyes with one hand, looked out to sea, and saw a faint scrap of white on the horizon, like a bit of the wing of a diving tern.

The white square grew bigger by the minute. Now the whole village was hurrying down to the beach, and Marrah with them. Stavan was there too, come from the fields, where he had been helping Rhom nurse a sick calf, and Arang, with half a dozen other children, all of them so excited it was all the adults could do to keep them from jumping into the water.

"I see the flag!" one of little ones cried.

"I see the carved figure on the bow!"

"It's the *Gannet!*"

"No, it's not. It's the *Gray Goose!*"

But it was the *Gannet*, crewed by Rhom's irresponsible cousins, plowing through the calm waters toward Lezentka with its blue-and-white flag fluttering in the spring breeze. The wind that filled its sails had brought it from Gira in record time, and as the five men and women who crewed it leaped into the surf and helped the villagers drag the boat onto logs and roll it beyond the reach of the waves, they called out bits of news. "Everyone well. No cargo lost. The Goddess gave us fair passage."

"We've brought back a load of honey-colored flint. . . ."

"And some things called pomegranates. . . ."

"Obsidian and olives."

"Hip belts and a new incense burner for the temple."

"The last old Yasha died this winter, and they're going to pick the new twin baby priestesses at the Snake Festival."

"It's going to be the greatest Snake Festival in living memory. The rumor is that this time the Queen of the West and her women are actually going to share joy with the dolphins so a pair of twin dolphin babies can be born to guide them through the hard times that the old Yasha predicted before she died. Now that's a sight I'd give a lot to see."

The trader who shouted out the news about the dolphins was a dark, wiry man who seemed to be in charge. Evidently that was the case because, as Marrah watched, Rhom walked over to him and began to upbraid him for sailing from Lezentka last summer without waiting for the jadeite axes and feather capes to arrive.

"But my dear cousin," the trader protested, "if we'd waited any longer for you three land snails to crawl out of the forest, we'd have been caught in the winter storms just like the divining shells predicted, and where would the five of us be now? Gone home to the Mother with our mouths full of seawater and the *Gannet* lost besides."

Rhom's other four cousins—two women and two men—joined in the argument, and although it was loud as usual, no one seemed to take it very seriously. There were some apologies, some hugs and backslapping, and some promises made that clearly no one intended to keep. Several clay jars of Giran wine were taken out of the hold, unsealed, and passed around, and by the time Rhom had a few swigs he was in a forgiving mood.

That night there was a welcome-home feast for the crew of the *Gannet*. Two weeks later, when her hull had been scraped and mended and her sails repaired, the village council gave its blessing, and the boat left for Gira, carrying Marrah, Arang, and Stavan.

Although she had expected to be sorry to part with Shema, Zastra, and Rhom, Marrah was surprised to discover she missed Lezentka itself. The village had become a kind of home over the past months, and it was odd at first—and even a little frightening—to be out of sight of land, but the weather was fair, the winds blew steadily, and no one got seasick. Before the voyage was over, even Stavan relaxed. By the third day, he was gambling with Rhom's cousins, losing imaginary fortunes in rare shells and phantom obsidian—for neither winners nor losers ever paid up, and when he tried to hand over one of his earrings, the Lezentkans laughed and pushed it away.

"In my land," he told Marrah, "we take our debts seriously," but he didn't seem displeased to keep his earring. Soon he got the knack of throwing the shell counters into just the right holes on the wooden gaming board, and by the end of the voyage he had won so often and so consistently the traders told him he could beat the best players in Eringah if he ever made it that far east. They expected him to be impressed when they mentioned a land so distant—one many weeks beyond Gira—but Stavan surprised them by knowing all about Eringah.

Marrah found all this highly entertaining. Eringah was in Sabalah's song, and at night when she and Arang sat in the bow of the *Gannet* softly singing it to each other, she felt as if they were flying toward the east guided by Sabalah. Sometimes she even imagined she could hear a third voice joining in, and when she closed her eyes she could feel her mother sitting beside her, invisible in the cool, windy darkness.

# CHAPTER NINE

When the Queen of the West
calls to her dolphins
the sea trembles,
white foam climbs her thighs.

Gira, island of soft nights.
Gira, island of love.
Gira, where the maidens dance
swinging their long black hair.

SABALAH'S SONG
VERSES 19–20

Gira

I tesh was the largest city on Gira and certainly the largest Marrah had ever seen. From the sea it had looked like a handful of white stones tossed carelessly along the fertile banks of the Usha River. Its hundred or so houses were built of the same gray-white granite that cropped out of the hills and made the dry upland forests fit only for hunting and obsidian mining, but here the starkness of the stone had been transformed into cheerful urban chaos. There were no streets as such: the one-story houses touched each other, turned their backs on each other, or faced each other at the whim of the mother families who inhabited them, some seeking a view of the sea, others looking toward the river and the fertile plain, where the olive trees were putting on new leaves and green shoots were sprouting in the vineyards.

Located in the Gulf of Hessa at the northwestern tip of the island, Itesh had no defenses: unwalled and vulnerable from both land and sea, it offered its famous temples and sacred caves to any traveler who needed refuge, healing, religious comfort, or—in the case of the Snake Festival—five days of wild celebration. You could always be sure of a warm welcome in Itesh, especially if you came when the spring moon was ripe and Hessa, the little steel-blue grass snake found only on the island, was shedding her old skin for a new one.

On the first day of the festival in the year we would have called 4371 B.C., the city was so crowded with pilgrims, foreign visitors, and mother clans from the surrounding villages that it seemed about to burst apart like a pod of dry chick-peas. There was only one spot of order: a sturdy rectangular wooden platform that towered over the crowd like an oversized table. The platform had a ramp sloping gently up one side, making it easy to reach the top, and for fifty-one weeks of the year it was the commercial and social center of the city. Depending on the occasion, it could be a stage, an open-air temple, a public forum, a court of justice, a threshing floor, a market for the trade goods that came into the port, or just a pleasant place to stand around gossiping; but during the week of the Snake Festival, poles were put into special holes around the edges, a large blue-and-white linen sunshade was raised on woven cords, and the platform was transformed into a reviewing stand.

On that warm spring afternoon, a mere two days after they arrived in Itesh, Marrah, Stavan, and Arang stood on the platform far above the crowd watching an endless procession of worshipers dance by, pounding their feet to the deafening beat of hundreds of drums. As Marrah watched, her feet tapped, her hips swayed, and her arms moved, but all very discreetly. Drums had always set her blood on fire and made her want to stamp and sing, but for reasons of propriety and that sticky thing called politeness, she was trapped up on the platform like an old woman whose dancing days were over. Ah, to be down there with them! she thought. Arang and Stavan must have been thinking the same thing because they too were dancing in place, which was understandable, because who could resist those drums? They pounded and echoed, drowning out everything, seducing you until your heart beat with every stroke of the sticks. She'd never heard such drumming. The drummers of Itesh were even better than Rhom's cousins had promised.

She looked longingly down at the dancers, who were already half lost in a state of ecstasy that would last the better part of a week. Mixed in among them were the various work and recreation societies of Itesh, each dressed in matching costumes. Most were animals: the Society of Cheesemakers pranced along in goatskin capes, the Society of Men and Women Who Hunt wore fox and marten masks, and the Society for Festivals had decided this year to costume its members as plump partridges. Each society carried a statue of the Goddess mounted on a wooden platform. The statues were huge, mostly made of wood or sometimes clay, some so heavy it took as many as twenty men and women to carry them, but from Marrah's viewpoint the Goddess-bearers looked as if they were holding air on their backs. They danced too, chanting and weaving back and forth in a serpentine pattern, and as they danced, the Goddesses on their backs danced with them so that, seen from above, dancers, bearers, and images all seemed to be part of one long brightly colored serpent that had wound its coils around the city.

Here came the Snake Goddess Herself, blue and glittering, made from a twisting frame of wicker covered with hundreds of carved wooden scales; here She came as Bird floating above the crowd, a giant kite of brilliant feathers. The Goddess as the Sea was alive and waving to everyone, throwing kisses from the back of a great dolphin made out of linen and wheat paste, while the Goddess as Bull Head sported giant red Horns of Consecration decorated with tassels that waved gaily in the wind. There was a lull, and then the Goddess of Death appeared, a stiffly stylized figure made to look exactly like the stiff bone and alabaster statues the people of Gira put in the graves of their dead. She was followed by a procession of men and women beating their breasts and singing laments in Old Language, but even the mourning songs sounded rather cheerful, and if you listened to the words, Marrah realized, they were frankly bawdy. Right behind the Goddess of Death, almost treading on her heels, came the Goddess of Fertility, woven of straw and flowers. She was borne along lying on her back with her legs in the air as dozens of small naked children scrambled out from between them, but it was her attendants who attracted the most attention. There must have been twenty or thirty of them, all dressed as giant babies. As they passed the reviewing stand, they shook their rattles and broke into a song about how they loved to suck at their Mother's breast.

The crowd roared with laughter, and Marrah, Stavan, and Arang laughed along with them and threw flower petals down on the "babies," who were growing more outrageous by the moment. On the other end of the platform, Desta and Olva, the twin priestess queens of the island, were also laughing, as was the Council of Elders. Itesh was a moderately sedate place for most of the year, but during festival time anything was permitted.

There was no one else on the reviewing stand, which was a pity, Marrah thought, because only from above could you really appreciate how long the snake of dancers really was, but the central platform was a place of honor—such honor that between bouts of longing to dance she felt guilty and a little embarrassed to have been put so high above the crowd. Their places should have gone to some old wise man or woman, or a priestess, or a visiting village mother, but the twin queens themselves had ordered them up, pointing to the pilgrim's necklaces around Arang and Marrah's necks and insisting that Marrah was their own niece, adopted by them both when she was hardly old enough to hold her head up.

That wasn't strictly true, of course. According to Sabalah, the Queen of the East and the Queen of the West had only blessed Marrah at birth, not adopted her, but no amount of protest could keep Desta and Olva from heaping hospitality on them. There had been a prophecy, they had informed Marrah not ten minutes after officially welcoming her to the island: the last Yasha, the old retired priestess queen who had died last winter, had told them she was coming and bringing her brother and a yellow-haired ghost with her. Well, this Stavan person was clearly not a ghost, but he did have yellow hair. Frankly, they confided, he was the biggest, ugliest-looking thing they had seen in a long time, but she needn't worry because they both adored all the wonderful and strange things the Goddess had placed on Her earth. Didn't Desta have a tiny lion-colored wildcat perfectly tame and no bigger than a rabbit that had been brought all the way from the hot lands of the south? And didn't Olva, who was head priestess of the Western Temple and thus Queen of Death and Water, have a strange lizard skull that was kept most respectfully on display in the temple for everyone to see and marvel at, a skull bigger than two grown men, one that might have belonged to the Goddess Earth Herself in those long-ago days when She took on animal forms to walk among the beings She had created?

Rhom's cousins could do as they pleased, but Marrah, Stavan, and Arang had to accept the place of honor on the reviewing stand. Anything else was out of the question. Everyone in the entire city of Itesh would be offended, not to mention annoyed, if they were deprived of a chance to gawk at the yellow-haired stranger. It didn't do to make people cross at Snake Festival time. It was bad luck. Hard feelings had been known to make Hessa coil her body and start an earthquake that toppled houses and swamped the boats in the harbor.

Stavan, who had not been at all offended by being called big and ugly, had smiled at the crazy idea that the Earth might move under them like a big snake, but Marrah had taken the warning seriously. Sabalah had told her about earthquakes, and besides, she had learned long ago that it was a good idea to listen when great priestesses were in a predicting mood. Besides, a request from Desta and Olva would have been hard to refuse even if they hadn't been priestess queens: they were small heavy women, in the prime of middle age, dark-browed and sharp-eyed, with wild blackish gray hair that hung down to their hips, and their voices, although sweet-toned, were loud and clear. They were so much alike that if Olva hadn't had a narrow band of pure white hair that began at her forehead and fell down her back like a scarf, no one would ever have been able to tell them apart. They reminded Marrah of two proud birds, falcons perhaps, though that might be too fierce a comparison, since they were motherly as well as queenly.

Together, the two queens were irresistible. So, swallowing their embarrassment, they had accepted the place on the reviewing stand, and now Marrah was glad of it—or as glad as she could be, considering the drums. She tried to tell herself that it was sweaty and crowded down below and she wouldn't enjoy being half trampled, but her feet kept on dancing.

More images of the Goddess came by, more dancers. The sun grew hot despite the shade, but she was too absorbed in the spectacle to care. Once she thought she spotted one of Rhom's cousins weaving back and forth behind a group of drummers, but she couldn't be sure. Five days of this, she thought, five days up here being the honored guest; I'm not going to be able to take it. I'm going to do something silly and disgrace all of us. I'm too young to hold still when the drums are beating.

She took Stavan's hand and held it for a while. She wanted to ask him if he too longed to join the procession, but the noise made any conversation impossible. Stavan smiled and kissed her on the cheek. Putting his mouth to her ear he yelled something: "Love . . . drums." Either he was saying that he loved her or loved the drums, she couldn't tell which. Putting her arm around his waist, she drew him close, and they stood together watching the procession pass.

That night as they sat in the small, simply furnished guest room of the Eastern Temple, drinking cups of spiced wine that the queens had sent over with their compliments, Stavan talked about how excited he'd been by the first day of the festival. Arang was even more enthusiastic. Getting to his feet, he danced around the room to the sound of the drumming, which could still be plainly heard, although it was a bit muffled now, having taken itself over to the other side of town.

"I'd give anything to be out there dancing!" Arang panted as he fell back on the cushions, his cheeks pink with excitement. "Why, I'd get in front and lead that snake around the city so fast you two old people couldn't keep up."

They laughed and said they could outdance him any day, but none of them had the nerve to tell Desta and Olva how much they longed to sweat and bend and stamp their feet to the beat of the drums, so the next morning they were all back on the platform again being honored.

This time there was no procession of images. It was the day the new baby twin priestesses were to be chosen, and mothers had come from all over the island, bringing their twin daughters with them. It was quite a sight to see so many pairs of identical babies crawling toward the pile of sacred objects that would determine which two would someday be queens, but other than that Marrah remembered little of the ceremony. A few of the babies pulled at her skirt and even crawled up in her lap, and she spent a pleasant enough morning cooing to them and rocking them in her arms.

In the end two little girls from the southern part of the island were chosen—or, rather, chose themselves by picking the right objects—and Desta and Olva consecrated them by rubbing olive oil mixed with red ocher on their foreheads and giving them big kisses while everyone cheered and stamped their feet to show they approved. Meanwhile the snake dancing went on elsewhere; in fact, it never stopped, so everything in Itesh was done to the beat of the drums.

By the third day, Marrah had had enough of being a spectator. All night the drums had pounded in her dreams, and she had danced imaginary dances of great beauty. It was disappointing to wake to the prospect of still another day on the reviewing platform, and as she lay in the cool predawn light listening to the real drums beating, she decided it couldn't do any harm to ask one more time for permission to dance.

She left Stavan and Arang asleep in the temple guest room and made her way to Desta's house, which she found by asking directions from a group of bleary-eyed people who were staggering toward the beach to sleep off the effects of the Snake Dance, which was (of course) still going on.

The house of the Queen of the East was like dozens of others, shaped like an oval with cobbled floors and red goddess signs painted above all the doors; big enough to accommodate Desta's children and grandchildren but not luxurious in any way. "Priestess Queen" was a religious title that conferred many duties but few honors on the women who bore it. In exchange for helping Olva preside over the Greater Island Council and leading her half of the ceremonies, Desta got a good seat on the platform at festival time, but neither she nor Olva had a palace, much less attendants or luxuries. They worked like everyone else, only harder—wove and farmed and cooked and fished and mothered and governed as the mood struck them—and when they had served as queens for twenty years they were expected to retire without protest and let the new twin queens take over. It had never occurred to anyone that they needed guards at their doors or special clothing or delicate food. The beautiful robes and adornments they wore on public occasions were the property of the temples and would be passed on to the next queens.

Marrah found Desta already awake and putting wood on the family cooking fire. She was wearing a simple linen shift, but her hair had already been woven into the formal braids she would wear on the reviewing platform.

"What can I do for you?" she asked briskly when she spotted Marrah in her doorway. Flushed with embarrassment and stumbling over the words, Marrah begged to be allowed to dance with the others.

"It's not that I don't appreciate the honor of being on the reviewing platform," she explained, "but they all look like they're having such fun down there."

To her relief, Desta laughed. "Go on," she said. "Go dance if you want. Olva and I didn't mean to hold you captive. I've seen your feet twitching and your hips swaying. We've honored you quite enough, haven't we? I forgot how young you are. Why, when I was your age, I danced through a pair of sandals every festival. But if I were you, I'd make my little brother stay out of the crowd. I know he wants to dance too, but he's too young and too short; he might accidentally get stepped on. Also, there are religious customs connected with the dance that might make a boy of his age uncomfortable." She smiled.

The
Year
the
Horses
Came

181

"I know it won't be easy breaking the news to him; I can see he's a born dancer, but tell him there'll be a special Children's Snake on the last day and he can join it if he likes. Tell him I'll even see to it that he gets a mask—something exciting like a white-tailed eagle or a speckled whip snake."

Marrah promised to do her best to keep Arang up on the reviewing stand. He wasn't going to like the idea of waiting two more days to dance, but Desta was probably right: from what she had seen of the Snake Dance it didn't look suitable for children. Thanking the queen, she turned to go, but she was no more than two steps out the door when she remembered she'd promised to ask permission for Stavan too. Going back, she interrupted Desta's breakfast preparations a second time.

"Of course," Desta said graciously, not looking the least annoyed. "Let the stranger join in. Everyone's had a good view of your peculiar yellow-haired lover—excuse me, I mean no offense, but you must admit he's an odd-looking man—so take him dancing with you. Only"—she winked—"I wouldn't count on keeping track of him once the Snake starts twisting."

Thanking her profusely, Marrah went back to the temple to tell Stavan the good news and break the bad news to Arang as gently as possible.

Beat. Off beat. Beat. Off beat. This was the rhythm of her heart. This was the rise and flow of her own blood. This was the Snake Dance of Gira done to the beat of the drums.

Coil forward. Coil sideways. Coil back. Stamp your left foot. Stamp your right foot. Be the Snake. Become the Snake. Hold the person in front of you around the waist. Hold her tightly. Press yourself against him. Let yourself be held. Let yourself be pressed against. Go back one step. Go forward one step. Forget who you are. Forget what you are. Forget man; forget woman. Be a single body. Be a ripple of energy. Be life. The Snake is life. Hessa is life. She is all there is. There is nothing but Her. There is nothing but Her drums. Step. Go forward one step. Step. Go back one step. Hold. Let yourself be held.

That afternoon Marrah and Stavan danced the Snake Dance together; or rather they started out together, but soon Marrah wasn't sure whose hands held her around the waist. The dancing area was so crowded that people pressed against her from all sides, all moving to the same rhythms. Bare legs touched her legs and bare arms slid over her arms coated with sweat until she couldn't tell her own legs and arms and heat from the heat and arms and legs that surrounded her. The Snake Dancers were chanting a few simple words, chanting them over and over to the beat of the drums, and she was chanting them too although she was on the verge of forgetting which voice was hers.

> Come into us, Hessa.
> Come into us, Hessa.
> Give us new skin.
> Give us new life.

A man's face floated toward her, dark-eyed and unfamiliar. As he passed, he reached out and kissed her on the lips, and she kissed him back. A woman wearing only a linen skirt and a hip belt of shells was trapped against her in a passing coil. Reaching out, she and Marrah put their arms around each other and kissed. The kiss of peace; the kiss of life itself.

Marrah could feel the Over-mind hovering over her, the mind that was neither woman nor man. Soon It too would kiss her just as It had kissed her at Hoza when she had danced around the Tree of Life, and Its message of love would fill her heart.

This was the new skin the Girans were asking for. Once the spirit of the Over-mind descended on them, they could dance all day without hunger or fatigue. But they could also stop dancing. Two strangers could fall into each other's arms and walk away from the Snake. They could go to the beach or into one of the houses that had intentionally been left open and marked with chains of flowers and bunches of green leaves. Two strangers who had never seen each other before, and who might never see each other again, could go off together and share joy because they had been given to each other by the Goddess. This was accepted and understood and even expected.

More faces drifted by Marrah. More hugs and kisses. No one was in a hurry, and the drums went on beating. The day grew hot and then cooler and the shadows lengthened, but she no longer noticed the passage of time. She could feel her new body, her long graceful snake body, coiling through the city of Itesh. Every human head was a scale, every pair of feet a muscle. The Snake caressed the houses; She lifted Her great head and put out Her delicate forked tongue to savor the salt air.

The
Year
the
Horses
Came

183

A man took Marrah in his arms and kissed her. He too had dark eyes, but they were shot through with bits of light the color of the stone the priestess of Nar had given her. There was no butterfly trapped in them, but he looked like a kind man. Gently he disentangled her from the crowd and gently he led her to the edge of the dance. They leaned up against a wall and kissed some more as the Snake coiled by. He was short, exactly her height, with strong hands. A mask made of partridge feathers dangled from a cord around his neck. As she kissed him, some part of her realized that he was a member of the Society for Festivals.

The Giran brushed her hair out of her eyes, and she touched his face lightly with her fingertips. Yes? he asked with his eyes, because even now, even in a state where they were filled with the ecstasy of the Goddess and not quite sure where they were or what they were called, he would never forget to ask. Even those who had kissed her in the crowd had asked first, by a word, a lifted eyebrow, a gesture.

Yes, she nodded. The Giran kissed her again and began to lead her toward a house marked with chains of fresh flowers and a bunch of green laurel leaves. It was dark inside, but through the open doorway she could see a few soft pallets and several couples wrapped in each other's arms, already sharing joy. Mindful of their privacy, she looked away.

The Giran led her to a pallet in the far corner and began to make love to her. He was very slow, very sweet. Afterward she fell asleep, and when she opened her eyes, he was gone and it was dark, but the drums were still beating and the Snake Dance was still going on.

She sat for a while in the doorway of the house, watching the dancers pass by. When the sun went down, the Society for Festivals distributed torches. The Great Snake was now a coiling ribbon of light that stretched from the river to the sea. Shadows flickered on the walls of the houses, moving up and down to the beat of the drums. It was as if another snake, a snake made of shadows, had joined the first one. From time to time the torchlight would illuminate the face of one of the dancers, and she would catch a brief glimpse of an ecstatic smile or a pair of eyes that looked at her without seeing her.

The drums went on calling to her to join in, but she no longer had any desire to dance. She felt relaxed and at peace. Time passed. Finally, she got to her feet and began to make her way back to the temple. As she walked away from the Snake, the crowd thinned and she began to come upon whole families sleeping in the spaces between the houses. Young children curled in their mothers' arms; partners lay side by side; old people snored, their heads pillowed comfortably on small packs or rolled up cloaks. They slept under the stars as calmly as if they had been in their own homes.

Marrah walked carefully, trying not to step on anyone. Soon she saw the low, white, bullhead-shaped entrance of the Western Temple. Behind it the sea shone dully in the moonlight like a piece of gray linen.

Oh, bother! she thought. I've walked in the wrong direction. She picked her way back across the city toward the Eastern Temple, where babies were born and special guests were housed. The Temple of the East was a two-story stone structure, decorated with womb signs. Hedgehogs, toads, and fish swam across its whitewashed walls, and a large red triangle had been drawn above its main entrance. Although there were half a dozen similar temples in Itesh, this one was remarkable for several egg-shaped cells that had been hollowed out under it several generations ago by a pair of priestess queens the Girans always referred to as the Blessed Ones.

The Blessed Ones had been born in the highland forests where the Goddess was worshiped in caves and the dead were laid to rest in egg-shaped tombs. According to the memory songs, the two old twins had been homesick for the mountains, so they decided after they retired to bring the mountains to Itesh. Chipping away at the rock until they were well into their seventies, they had made three sanctuaries where women could come to give birth and sick people could come to sleep and be healed. Each subsequent pair of queens had added another cell, until by now the temple sat over seven "eggs." Whether the eggs were supposed to be bird eggs or snake eggs had never been clear to Marrah, but perhaps it didn't matter since the Girans held both kinds sacred.

A small guest room was attached to the right side of the temple for the use of pilgrims who didn't care to pass their nights underground. In front of it was a porch made of smooth stones, a bread oven, and two wooden benches. As Marrah drew closer, she realized someone was sitting on one of the benches. The man was tall with hair that looked white in the moonlight.

"Stavan?" she whispered, not wanting to wake Arang, who lay asleep inside. He turned toward her, but said nothing. "What's wrong? Couldn't you sleep?"

"No," he whispered in a husky voice that hardly sounded like his own. Sure that something was wrong, she hurried up to him, but instead of rising and embracing her as he usually did, he just sat there.

The
Year
the
Horses
Came

185

She stood in front of him, not knowing what to do. She wanted to give him a hug but something about the rigid way he was holding his body told her he didn't want to be hugged.

"What's wrong?" she asked again. Still he said nothing. "Speak to me, please. Tell me what's happened. Are you hurt? Are you sick?" A terrible thought struck her. "Has anything happened to Arang?"

"Arang's fine," he said, in that same strange voice.

Relieved that at least Arang was in no danger, she sat down beside him and took his hand in hers. It felt cold. He made a motion as if to draw it back and then reconsidered. They sat together in silence for a while as he looked away from her into the darkness. She did her best to hold her peace and not rush him. Finally he spoke.

"Where were you?"

"Where was I? Why, out dancing in the Snake, of course. Isn't that what you were doing?"

"Yes, but I came back early."

"You didn't enjoy it?"

"No." He didn't seem inclined to elaborate.

"Why not?" she persisted.

He made an exasperated motion with his free hand. "Forgive me for saying so, but I don't like the customs of your people."

She still had no idea what he meant, and she told him so. "Explain," she begged. "What customs do you mean? Is there one in particular?"

He looked at her intently for a moment and shook his head. "You really don't know, do you?"

"Stavan," she cried in frustration, "of course I don't know or I wouldn't be asking! Talk to me plainly, please. It's hard enough for us to understand each other in Shambah without your turning everything into riddles. What in the name of the blessed Goddess has you so upset?"

"You can't imagine? You have no idea?" He raised her hand to his lips and began to kiss her fingers slowly as if reluctant to go on. There was an odd expression on his face, and his blue eyes looked almost white in the moonlight. "Let me make it simple. Did you sleep with another man tonight?"

"'Sleep with another man?' What do you mean?" The expression wasn't familiar to her and didn't make any sense. Clearly she'd come back to the temple to sleep, as Stavan could plainly see.

"I mean, did you 'share joy' with someone?" He said the two words slowly as if they stuck in his throat.

She was relieved to understand the question at last. "Why of course," she said. "Didn't you?"

He dropped her hand. "No, I didn't." And then as she sat listening in amazement, he began to explain that this very simple, natural thing she had done had hurt him terribly. He had lost her in the crowd, he told her, and searched for her everywhere, not realizing at first that people who danced in the Snake Dance were meant to lose track of each other. Soon he had become aware that complete strangers were kissing and hugging each other, and he had seen couples going off together. Then he had known that the Snake Dance was like the dance he had seen her do in Hoza, and he'd become half crazy with jealousy, but still he couldn't find her. Women had embraced him, but he had pushed them away, and men had embraced him too, but he had turned away from all of them. He had walked along the Snake, back and forth, following its coils from one end of the city to the other, but there were too many people. He never once saw her, and after a while, after he saw the houses marked with flowers and bunches of green leaves and saw what was going on inside, he knew it was too late. So he had come back to the Eastern Temple to wait for her—angry at first, then coming to his senses and understanding that she hadn't meant to betray him, only the understanding hadn't made the pain any less.

"I called out your name and paced back and forth like a fool, no doubt entertaining everyone who passed by. And after a time I realized there was only one thing I wanted." He took her face in his hands and looked at her, not with anger but so gently, and with so much love, that she was seized with an irrational urge to cry even though she still didn't fully understand. "I realized I wanted you for my own. I realized I had to have you whatever it took. Do you understand what I'm saying?"

She wanted to say yes, but she was growing more confused by the minute. "You're saying you want me, and that's wonderful, but . . . but I don't understand why you're saying it. As far as I can see, you already have me—or rather we have each other. We're lovers; we're happy; we share joy. What more of each other could we have?"

Stavan kissed her. "We could have a lifetime."

"A what?" She looked at him blankly.

He kissed her again. "I want to marry you. I've wanted to marry you for months only I don't know how. I don't even know if your people marry. I only know I can't buy you like I could a woman

The
Year
the
Horses
Came

187

back in the Sea of Grass. You're not for sale. And even if I could buy you, I wouldn't want to. I won't be happy unless you become my wife of your own free will. Most of all, I want you to promise me that you'll never share joy with another man as long as you live."

She only had the vaguest idea what he meant by the words "wife" and "marriage," and as for promising not to share joy with another man—when the Goddess gave two people to each other at a festival, they were expected to celebrate life together. She decided he must not have understood what the Snake Dance was about.

"It's holy," she explained. "I thought you understood that. When I danced in the Snake, it wasn't like I was out looking for a new lover. I love you as much as you love me, but I'm a priestess and sharing joy with strangers is one of the ways my people pray. We don't do it often—once a year, perhaps—but we do it with reverence. When we dance and chant and make love, Her spirit flows into us and makes us One, not just with each other but with everything: the animals, the trees, the ancestors, the—"

He interrupted her impatiently. "And when you do it, it hurts me beyond words."

"But why? Why should such a beautiful custom hurt you?"

"Because in my land women only have one man."

"That may be true, but you've told me yourself often enough that your men have many women."

"That's different."

"How is it different? If a Hansi man can have all those wives and concubines, why can't a woman share joy with any man she wants?"

"Women are different from men. They don't have the same feelings about sex."

"Around here they do." She was beginning to get annoyed. Sometimes it seemed as if all she did was explain to him how her world was different from his.

"Marrah, I'm asking you to do this for your own good. You'll be happier as my wife, I promise. Everyone knows a decent woman really doesn't want more than one lover, and I'd make you a good husband."

"Stavan, open your eyes and take a look around. What do you think's going on out there?" She waved in the direction of the drums. "Do you think the men on this island are tricking the women into the love houses? In ancient times only the women could invite the men to follow them out of the Snake line. Then the priestess queens decided in their wisdom that everyone should have an equal say, and that's the way it's been ever since. If you want me to stop sharing joy with other men for the rest of my life, the very least you can do is offer to give up all other women."

Stavan folded his arms across his chest and looked at her stubbornly. "That wouldn't be manly."

They were getting nowhere. She shook her head, turned around, walked over to the fountain, and got herself a drink of water. When she came back, he was still sitting where she had left him. She spoke gently but firmly. "I know you're unhappy and I'm sorry to have done anything to make you suffer, but I can't become this thing you call a 'wife.' I'm much too young to take a permanent partner, and to be honest it doesn't seem fair that Hansi men should have so many women while the women are expected to share joy with only one man. Surely things can't really be that way; surely even 'wives' must lie with more than one man before they choose a 'husband.' Otherwise how would they know if they were getting the right partner? They'd have no one to compare him to."

"No." Stavan pressed his lips together and shook his head. "If a woman sleeps with any man besides her husband or master, terrible things happen to her."

"What sort of things?"

He shuddered slightly. "I can't tell you. It's too awful. It has to do with honor." He rose to his feet. "Marrah, listen, I can't help suffering at the thought of some other man touching you. It makes me half crazy. Where I come from decent women just don't lie with strangers. You seem to want me to be delirious with joy every time you dance into some other man's arms, but I can promise you, it's not going to happen. My love for you runs too deep. I was brought up to see life a certain way. I've changed a lot since we met, but there are some strong feelings inside me that will never change. You don't seem to understand that if I weren't jealous, it would be a bad sign. It would mean I didn't love you. But I do love you. And when a man of my people loves a woman, he wants her all to himself."

She was touched by his sincerity, but also annoyed. Why couldn't he see he was being unfair? What he wanted was impossible. How could she promise to give up one of the most sacred customs of her people? How could she abandon such an important part of her religion for any man, no matter how much she loved him? She tried to imagine herself living only for him, but it seemed like a selfish thing to do. You lived for your village and your community and for the blessed Earth under your feet.

They talked for a long time after that, getting nowhere, not angry with each other but greatly confused. Finally she suggested they give up and try to go to sleep. "We're too tired," she said. "We're going in circles. What it comes down to is that I love you and you love me, and somehow we'll work this out." Reluctantly, he agreed. Taking each other's hands, they tiptoed into the guest room and settled down quietly beside Arang, who was snoring softly.

They slept together that night like two children, curled in each other's arms, but even in sleep Stavan went on suffering. Sometimes he moved his lips as if continuing their conversation, and sometimes he moaned. Marrah—who really did love him as much as he loved her—felt his pain as if it were her own. "Hush, hush," she whispered. "Rest easy, darling." Once or twice he seemed to take comfort from the sound of her voice, but more often he didn't.

She would have given anything to talk to Sabalah or Mother Asha about Stavan, but Sabalah was far away in Xori and Mother Asha in Gurasoak, so the next morning she went in search of Desta and Olva. She was embarrassed to bother them. After all, the queens were in charge of the entire festival and no doubt had better things to do than listen to a young woman complain about her lover, but they were the closest thing she had to a family, so, swallowing her pride, she spent the morning tracking them down—not an easy task since they had evidently thrown dignity aside and joined the Snake. In fact, it was not until the sun was high in the sky that she finally came across them sitting under a tree, taking their midday meal together as was their custom. They had their sandals off and were nursing their blisters, but the dancing had put them in a good mood and they gave Marrah a warm reception.

"You're absolutely right," Desta said when Marrah finished explaining her problem. "You're much too young to take a permanent partner, and I'm sure if your mother were here she'd tell you the same thing."

Mary
Mackey

190

Olva agreed. "Fourteen isn't an age for making promises you might regret." She spread some crushed olives and cheese on a piece of bread and offered it to Marrah. Marrah accepted the food with a gesture of thanks. Somewhere in the distance, the drums of the Snake Dance were still beating.

"Of course"—Desta smiled and bit into her own piece of bread— "you're a grown woman, so the decision is yours. We only advise."

"Never command," Olva agreed.

"But, dear mothers, tell me: have you ever heard of such a thing before? Stavan wants me to give up all other men forever, even at festival time."

Desta and Olva exchange an amused glance. "I've heard of such things," Olva said, taking a sip of wine. "I'm old enough to have heard of almost everything. But such extreme jealousy is rare."

Desta nodded. "Rare indeed. As you know, partners often promise only to share joy with each other, but the promise doesn't include ceremonies like the Snake Dance. And then there are those who for some reason or other have given up sharing joy altogether, like the priestesses of Nar, who take the Goddess Earth for their only lover, or those men and women who have no desire. The Goddess, after all, makes many kinds of people. But what your lover is asking of you is unusual."

"And has some distressing implications," Olva added. "If you take the kind of vow he wants you to take, you'll have to let him help you start your children. Why"—she looked slightly scandalized—"you'd have to have all of them by the same man, and perhaps he'd even insist on being their aita."

"On the other hand," Desta observed, "you can't go on making him suffer. To hurt someone you share joy with is one of the worst things you can do, so you must make a choice. Either do as he asks and promise him you'll make love only with him until you're so old that sex no longer interests you, which"—she chuckled—"I think will happen when you're about ninety, because you look like the sort of woman who will be praising the Goddess with her body as long as she can, or . . ." She paused.

"Or stop sharing joy with him altogether," Marrah said glumly.

Desta and Olva both laughed. "My dear girl," Desta said, "who suggested any such thing? Olva and I can tell by looking at you that you could no more give up your odd, ugly lover than a butterfly can give up the flowers. No, don't stop sharing joy with him; compromise. Take a summer vow."

"My thought exactly." Olva nodded. "A summer vow would be just the thing in this case." She passed Marrah another piece of bread and motioned for her to help herself to the wine. "One might say the Goddess in Her wisdom made summer vows for just such occasions."

"But what's a summer vow?" Marrah looked from one queen to the other.

The
Year
the
Horses
Came

191

They appeared surprised. "You don't have them in the West Beyond the West?" Marrah shook her head. "How odd."

"Well, we have them in Gira," Olva explained. "You see this young man of yours isn't the first to suffer jealousy when the drums of the Snake Festival start beating." She sighed. "Ah, young men, how sweet they are and how impractical."

"Young women too," Desta insisted.

"Yes," Olva acknowledged, "young women too, certainly. But in my experience, it's the young men who are the dreamers; they think they'll love the same woman forever. Sometimes, I have to admit, they're right. But more often both partners develop new interests, which is why it's customary for people to wait until they're more—how shall I put it?" She looked at Marrah thoughtfully, clearly not wanting to give offense. "Until they're old enough to know their own preferences. Meanwhile"—she smiled—"there are summer vows to take away the sufferings of youth. When two people take a summer vow they both promise—"

"To share joy with each other, and only each other, for an entire summer." Desta laughed. She held up her index finger and wagged it in front of Marrah's nose. "No sharing joy with strangers at ceremonies, no casual trips into the fields with anyone else when the moon's full and you're feeling bored, and absolutely no lying of any kind; vow to terminate at the first rains."

"When you can take a winter vow if you're still in the mood." Olva chuckled.

Marrah wasn't sure how Stavan would react to the idea of a summer vow, but she thanked the queens for the suggestion. They nodded and smiled as if everything had been solved, which Marrah hoped was the case.

"Now finish your wine," Olva said, "and run tell your rash young lover the good news: that you'll be his and only his until the rains fall. Perhaps by then he'll have come to his senses. And let me give you one more piece of advice, just between the three of us: you may find as you get older that you don't want a partner. I don't have one. Oh, I have lovers, of course, but my children and my family are enough for me; they fill my heart. You see, the Goddess made some people to be paired and some people not to be paired, and the secret of happiness is to figure out which kind of person you are."

"Not to mention that there are other things in life," Desta said. "Tomorrow, for example, we take the ashes of the old Yasha to the

Sea and call up the dolphins to receive her soul. It's a beautiful ceremony." She put the tips of her fingers together and bowed formally to Marrah. "And we would be honored if Sabalah's daughter would be part of it."

The invitation took Marrah completely by surprise. She hadn't expected to be asked. Putting her own fingertips together, she thanked the queens. It was an oddly formal moment, coming at the end of so much motherly advice, but strangely satisfying. Olva and Desta had sympathized with her dilemma, but they hadn't let her forget that she was also a priestess from a long line of priestesses. She might love Stavan, but no matter how much happiness or pain that love brought her, she was still Sabalah's daughter, and, as Desta had said, there were other things in life.

As she had suspected, Stavan didn't particularly like the idea of a summer vow, but he was relieved that she was willing to make any kind of promise at all, especially since the drums of the Snake Dance were still beating. "I want you all to myself," he told her, "and if that means I have to promise not to have other women—well, I've been thinking it over, and I've decided it's worth sacrificing some of my pride so we can have peace. It's not the kind of bargain any warrior in his right mind would make with a woman, and I'd be the laughingstock of my whole tribe if they found out, but I have to face the fact that things are different here and you're no ordinary woman, so, by Han, I'll do it! By winter I'll have persuaded you to take a longer vow, and sooner or later . . ." He didn't finish the sentence, but she could see he was still hoping she would take him as that thing he called a "husband." Well, let him hope. How did she know what she would feel by the time the rains came? They could be in Shara by then, and everything might be different.

That evening the two of them went into one of the small egg-shaped caves beneath the Eastern Temple and took their summer vow in front of a small statue of Hessa, the little Snake Goddess.

"This is our wedding day," Stavan said. "Back in the Sea of Grass all our relatives would be here, and we'd be having a great feast. You'd be wearing a white shawl and covering your face like a modest young woman"—he laughed and kissed her—"and I'd ride up on a fine stallion and carry you off while you screamed and scratched— or, rather, pretended to. Afterward the women would dance and the men would drink until dawn while we made love in a special white tent decorated with my father's clan signs."

As usual, when he spoke of the ways of his people, Marrah was puzzled. "What would be the point of pretending to steal me?" she said. "It sounds unpleasant and certainly unnecessary, and that long shawl would get in the way. I'd rather take vows as my people always take them, alone with only the Goddess to hear us."

Stavan couldn't explain why his people did what they did. Kissing her formally on the forehead, he took off one of Achan's gold bracelets and slipped it on her arm. "We'll do whatever makes you happy," he promised. And putting his hand on Hessa's round, coiled belly, he swore to love Marrah all summer, first in Hansi and then again in Shambah so she'd understand.

Things went well after that, and they were happy again for a long time.

The next morning, on the fifth and last day of the festival, Marrah joined the priestesses of Gira in a ceremony so strange and beautiful that no memory song had ever done it justice. The ceremony, which was known as the Calling of the Dolphins, took place shortly before sunrise when the sky was streaked with red and pink and the sea was as calm and flat as the palm of a hand.

Earlier, when it was still dark, Desta had walked from the Eastern Temple carrying the ashes of the dead Yasha in a small clay bowl shaped like an egg. As Queen of the East, Desta was responsible for all rites of birth and life, and as she passed through the city, followed by Marrah and several hundred white-robed priestesses, she sang a song she had composed herself. The song told the story of the dead Yasha's life. Like all funeral songs it wasn't entirely reverent, but the old Yasha and her dead twin had served the island people well in their time, and the history of their exploits was lovingly told, accompanied by flutes and harps and the high voices of a special group of young children who joined Desta in the chorus.

When Desta reached the Western Temple, she handed the egg full of ashes to Olva, who stood waiting for her by the edge of the sea. As Queen of the West, Olva was responsible for everything having to do with death and regeneration. Taking the bowl from her sister, she knelt and kissed the earth, and as her lips touched the sand, six priestesses came forward with their arms full of white flowers and made a path of petals that led down to the water.

Marrah was one of those priestesses, and as she bent down, scattering the fragrant blossoms on the beach, she felt a thrill of anticipation. Was it her imagination, or was the sea already beginning to ripple? Tossing the last of the flowers, she stood and looked at the water, but it was still glassy. Almost imperceptible waves lapped at the shore; the only sign of movement was a single gull flying toward the West, its white underbelly shining dimly in the early morning light.

Olva rose and handed the egg to the oldest woman on the island, an ancient village mother named Shadaz who stood supported on either side by her two eldest sons. Shadaz, in turn, handed Olva a ram's horn. Putting the horn to her lips, Olva blew a single powerful blast that echoed off the houses of Itesh. At the sound of the horn, the six priestesses threw off their robes and stood naked facing the sea. Linking hands, they walked into the water until the waves lapped at their breasts.

Up to that point, the ceremony had been interesting but not that different from dozens of others Marrah had witnessed. But what happened next was so amazing that later she could hardly believe she hadn't dreamed it. Again Olva blew on the horn, and at the sound of the second blast the water began to churn. A single smooth black fin appeared, cutting through the waves, then another. White and black bodies leapt in the air, splashing the priestesses and falling back with a smack. The dolphins of Gira had come.

There must have been at least twenty of them, perhaps more. Fed every day with the best fish the temples of Itesh had to offer, and never hunted or harmed in any way, they had no fear. Circling the naked women, they nudged at them with their long beaks and bumped up against them playfully.

The priestesses called to the dolphins, making high, whistling noises that Marrah tried to imitate. One by one, they caught the beasts, climbed on their backs, and rode them through the churning water. Marrah too caught and rode a dolphin, not because she was skilled—she was as clumsy as anyone could have been—but because the animal was patient with her, treating her, she decided later, as if she were a baby who hadn't quite learned to swim. The dolphin's body was slick and she slipped off several times, but each time the dolphin waited for her, circling and nudging her until she climbed back up.

Back on shore, Olva had taken off her own robes and walked into the sea to scatter the old Yasha's ashes, but Marrah hardly noticed that part of the ceremony. She was too thrilled by the rolling ride, the wind in her wet hair, the slim black and white dolphin, strong and lovely under her, bearing her through the water.

A few days later, after saying goodbye to Rhom's cousins, who were returning to Lezentka, Marrah, Stavan, and Arang left Gira on a boat full of obsidian headed east toward the mainland. The tide wasn't with them until well into the afternoon, so it was a late departure. That morning, while Marrah was sitting on one of the benches in front of the temple waiting impatiently for Arang and Stavan to come back with dried dates and other provisions, Desta and Olva appeared carrying a bundle wrapped in white linen. Inside the bundle was a small, beautifully decorated cup that showed a circle of dancing priestesses surrounded by a ring of dolphins. The priestesses were swinging their long black hair just like the priestesses in Sabalah's song, and the dolphins were leaping and rolling through the waves that lapped over the edge.

"It's a farewell gift," Olva said. "Something for you to remember Gira by." And kissing her on both cheeks, the queens gave her their blessing and wished her a safe journey to Shara.

CHAPTER TEN

Travel fast, my darling children,
travel safely on to Shara.
Sabalah's love for you is sweeter
than all the honey cakes of Kaza,

more beautiful than the breast-vases of Hita,
more powerful than the smoking mountain
that towers over the Bay of Omu,
draped with clouds and filled with fire.

SABALAH'S SONG
VERSES 23–24

East from Gira

Once again the wind filled the sail of their *raspa*, blowing them east across the morning-glory–colored sea, and once again a new city appeared on the horizon, but Marrah never got to know it the way she knew Itesh. Like so many of the cities to come, the first city of the mainland was a place she passed through so quickly that only a vague impression remained behind: a wide bay, a smoking mountain, a cluster of stone houses, temples filled with yellow jasmine, hospitable people, swift passage overland. From the moment they left Gira, they were constantly on the move: crossing from Omu to Sula, from Sula to Eringah, from Eringah to Chutku, where the streams flowed east into the land of the Hita and joined the River of Smoke, which ran like a long watery snake through the heart of the world.

Thanks to Marrah and Arang's pilgrim necklaces, they were rarely delayed for more than a few days. One look at the shell triangles, and strangers placed food before them and offered them warm beds and

197

whatever help they needed. Whole villages sometimes gathered around asking to be blessed, and it was not unusual for Marrah and Arang to wake up in the morning to find their hosts had quietly placed offerings of fruit and flowers at their feet.

If Marrah had any home at all that summer, it was the cloak she drew around herself at night to keep off the chill and Stavan's shoulder where she laid her head. It was exhilarating to move so quickly and see so many new things, but it was confusing too, and sometimes when she woke in still another strange place she experienced the odd sensation of not knowing exactly why she was there. Then she would touch the little yellow stone that hung from the thong around her neck and remember she was Marrah of Xori, Sabalah's daughter, taking a warning to her mother's people. Reassured, she would get up, put on her dress and sandals, and go to look for Stavan, who was often up before her. The two of them would have a few minutes together to discuss the weather or the prospects for breakfast before they woke Arang, and then the day would begin. Packing their carrying baskets, they would eat whatever was offered, thank their hosts, join the traders who were guiding them, and set off, not stopping again until midday.

Yet although they moved swiftly, Marrah took time to savor the world. She was fourteen now, and she had traveled long enough to know she might never come exactly the same way again, so as she walked down a trail or floated past a village, she kept her eyes open, trying to learn as much as she could. If the guides happened to know how the local plants were used, she would walk beside them and ask them to share their knowledge. "In the land of the Shore People we use this for broken bones," she would say, holding up a bit of comfrey. "What do you use it for? We sometimes make a soup out of nettles. Do you?"

Sometimes they could tell her what she wanted to know and sometimes they couldn't, but one question always led to another, and soon they would be discussing other things: what customs surrounded the birth of twins, how hot a mineral spring had to be to ease aching bones, what clay was best for making cooking pots, how salt could be extracted from seawater. Although her days were long and tiring, they were never dull. Later, she put those conversations to good use, and in the end they proved to be the best education a priestess could possibly have had.

But there was more to that summer than just putting one foot before the other. In the years to come, Marrah never forgot the mountain villages of Chutku, where naked women wrestled each other in honor of the Bear Goddess, or the crescent-shaped reservoirs of Sula shining like a heap of new moons strewn carelessly across the lowlands. The world was full of unexpected beauty and exotic customs, and she rarely traveled more than a few days without seeing something memorable.

Three things stood out from all the rest. The first was a copper mine in a place called Shifaz. They came on the mine at midday when the sun was high overhead and the rocks burned under the soles of their sandals. Half a dozen men and women were standing in a long trench, digging the raw ore out of the earth with stone mallets and deer-antler picks. As they worked they sang, beating out the rhythm with their tools. Their songs were haunting, like the howling of wolves or the crying of birds, and when Marrah asked to have one translated into Old Language, she discovered it was an apology to the Goddess Earth, much like the sort of apology her own people offered to animals. "Thank you, dear Mother, for giving us your bones," the miners were singing. "Forgive us for taking the copper that grew in Your womb."

Smoke swirled around them as they sang, and the fires they had built to crack the rocks smoldered and leapt. Picking up clay jars half the size of a man, they splashed ice-cold water on the hot rocks, releasing the green and blue lumps of ore, and when Marrah and Arang left, they gave them each a small copper bead no bigger than a raindrop.

The second memorable sight was the pottery of Hita. Hita was a vast region that included everything from remote mountain villages to several large cities that lay on the River of Smoke. Although its people all spoke the same language, they lived in many ways, following many different customs. The one thing they shared besides a common tongue was a genius for taking the red and brown clays of their native soil and turning them into ceramics so beautiful that Marrah could only look at them in awe, amazed that mere human beings could create such loveliness. Every temple, no matter how small, had a pottery workshop, and the Hitan priestesses knew special recipes for mixing paints and glazes.

The pottery of the Hitans came in every possible shape. There were frogs, snakes, dogs, rams; ceremonial cups, libation bowls; masks as light as straw; platters too heavy to lift. But the greatest pieces of Hitan pottery were the temples of Takash. Takash, which lay on the River of Smoke, had been a wealthy trading center for

The
Year
the
Horses
Came

199

generations. It had twenty-three temples, and each one was a single piece of glazed clay four times as tall as a man and big enough to hold a dozen people. Most of the gigantic sculptured temples were shaped like the Bird Goddess, with a beaked mouth, breasts, and a womb door, but there were mother bears larger than any bear that had ever lived, great snakes that spiraled toward the sky, and even a water temple whose walls flowed forever in green and blue glaze like the River of Smoke that flowed at its feet.

Marrah learned that the clay temples of Takash were fired from within by a great blaze that turned the wet bricks solid. Often in later years she dreamed of those temples rising above the city like guardian spirits. When she became a master potter, she would take a ball of raw clay in her hands and sit for a moment praying for inspiration, and the temples would come into her mind's eye, gleaming and beautiful. Then the clay would take on a life of its own, and she would only need to guide the pot or cup as it took shape.

Compared to the temples of Takash, the third great sight of the journey seemed like nothing at all when she first laid eyes on it. It didn't have the drama of the copper mines of Shifaz or the breathtaking beauty of a Bird Goddess big enough to hold a dozen people; it was only a piece of cured leather about two hands wide and three hands long, frayed at one corner and thin with use. An old priestess showed it to her one afternoon in a small village on the River of Smoke, hurrying out to the landing at the sight of their dugout to hail them over to shore. The leather was rolled in a piece of fleece like a sleeping baby, and the old priestess unrolled it reverently. There were some marks on it: triangles, comblike shapes, dots, water lines, and so forth, not set in any particular pattern but scattered randomly—or so Marrah thought.

"These speak," the old woman said, pointing to the marks.

Marrah peered at them, trying to figure out what "speak" could possibly mean when it was obvious the marks were silent. Some, like the triangle, were familiar signs for the Goddess, but the rest could have been the scribblings of an idle child.

"Thank you for showing me this, Grandmother," she said politely and started to make her way back to the boat.

The old priestess caught her by the elbow, smiled a toothless smile, smoothed out the piece of leather with the tip of one finger, and began to sing a healing song that Marrah had never heard before. The song was in Old Language, and it described how, by combining certain roots and leaves, wine-red birthmarks could be removed from the faces of newborn children. Marrah listened politely, mystified since there were clearly no newborn children in sight, and when the old priestess had finished, she thanked her again, climbed back into the dugout, continued down the river, and thought no more about it.

Only many months later when she was admitted to the inner sanctuary of the Owl Temple in Shara and saw thirty rolled strips of leather, each in its own wooden nest, did she come to understand that the old priestess had shown her a thing called "writing." The priestess had not been singing a memory song as Marrah had supposed; she had been reading from a frayed leather scroll. It had been a great honor, one she had been too ignorant to appreciate at the time, but later, as she sat in the temple, slowly puzzling out the sacred script and hearing the voices of generations long dead, she realized that only her pilgrim's necklace could have given her a glimpse of such a powerful piece of magic before she had taken her final vows of initiation.

But the greatest sight of all wasn't a scroll or a temple or a copper mine; it was the world itself. Sabalah had sung that the heart of Earth lay in the East, and now Marrah saw that heart alive and beating with commerce and civilization. Along the River of Smoke alone, there were hundreds of villages and dozens of cities. There were more people than she had ever imagined, and all of them had their own customs, their own way of dressing, their own languages, and their own way of praying. Only the Goddess Earth united them, and even She came in different forms. But whether She was worshiped as a bear or a butterfly, a fish or a bee, wherever the people prayed to Her, children were cherished, women were honored, old people were respected, and quarrels between villages were settled peacefully.

Stavan, who had seen more of the world than she had, was just as impressed as Marrah. Often, as they drifted down the river, passing village after village surrounded by green fields of wheat and barley, he would shake his head in amazement. "If my people lived here," he would tell Marrah, "they wouldn't pitch their camps on the banks of the river. They'd be up in the hills where they could defend themselves. But then these people don't have any enemies, do they? They just build wherever the ground's the best for growing wheat and vegetables, and they never give a thought to the fact that they're vulnerable on all four sides."

Sometimes when a village lay on a bit of flatland that jutted out into the river, he would laugh. "Why, a Hansi war party could take that village so fast they'd never know what hit them! But that won't

The
Year
the
Horses
Came

201

ever happen, because my people don't have any idea such villages exist. Bless your sweet Goddess for that, Marrah, and pray they never do."

Marrah would look at the village and hold her tongue. She was often tempted to tell him about the prophecy, especially when he went on about how defenseless the river villages were, but the vision she had been granted when she ate the Bread of Darkness was sacred knowledge that could only be told to another priestess. Still, she sometimes felt bad about not speaking. She loved Stavan and trusted him, and when you loved someone it was hard to take him to your mother's city and present him as an example of the evil men who were coming to kill its people and burn down its temples: at least not unless you told him straight out what was in store for him. But no matter how much she loved him, her duty to her own people came first. One thing a priestess never did was break a promise, especially a promise made to her own mother.

Even though she couldn't tell him everything, they were very close. Thrown together day after day, they talked endlessly until she was convinced she knew almost as much about the Sea of Grass as he did. Later she was to discover he had kept a number of things from her out of kindness, but at the time she never suspected that he too had secrets. As the days went by, he began to act more and more like a man of her own people and even began to look like one. Not long after they reached the River of Smoke and joined some traders going downstream he cut off his beard and discarded his matted fur tunic and boots for sandals and a linen kilt like the ones the local men wore. The sun had darkened his skin, and if it hadn't been for his light hair and blue eyes, he might have been mistaken for a trader traveling east with some odd knives, a finely made quiver, and a strange bow he intended to exchange for rare herbs or a few jars of good wine.

And so the days passed, and they grew to be good friends as well as lovers. When the river was wide and slow, they would dive off the side of the dugout and call to Arang to join them. Laughing and splashing, they would invent games to pass the time. Arang liked to play tag, swimming away so fast that no one could catch him, but when they competed to see who could stay under water the longest, Marrah almost always won. Stavan, on the other hand, was clearly the strongest swimmer.

Afterward, when they'd tired of games, he would sit beside her with his arm around her waist, and they would watch the heart of the world flow by, village after village. When her hair was partly dry, he would comb it until it shone or take out his knife and carve Arang a whistle, but mostly they simply sat quietly, enjoying each other's company.

At midday, when the heat was fierce and even the shadows seemed to glow, the traders would guide the dugouts over to some shady place for the midday meal. They would all strip off their clothes and take another bath in the cool river, eat, and then lie down to rest until the sun began to dip toward the western horizon.

On those days, when Arang was asleep and the traders were snoring peacefully, Marrah and Stavan would sometimes go off by themselves a little distance from the rest and make love quietly so as not to disturb the others. When she came, he would draw her hair over her mouth to muffle her cries; and when he came, she would place the palm of her hand lightly against his lips. There was something sweet about making love in silence; it gave the afternoons a dreamlike quality. Sometimes, as they sat whispering and laughing afterward, sharing sips of fruit juice from a clay jar that had been cooled in the river, she would tease him about being a dream and he would tease back, saying no, he was her demon lover. In the Sea of Grass, he'd tell her, the gods from the underworld often came up to mate with mortal women, and everyone knew the gods could never be satisfied.

"No man of flesh and blood could kiss you like this," he'd say, kissing her until she could hardly breathe, and she'd escape for a moment and roll out of reach, laughing so hard she had to put her hands over her mouth to keep from waking everyone up.

When they were delayed in some remote village for more than a few days, they would explore the forests, sometimes climbing a hill to get a better look at what lay downriver. In the mornings the River of Smoke was true to its name. Streamers of white mist rose slowly off its surface, and it seemed as broad and calm as a lake. But as the day progressed, the water turned blue-green; great trees floated by, their roots sticking up like fingers, and you could see powerful currents twisting at the banks in an endless, sinuous curve that reminded Marrah of the Snake Dance.

After they had looked their fill at the river, she would walk around keeping an eye out for unfamiliar plants, Arang would practice with his bow and arrow, and Stavan would hunt birds or other small animals. Sometimes, when he grew bored with hunting or was having no luck, he'd take them farther into the forest and teach them interesting things: how to track an animal by looking for overturned rocks or broken twigs; how to imitate birdsongs so perfectly the birds themselves couldn't tell the difference; how to find dry wood in wet weather or shoot his brother's singing bow. She and Arang had known many of these things long before they met him, of course. Every child of the Shore People did. But he knew the forest better than they did. There was nothing he couldn't track when he set his mind to it; when he whistled the birds flew down and landed at his feet; when he stood still and willed himself to blend into the shadows, he was invisible.

And so they traveled east, teaching each other and changing each other, until a day came when Marrah could send an arrow into a target and Stavan could look at her and say with all sincerity that he never wanted to go back to the Sea of Grass.

The day he told her he no longer felt like going home was an ordinary day that began like any other. In the morning he and Arang caught some fish, and later one of the traders snared a turtle. At midday they arrived at a small dusty village where a festival was in progress, lured to it by the smell of roasting goat and the sound of drums. Pulling the boats out of the water, they hurried toward the sound and found all the village *aitas* gathered around the central fire pit being honored by their children and their children's mothers. Decked out in flowers, the men were sprawled on grass mats eating roast goat, ripe purple grapes, and cakes that dripped with honey from their own hives.

The villagers greeted Marrah and Arang warmly, as usual, bowing at the sight of their pilgrim's necklaces, but that afternoon Stavan was the center of attention—and not because his hair was yellow and his eyes were blue. The villagers hardly seemed to notice that he was different, but when Arang told them proudly that Stavan was also an *aita*, the men grabbed him by the hands and led him laughing and protesting to the fire pit, where they installed him on a pile of down-filled pillows and handed him a cup of fermented honey water.

"Our Lady must have sent you to us to be honored," the village mothers told him, draping a garland of red and yellow flowers around his neck. Putting the tips of their fingers together, they bowed to him as if he were a sacred messenger in disguise, and then the oldest woman kissed him full on the lips to welcome him.

That having been settled, the festival went on in the usual noisy, disorganized way: drums played, dogs barked, people clapped; the

Society of Children sang a song about the goodness of *aitas*; and everyone joined in the chorus whether they could sing or not.

One by one, children came forward to thank the men who had raised them, kissing their *aitas* on each cheek and laying flowers at their feet. Arang was given a great bunch of sweet-smelling honeysuckle to offer to Stavan, which he did, stumbling a little from shyness but winning a round of applause from the villagers when he threw his arms around Stavan's neck and hugged him.

When all the *aitas* had been thanked and honored by their children, the mothers of the children danced for them and sang more songs wishing them happiness and long lives. Finally, the *aitas* themselves danced.

The last to dance was Stavan. Pleading to be excused, he tried to get away without performing, but the villagers wouldn't hear of such a thing.

"You have to dance," they insisted. "Everything dances in our village. The flowers dance in the wind, the waves dance on the river, the birds dance above us, and the Goddess dances around us. How can you not dance too?"

Laughing and shaking his head, Stavan gave in, saying that he was no match for their poetry. "But I warn you: my people don't dance as well as yours do."

"Dance!" they cried. "Don't talk, just dance!"

So Stavan danced. Leaping and waving his arms, he moved to the beat of the drums, not with the fluid grace of the villagers but with the wild energy of a Hansi warrior. And yet the dance he did wasn't Hansi. Marrah knew this because he had once shown her a Hansi dance back in Lezentka when they were first getting to know each other. He hadn't wanted to do it, but she had begged, kissing his cheeks and ruffling his hair until he gave in. Afterward, she had been sorry. The Hansi danced without joy, with a spear in one hand and a dagger in the other. Feinting, thrusting, and ducking in time to the drums, they pretended to fight their enemies and kill them. It was a terrifying spectacle, one she never asked him to repeat.

Stavan must have realized he would only upset the villagers if he danced the way his people danced, so instead he—usually so graceful—elected to be awkward. Instead of landing on the balls of his feet and turning fiercely to attack an imaginary opponent, he danced in no particular pattern, stumbling sometimes when he lost the beat and waving his arms in a way that looked a little silly, but not at all threatening. He didn't dance very long, and when he was finished,

The
Year
the
Horses
Came

205

he smiled and bowed to the crowd, who cheered and threw flowers at him, obviously delighted. Marrah could see that not one of them suspected he could do better. He's given them his pride, she thought, and they don't even know it.

That night, as they lay together on the riverbank sharing the same pile of soft moss, she whispered to him that what he had done made her respect him more than ever. He was silent for a long time. Finally he rose to his feet, took her hand, and led her to a place where they could talk without waking Arang.

"I'm changing," he said.

She nodded and pressed his hand. "Yes," she agreed. She thought how different he was from the stranger she had found on the beach a year ago. He'd been so fierce, so suspicious, so hard to get along with that even Mother Asha had given up on him. What would she think now if she could see him talking to Arang or gathering fire-wood or taking his turn at the paddles?

They stood quietly for a moment, not speaking. In the distance an owl called, and the great river flowed on toward Shara. Finally he spoke again. "I'm not sure how to say this, Marrah, but I think your people love one another in ways mine don't, and I want to be part of that love. Did you see how those men welcomed me this afternoon, how they all stretched out their hands to me without fear?"

"Of course they welcomed you. Why should they have been afraid? You were one of them, Stavan."

"No, I wasn't. I was a stranger—a big, odd-looking stranger who walked into their village without asking permission. How did they know I came in peace? Where I come from, no one ever trusts a stranger. When you meet a man you don't know, you put a knife to his throat until he tells you his father's name, and even after he's managed to convince you he isn't a spy, you can never be sure he won't creep up on you and knife you in the back. The Hansi have a saying: 'All men are born enemies except brothers, but don't turn your back on your brother.'"

He put his arms around Marrah and drew her close. She waited, knowing there was more to come. "Some of the men who danced this afternoon were so old they could hardly move, but whenever one stumbled, there was a younger arm to support him, and if he missed a step or stopped to get his breath, the others waited until he was ready to begin again." He pressed his lips together and looked off into the darkness again.

"Do you have any idea how strange it was for me to see those old men and young men dancing together? Where I come from only chiefs are treated with so much respect. When an ordinary man gets too old to fight or hunt, he ends up sitting at the back of his oldest son's tent, eating whatever scraps the women are willing to throw his way—that is, if his sons don't kill him for his horses. But here every man's treated like a chief—and every woman too, for that matter. Even the children are honored. I've never seen anything like it. And I want it. I think I've always wanted it, but before I came west I never knew it was possible."

He kissed her on the forehead. "So tonight I want to ask you a great favor: teach me more of your ways. Let me learn how to become part of your world, because I don't fit into mine anymore. Tonight I don't feel like a Hansi. I don't know what I am exactly or what tribe I belong to, but I know it's not the one I was born in."

He touched the copper sun signs that hung around his neck. "I'm not saying I'm ready to take these off and put one of your Goddesses in their place. I still believe Lord Han is so powerful that if I turn away from Him He'll curse me in some terrible way. And I still feel love for my father and my people. If they needed defending, I'd defend them, and no matter how peacefully we live, some part of me will always be a warrior—a reluctant warrior, but a warrior all the same. Still, the next time you go into a temple to offer the Goddess Earth flowers, I'm ready to go with you." He reached out and touched the yellow stone the priestesses of Nar had given her. "In time, who knows what may happen? Someday I may take off these suns and scatter them at your feet like so many fallen stars."

The
Year
the
Horses
Came

CHAPTER ELEVEN

*I saw Shara gleaming,*
*its white houses*
*sparkling in the sun.*

*Most beautiful of cities,*
*built on the rim*
*of the wine-dark sea,*

*Sabalah has sent you*
*her dearest treasures.*
*Sabalah has sent you*
*the children of her heart.*

SABALAH'S SONG
THE FINAL THREE VERSES
(SUNG WEST TO EAST)

Shemsheme to the Sweetwater Sea

For all practical purposes the River of Smoke
was two rivers separated by a narrow gorge of
boiling rapids that cut the trade routes in half.
Known as Shemsheme or the Goddess's Knees,
the gorge was famous in memory songs for the number of boats that
had been dashed to pieces on its rocks while trying to pass from one
end to the other, and as Marrah, Stavan, and Arang traveled closer,
they were treated to an endless string of terrifying stories. Above
Shemsheme the river was a misty, silent expanse of gray-green water
that flowed between low hills. There were no currents to speak of,
and on ordinary days it was so calm the villagers could soak their
flax in the main channel. Cattle stood knee-deep in the sluggish flow,
patiently chewing their cuds while small children washed them,

209

splashing each other and laughing. At sunset the river became a mirror filled with red, blue, and purple light, and unless a gust of wind curled the water into ripples or a flight of birds called out noisily as they flew overhead, nothing disturbed the brooding calm.

Below Shemsheme, according to all accounts, the river was much the same. Broad and lazy, it wandered across a great flat plain, with currents so slow that a bit of straw tossed out of a boat hardly seemed to move. At last it turned north and then east, splitting into smaller channels and threading its way through a reed-filled delta before it emptied into the Sweetwater Sea. But at Shemsheme itself, the river became a wild thing. Roaring and boiling as it plunged between the Goddess's knees, it kicked up waves taller than a grown man.

"You'll be dashed against the cliffs," the villagers assured Marrah when she told them where they were headed. "And if by some miracle you survive the wreck of your boat, the whirlpools will drag you down. If you're really determined to go all the way to the Sweetwater Sea, get out and walk around Shemsheme. We know some traders say they're willing to try to shoot the rapids, but they're crazy. Don't listen to them."

But the traders who were guiding Marrah's party had no intention of risking their cargo. As soon as they came to the jagged cliffs that marked the entrance to Shemsheme, they ordered everyone out of the boats. For the next five days they all hiked overland, lugging the dugouts up trails not fit for a goat. Sometimes they saw white-tailed eagles perched above them, but no matter how far they climbed they could always hear the voice of the river.

Gradually the tumult grew fainter. On the final night of the portage, they walked down the slope and camped at the base of the cliffs on a narrow strip of white gravel, waking to fair weather the next morning. Putting the boats back in, they spent the whole day gliding through the gorge, until at last the wild river burst out onto a broad plain and became tame again.

That evening, as Marrah, Stavan, and Arang sat around the campfire, they agreed that the most dangerous part of the trip was over. Soon they would reach the Sweetwater Sea, and from there, according to Sabalah's Song, it would only be four or five days to Shara.

As they congratulated each other on a job well done, they looked out at the river. It seemed almost yellow in the dusk, like a great flower petal covered with pollen. On the far shore, a flock of geese swam slowly toward the reeds where they would sleep until morning.

Arang put his head in Marrah's lap and yawned. "I'm glad there aren't any more rapids. They looked really nasty, and even though we were so far above them I was a little scared."

"I was a little scared too," Marrah admitted, "but don't worry; from here on there's nothing to be afraid of."

Later she would wonder if one of the evil spirits Stavan believed in had heard her and taken offense.


Several days passed as they drifted downriver at a leisurely pace, stopping often to rest and swim. Then, without warning, something completely unexpected happened. It started out as nothing: just a sick woman who wouldn't talk.

The day was unusually hot and still, and the traders who had taken them around Shemsheme were singing a new song, but otherwise nothing remarkable was going on. The river hardly seemed to have a current at this point, and although the villages along its banks looked a little larger than the villages upriver, they were more compact.

There seemed to be no stone houses downstream from Shemsheme. Everything in sight was built of split logs and wicker, daubed with clay and painted with gaudy black and yellow designs that on closer inspection usually proved to be bees. There were thousands of bees, none bigger than a fingertip, painted so they appeared to be swarming up the walls, clustering over the doors, and hanging from the edges of the smoke holes. Here and there, some mother family with an artistic bent had added a few flowers with green stems and big red petals or a splash of golden-colored stuff that looked like honey. Every time they came to a settlement, Marrah imagined for a moment that some potter had left a pile of clay hives out to cure in the sun. The biggest hive of all was always the temple; often you could see its round windows and peaked roof before you could see anything else.

The name of this land where the Bee Goddess was worshiped was Kaza. The Kazans were friendly people who gathered on the riverbank to wave at passing boats. Sometimes half a dozen of the older boys and girls would swim out to them and ask the traders for news, speaking in broken Old Language with a soft, lilting accent that was almost like a lisp. But this particular afternoon, the boys and girls who swam out to the boats had a different request. They were small dark-haired children with graceful arms and legs, so quick in the

The
Year
the
Horses
Came

211

water they could outrace the fish, but unlike the other children Marrah had seen since they left Shemsheme, they didn't laugh and joke as they approached. Instead they came up solemnly, swimming with long, quick strokes until they were close enough to be heard.

"Is the great priestess Marrah of Xori with you?" the oldest girl called.

Surprised to hear herself referred to as a "great priestess," Marrah started to protest, but the traders were too quick for her.

"We carry Marrah of Xori, daughter of Sabalah," one of them cried. "We're taking her and her brother to Shara. And a giant too. One with a young face and old hair."

"Then you're the traders we've been looking for," the girl said, swimming closer. She treaded water and looked at the two boats for a moment until she spotted Marrah. "Good Mother Marrah," she cried, "our Council of Elders begs you to come ashore and grace our village with your presence."

"Me?" Marrah knew she was no one's mother. The girl was paying her entirely too much honor. "I'm happy to come, but why should your village council want me?"

"Good Mother, the sister of my aunt's partner has a strange sickness, and the traders who came past last week told us you have great healing powers."

Marrah was amazed that news could travel so fast downriver and upset that it had been so inaccurate. She began to explain that she had no extraordinary powers and then realized this was no conversation to have with someone treading water. "I'll come," she called.

"Bless you, good Mother," the children cried, and turning, they swam toward shore, leaving Marrah embarrassed and more than a little confused.

"I wonder what gave them the idea that I have special healing powers," she said to Stavan as they paddled after the children. Stavan shrugged and shook his head.

"Bless you, good Mother." Arang giggled. "Oh, Marrah, you're in for it!"

"Stop that right now," she ordered. "It's not nice to make fun of people when they're being polite."

The village was smaller than most, a cluster of not more than fifteen houses separated by two main streets and a wooden fence designed to keep cattle from wandering in uninvited. The Council of Elders met Marrah as she stepped off the boat. Bowing to her, they offered her a bowl of honey mixed with a strange sort of thickened milk.

"Welcome, good Mother," they said. Ignoring Arang's snickers, Marrah accepted the bowl with both hands and drank from it, doing her best not to make a face. The thick milk was sour despite the honey, but since it was hardly likely that they would have offered her something spoiled, it had to be a local delicacy.

"Thank you," she said, handing the bowl back to the woman who had given it to her. She looked at the elders: there were half a dozen of them, all white-haired, men and women dressed in spotless linen as if they were about to participate in some important festival. They'd clearly put on their best clothes to welcome her. How was she going to tell them they'd made a mistake?

The oldest woman put the tips of her fingers together, bowed to Marrah a second time, and launched into a formal greeting. It was clear from the way the others immediately fell silent that she was the village mother. "O great healer," she said, "beloved of the Goddess, we of the village of Sebol—"

"Please," Marrah protested. "I'm sorry, excuse me, but you do me too much honor. I'm not a great healer."

The village mother stopped in mid-sentence, obviously surprised to have been interrupted. "What did you say?" Marrah repeated that she had no special healing talents. A murmur of disbelief rose from the villagers who understood this exchange. "You don't?" the village mother said.

"No." Marrah shook her head, wishing she could sink into the ground. Behind her, she could feel Stavan and Arang struggling to keep straight faces. "I've had some training as a healer from my mother, but I still have a lot to learn."

"Are you being modest?"

"I'm afraid not."

The old woman clicked her tongue and shook her head. "Well, this is a pretty mess. Here we thought you'd heal Nurga. You're sure you don't have magic powers? After all, you're the daughter of a priestess of Shara, aren't you? Shara's famous all up and down the river. Why, my mother's third cousin went there once many years ago, and when he came back he told us you had a sacred hot spring that could cure anything. Shara's waters make the blind see and the deaf hear, he said, and its priestesses are all great healers."

"I've never been to Shara."

The
Year
the
Horses
Came

213

"Surely you're joking?"

"No, it's true my mother's from Shara, but she left before I was born. I was brought up in the West Beyond the West, in a village called Xori on the shore of the Sea of Gray Waves."

"Sixteen curses!" the village mother exclaimed. "Then you probably don't even know one healing plant from another in this part of the world. You're going to be no use to Nurga at all." The elders muttered among themselves, clearly disappointed, and some of them gave Marrah disapproving looks as if she had deceived them on purpose, but the village mother was more sensible. "Well, I suppose it's not your fault we took you for a great healer. That's what we get for listening to the gossip the traders pass off as news. Here comes Nurga now, poor thing."

There was a stir at the back of the crowd. People moved aside, and two women came forward carrying a sick woman between them. She was perhaps seventeen, ordinary looking, with dark eyes and neatly combed hair that had been braided and tied back with a leather thong. Her feet were bare, and she was dressed in the sort of linen shift the sick sometimes wore when they came to a temple to pray for a healing, but it was clear she hadn't put it on herself, because Marrah could see at once that she wasn't in the world in the ordinary sense. She sat rigidly with her eyes wide open, looking neither to right nor left, as if frozen. Only when she passed Stavan did something flicker in the depths of her eyes, a flame of pure terror so quickly extinguished that Marrah thought she might have imagined it.

The women placed the sick woman down on a clean straw mat, arranged her arms and legs, bowed, and withdrew into the crowd.

"This is Nurga." The village mother sighed and brushed a wisp of hair off the woman's forehead. "A year ago she was as happy and lively as any young woman in the village. She was a trader who worked with her aunt, her brother, and her partner, my oldest grandson, Erdin. The four of them used to go down the River of Smoke to bring back shells or north to get salt and the powdered gold we use to decorate our pottery. Last spring they went north. We expected them back by the end of the summer, but they never showed up."

The village mother caressed Nurga again, but Nurga didn't seem to notice. "We waited all winter, worrying and wondering what had happened to them. Two weeks ago, Nurga came back alone, or rather what was left of her came back. She staggered through the gate one morning so covered with dirt she hardly looked human, and she

Mary
Mackey

214

hasn't said a word to anyone since. She hardly eats, and at night she screams in her sleep as if she's having nightmares. We've all been beside ourselves worrying about Erdin and the others, but when we ask her where they are, she looks right through us. At first we thought she must have witnessed some terrible accident that deprived her of her senses, but yesterday her mother noticed something that makes us think she has some strange kind of sickness."

She sighed. "I suppose as long as you're here you might as well take a look at it. After all, you've come a long way, and even if you aren't a great healer maybe you can tell us if you've seen anything like it before."

She gently inserted her finger between Nurga's lips; Nurga opened her mouth, but other than that she gave no sign that she knew any of them were there. "You see those white spots on her tongue and throat?"

Marrah bent over to have a look. Putting her finger on Nurga's tongue, she pressed it down so she could see her throat. The tongue and the entire inside of the sick woman's mouth were indeed covered with small white spots that looked like blisters.

"Ever see anything like them before?"

Marrah was forced to admit that she hadn't. The village mother looked disappointed. "How about this?" Picking up Nurga's braid, she exposed her neck and pointed to several small red spots that looked like insect bites.

"Fleas?" Marrah guessed.

"We don't think so. It isn't the season, and besides she has these things all over her. They came all at once like a rash."

"Perhaps it is a rash. Have you tried bathing her in camomile tea?"

"Great Goddess!" the village mother said sharply. "What kind of fools do you take us for? Of course we bathed her in camomile and pennyroyal and all the other usual things, including river mud, which usually sucks the itching out of the most stubborn rash, but none of them did a bit of good, and—" The expression on Marrah's face brought her to a stop. "I'm sorry. I didn't mean to snap at you. You're our guest. We dragged you off the river because we thought you could heal Nurga, and even though it's obvious you can't, I don't have any right to blame you." She put the tips of her fingers together and bowed. "Forgive me." Tears came to her eyes. "It's just that I love this girl like my own daughter, and I hoped you'd be able to help her."

The
Year
the
Horses
Came

215

"Excuse me," Stavan interrupted in halting Old Language.

They both turned, surprised to hear him speak.

"Spots"—he pointed—"small ones. Sea of Grass get."

The village mother wiped her eyes on her sleeve and looked at Stavan as if she had just noticed him for the first time. "What's he saying? What's all this about spots and seas of grass?"

Stavan gave up trying to make himself understood in Old Language. Lapsing into Shambah, he asked Marrah to translate. "Please tell her that the rash on that woman's neck looks like the kind of rash children get when they have *ashishna.*"

"*Ashishna?*" The word was Hansi. Stavan translated.

"It means 'redberry fever'; it's usually not very serious. Sometimes the little ones get pretty sick, but after the rash breaks out, they're usually well in three or four days. I had it myself when I was a boy." He pointed to a small pockmark on his arm. "Once you have it, you never get it again."

Redberry fever, a sweet name for something unpleasant, but not too dangerous. Marrah told the village mother the good news and was rewarded with the first smile of the morning.

"Bless the giant!" she exclaimed, and the crowd murmured in agreement. "Ask him how his people cure this fever of red berries."

But there Stavan was no help. It seemed there was some kind of mint that grew along riverbanks in the Sea of Grass that the women of his people made into a tea and fed to sick children, and also a bitter yellow flower, but he hadn't seen any such plants on the way downriver.

"He means well," Marrah told the disappointed village mother, "but he's even less of a healer than I am. Still, he keeps telling me to reassure you that redberry fever usually doesn't need to be cured. It cures itself."

That proved to be the best they could offer, although they went on talking for some time and the villagers even brought out samples of mint and yellow flowers for Stavan to look at. Finally the village mother gave up.

As they got back into the boats and pushed off into the main current, everyone was unusually quiet. Soon they rounded a bend and the village of Sebol disappeared.

That night as they sat beside the river eating cheese and bread the villagers had given them, Stavan said something that Marrah remembered when it was much too late. "You know," he said, "there was something else wrong with that woman." When Marrah asked him what he meant, he hesitated. Finally he spoke. "It wasn't just *ashishna* she had, if she did have *ashishna*. You don't stop speaking and eating when you have the fever. She had a look on her face I've seen before."

"Where?" Marrah asked.

Stavan claimed not to remember, but for the first time she had the feeling he was intentionally keeping something from her. That night as she lay beside him, she wondered what it was and why he didn't want her to know. I'll ask him again, she thought, but when she turned to him, she found he was already asleep. By the next morning, she had forgotten her suspicions.

A few days later something happened to drive all other thoughts from her mind. The trouble began as most troubles do, in so small a way that at the time it seemed like nothing more than a minor inconvenience.

"I have a headache," Arang complained. It was hot and sultry. They had stopped for their midday meal as usual, but everyone seemed out of sorts, especially Marrah, who had a stuffed-up nose and the beginnings of a sore throat. The standard remedy for headaches was to warm a large jar of water and soak your hands in it, but Marrah didn't feel up to trying to persuade the traders to empty out one of their wine jars, so she made Arang a cup of broth instead, chopping the dried meat into small pieces and boiling it with a handful of wild greens and a pinch of salt.

The traders who had taken them around Shemsheme had passed them along to a new group who were going all the way to the Sweetwater Sea. The new traders weren't nearly as friendly or as much fun as the old ones. They never sang or stood up in the boats to wave to the passing villagers, and when they bathed in the river they did so solemnly without splashing or laughing. There were four: a mother, her two eldest daughters, and a man who was either a partner of one of the daughters or their first cousin, Marrah was never really sure which. They came from a small village well to the north of the River of Smoke, and they spoke a strange dialect only they could understand, lapsing into broken Old Language only when there was no other way they could make themselves understood. Mostly they communicated by gestures, waving at Stavan and Marrah when they wanted them to paddle, pointing when they wanted them

The
Year
the
Horses
Came

217

to head toward shore, dropping an armful of firewood at their feet when they thought it was time for dinner. Somehow Marrah, Stavan, and Arang had become the keepers of the camp, and although Marrah knew this was only fair, it had begun to annoy her that the traders obviously expected their guests to cook, clean up, and tend the fires. Worse yet, they had an odd custom of not eating from a common pot. Instead they ladled their food into special clay cups they carried tied to their belts, and went off to eat in privacy, which Marrah found positively rude.

Perhaps she had been coddled too long on the strength of her pilgrim's necklace, or perhaps she was just getting impatient with Shara so close at hand, but in any event she was feeling more irritable than usual. The paddle had seemed heavier in her hands this morning, the current stronger, the traders ruder, and the sun too hot to bear.

After she made Arang the broth, she went off by herself to sit in the shade and cultivate self-pity. She thought of the cool winds and fogs of Xori; she thought of her mother standing on the beach waving goodbye; she even thought of Bere and how sweet his kisses had been, which wasn't fair to Stavan, but then she was annoyed with Stavan and in no mood to be fair. Why she felt so irritated with him was something of a mystery. He hadn't done anything out of the ordinary; in fact, when she reviewed the morning, she had to admit he'd paddled the dugout a little harder to take up her slack. He just seemed so loud and full of energy. His voice hurt her ears, and when he'd jumped over the side of the boat to swim alongside, he'd kicked up so much water she'd had an urge to reach out and dunk him in retaliation.

Thinking about home made her feel like crying. She closed her eyes and tried to tell herself it was a beautiful day, the journey was almost over, and she was being unreasonable, but a vague throbbing in her temples distracted her. Sixteen curses! she thought, opening her eyes and glaring at the river. The sunlight on the water was molten; she squinted at it, wishing it would go away. The very sight of it hurt. Was she getting a headache too? Oh, wonderful. Oh, perfect. This was just what she needed. Everyone knew there was nothing harder to get rid of than a summer cold.

The day went from bad to worse. Arang whined and she alternated between snapping at Stavan and apologizing. Stavan was remarkably patient with both of them, and for once Marrah was glad the traders couldn't understand a word she said.

By the time they stopped to pitch camp, it was clear both she and Arang were sick. Stretching out on the ground, she refused dinner; Arang ate some stew but threw it up. Lying down beside Marrah, he put his head on her chest and began to whimper.

"I hate this trip. I hate you for making me come. I want to go home."

"Well, you can't go home and neither can I, so you'll just have to put up with it."

Stavan walked over to where they were lying and stood over them, looking concerned. "What's going on here?"

"I think we're fighting," Marrah said, "only I feel too rotten to keep up my half."

Stavan put his hand on Arang's forehead and then on hers. "You both feel feverish," he announced. At this, Arang began to cry. Picking him up in his arms, Stavan tried to soothe him, but he only cried harder.

"I think he's really sick," he told Marrah.

Marrah sat up. Her head was spinning, and the throbbing had turned into a drumming. It was dusk, but even the firelight hurt her eyes. She asked Stavan to bring her medicine bag. The strings were hard to untie, but she managed to locate a packet of rosemary. "Boil this in some water and give it to Arang," she said, and then she lay back down and closed her eyes.

A little while later, Stavan brought her and Arang cups of rosemary tea. Thanking him, Marrah drank hers, but Arang had to be persuaded, sip by sip. Later still, Marrah felt Stavan lift her up, carry her closer to the fire, put her down on a bed of soft moss, and cover her with her cloak, but by then she felt too sick to do anything more than mumble an apology for being so hard on him all day.

"Don't worry about it," he whispered, kissing her on the forehead as he tucked the cloak in around her. The fire crackled and flames leapt up, casting strange shadows. Marrah saw the four traders looking at her with concern. Why, they're not so bad after all, she thought. She wondered if rosemary tea had been the right thing to give Arang. If not, she had plenty of other herbs with her. In the morning, she'd ask Stavan to make a tea of—what? What was wrong with them? What sickness did they have?

Just a summer cold, her mind sang. Just a summer cold.

The
Year
the
Horses
Came

219

Cold. She felt cold in spite of the fire. Curling up, she wrapped her arms around her knees and fell asleep.

She remembered very little of the next four days. Sometimes she was conscious enough to realize she was very sick, but mostly she burned with fever. She remembered Stavan forcing her to take sips of broth and herbal teas, and once she woke to find him cutting off her hair.

"Stop," she begged as her curls fell to the ground, but even as she begged him to stop she knew he was doing the right thing because if she didn't get cooler somehow she was going to burn up. Later, when he picked her up, walked into the river with her, and held her in the cool current, she tried to fight him, but he was too strong and she was too weak.

"Let go of me!" she yelled. But it was the delirium talking, and when she came back to her senses and saw how gentle he was being with her, she put her head on his shoulder and cried.

Another time, she realized he was crying. It was the oddest sight, and she laughed at it.

"I think Arang's dying," he told her.

She wanted to cry too, but she couldn't stop laughing. "Beast-man," she said, "I'm taking you to Shara so everyone can see how funny you look." It was a horrible thing to say, and the minute she uttered the words she was ashamed of herself, but Stavan only kissed her and held her closer.

"I know," he said. "I've known for a long time. And I don't care. Marrah, please get well. I love you."

"Bring me Arang," she begged. He brought Arang to her, putting him gently down beside her. Arang seemed to be asleep. Kissing him on the lips, Marrah cradled him in her arms. He couldn't be dead yet because he was still hot with fever. She took off the yellow stone the priestesses of Nar had given her and put it around his neck. As long as he wears this and I hold him, she thought, his soul won't be able to leave. Clutching him, she fell asleep.

Time passed: bad time, full of troubled dreams. In the middle of the night she woke to find Arang gone.

"Arang!" she cried. One of the traders bent over her. It was the mother. The moonlight shone on her gray hair, making it look like the white water that swirled against the rocks at Shemsheme.

"Hush," the old woman whispered. "Don't worry. The big man's taken the little boy down to the river again to cool him off." Marrah tried to protest, but the trader was gone before she could get the words in the right order.

The next afternoon her fever broke, and she woke drenched with sweat. Her skin was raw, and the palms of her hands burned as if she had plunged them into hot water. Uncovering herself, she looked at her arms and legs. They were covered with tiny red spots. She thought of camomile and pennyroyal and then of the village of Sebol and of Nurga who couldn't speak. "Stavan!" she cried. He was beside her in an instant, holding a cup of cool water.

"Do I have . . . ?" Her tongue was thick, and she couldn't remember what it was called, the disease that had made Nurga act so strangely. "How sick am I?"

Stavan dropped the cup to the ground. Putting his hand on her forehead, he felt the coolness. "Praise Han!" he cried. He took her in his arms and began to kiss her cheeks and forehead. "Praise the sweet little Goddess who guards you! You were very sick, but you're getting better."

She had one more question to ask him, but she wasn't sure she could bear the answer. She reached down and touched Earth, and her fingers trembled. "Is Arang alive?"

"Yes," Stavan said, "but he was very sick. I had to hold him in the river all last night. This morning his fever broke. He drank some broth and now he's resting."

"Bless you, Stavan! You saved both our lives."

"Don't say that," he begged, but she hardly heard him. She was too happy.

"I want to see Arang." She tried to get to her feet, but her legs gave out under her. Stavan caught her, picked her up, carried her over to Arang, and put her down beside him. She took Arang in her arms and curled around him again. When she woke, he was sitting up, calling for Stavan to bring him something to eat.

They both recovered rapidly, and in a few days they were back on the river again, floating down to the Sweetwater Sea as if they had never been on the edge of death. The only difference was that the traders and Stavan had to paddle a little harder when they hit crosscurrents since both Marrah and Arang were too weak to do much more than sit and watch the world flow by.

Although the fever was soon only a memory, it had an unexpected consequence. Before she got sick, Marrah had been sure the traders were the four rudest people on earth, but it turned out she had misjudged them. Not only had they stayed around to make sure she and Arang recovered, they weren't hostile at all, only painfully shy.

"We thought you were as important as the Goddess Herself," one of the younger women told Marrah in halting Old Language, "but now that we've seen you and your brother get sick like ordinary people, we aren't so afraid of you." Breaking into a large grin that revealed two missing front teeth, she gave Marrah a friendly slap on the back. "We're all glad you didn't die, girl, but your hair's a real mess. I've got a pretty blue-and-white scarf in my basket that I was taking down to the Sweetwater Sea to trade for shells. Maybe when we stop this evening I can do something to make you look less bald-headed."

Marrah took this for the kind remark it was clearly meant to be and thanked her. A few minutes later the trader and her sister broke into a loud river song, beating out the rhythms with their paddles, and after that there was hardly a moment when the four of them weren't either singing or joking with one another in their own language.


That night she was sitting beside the river wearing the blue-and-white scarf around her head and watching a pair of white egrets stalking tadpoles in the shallows when Stavan came up and sat down beside her. It was her favorite time of day, halfway between the evening meal and sunset, when colors were beginning to fade and the air was cool and sweet. He put his arm around her shoulder, and they watched the birds silently until the sun began to sink and the egrets were no more than white shadows against a glowing dusk. Finally he spoke.

"I've been thinking." He sounded somber and tired.

"Thinking about what?"

"About what's going to happen when we finally get to Shara." He took her hand. "Do you remember the things you said to me when you were so sick?"

"No, not really." She thought back to the days of high fever; she could remember Stavan's face bending over her, the shock of the cold river, the way she had held Arang to keep his soul from leaving his body, but mostly it was all a jumble of confused images and bad dreams surrounded by long blank spaces when she had hardly seemed to exist.

He lifted her hand to his lips and kissed it. "You talked a lot."

"I did?"

"Some of it was just delirium, but a lot of it made sense. You really don't remember?"

"Not a word. What did I say?"

He waited so long before he spoke that she thought perhaps he wasn't going to tell her. "You kept talking about a prophecy that had been given to either you or your mother, I couldn't tell which. You kept asking me to take something called the Bread of Darkness out of your mouth so you wouldn't have to see what was coming, and then you'd cry and shudder and cling to me and beg me to take you back to Xori where the beastmen couldn't get you. At first I thought it was just the fever talking, but after a while the pieces began to fall into place. These beastmen you were so afraid of weren't just bad dreams; they were men on horseback, and you or your mother had been warned that they were coming to destroy Shara. Once I figured that out, I understood what we were doing." He pointed to the boats tied up and bobbing slowly in the current. "We're going to warn your people about mine, aren't we?"

She was upset that she'd given away so much. "I wasn't supposed to tell you!" She pulled her hand out of his. "I've broken a solemn vow." She felt terrible and yet, at the same time, relieved. So he knew. The truth was out, and she wasn't to blame. The fever had spoken for her.

There was an awkward silence. He cleared his throat. "If it's any comfort to you, I'd guessed most of it a long time ago. Of course I didn't know there'd actually been a prophecy, but I would have had to be a fool not to figure out you were carrying a warning of some kind. One day your mother is talking to me about the Sea of Grass, asking me how many warriors the Hansi have and how fast they can ride west. A few days later, she's sent the three of us off to Shara with orders to move as fast as we can. What could she have been doing but warning your people against mine? And why would she have wanted me to go with you except as proof?"

"You've known all these months?"

He nodded.

"And you never once mentioned it!"

"Why should I? At first—before we came to love each other—I found it amusing that you were carrying me off to the East to serve as a bad example. I thought, Well, I'll have plenty of food, a warm

The
Year
the
Horses
Came

223

bed, and fast traveling as long as I stay with her and her brother, so why not let them take me east in style? I was planning to win my life back from you and leave at the first opportunity. And that's just the problem." He paused again. "I did win my life back."

There was something strange in his voice. She looked at him in surprise, trying to read what was in his eyes, but his face was only a white oval in the darkness. "I don't understand."

"I saved your life," he repeated.

"Yes," she agreed, "you did. And Arang's too. I'll never be able to thank you enough for that. The traders would never have thought of holding us in the river to cool our fevers. You're a born healer. If you hadn't—"

"You don't understand," he interrupted. "I *saved your life*. That means we're even. It means you're not my chief anymore. It means that according to the laws of the Hansi I don't owe you anything. If you had horses I could take them, and if you had cattle I could steal them. I have a new chief now—or, rather, an old one—my father. I owe him the loyalty I used to owe you. In fact, if I were a good son, I'd already be on my way back to the Sea of Grass to tell him how Achan died and to warn him about your people. No, it's worse than that: I wouldn't be on my way to warn him. Your people aren't ever going to attack mine. They don't have horses or spears or decent bows, and they'd make laughable warriors. No, I'd be on my way to tell him that there were rich pickings in the West: cities full of gold without so much as a wall to defend them, fat cattle, women, slaves—"

"Stop!" she leapt to her feet. "You can't mean this!"

He was beside her in an instant with his arms around her. "Marrah, I'm sorry; Marrah, listen. Of course I don't mean it. I'd never betray your people; I swear by all that's sacred that I'd die myself before I let any harm come to them. Forgive me; I'm tired and overwrought. I've been worrying for days about this. I didn't mean to upset you so much. I just wanted you to understand how my people would react if they heard how your people live. They wouldn't admire you for living peacefully with one another; they wouldn't care about your fine pottery or your temples. They'd only think—"

He stopped in mid-sentence and held her closer. "You're trembling. I'm still upsetting you. Come, sit back down and let me go more slowly. I'm sorry. Sometimes I have all the tact of a stampeding bull."

She was more than upset: she was furious, but she had known Stavan a long time and loved him too well to doubt him when he said he'd never betray her people, so she sat back down, swallowed all the bitter words on the tip of her tongue, and let him talk.

What he had to say turned out to be simple in the way unpleasant truths were often simple: he had decided there was no use taking a warning to Shara. He'd given it a lot of thought, he said, and it had become clear to him that her people would have no idea what to do when she appeared to tell them they were about to be attacked. Perhaps they'd believe her, since she was Sabalah's daughter, and perhaps they wouldn't, but in any event it wouldn't matter in the long run. The Hansi knew everything about war, and the Sharans knew nothing.

Was Shara as open and undefended as all the cities they'd seen along the River of Smoke? he asked, and she had to admit it was. Did the city contain a single man or woman who had been trained to kill? Did its people have scouts, weapons, enough supplies to withstand a long siege if the fields were burned and the wells poisoned? Were its people even capable of running away? Could they, for example, retreat to the hills and live off the land, coming down only at night in small bands to attack? They were farmers, weren't they? Farmers, craftspeople, fishermen? Some of them could hunt, yes, but they grew most of what they ate. What did they know about building a fire so the smoke couldn't be seen or smelled? What did they know about walking so they left no prints for dogs and trackers to follow?

"Nothing," Marrah was forced to say again and again. "You're right. They know nothing. They don't think that way. Just the idea of killing another person would horrify them." She wrung her hands and wept. "You're right; they can't all run west like my mother did. They'll be slaughtered."

"Slaughtered or captured," he agreed, "but it doesn't have to happen." He got to his feet again and began to pace. His words came quickly, tumbling over one another. "While you and Arang were sick, I couldn't sleep. I lay awake night after night worrying, and for once my worrying paid off. I have a plan to save your people, and I think it will work." Again he pointed to the boats that lay bobbing in the river. "Tomorrow or the next day we'll reach the Sweetwater Sea. You and Arang will turn south toward Shara, but I'll go north, back to the Sea of Grass, and find my tribe before winter sets in." She started to object, but he gestured for her to let him continue.

"It won't be easy to cross the steppes on foot, but with a little luck I'll get a horse from some subchief who owes my father a favor. I'm a good tracker, and I know the places the Hansi usually make

The
Year
the
Horses
Came

225

camp. When I'm brought before my father, I'll bow down to him like a faithful son and tell him the bad news: that Achan died looking for the golden tents of Han. Achan was my father's only legitimate heir; he would have been the Great Chief of all the Hansi if he'd lived, and when I announce his death, the women will scream and moan. My father will tear his clothes and smear ashes on his face and curse the gods for letting me come back alive when Achan lies in a grave in a strange land. He'll demand to know if I made the proper sacrifices to Han to put Achan's soul to rest, and I'll lie and say I did, because . . ." He paused. "Well, that's another story, one we don't need to go into. Enough to say that Achan had several concubines who will be overjoyed to learn that the most important funeral sacrifices have already been taken care of, and with luck Changar, our diviner, will demand no more."

He held up his right hand and began to count off time on his fingers. "After I deliver the message, there'll be funeral games, horse sacrifices, and six months of mourning. By the time my father has put off his torn cape and washed the ashes of grief from his body, it will be spring and I can come back to you, but meanwhile I'll become a great storyteller, a poet worthy of your memory songs. I'll tell my people about my adventures in the West, and what adventures they'll be. The West of my stories won't be a green river valley; it will be a dense forest filled with vicious little knock-kneed savages who have no cities, no gold, and no cattle."

" 'Go west?' I'll say. 'No man in his right mind would ride in that direction. There's nothing worth taking.' And then I'll spit on the ground as if cursing the whole place and look sullen and disappointed as befits a man who has wasted years of his life wandering in a wilderness where there's not a woman worth fucking or a horse worth stealing."

Marrah was silent for a long time. As he was speaking, she had briefly wondered if he was lying to her. It would be so easy for him to betray her people. All he had to do was go back and tell his father that the cities of the West were rich and defenseless. But those were the thoughts of a moment only. She knew him as well as she had ever known anyone, and if he had been lying she would have seen through him; if he even had been ambivalent, she would have sensed it the way she could sense an approaching thunderstorm.

By the time he finished, she was sure he was absolutely sincere. There was no question that he wanted to save her people. The only problem was, his plan wouldn't work. At least she didn't think it would, and realizing that made her more than a little frightened, because if it didn't, what other choice was there?

When she finally spoke, her voice was steady, but even she could hear the fear in it. She told him frankly that she wanted to believe he could save Shara, but she couldn't. Weren't there already women who spoke Shambah living in the tents of the Hansi? Didn't his people already know there were cities in the West? She realized he had offered to take a great risk for her sake and the sake of her people, and she honored him for his loyalty and courage, but what good was his plan when some little fact smaller than his thumbnail could bring everything tumbling down? So many things could go wrong. Perhaps some poor captured woman, sick with longing, had already bragged of the rich temples of her city, or perhaps some young girl, lonely for her mother, had cried out angrily that the sheep were fatter and the honey sweeter in the West.

"No," he kept insisting. "No, you're worrying unnecessarily." He sat down, drew her close, and held her. His body was warm, like a shield against the cold possibility of failure. Slowly, and with great conviction, he explained why her fears were groundless. All the captured women had come from small villages, and if they spoke of great cities to the West no one would believe them anyway because women, he was sorry to say, weren't listened to in a Hansi camp. No warrior had ever seen a real city or even imagined one, and only warriors had the power to make things happen. So surely his father would believe him. Then, too, although he never liked to bend the truth, he had a gift for storytelling. When he was a young boy people had said he had been born to go from camp to camp singing of the gods and heroes, but then he had grown older and his voice had changed from a sweet bell to a frog's croak. Still, he had the gift. She had to understand that this was their best chance, perhaps their only chance, and it was a good one; he promised her it was. Unless he went back to the Sea of Grass, the Hansi would ride west someday. Hadn't her own Goddess warned of an invasion?

She considered two versions of the future: in one, the Hansi warriors rode down on Shara and burned it to the ground; in the other, Shara was spared. And not only Shara was saved: the cities along the River of Smoke, the villages of Kaza, the temples of Takash, all the beauty and peace of the world was saved too—at least for a while. Stavan's plan did make sense and it just might work, but something still bothered her about it, something that went beyond the pain of being separated from him for so many months.

"How dangerous is this?" she asked at last.

"What do you mean?" He shifted his weight uneasily, and she knew she had touched on the one thing he'd hoped she'd overlook.

"What if your father and the other warriors don't believe you?"

"Oh, they'll believe me."

"And if they don't?"

"Then I suppose they'll call me a traitor."

"What's a 'traitor'?"

His answer was a long time coming. "Someone who betrays his people."

"And what do your people do when they find out someone's betrayed them?"

"Don't worry so much. There's no use borrowing trouble. My people will believe me. No Hansi would lie to his father unless he was planning to kill him, and everyone knows I don't want to be Great Chief. Now Vlahan, my father's bastard, is different. If Vlahan told my father the sky was blue my father would step outside his tent to see if it was true, but I have always had a reputation for being honest to a fault."

She took a deep breath. "Stavan," she said. She paused, trying to make her voice firm because again she could hear the fear in it. "I know you're doing your best to keep me from worrying about you, but I don't want to be spared the truth. We both know if you go back to the Sea of Grass you may not come back. You could die of hunger or cold before you even reached your people. I don't like either of these possibilities. They scare me. But there's one thing that scares me even more, and that's the idea that your own people might do something terrible to you if they found out you weren't telling them the truth. Would they, Stavan?"

He nodded reluctantly.

"What would they do?"

Once again his answer was a long time coming. "Kill me, I suppose."

"Quickly?"

He shook his head.

"I thought so." She took him in her arms and kissed him. "How can I let you do this? I love you so much, and it's practically suicide!"

"I'll come back."

"Will you?"

"I swear it."

"How do you know?"

He shrugged. "I have a feeling."

"A feeling isn't good enough." Impulsively, she reached up, untied the leather cord that held the Tear of Compassion, and retied it around his neck. "Take this. It saved Arang when he was dying from the fever, and it will protect you."

"Marrah, I can't take your magic charm. The priestess of Nar gave you this."

"What do you think they gave it to me for, you sweet fool? Take it and save my people, and may the Goddess bless you and protect you and bring you back safely." She leaned forward and kissed the butterfly that lay frozen in the depths of the yellow stone, and then she kissed Stavan, who was going into such great danger with only this small bit of magic to protect him.

That night they made love, but their hearts weren't in it. They were both too sad. Afterward they lay awake for a long time talking to each other. They made plans and promises, and when they ran out of reassurances, they went on talking, afraid to let go of each other's voices.

I can feel him leaving already, she thought, as she ran her fingers through his pale hair, seeing smoke and clouds and moonlight and white bones and loneliness.

The next afternoon, after passing through the last of the delta, they finally reached the Sweetwater Sea. From the moment they sighted open water, events moved so quickly that almost before she had time to say goodbye, he was gone, headed north with three traders who were on their way to Shambah in a dugout filled with jars of wine.

His boat had hardly rounded the point before two salmon fishers spotted Marrah and Arang's pilgrim necklaces and volunteered to take them south. So, following the coast and blown by good breezes, the two of them came at last to Shara, whose white houses sparkled in the sun just as brightly and beautifully as Sabalah's song had promised.

The
Year
the
Horses
Came

229

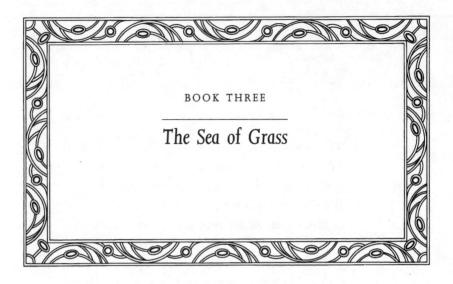

BOOK THREE

The Sea of Grass

"The women of the West are ugly," the hero told his people. "They have faces like rats, skin like toads, and smell like male goats in rut. They live in caves like animals and eat filth. Don't bother to ride west, my kinsmen. You won't find gold or horses there. All the West has to offer is death."

"He lies!" cried his brother. "The West is rich!"

"He's a traitor!" cried his uncles. "Put him to death!"

But the Great Chief was wiser than the rest. He ripped open the hero's shirt and a piece of the sun fell out. "Look!" the Great Chief cried. "Stavan isn't lying. He doesn't know what he's saying; he's been bewitched!"

FROM "STAVAN AND THE WITCH"
A HANSI FOLK TALE

## CHAPTER TWELVE

*Shara: Two Years Later*

On her seventeenth birthday Marrah's grandmother called her to the temple that had been built beside the Dreaming Cave where Sabalah had had her vision of the beastmen so many years ago. It was a cold winter day that promised icy rain by evening, and a stiff breeze was blowing from the northeast, stirring the Sweetwater Sea into whitecaps and sending clouds scudding west to pile up behind the hills. As she climbed the path that led to the cliff above the city, Marrah could see two trading boats coming quickly down the coast, one a white-sailed *raspa* and the other a small dugout propelled by two figures who were hunched over their paddles and pulling to the rhythm of a sea song—a fast one by the look of it.

She stood for a moment with her back to a wall of honey-colored granite and let the wind whip her hair into snarls as she watched the boats pitch and slap through the waves, hoping, as she always hoped, that Stavan was on one of them, but even from this distance she could see that none of the traders had yellow hair. They were all small and dark, dressed in brightly colored cloaks dyed with clan

233

signs. The city of Shara was in the middle of the midwinter holy days, and despite the bone-chilling winds that always blew this time of year a few hardy pilgrims never failed to show up to bathe in the sacred hot spring and hear what the new year had in store for them.

Marrah shivered and drew her fur-lined cloak closer. She wished she knew what the new year held for her, but she wasn't as lucky as the pilgrims. Although she'd lain in the Dreaming Cave four times now, she'd seen nothing, and neither had anyone else who'd looked for her, including Lalah, her own grandmother, who as priestess queen of Shara should have been granted a vision if there were any visions to be had. The Goddess Batal was willing to tell village elders how good their spring harvest would be, advise women whether or not to bear children, and predict an unusually wet summer, but when it came to the subject of Stavan or the possibility of an invasion from the east, She was stubbornly silent. When the priestesses inhaled the sacred smoke, drank the poppy wine, and begged to be told if the beastmen were still a threat, all they got was a long nap and a headache. This absence of omens was a bad state of affairs and was making everyone nervous, especially Marrah.

She sighed and gave up trying to see Stavan standing at the bow of the *raspa* or hiding behind the baskets piled at the center of the dugout. She had waited two years for him to come back from the Sea of Grass—two years and three months to be precise. She'd met every boat as it docked, asked every pilgrim coming down from the north if they'd heard any news of a tall yellow-haired man, and there'd been nothing. Now she was a year older, and still he hadn't come. Despite the fact that Arang had promised to dance for her this evening, this was going to be a cold birthday in more ways than one.

She looked away from the sea, beyond the delta to Shara, which twisted its way along the south bank of the river just as it had in Sabalah's time. The site had been sacred to the Snake Goddess for countless generations, and everything about the city proclaimed this good fortune. Built in coils like a snake, it was composed of a hundred mother houses and a dozen temples, all faced with smooth white clay. Every wall had been lovingly painted with colored lozenges and sprinkled with crushed mica so that a stranger's first impression was a line of glittering scales moving through fertile fields. The fields were brown this time of year, and the short-haired sheep huddled in small flocks, grazing on hay and dried vetch, looked awkward and fat under their winter fleeces.

The sight of the city cheered Marrah a little. It wasn't Xori and never would be, but after two years it felt like home—or at least as much home as she was likely to have for a long time. She still missed her mother terribly, and Great-Grandmother Ama, and all the friends she'd left behind in the West, including Bere, whom she often thought of with affection; but now, for the first time in her life, she had blood relatives: uncles and aunts and cousins, all of whom had loved her mother and who immediately loved her as well.

At first she'd been reluctant to love them back; it had been over-whelming to step out of the boat after a trip of many months and find a whole new family waiting for her, but the Sharans were like the Girans: easygoing, warm, emotionally expressive. They'd wept and hugged her when they learned she was Sabalah's daughter, and then they had swept Arang up in their arms and passed him from embrace to embrace until he was so embarrassed she had to rescue him.

When she'd asked after her great-aunt, Queen Nasula, they'd cried some more and told her that, alas, Nasula had died long ago, but Marrah wasn't to grieve because Nasula had ruled well and now Marrah's own grandmother was the priestess queen. It was quite an experience to suddenly find yourself with a new grandmother when you were already a woman. Marrah had been timid at first, but her timidity didn't survive Lalah's first enthusiastic kiss.

The people of Shara have been good to me, she thought, and she stood for a moment, remembering what they had done and being grateful for it. Their priestesses and priests of the city lived at the center of things, and they had trained her in ways Sabalah never could have. Great-Uncle Bindar, her mother's *aita*, had taught her the sacred art of pottery making, and now, although she still wasn't as skilled as the Hitan potters, she could finish a piece of work and put it in the temple kiln knowing it would come out in one piece. She was even responsible for the new temple, the one she was climbing toward this very morning. She hadn't actually built it, of course. Uncle Bindar had done that. But she had told him how to smooth the clay bricks into a single block, cover the windows with thin sheets of clay, and fire it from the inside the way the temples of Takash were fired.

As for Arang: Uncle Bindar's partner, the great dancer Enal, had taken him for a pupil, practically grabbed him the moment he stepped on shore. "The boy's born to dance," Enal had informed Marrah. He was a little man, short the way all good dancers were; strong, with a compact body, forty years old and not looking a day over thirty, and he had a way of barking that could be intimidating until you got to know him. "Look how your brother walks; look at the sense of balance he has. Give him to me, and I promise I'll make something of him. How could you Westerners not have noticed what a treasure he is?"

Marrah hadn't liked Enal at first and she'd refused, but once Arang heard about the offer, she got no rest until she gave in and let him take lessons. Within two months Enal had Arang doing backflips, and by the time a year was up he was performing by himself, moving to the rhythm of the drums and the sweet droning of the three-stringed *ashad* in ways that made spectators catch their breath and throw flowers to him when he was finished.

"Enal knows everything there is to know about dancing," Arang had told Marrah one day, and then, seeing the expression on her face, he had caught her hand and added, "Of course, I don't love him the way I love Stavan. Don't worry, Marrah; Stavan will come back to us this summer, I know he will."

Her heart had leapt at his words, and for less time than it took to draw a breath she had been convinced that the Goddess Batal had come to Arang and told him Stavan was on his way back from the Sea of Grass; then she had come to her senses and seen he was just talking to comfort her.

That had been well over a year ago. Now she was hoping again, even while she knew she was a fool to hope, which was why she was standing here looking at Shara instead of hurrying up the hill to see what her grandmother wanted. She was taking as long as possible, being rude, making her grandmother wait, because as long as she was on the path, she could go on telling herself that there was news waiting for her. There wasn't, of course. Perhaps there never would be, but when you loved someone as much as she loved Stavan you didn't give up easily.

She turned away from the sight of the city and began to climb the trail, lost in thought. She knew it was selfish to brood this way when there were so many beautiful things in the world and so many people who loved her, but it was hard to face another birthday with no word from him. Time was passing. I'm getting old, she thought. She imagined herself many years from now, wrinkled and bent, her whole life wasted, tottering up to a gray-haired Stavan who didn't recognize her.

Suddenly she stopped in the middle of the path and began to laugh. A flock of startled seagulls took flight at the sound, whirring with harsh cries. Sometimes you had to go to the bottom of self-pity to get through it. A wasted life indeed! She was only seventeen, and with or without Stavan, she was going to have an interesting life, lots of children, lovers if she wanted them, even a partner some day. Feeling considerably more cheerful, she hurried toward the temple, ashamed to have made her grandmother wait so long.

Soon she saw it, perched on the top of the cliff directly above the entrance to the Dreaming Cave. It was an unusual temple, perhaps the most unusual one east of the land of the Hita. Large enough to hold over a dozen worshipers, the temple had been formed in the shape of a breast surrounded by the coils of the Snake Goddess, whose head rose above the roof for fifteen handspans. Like all the snake sculptures of Shara, this Batal had a human nose, but Her eyes were the round, hypnotic eyes of a snake. As Marrah looked up, Batal's long neck seemed to sway in the wind. It was only an illusion caused by the clouds scudding behind Her head, but impressive nevertheless.

All this would have been enough to make the temple one of the wonders of the Sweetwater Sea, but there was more. The official name of the building was the Temple of Children's Dreams. At Marrah's suggestion, the children of Shara had been invited to etch pictures of their dreams in the wet clay of Batal's coils before they were fired. The smallest ones had only left handprints, but some of the older children had drawn fantastic scenes: flying bird-women, talking fish, flowers with faces, and so forth. When the pilgrims bathing in the sacred hot spring looked up at the temple, they saw coils of dreams rising into the air like frozen smoke.

There were half a dozen pilgrims in the water now, several clearly ill but others simply bathing for blessings and good luck. As Marrah passed they called out formal greetings, putting the pink, steaming tips of their fingers together in the universal sign of respect. It occurred to Marrah that even when she was in a hurry, dressed in an ordinary cloak with wind snarls in her hair and boots that could use mending, the pilgrims could tell she was a priestess. As she climbed the last few steps to the temple, she wondered what it was that gave her away.

The
Year
the
Horses
Came

237

"You certainly took your time," Lalah said as Marrah pushed aside the leather door curtain. She looked at her sharply as if she was thinking about giving her a lecture on the virtues of punctuality, but there were guests present and Queen Lalah never liked to criticize her own in front of strangers. Turning to the two women who sat to her left, she smiled with studied courtesy. You would have had to have known her well indeed to guess she was annoyed.

"Now that my granddaughter, Marrah, has arrived, I think we can begin." The women smiled back, put completely at ease, which was exactly what she had intended. As the twenty-seventh priestess queen in a direct line that had passed from mother to daughter or sister to sister from time out of mind, Lalah of Shara knew she always ran the risk of intimidating people, but fortunately she looked motherly and harmless, which was not to say she lacked a keen mind or the ability to strike as quickly as Batal Herself when order had to be imposed. In her youth, she'd had a reputation for sarcasm, a quick wit, and a sharp tongue, but self-control had come with age and now strangers often mistook her for a sweet old woman.

Marrah knew better. Lalah's face was like a mirror that showed her what she herself might be like in forty years or so. Although her grandmother was taller than she was, she had given Marrah her long nose, full lips, curly hair, and prominent cheekbones. Behind her sweet face lay a quick temper, passionate curiosity, and a longing for adventure that she often satisfied by interrogating travelers until they were too weary to go on talking. Marrah hoped that this afternoon her grandmother would be brief. If she didn't get back to the city in plenty of time for the feasting and dancing in her honor, everyone was going to be disappointed.

To her relief, Queen Lalah got straight to the point. "Tell Marrah what you just told me," she suggested, motioning to the strangers to draw closer to the clay brazier and warm themselves. The women approached the glowing charcoal and held out their hands. Both were dressed in stout leather boots and long hooded robes woven from strands of mud-colored fur mixed with flax. Marrah had the feeling that she'd seen that kind of fur before, but for the moment she couldn't remember where. In any case, it was obvious they'd come from far away. No one in Shara dressed in hooded robes; they looked enviously warm.

The elder cleared her throat and bowed in an odd, bobbing way, first to Lalah and then to Marrah and then to her companion, as if not knowing whether to salute her too or leave her out altogether. She was a countrywoman, not used to the politer forms of city life.

"Mother Marrah," she said, although it would have been clear to anyone that Marrah was younger than she was by several years, "my name is Nisig. My sister and I come from the village of Nemsha, which rests on the edge of the world. We're farmers, my sisters and mother and me; we grow barley mostly, which does well because it's colder in our land."

Marrah stared at her in astonishment. The woman was speaking perfect Shambah. "Do you come from the edge of the Sea of Grass?" she asked eagerly, hoping for news of Stavan.

Nisig stopped in mid-sentence, clearly puzzled by the question. "I've never heard of such a sea, dear Mother, but there's much grass where we live. The forest ends not far from our village, and where it begins again no one knows." She looked at her sister, who nodded. Encouraged, she continued.

"Two years ago, in the month of first frosts, a man walked out of the forest and asked for a warm bed by our fire. He was strange-looking—very tall—but in those days we had no fear of strangers, so we fed him, and when he left, our village elders offered him dried food and a warm cloak because he said he was going north and winter was coming on. To thank us, he gave us a warning. A great priestess called Marrah of Xori had had a vision that the world was about to end. Men sitting on the backs of some kind of big animal"—she paused and smiled shyly as if embarrassed by the foolishness of such an idea—"were going to come out of the east and kill us, so we'd better leave our village right away before they arrived."

She shook her head. "Well, we all thought he was crazy and we told him so. 'Thank you,' we said, 'but we've lived here all our lives and we love this land, so we're not going anywhere.' When he saw we were staying put, he got mad and called us a flock of sheep, but since he was a crazy man and sacred to the Goddess because of his madness, we gave him soft answers. I think he must have liked us for that, because instead of stamping off with a curse, he gave us another warning before he left. 'If anything bad happens,' he said, 'go to the city of Shambah and let them know; and after you've told the elders there, go on to the city of Shara and ask for Marrah of Xori, and when you find her say Stavan the Hansi sends his love to her and'—dear Mother, are you ill?"

It was a reasonable question. Marrah had cried out at the sound of Stavan's name, and now she was sitting on one of the clay benches, white-faced and trembling.

"No," she said. "Go on. What more did he say? Please, tell me quickly."

"Nothing, Mother. That was the whole message. I'm sorry. Should there have been more?"

"You forgot the seeds," her sister said. "Give the mother priestess the seeds, you silly goat."

Nisig turned almost purple with embarrassment. Fumbling in the leather pocket that hung from her belt, she pulled out a linen packet of seeds and offered it to Marrah. "The stranger said we should give these to you, Mother; he said you'd know what to do with them; he said they were berry seeds, but I'm sorry to say he was wrong. Any farmer could tell you there are two different kinds of seeds here and neither of them will produce berries. Why, just look how big they are. Berry seeds are tiny little things that . . ." Her voice trailed off, and she looked at Marrah with unconcealed curiosity as Marrah eagerly poured the seeds into the palm of her hand.

"Marrah," Lalah said sharply, "there'll be time enough for that later. I know this is the news you've been waiting for, but dry your tears of joy and listen. These women have more to tell us, and it's nothing to rejoice over."

Sobered by her grandmother's reprimand, Marrah poured the seeds back into the packet.

"Tell my granddaughter why you came south to Shara."

Nisig swallowed hard and looked at her sister. "The summer before last, people started showing up in our village. They weren't traders because there were old people and little children among them, and they were carrying things they had no intention of selling. Some of them were driving a few cows or goats, and others had temple goddesses on their backs. They didn't speak our language, but we could tell they were scared of something. They kept pointing to the east and crying, but we couldn't understand what had happened, so we fed them and gave them a warm place to sleep and watched them move on. After a while, they stopped coming and everything went back to normal, and then—"

She swallowed hard again and pressed her lips together as if she was trying not to cry. "A few months ago a whole village to the east of ours just disappeared—all of it: every woman, man, and child. I had two brothers and five cousins in that village. They used to come to our celebrations, and sometimes we'd help one another at harvest-time."

She looked from Lalah to Marrah. "We saw the smoke in Nemsha, but by the time we got there, there was nothing left but burned clan houses. The barley'd been trampled and the cows were gone. We found the village dogs with their throats slit, and we found this." She walked over to Marrah, bowed, and placed something in her hand. It was a small piece of copper, thin as a fingernail, blackened by smoke.

"Do you have any idea what it is?" Lalah said.

Marrah nodded, too sickened to speak.

"Well, don't just sit there. Tell us."

"It's the beast that's coming from the east," Marrah said through clenched teeth. "It's called a horse." She handed the ornament back to her grandmother. "It's an evil charm; it doesn't belong in a temple dedicated to the dreams of children."

Lalah turned the ornament over in her hand, inspecting it from all angles. Then, without another word, she rose to her feet, walked over to the brazier, and dropped the horse on the hot coals. The copper melted almost instantly, sending up a trail of greenish smoke. Lalah wrinkled her nose. "It leaves behind a bad smell." She pointed to the leather window curtains. "Open those up, and let's have some fresh air in here."


The rest of the winter was long and unseasonably cold. The two farmers who had brought the news of the burned village stayed only long enough to bathe in the sacred spring before they boarded a boat going north, but like the bitter winds, their presence lingered. For days on end, the Council of Elders met, trying to decide what to do, but as Stavan had predicted, they had no practical solutions to offer. In the streets of Shara people clustered in small, worried groups, and the holy days of midwinter, which were usually so festive, were celebrated in a distracted way that left everyone feeling vaguely out of sorts. Something seemed out of tune at the heart of the city, something not even Arang's quick feet and bright smile could dance back into harmony.

Everyone knew about the prophecy, and now the rumors began: a great fire was burning in the east, consuming everything; Shambah had been destroyed; all the cities along the River of Smoke had vanished. Sharans were great storytellers, and as they sat in their snug houses, drinking warm wine, they created elaborate fantasies like children frightening each other after the grown-ups have gone to sleep. At least that was the way Marrah felt when she heard them. Had the end of the world really begun? If so, you wouldn't have guessed it from the way those same storytellers went about their daily business. Occasionally she would hear someone make a sensible suggestion like posting guards around the city, but when it came to drawing lots to see who would stand out in the cold all night there were never any takers. When she herself suggested more drastic measures—like building walls around Shara or moving the whole city to the top of the cliffs—people made polite noises, but she could see that even her own grandmother thought she was slightly crazed.

Move Shara? Lalah cried. Move a city that had sat at the center of the civilized world for countless generations? You might just as well try to pick up the Sweetwater Sea and put it in the west or pluck the moon out of the sky and use it for a lamp. No matter what visions the priestesses were given, no matter what warnings Sabalah sent from the West or what news came from the north, Lalah wasn't about to wall up the spiral of life energy or move the great snake of the city from holy ground. Whatever was coming, they'd survive.

"When you live in Shara," she told Marrah, "you live under the protection of Batal; this business of the beastmen may get nasty, but the Snake Goddess will show us what to do when the time comes."

Thwarted at every turn, Marrah chalked up her grandmother's courage to a failure of imagination. She had heard these same reassurances when she and Arang first came to the city two years ago. Then too the Council of Elders had met in emergency session, and then too the people had frightened one another with stories of impending doom, and what had come of all the worrying? Nothing. Soon life had returned to normal, and except for the priestess who lay in the Dreaming Cave trying to get Batal to speak, everyone went back to thinking about more pleasant things like spring festivals, the children who were about to come of age, the weather, and the crops. No doubt the same process would be repeated. People would worry for a while and rumors would be passed from house to house, but by spring they would have grown bored with the subject. The unlucky village would still be remembered, but gradually people would forget the slaughtered dogs and the trampled crops. They'd begin to think about planting their own fields. Lots would be drawn, the Society for Fertility would tune its drums and gather flowers, streamers of seaweed would be brought to sweeten the land, and there would be no more talk of the sisters who came down from the north to tell of burned mother houses.

"Do something!" Marrah pleaded at the council meetings. "Do it now before it's too late!" But she was like the young priestess in the memory song, the one who stole a magic eye from the Goddess Earth without waiting for it to be given to her; she could see the future but no one listened. Or rather they listened, but they didn't understand. The elders gave her a respectful hearing, but few of them had ever been as far north as the River of Smoke, and most had never walked out of sight of the sacred coil of the city. The grasslands north of Shambah seemed more like a dream than a real place. They were wise, but they had no idea how fast men on horseback could move. Marrah wouldn't have understood it herself if she hadn't lain by Stavan night after night listening to him talk.

After a while, she gave up in despair and stopped going to the council meetings. Retreating to one of the temple workshops, she spent the rest of the winter making pottery. She would mix the powdered clay with tempering earth and water, knead it into a smooth paste, roll the warm damp dough between her palms, and begin to build a bowl, starting with a round coil for the base.

As she worked she thought of nothing but the clay. Sometimes she would chant a prayer: to Amonah if the bowl was to be decorated with water signs, to Xori if birds would fly around it, to Batal or Hessa if she intended to paint a snake coiling from base to rim. She would ask one of the Goddesses to inhabit her hands and give her the grace and power to make the bowl come alive, and when she was done she would set the result on a shelf to dry.

Later she would decide if the Goddess had heard her prayer, and if the bowl was worthy she would paint it, measuring it first with her fingers so the designs would be pleasingly spaced. She would sit with a row of seashells beside her, dipping a fine brush into crimson, scarlet, pink, orange, yellow, green, brown, gray, black, and as many blues as a week of skies, and when she was finished, she would carry the result outside to an old priestess, who would take it from her and, holding it as gently as an eggshell, put it into the kiln.

The pottery making kept her sane. As long as her hands were damp with clay and her paints were sitting beside her waiting to be mixed, she could put the vision of the beastmen out of her mind. But sometimes the outside world intruded into the temple, catching her by surprise. Once when she was making a cup, she suddenly thought of the dolphin cup Olva and Desta had given her on the day she left Gira and how she and Stavan had marveled over it. Her hands trembled and she spoiled a whole morning's work. Bowing her head, she closed her eyes and prayed for more patience and serenity.

When spring came, she left the temple and with Lalah's permission went to the fields, where she planted the seeds Stavan had sent her, setting aside two small plots, carefully fenced with thorns so no stray sheep or goats would make a meal of the new shoots. Every day she went out to look at them, weeding and watering the new growth by hand when the rains stopped.

"What are they?" Arang asked one afternoon when she took him with her to eat their midday meal beside the little garden.

"I have no idea." She shrugged. "A message, perhaps."

"From Stavan?"

She nodded.

Arang bent over the small green plants and poked one finger into the dirt. "I wish he'd come back to us." And putting their arms around each other, he and Marrah stood for a while looking at the garden, wondering what, if anything, the plants would have to say.

Spring turned to early summer and there was no more news from the north, but the plants grew quickly and by the time the days were long Marrah was finally able to read Stavan's message. One of the seeds produced a small yellow flower, so bitter that when she first tasted it she spat it out in disgust. The other was very much like mint, fragrant and sweet but without the square stems real mint had.

"They're the cures for redberry fever," she told Arang, handing him a sample of each. "Remember? Stavan said his people used a mint and a bitter yellow flower that grew in the Sea of Grass. He must have found some on his way north and sent the seeds back to us, but why would he do a thing like that when he was in such a hurry?"

"Maybe he was afraid we'd get sick again." Arang bit into the yellow flower and made a face. "Ugh, this stuff is horrible."

"But he told the village mother back on the River of Smoke that once you had the fever you could never get it again." She looked at the plants and frowned. "No, I think it's more than that. I think he knows something we don't. Perhaps something he discovered after he left us."

Arang tore off a bit of the mintlike plant and put it in his mouth. "This one's much better. It would make a great tea."

"You shouldn't eat that," she warned. "Who knows what it does besides cure the fever? Medicine plants are nothing to play with."

Arang obediently spat out the leaf. "I'm sorry. You're right. It was a dumb thing to do. At least there's a lot of the stuff."

She grew thoughtful. He was right. There was indeed a lot of both kinds of plants. Why *had* Stavan taken time to collect so many seeds when he was supposed to be hurrying to reach his tribe before winter set in? Did he think she was going to need so many herbs? She certainly hoped not. Perhaps she hadn't read his message correctly.

Time passed and the days grew hotter. The yellow flowers and mint were no more than a week harvested and hung in the temple storehouse to dry when more messengers came from the north. These were no farmers from the edge of the world but envoys from the city of Shambah. There were two of them, one a frail man of perhaps seventeen and the other a boy a year or so younger than Arang. They were dressed in holy adornments and the fine linen robes Shambah was famous for, but there was nothing festive about their appearance. They walked slowly, supporting one another, and their faces were pale, pitted with little round scars that looked like water dripped on dust.

"They look sick," Arang whispered to Marrah as the envoys passed by on their way to the center of the city, but he was wrong: these were the well ones.

The envoys climbed onto the public platform and claimed the right to speak by touching the lips of a small statue of Batal. "Greetings to the people of Shara from the people of Shambah," the boy called to the crowd who had gathered around the platform. It was very unusual for a boy to be an envoy, and he was nervous. His voice was wispy and weak like an old woman's. "I'm Nacah, grandson of the priestess queen Aimbah and son of her youngest daughter, Dashlah. This is my *aita's* brother, Cyen." He swallowed hard and bit his lower lip anxiously. "I know I'm supposed to make a long speech about how glad Cyen and I are to be here, but I can't. We're happy to be in Shara, really we are, but I wasn't trained to be an envoy. No one ever taught me how to do it. I was just the only one of my grandmother's family well enough to travel, and, as you can see, Cyen and I have both been sick. I don't think either of us is really well yet. On the way down the coast Cyen threw up a dozen times." He came to a full stop and turned bright red. "I'm sorry. I'm making a mess of this."

Motioning for people not to laugh, Lalah stepped out of the crowd, put the tips of her fingers together, and saluted the child with as much respect as if he'd been an old man. "Welcome to Shara, grandson of Aimbah. By the grace of the Goddess, I'm the mother of this city. Don't worry about being polite; just tell us what we can do for you."

The boy swallowed hard and bowed back. "We need your help, Mother," he said, and then he began to cry, an unheard-of thing for an envoy to do, but he was very young and very scared. "My mother's dead and my grandmother's dying. Everyone in Shambah's getting sick, and hardly anyone except Cyen and me has gotten well. We think we must have done something terrible to bring such a curse on our city, but our priestesses can't figure out why the Goddess is punishing us so."

"There, there," Lalah said, "just take your time, child. Of course you're upset. This sounds terrible. Cry all you want, and when you've cried your fill, tell us more."

The boy sniffed, wiped away his tears, and looked hopefully at her. "It's terrible, dear Mother. The worst of it is that we were warned but we didn't listen. Last fall two farmers from a village way north of us came to my grandmother and told her that there'd been a prophecy that really bad things were going to happen, and when they did we should send someone to Shara to ask for the priestess Marrah. We didn't pay much attention to them at the time. A lot of those northern farmers smoke the hemp that grows wild in the grasslands and they have visions all the time, but then this great sickness came." He began to cry again. "Is there a priestess here named Marrah?"

"Marrah," Lalah called. "Come forward."

Marrah stepped out of the crowd.

"This is the great priestess?" the man called Cyen cried. "Oh, this is terrible. She's much too young. We need an old wise woman, a great healer, a—"

"Marrah is my granddaughter," Lalah said firmly, putting her arm around Marrah's waist. "She's walked across the world and seen more things than you ever will. She's a skilled healer and I'd trust her with my life."

On any other occasion Marrah would have been embarrassed to hear her grandmother praise her so highly in public, but she was too worried. She looked at the boy and the young man. She'd seen scars like the ones on their faces; she had several on her own chest, and Arang had one on his right arm. They were the marks of redberry fever.

"You say everyone in Shambah is sick?" Lalah continued, turning back to the boy, who was shifting his weight nervously from one foot to the other.

He nodded unhappily. "Everyone, dear mother."

"How many would that be, ten? A hundred?"

"Great Goddess!" Cyen cried. He stretched out his arms to Lalah, Marrah, and the people of Shara. "Don't you understand? The whole city's dying! The Towers of Silence were full weeks ago, and there aren't enough well people left to build new ones. Children are crying for milk from mothers who have gone back to the Goddess; dogs roam the streets looking for food; the weeds are taking over the fields because nobody's well enough to chop them out."

He went on and on, describing one horror after another. The crowd fell silent, and people exchanged sympathetic glances. The young man from Shambah was overwrought and exaggerating. What he was saying couldn't possibly be true. There had been serious epidemics a few generations ago, but everyone knew there was no such thing as a sickness that could sweep through an entire city.

Only Marrah understood his despair. She knew now what Stavan had seen to make him stop on his way to the Sea of Grass to gather that packet of seeds.

Five days later, when the two young envoys returned to Shambah, Marrah went with them. Knowing the prophecy, Lalah and the Council of Elders had been reluctant to give her permission, but she had insisted.

"Let me go north," she had begged. "I have the cure, and what's more, I've had the fever. I can treat the sick without getting sick myself." She had looked around the council room at the thirteen men and women who, with Lalah, governed Shara. She was related to half of them, and all were older and wiser than she was by many years. "Dearest mothers and uncles, the people of Shambah have come to us begging help in the name of the Goddess. How can we let them die without sending it? I admit I'm afraid the prophecy Batal gave to my mother will be fulfilled, but what kind of priestess would I be if I let fear keep me from my duty?"

She argued for a long time in the same vein, and finally, when they saw she was absolutely determined to go, the council consented.

The journey to Shambah got off to a good start. They left in a *raspa*, with fair weather and fine winds blowing them north. The boat was crewed by three women. Like most work teams, they were related— two aunts and a niece—all skilled sailors who knew how to catch every breeze, and although none of them had been as far north as Shambah, they were confident they could steer clear of the sandbars that plagued the coast above the mouth of the River of Smoke. But despite the crew's easy way with the sails, Cyen and Nacah were both nervous at the prospect of another sea voyage.

"With this crew we're not going to have any problems," Marrah promised them. "The Goddess Herself is blessing us, and we'll be in Shambah in no time."

She spoke too soon. Not long afterward, the first problem popped up—quite literally. It was Arang. Determined not to be left behind, he'd stowed away under a pile of hides.

Marrah was furious. "How could you do something so irresponsible?" she yelled as soon as she saw his head, and she would have run over to him and jerked him to his feet only the boat would have tipped.

Arang sat up, sneezed, brushed the dust out of his eyes, and grinned a maddeningly endearing grin. "Hello," he said to Cyen and Nacah and the startled crew of the *raspa*.

"Who's this?" Akoah asked. She was the youngest of the three sailors, sixteen or so, with arms tanned the color of doeskin and wide innocent eyes that seemed never to have looked on anything but blue skies and clear water.

"It's my fool of a brother," Marrah snapped. "And don't bother introducing yourself because you aren't going to have time to get to know him. He's going back to Shara."

But Arang wasn't to be put off so easily. "I'm not letting you go to Shambah all by yourself," he insisted, climbing out from under the pile of hides and helping himself to a handful of figs and a drink of water. "I've had the fever too, you know, and I can nurse those sick people as well as you can. We came all the way from Xori to Shara together, and if there are adventures to be had, I want to have them too. Besides, maybe we'll run into Stavan."

"This is a mission of mercy," she yelled, "not a pleasure trip. I'm putting you ashore at the next port, and you're going straight back to Shara."

"I won't." Arang tossed the fig stems in the water, folded his arms across his chest, and looked at Nacah. "I'm older than he is, and if he can be an envoy, I can be a healer, or an apprentice healer, or whatever you want to call me. I'm almost a man now, and if you put me ashore I'll get on another boat and follow you to Shambah. Face it, you're stuck with me."

"We'll see about that," Marrah said grimly. But she knew she was powerless. If Arang was determined to follow her to Shambah, there wasn't much she could do to stop him.

That day and the next she barely spoke to him, but either he didn't care or he was good at pretending. She never carried out her threat to put him ashore, and by the third day she knew, and Arang knew, that she was taking him to Shambah.

The
Year
the
Horses
Came

249

CHAPTER THIRTEEN

A lthough Shambah was the largest city on the northwest coast of the Sweetwater Sea, it was considerably smaller than Shara and considerably less convenient. Built on the eastern shore of a shallow, salty lagoon, its hundred or so mother houses were cut off from open water by a wide bar of silt that forced traders to leave their boats behind and carry everything on their backs the last stretch of the way. It had little to offer: only linen, which was traded as far south as the mouth of the River of Smoke, and salt, which was hauled into the interior. Still, it was a pretty town, and as Marrah and Arang traveled toward it, the two young envoys entertained them by describing their home in loving detail.

The houses of Shambah, they told Marrah, weren't set in snake coils, like those of Shara, but built partly underground so they were warm in winter and cool in summer. The roofs were dome-shaped, made of mud and willow twigs plastered over with white clay. Each roof had been painted with a different flower so at first sight the city looked like a garden.

"Shambah's the old word for butterfly," Cyen explained. "We worship the butterfly as Her messenger so we grow flowers every- where, especially the purple, white, and yellow ones the butterflies love. Our trading families have brought us plants from all over. Sometimes it's hard to keep the delicate ones alive, especially when the cold winds blow down from the north, but we cover them with straw when the frosts come. Of course there are winters when nearly everything freezes, but the honeysuckle and blue delphiniums have been beautiful this year." He smiled. "My mother always says you can smell the flowers of Shambah before you can see the city itself."

But what they smelled when they drew near Shambah wasn't flowers but smoke. Arang was the first to see it, rising up like a thin black thread some distance ahead of them.

"What's that?" he asked.

Marrah shaded her eyes and looked. "A forest fire," she told him, but even as she spoke she knew the smoke was the wrong color to come from burning wood.

They sailed closer, and with each passing moment it became more obvious that the smoke was coming from the direction of Shambah. "Perhaps they're burning barley stubble," Nacah murmured, but even he was old enough to know the barley hadn't been harvested yet. Cyen said nothing. He sat in the bow of the boat, staring at the smoke, clasping and unclasping his hands.

"My mother was alive when I left," he said once to no one in particular. Marrah started to reassure him that no doubt his mother was still alive and waiting for him, but the look he gave her stopped her in mid-sentence. Arang sat down beside her and put his arm around her, and they watched the smoke getting thicker. It looked like a ribbon now, furled by the same wind that was blowing them toward shore.

"What could it be?" he whispered.

Marrah could only think of one thing the people of Shambah could be burning with such a fire, but it was no thought for Arang's ears. She drew him closer. "We'll find out soon enough."

The wind held, bringing them in sight of the sandbar that blocked the entrance to the lagoon. Afraid to risk the boat in shallow water, the sailors anchored some distance offshore, and everyone strapped carrying baskets on their backs, took off their sandals, and waded to dry land. The wind was shifting; a few puffs of black smoke blew in their direction, making their eyes sting. Marrah took a breath and coughed.

"It smells terrible," Arang complained, pinching his nose shut. Something did smell terrible, and it wasn't just the smoke. There was another smell, altogether foul, that came to them every time the wind blew seaward.

As they made their way along the bank of the lagoon toward the city, it was very quiet. Not a bird sang, not a dog barked. If people had still been dying from the fever, Marrah would have expected to hear laments and funeral drums. The stillness was eerie. She wondered if the cattle and pigs had caught the fever too. Maybe everything in the city was already dead and they'd come for no reason. She looked at the two young envoys. Their faces were unreadable, but she could imagine what they must be feeling. As they hurried forward, no one spoke.

Soon they came to a field of barley that had been flattened as if a strong wind or a great herd of cattle had passed over it.

Cyen stopped. He looked stunned and puzzled. He turned to Nacah. "Have you ever heard of it hailing this time of year, cousin?" Nacah shook his head, and the two of them stood for a moment like people caught in a nightmare. Marrah knelt and inspected the mud at the edge of the field. It was all churned up, and there were hoof-prints everywhere. They looked more or less like the kind of marks a herd of cattle might leave, which would account for the trampled crops, but they were different somehow: smaller and deeper.

She felt her mouth go dry. Smoke and trampled fields and what else? Would they find the dogs of the city with their throats slit? Would Shambah be empty? She remembered the two farmers who had come from the north last winter and her own vision of the beastmen riding west, burning everything in their path. These prints could be the mark of horses, and they were fresh.

She stood up quickly and looked around, but there were no beastmen in sight, only smoke, trampled grain, a row of trees. "We have to go back to the boat immediately," she said. She pointed to the hoof-prints and tried to explain, but only Arang understood. The rest of them just looked at her as if she were speaking an unknown language.

"Beastmen?" Cyen exchanged a bewildered glance with Nacah. "What are beastmen?" He was respectful but perplexed. "We can't go back to the boat. At least Nacah and I can't. We have to go on to Shambah. It isn't far. Look at that smoke. Maybe some of the houses caught fire and everyone's too sick to put it out. We have to help. My mother's there, and my *aita*, my sisters, my—"

"Listen to me!" Marrah cried. "You're in danger. We're all in danger!"

"Calm down." The captain of the *raspa* placed her hands on Marrah's shoulders. She was a burly, barrel-chested woman of about forty, the kind of sailor who was afraid of nothing on land or water. "What's all this talk of danger? All we have here is a field of spoiled barley and maybe a big fire."

Marrah was angry at the insinuation that she was a coward, but this was no time to argue. She removed the captain's hands and stepped back. "Please listen to me: if we keep walking in this direction, something terrible's going to happen to us." She described the beastmen again and pointed to the tracks, but everyone except Arang was convinced they'd been made by cows.

The two envoys and the three sailors continued on toward the column of black smoke, leaving Marrah and Arang standing beside the ruined field. Now what? Should they try to make it back to the boat? There seemed to be a good chance they could sail to safety, but that would mean leaving the others stranded and at the mercy of whatever lay ahead. She couldn't abandon them, and when she asked Arang he felt the same.

"Maybe we'll be safer if we all stick together," he said. Marrah didn't think so, but what choice did they have? Breaking into a run, they hurried after the others.

And so they saw Shambah, not the Shambah of blue delphiniums, honeysuckle, and white-domed mother houses that Cyen had described, but a city on fire. Making their way through a thicket of bulrushes and sweet flag, they came on a scene of devastation. Yellow flames licked the air, crackling as they consumed everything in their path. Here and there, Marrah could see what was left of a roof, blackened and cracked like an eggshell, but most of the mother houses had already collapsed under the heat. Where the butterfly gardens of Shambah had been, there were only ashes, and where its temples had stood, there were only charred beams, shards of pottery, loom weights, and the remains of kilns.

*Mary Mackey*

254

If that had been all, it would have been terrible enough, but it was only the beginning. They saw other things that morning, things so unspeakable that for the rest of her life Marrah could never think of them without shuddering. Shambah hadn't just burned; it had been attacked and looted.

"Sweet Goddess Earth!" the captain of the *raspa* cried. "What terrible curse is this?" No one answered. Akoah and her younger aunt sat down on the ground, put their hands over their eyes, and began to moan. Arang hid his face in Marrah's dress. Cyen and Nacah stood side by side, staring at their city like people turned to stone. As for Marrah, the sight of Shambah in flames was worse than her darkest vision.

She should have turned and run; they all should have, but they were in shock. Marrah took one step forward, then another. The others followed, and soon they were standing in what was left of the city. In front of them several streets ran past charred holes that had once been homes. A little while ago these same streets had been clean and smooth, paved with small white stones. The people of Shambah had set each stone carefully in the sandy earth, arranging thousands of them in intricate patterns. You could still see seashells and butterflies and flowers, but now, like everything else, they were dirty black.

Dazed, they wandered through the ashes. There were signs of struggle everywhere: heaps of broken household goods thrown in smoldering piles; headless statues; a temple robe slashed to rags and half burned, stained on one side as if someone had tried to douse the flames with a jug of wine. The poor dogs of the city had been killed just as they'd been killed in the northern village: throats slit, heads bashed in. Someone had even tossed a litter of puppies on one of the fires. But there was worse, much worse.

As they walked toward the center, they began to see human bodies. The people of Shambah had died horribly. Old men and women lay in the streets, hacked to pieces. Babies with smashed skulls had been thrown aside like so much trash. There was no sign of the younger women or children except for the bodies of a few young girls, but when Marrah saw what had happened to them she clasped her hands over Arang's eyes and made him turn away. Their bodies were naked, and a great sacrilege had been committed on them. There was not even any name for what had been done to those girls, but it was terrible beyond description and it had killed them.

Cyen and Nacah lost their minds when they saw it. They walked from body to body, calling out the names of people they'd loved and pleading with the dead to return. "Don't go to the Mother without us!" they cried. "Don't leave us." Picking up babies, they cradled them in their arms, wiped the blood and ashes off their faces, and wept uncontrollably.

When Marrah saw the slaughtered children, she came to her senses. "Come away," she begged. "Let your dead lie where they are.

The
Year
the
Horses
Came

255

There's nothing any of us can do for them." She tugged at the men's clothes and grabbed their arms, and this time the terrified sailors helped her, but Cyen and Nacah pulled away.

"We have to lay out our relatives," they insisted. "We have to put their bodies on the Towers of Silence so the Bird Goddess can accept their souls." They bent down, picked up the body of an old woman, and began to stagger toward the forest. "This is the body of Queen Aimbah," they cried. "How can we let her lie untended?"

"In the name of the sweet Goddess," Nacah pleaded, "at least let us put my grandmother to rest."

And so, hoping that after they laid Queen Aimbah's body on a tower, Cyen and Nacah would consent to return to the boat, Marrah and Arang and the three sailors followed them to the place where the Shambans laid out their dead and came on the worst horror of all: the young men.

There were perhaps a hundred, and they'd not died easily. Most had been strangled, but the best and strongest had been spitted alive on the posts of the Towers of Silence.

When they saw the massacre, Cyen and Nacah gave a cry of terror and let Queen Aimbah's body fall to the ground. There was no more talk of funeral rites. They just ran back across the smoking rubble of Shambah toward the sea, but it was already too late.

As they passed the field of trampled barley, Marrah heard a pounding. She looked up and saw three beasts charging out of the forest. The beasts had short manes, powerful legs, glittering eyes, and bodies covered with shaggy fur. On their backs sat naked men—tall pale men with yellow hair that gleamed in the sun like dead bone.

"Run!" she screamed, but they were already running as fast as they could. The horses thundered over the field, kicking up clods of dirt. As they drew closer, one of the riders let out an earsplitting cry, raised his bow, and took aim at the captain of the *raspa*. An arrow whistled past Marrah's ear, and she saw the captain suddenly leap into the air like a wounded deer and fall to the ground. In the moment of horror before they were all overtaken, she saw another warrior bend down and swoop up Nacah by the hair. The man grinned and made a slashing movement with his knife, and Nacah screamed. The man screamed too, but it was a scream of triumph. In his hand he held something terrible spattered with blood.

The third warrior rode past them and wheeled around. His beast reared, and Marrah saw two powerful legs and two great hoofs coming down on her. Screaming, she turned and ran, and the man pursued her, herding her toward the edge of the field like a cow. Her breath burned in her chest, but she kept on running. Every time she tried to turn, he cut her off; every time she went one way, he was there before her. It was like some kind of terrible game. At last, totally exhausted, she stumbled, and as she fell, he bent down, caught her by the hair, and jerked her into the air. She smelled the rank odor of the man and saw his grinning face, painted with blood and ashes and yellow lines. His eyes were the same color as Stavan's, but they were hard and contemptuous.

She yelled and flailed out with both hands, and her nails scraped against something. A thin line of blood appeared on the man's cheek. For an instant he looked surprised. Then he gave a roar of anger, threw her to the ground, leaped off his horse, and began to beat and kick her. She tried to ward off the blows, but there was no way she could defend herself. Crying and almost senseless, she lay face down in the mud as he struck her again and again. When he was finished, he turned her over, and spat on her. Then he raised his knife, slipped the blade under the edge of her dress, and cut it from neck to knee in one swift movement so that she lay naked in front of him.

She put her hands over her breasts and tried to move away, but he grabbed her by the ankle and pulled her flat, knocking the wind out of her. She lay there, panting and terrified. She had no idea what was coming next except that she was soon going to die. Later she found out that instant death wasn't usually the fate of young women taken in war, but mercifully she didn't know what the nomads did to their female captives.

She could see now that the man wasn't naked after all but wore a leather loincloth. A string of wolf teeth hung around his neck, mixed with other things that looked like they might have once been temple adornments. Most of the ornaments were clay or copper, but here and there a bit of gold glinted. Like Stavan he was tattooed with blue marks, but they covered his whole chest and part of his face. His hands were spattered with blood, and there was more blood matted in his hair. He looked fierce and terrible, like some kind of animal that had just attacked and eaten its prey.

"Let me go!" she screamed.

The man smiled at her in an ugly way, exposing a row of uneven teeth. He reached down and started to unhook the wide leather belt that held his quiver and scabbard, but before his fingers found the bone buckle, one of his companions rode up in a spray of mud and a thud of hooves. Pointing to Marrah, the man cried something in a harsh, guttural language that sounded like Hansi, although she couldn't understand it. The warrior who'd been about to take off his belt looked annoyed. He said something to the rider—something angry by the sound of it—grabbed Marrah by the arm, and pulled her to her feet. Still grumbling, he pulled a leather thong out of his hair, jerked her wrists behind her back, and tied them so tightly she cried out in pain. Then he put the flat of his hand on the back of her neck and shoved her in the direction of the newcomer. Bruised and sobbing, she stumbled forward, scarcely able to see where she was going.

The second man was carrying a long spear that reached almost to the ground. Putting the point in the middle of Marrah's back, he forced her to walk in front of him. Every step she took was agony, but with the possible exception of a cracked rib nothing seemed broken. As she limped across the field, she saw Nacah, Cyen, the captain, and one of the sailors sprawled in the mud. All four looked dead. She felt sick with grief and terror, but at least Arang was nowhere in sight and neither was Akoah. Perhaps they'd escaped somehow. The thought gave her hope.

The rider herded her toward the forest and down a path that had probably once led to the place where the people of Shambah washed their clothes. Whenever she slowed down, he grunted a rough command and prodded her between the shoulder blades. After a while, she smelled smoke—not the smoke of Shambah but the smoke of a campfire. Someone was cooking meat. The horse must have smelled the smoke too because it made a strange, high-pitched sound, and an answering sound came from up ahead.

Suddenly, without warning, a woman started screaming. The scream wasn't like anything Marrah had ever heard. She froze, paralyzed by the horrible, high-pitched cries. The rider grunted and prodded her impatiently. She looked back and saw him regarding her with indifference. The terrible screams evidently meant nothing to him. He seemed used to them.

She limped on, and the screams stopped just as quickly as they'd begun. They crossed the stream on a fine wooden bridge, built no doubt by some Shamban carpenter. The rails had been carved with goddess signs; brightly painted flowers and vines twined in a triangle of fertility, and small, pretty butterflies fluttered along above the water. Marrah stared at it as if she'd never seen a bridge before. Already it seemed to belong to another world.

They started along the opposite bank, following a smooth, white-shelled path. After a while they came to a clearing. Once it had been planted with chick-peas, but now it was so thrashed up it looked like a muddy pond. A fire was burning in the center of the trampled space, and a dozen or so warriors sat near it watching meat roast on a wooden spit. Their horses were hobbled nearby, peacefully munching what bits of bean vines were left.

The most chilling thing about the scene was how normal it looked. The men seemed relaxed and even slightly bored, as if the atrocities they had just committed were all in a day's work. Some of them were sharpening their weapons; others were talking; one even appeared to be taking a nap. Heaped up on a blanket beside the sleeping man were things he and his companions had stolen from the city—gold and copper temple adornments, mostly, but other things too: mirrors, knives, woodworking tools, cups, fine linen skirts, fishhooks, a child's doll with a clay face and a red skirt, even several links of sausages. There were clay wine jars scattered around the clearing—no doubt also taken from Shambah, since most displayed a brightly painted butterfly stamped on one side. It was common to reuse wine jars—a good one could last as long as twenty years—but two-thirds of these were broken, and as Marrah watched, a warrior finished off the wine in another and threw it over his shoulder.

When the men saw Marrah, several of them got to their feet, smiling in the same nasty way as the man who had beat her, but the rider said something gruff to them and they sat back down looking disappointed. The man herded her over to the booty at spear point and indicated that she should stand still on pain of being run through. Then he wheeled around and rode out of the clearing.

She stood absolutely still for a few minutes, afraid he might come back and kill her. Her whole body ached and she was trembling with terror, but she was also so angry she could hardly think. No one had ever hit her before; no one had so much as ever raised a hand to her. She glared at the warriors, who were paying no attention to her, feeling humiliated by her nakedness. Ordinarily she didn't mind being without clothes in hot weather—in Shara she swam naked in the ocean all summer—but these men had turned nakedness into something that made her feel vulnerable.

She examined the bruises on her arms and thought of how these men, who were sitting so convivially around the fire chatting with one another, had burned Shambah, massacred its people, killed

The
Year
the
Horses
Came

259

Nacah and Cyen and the two sailors, and done the Goddess only knew what to Akoah and Arang; and for the first time in her life she knew what it was to want revenge. If they'd touched her brother, if they'd so much as harmed a hair on his head, she'd—

What would she do? She stood still, paralyzed by rage and fear and appalled by the fierceness of her own hatred. The beastmen had called some sort of evil into the world that could infect even peaceful people. They were frightening enough in themselves, but equally frightening was the idea that she, who had always worshiped the Goddess Earth and kept Her commandments, could long to kill them.

The men laughed at some joke and she turned away, repelled by the sight of them. Slowly, step by step, she started to move toward the forest, hoping none of the warriors would notice her until she was close enough to the trees to make a run for it, but they were as sharp-eyed as hawks. She hadn't gone more than ten paces before one of them jumped to his feet, came over, grabbed her by the wrists, and pulled her to the ground. She sat down so hard her stomach turned over and her teeth slammed together with a click. Putting the tip of his knife under her throat, he uttered a quick, harsh command. Marrah didn't have to speak his language to know what he meant. She nodded to reassure him that she understood.

The man grinned a long, slow grin, as if it pleased him to have such power over her. Reaching down, he grabbed her pubic hair and pulled it so hard she yelled. Then he cut off a tuft, stuck it behind his ear, and sauntered back to his companions, who laughed and slapped him on the back as if this were a great joke.

After that she sat still, not wanting to risk attracting their attention again. Soon the rider who had left returned with another rider, a big man with long brown hair and a curly brown beard. The brown-bearded man wore a number of copper bracelets on his arms. Obviously he was someone of importance, because all the other warriors rose to their feet when they saw him coming, and even the sleeping man was kicked awake.

Riding up to Marrah, he looked down at her thoughtfully. There was no greed or hatred in his eyes, only a kind of cool appraisal. He made a quick motion with his index finger, and one of the warriors instantly ran over, pulled her to her feet, and cut the leather thong, setting her hands free. The blood surged back to her wrists, stinging her fingers. The brown-bearded man pointed toward the forest.

"*Kashw?*" he demanded.

Marrah shook her head. The word was definitely Hansi or something like it, but it meant nothing to her. Stavan had only taught her a few things: "yes," "no," "it's a beautiful day," "I love you."

The man looked disappointed, as if for some reason he had expected her to speak his language. He persisted, but she just kept shaking her head. Finally he gave up. Reaching into the pouch that hung from his war belt, he produced a gold bracelet and threw it at her. She tried to catch but missed, and the thin circle of gold fell spinning at her feet. She knew it was going to hurt to bend down and pick it up, but that was what she was expected to do, so she did. When she saw the bracelet up close, she gave an exclamation of surprise. It was the one Stavan had given her when they took their summer vows. The warrior who beat her must have stripped it off her arm while she was lying in the mud. She hadn't even missed it.

"*Votoah?*" the man demanded, pointing first to the bracelet and then to her.

"*De.*" She nodded, offering him one of the few words of Hansi she knew. She hoped he was asking if the bracelet was hers because she'd said yes. She pointed to the pale band of skin on her upper arm where the bracelet had been for so many months. Slipping it over her wrist, she pushed it into place.

Encouraged by the word *de*, the brown-bearded man let loose another barrage of incomprehensible questions. She shrugged and shook her head. At last he stopped trying to get her to understand. Pointing to the pile of booty, he said a few words to one of the warriors who were standing at a respectful distance, watching the whole interrogation. Then he turned, kicked his horse, and rode out of the clearing.

Although she didn't understand what had happened until much later, she could tell immediately that the warriors were no longer treating her with contempt. The man who had put the knife under her chin and cut off her pubic hair came up to her with downcast eyes and said something that might have been an apology. Motioning for her to make herself comfortable on the blanket, he sorted through the loot, pulled out the best linen dress, and, instead of tossing it at her, handed it to her with a sort of half bow. The dress was the long kind that older, important priestesses often wore on ceremonial occasions. Embroidered with Goddess signs and bordered with tiny blue beads made of clay, it must have been woven in the temple workshops of Shambah. As Marrah slipped it over her head, she wondered if perhaps it had belonged to Queen Aimbah. The linen was cool against her bruised flesh, and she settled into it gratefully.

But the warrior wasn't finished dressing her. Next he selected a belt, a tunic, a cape, and a white towel of the sort priestesses used to wrap delicate ceremonial objects in. As if that weren't enough, he then went over to one of the horses, opened a leather carrying bag, and drew out a pair of boots and some matted fur leggings. Marrah stared at the pile of clothes in amazement. Surely he didn't expect her to put all of them on, not in such hot weather.

But he did; in fact, he insisted. Since there was no way of knowing what would happen if she refused, she climbed reluctantly into the outfit, which was warm enough to carry her through a winter in Xori, only managing to hang onto her sandals when it became clear that the boots were much too large. When she had finished rolling up the ends of the leggings so they wouldn't drag on the ground, the man motioned for her to drape the towel over her head so that it covered her hair and part of her face, which was ridiculous, but once again she obeyed. By the time she was dressed to his satisfaction, she felt like someone costumed for one of the comic roles in the Snake Festival.

After that, he left her alone in the shade to sweat and wonder what was going to happen next. All in all, being muffled up in layers of clothing was better than being naked in front of murderers, but the leggings itched like crazy. She remembered Stavan had had a similar pair when he first came to Xori; he had told her they were made from wool plucked from the fleece of long-haired sheep.

She thought a lot about Stavan that afternoon. Mostly she wondered how such a good man had ever come out of such a terrible people. She knew now that he'd kept a lot of things from her—probably because he was ashamed of them—and she wondered if, after today, she could ever touch his hair or look into his eyes without shuddering.

Time passed and the shadows grew longer. The meat was cooked and eaten, and she was even brought a share, which she fell on hungrily despite the pain in her stomach and her growing dread that Arang had been killed along with the others. Sometimes riders came into the clearing and left again, but their weapons were put away and there seemed to be no fighting going on, perhaps because there was no one left to fight. Once a tall man rode up and dumped a small, dirty bundle at her feet. When she unfolded it, she found it contained her ruined dress, her belt, and her leather medicine pouch. The charms the priestess of Nar had given her were still inside the pouch. It didn't look as if she was going to have a chance to use them, but knowing they hadn't been lost made her feel a little more confident.

She was just beginning to think about making another attempt to escape when five new men rode up, laughing and joking among themselves. One of them had a large deerskin package slung across the rump of his horse. Dismounting, he untied the bundle, tossed it casually on the ground, and went over to the others to share a jar of wine. For lack of anything better to do, Marrah stared at the package, wondering what was inside. Suddenly the deerskin moved, and she saw a woman's bare foot protrude from one end.

Horrified, she limped over, untied the leather thongs, and threw the skins aside. A young woman looked up at her, her face so bruised and covered with mud that at first Marrah didn't recognize her. Then she realized who it was.

"Akoah?" she whispered. It was the youngest sailor. At the sound of her name, Akoah's face contorted with fear. "Don't be afraid; it's me, Marrah. I'm not going to hurt you." She caught the young woman's hands and began to untie them, working out the worst knots with her teeth. When she'd freed her, she kissed her gently and smoothed her tangled hair out of her eyes.

"Akoah, talk to me. What happened? What did they do to you? Did they beat you the way they beat me?" Akoah said nothing. She was naked as Marrah had been, but other than several nasty bruises on her face and the terrified look in her eyes, she seemed unharmed.

For a long time Marrah sat beside her, holding her hands and talking to her soothingly. If the warriors noticed what she was doing, they didn't care. Finally Akoah seemed to come to her senses. Sitting up, she cast a fearful glance in the direction of the men. "We have to get out of here," she whispered.

"Yes," Marrah agreed. "We will as soon as we can."

"You don't understand." Akoah shuddered and bit her bottom lip. "Those things over there aren't really men. They're something else. They don't act like men. They do things no men would do." She moved closer to Marrah and put her mouth to Marrah's ear. "I think they may be ghosts. Bad ghosts. Things that died and never went back to the Mother." She grabbed Marrah's arm and hung on to it. "They killed both my aunts with their arrows, didn't they?"

Marrah nodded reluctantly, thinking Akoah was in no shape to hear such news, but to her astonishment she seemed relieved. "Thank the Goddess, then they're beyond harm." Marrah asked her

The
Year
the
Horses
Came

263

what she meant, and tears came to Akoah's eyes. "They do things to women we don't have words for. Do it until it kills them. Better my aunts died quickly."

There was something chilling about the way she accepted her aunts' death that made the hair stand up on the back of Marrah's neck. "What do you mean?"

The young sailor wiped away her tears and looked at Marrah angrily. Her eyes were no longer wide and innocent; they were filled with loathing. "Those five ghosts who brought me here forced me to copulate with them," she whispered. "I use the word we use for animals, but not even animals copulate in such a way. They fell on me like dogs, but even a pack of dogs will leave a bitch alone if she's not in the mood. They tore me in front and in back, and when I tried to fight them off, they hit me in the face." She pointed to the inside of her thighs. "See that. That's dried blood. And I was lucky. There was another woman they forced sex on, a young priestess from Shambah, and they killed her. Ten of them went at her, and she screamed a scream I'll hear in my nightmares until I'm an old woman." She put her thumb and index finger together in the sign of the round-eyed Owl Goddess. "May She Who Brings Death curse them with no family and no joy, and when they die, may She refuse to accept their souls."

Marrah wanted to say something, but she was too frightened to do anything but take Akoah's hand and squeeze it. As she did, her own fingers trembled. She knew now what had nearly happened to her. The idea that Akoah had been forced to have sex with five men made her sick.

They were both silent for a moment. Then Akoah sighed. "Well, I can't keep thinking about what they did to me or I'll go crazy." She ran her fingers through her hair and began to pick out the leaves and bits of grass. "Right now I'd give anything to wash their stink off, but I suppose if I tried to get to the creek, they'd stop me."

Marrah looked at the warriors, who were still sitting around the campfire ignoring them. Ever since the brown-bearded man had thrown her the bracelet, they had been letting her do pretty much whatever she wanted except escape.

"Let's give it a try," she suggested. She helped Akoah to her feet and led her toward the creek, praying that their luck would hold. The men looked up as they passed, but they didn't stop them, although one rose to his feet, took up his spear, and followed along, making it clear there'd be no chance to run for the woods. At the edge of the creek, Marrah pulled off her hot, sticky clothes and threw them in a pile. Later she learned that she'd been lucky not to be beaten for stripping in public, but the warrior, who still considered her a savage, just grunted and looked in the other direction.

Hand in hand, the two women stepped into the warm water. Akoah flinched as it touched her thighs, but soon she relaxed with a sigh and began to wash herself. When she and Marrah had removed the last bits of blood and mud from their bodies, they took turns washing each other's hair.

So far, the guard had left them in peace, but when they climbed out to sit on the bank and dry off, he pointed to Marrah's clothes and insisted she climb back into them at once. When she tried to offer her tunic to Akoah, he pulled it out of her hand with a rough reprimand. Evidently Marrah was to be dressed so that only the tip of her nose showed, and Akoah was to remain naked. The warrior put his spear tip in the middle of Akoah's back, in what was by now a familiar gesture, and prodded her back toward the pile of booty, and Marrah followed. When they were alone again, sitting on the blanket with their arms around each other, Akoah turned to her.

"Bless you for the comfort you've given me," she said. "I'll hate them forever, but at least I feel clean." She paused and looked at the warriors, who had fallen to playing some kind of gambling game with their hands. "Do you think they'll try to force sex on me again?" Marrah said she hoped not. Akoah sighed. "Why do you think they attacked me? It couldn't have been for pleasure, because there was no pleasure in it. It wasn't anything like sharing joy; it was more like they were sneezing or pissing or beating me up with their penises. They must be ghosts. No real man would take something as sweet as his penis and turn it into a club. Only a ghost would hurt a woman so much." And with that, she buried her face in Marrah's dress and began to cry quietly until at last, exhausted, she fell asleep.

Akoah slept through most of the rest of the afternoon, but Marrah couldn't, although she was almost sick with weariness. Every once in a while her eyes closed for a few seconds, but every noise brought her bolt upright. Sometimes the sound that woke her was only the cawing of a crow or the laughter of the warriors, but often it was the thud of horses' hooves. She had never heard that rhythmic clopping until today, but already it spelled danger.

The sun was just about to set when three riders appeared. They must have come from far away because the fur of their horses was wet with sweat. Galloping up to the campfire, they dismounted, handed over their beasts, and exchanged some greetings in low voices. Then they turned and headed toward Marrah and Akoah.

"Wake up," Marrah whispered. Akoah opened her eyes, smiled, and then, remembering where she was, clutched at Marrah and sat up.

"What's wrong? Have they come for us?"

"I don't know. I hope not."

As the three drew closer, Marrah saw that one of them was the same brown-bearded man who'd thrown her the bracelet, the other man was a middle-aged warrior with a nasty scar across his left cheek, and the third was a young woman of perhaps seventeen. This was the first beastwoman Marrah had seen and she inspected her closely, but it was hard to make out her features. The woman was dressed in a long, shapeless brown tunic, leggings, and dark brown shawl, which she had draped over her head, partly concealing her face. The shawl was secured with a sort of headband made of coarse, twisted black hair that ended in several red tassels that fringed her forehead. Like the men, she wore leather boots tied at the ankles, but hers were embroidered with shells. There were more shells on the arms of her tunic, as well as copper and clay beads, but it was her adornments that surprised Marrah the most—they were heaped around her neck in string after string, jingling softly like tiny bells: some copper, some stone, some animal teeth; she wore bracelets too, three rings in each ear, and a ring on each finger. As if all that weren't strange enough, her eyes were circled with black grease, her cheeks and lips were stained red, and blue tattoo marks as delicate as vines spiraled down her cheeks.

"A priestess!" Akoah cried, jumping to her feet. "She must be a priestess! Who else would wear so many adornments? Oh, Marrah, we're saved! Look at that paint, that medicine bag at her belt!" Marrah tried to grab her hand, but Akoah pulled away and ran forward calling out greetings and prayers. "Hail, sweet priestess; hail, dear one who comes in Her name!"

"Akoah, come back!" Marrah begged. "She's not a priestess, she's wearing sun signs; she's—" But the warning came too late. As Akoah drew near the beastwoman, the warrior with the scarred face stepped between them, lifted his knee, and sent her sprawling to the ground like a bothersome dog. Then he stepped over her without a second look.

Akoah lay on the ground, blue-faced. Her lips were white and she didn't seem to be breathing. "You old goat turd!" Marrah cried.

"What have you done to her?" She started forward to help Akoah up, but the beastwoman called out to her in Shambah to be still. Startled by the sound of a language she could understand, Marrah froze.

The woman and the men came closer. One of them—the man with the scar—said something to the woman, and she bowed and replied in their language. Exchanging satisfied glances, the men folded their arms across their chests and stepped back. From that moment on they remained in the background, although Marrah was always conscious that they were close at hand, armed and fierce-looking as wolves.

The beastwoman turned to Marrah and gave so deep a bow that the red tassels on her forehead bobbed up and down. "Greetings in Her name, dearest sister," she said, in a firm, sweet voice. "I'm Dalish, daughter of the unfortunate Nashish, may her soul have found rest in the Mother. She and all my relatives were murdered by these hunks of human shit you see standing behind me, who fortunately are too stupid to speak Shambah. They've asked me to translate for them and told me if I say one word except what is absolutely necessary they'll cut me into small pieces and leave me for the crows, but over the years I've managed to convince them that it takes ten times as long to say anything in Shambah as it does in their own ugly tongue."

Marrah was so amazed by this unexpected speech that she couldn't think of a reply. "You're one of us?" she stammered.

The woman looked mildly insulted. "Of course, thank the Goddess. Do I look like one of them? If I'd been born to their people, I'd be as mindless as their women. Oh, you'll see them soon enough, those nomad women skulking around like whipped puppies with their damn shawls over their faces, jumping to attention every time one of their husbands or masters beckons." She straightened her shoulders proudly. "But I was trained to be a priestess. At six my grandmother dedicated me to the Bird Goddess, and I had four sweet years serving in Her temple before the nomads rode down on my village, burned it to the ground, and carried me away."

"My friend thought you were a priestess."

Dalish smiled wryly and looked at Akoah, who was sitting up looking bewildered. "Ah, yes, it still shows, doesn't it." She turned to Akoah. "Sit still, darling," she said in such a nasty tone of voice that Marrah jumped. "I'm sorry I have to talk to you this way, but those pieces of shit behind me have to think I'm on their side. If you move, they may decide to beat you to a pulp. It's their way of expressing affection."

She turned back to Marrah. "We have to get down to business before they get suspicious. Why don't you start by telling me your name and where you come from, and then I'll pass along the information as if it's taken us this long to get to it."

"My name is Marrah, daughter of Sabalah, and I come from the village of Xori."

Dalish turned to the men, bowed, and said something, and the brown-bearded man made a low, grumbling noise.

"Irehan the cowardly wants to know where Xori is."

"It's a fishing village on the shore of the Sea of Gray Waves."

Dalish frowned. "So far? I think I'm going to wait a bit before I tell him that. You and I have other things to settle first." She indicated Marrah's arm with the faintest of nods. "For example, where did you come by that gold bracelet? No, don't look at it; keep looking at me. I don't want them to guess I've asked you yet."

Marrah did as she was told. "I got the bracelet from a"—what had Dalish called them?—"nomad who washed up on our beach on my coming-of-age day." She began in a halting, embarrassed way to tell the story of how she and Stavan had met. Given what she had seen today, it seemed shameful ever to have loved him, and yet she had and still did. Before she could explain how he was different from the others, Dalish cut her off.

"Enough. I get the picture. He was your lover, yes?" Marrah nodded. "I take it he wasn't a thirty-year-old giant with a long black dagger tattooed on his penis?" Under any other circumstances Marrah might have laughed, but she was in no mood to laugh at anything. She shook her head.

"He was about seventeen when I first met him, tall, but no dagger."

Dalish was silent for some time, and when she finally spoke it was in a completely different voice. "Now listen to me and listen very closely, because if you don't do exactly as I say, you may get us both impaled. You saw what they did to the men of Shambah, yes? Just nod if you understand. Good. Well, that will be us if you don't pay attention. I'm about to risk my life for you, and I don't want it to go to waste."

She sat down and motioned for Marrah to sit beside her. "First, I want you to look confused so those bastards will believe that I'm having to explain things to you several times. I see that you don't know the word 'bastard.' Well, you will soon enough. Hansi is the best language in the world for swearing, but I'll try to restrain myself until you've picked up enough to appreciate my curses in the original."

Marrah sat down and did as Dalish had ordered. It was no trick to look confused. She was, thoroughly.

"I'm going to say this fast, so listen and remember. First: you're here and in one piece only by a miracle. That warrior who took you in battle was going to rape you—force you to have sex with him—and make you his slave girl, but his uncle liked your looks and decided to keep you for himself, so he brought you back here to await his pleasure. Meanwhile Irehan—the one with the brown beard—caught sight of that gold bracelet and demanded to know where it had come from. It's not an ordinary bracelet, you see. It has clan signs on it, important clan signs. The signs indicate"—she lifted her eyes just a fraction of an inch so they rested on the bracelet—"that it once belonged to Achan, only son of the Great Chief Zuhan."

"Yes," Marrah said, "it—"

Once again Dalish silenced her with a motion of her hand. "Never mind. You can tell me later how you came by it. The important thing for you to know is that you came within a handspan of being executed. When Irehan saw that bracelet, he quite reasonably assumed that some member of your immediate family had killed Achan and stripped it off his body as a spoil of war. Swift revenge is a nomad specialty. Irehan was actually in the process of picking out a stake to impale you on when I suggested there was a chance Achan might have given the bracelet to you. Since his mind works slowly, he had to stop for a while and think that one over, and while he was thinking, a messenger arrived with an interesting piece of news."

She paused. "I'm going to say something now that may make you want to cry out or make some gesture of delight. Instead, you must—you absolutely must—keep a face of stone." She shot a quick glance at the warriors, as if reassuring herself that they still had no idea what she was saying. "Your brother is still alive."

If Marrah hadn't been forewarned, she would have cried out with surprise and joy, but although the blood rushed to her face, she somehow managed to keep on staring impassively at Dalish.

"The warrior who rode him down would have slit his throat immediately, except that Slehan over there—the one with the scar on his face—had told them to take at least one live prisoner. They were planning a final thank-you sacrifice to Han, and all the men of Shambah had already been murdered or had run away. So they trussed your brother up like a little pig and carried him back to the main camp where—surprise!—they discovered that he wouldn't do for two reasons. In the first place, he had old redberry fever scars, and

The
Year
the
Horses
Came

269

sacrifices of gratitude have to be perfect; and second, he was wearing a gold earring, which, like your bracelet, was marked with Achan's clan sign."

She licked her lips nervously. "So here is where you stand at present. Thanks to me, they think there's a faint chance that your brother—he is your brother and not your son, yes?"

Marrah nodded.

"A faint chance that your brother is the legitimate son of the hero Achan. The timing isn't exactly right, but I didn't have the leisure to attend to minor details. I just talked as fast as I could and prayed to the Goddess for inspiration. Fortunately, every man in the Twenty Tribes knows Zuhan is desperate for a legitimate heir, and, even more fortunately for you, these boys are bad at numbers. Also, they think your brother's younger than I think he is. How old is he, by the way? They wouldn't let me talk to him."

"Twelve," Marrah whispered.

Dalish nodded. "Just as I thought. Well, they think he's ten. Luckily, he's small, and luckily everyone knows Achan went on a short trip west before he came back to announce that he was off to seek the golden tents of Han. So, as I pointed out to Slehan, Achan could have married a savage woman. Not exactly according to their ways, of course. There wouldn't have been a diviner present to slaughter the right number of horses and say the right prayers and all that, but Achan could just possibly have taken a wife, which—if it were true— would make your brother the only heir to the Great Chief. Are you following me?"

Marrah frowned. "Not entirely."

Mary
Mackey

270

"Let me make it simple. In a moment I'm going to turn around and pretend to translate. If you and your brother want to be alive this time tomorrow, remember this: from now on he's Achan's son. He's ten, not twelve. Achan gave him that earring when he recognized him as his heir. As for you, you're not your brother's sister; you're his aunt. Achan had to have married a virgin, so you can't possibly be anything but an aunt. You got your bracelet from Achan too. He gave it to your sister on their wedding day, but when the poor thing died in childbirth, he took it off her arm and placed it on yours, making you the boy's seeshma—sort of a cross between a stepmother and a wetnurse—a very respectable position for a woman, in Hansi terms. Now repeat that back to me, word for word."

Marrah did as she was told. When she was finished, Dalish nodded. "Good. Now forget everything else. What you've just said isn't a lie; it's the truth. There's no other story. You may be living with the Hansi for the rest of your life, but no matter how lonely you get or how much you're tempted to tell some sister from the south who you really are or how you really got that bracelet, don't. Not all women who once worshiped the Goddess hate these bastards as much as I do. But just to satisfy my curiosity, tell me one thing: How did your lover come by that bracelet? Did he kill Achan?"

"No." Marrah shook her head. "He took it off his arm before he buried him. Achan was his brother." She stopped talking and looked anxiously at Dalish, who had turned deadly pale under her paints.

"Was your lover named Stavan?" Dalish whispered so softly that her voice was less than a breath, and when Marrah indicated by a startled gesture that it was, she grabbed her by the wrist. "You must never, never tell anyone this! I wish I hadn't heard it myself. You don't know, of course, do you? There's no way you could. This lover of yours, this Stavan, came back to the Great Chief a year or two ago to tell him Achan was dead, but he acted so strange Zuhan decided he was bewitched. Changar, the diviner, read the stars and proclaimed that Zuhan was right; a beautiful witch had cast a spell on Stavan while he was in the West. Great Goddess, girl, don't you see? You're the witch! Why, they'll slice out your insides if they find out you so much as knew Zuhan's son."

The scar-faced warrior suddenly walked up to Dalish and said something to her. He pointed to the hand that was touching Marrah's wrist, and Dalish removed it very slowly. She said something to the warrior, and then she turned to Marrah. "Slehan the shit-faced has just reprimanded me for befriending you. I have explained to him that I was moved to make such an improper gesture when I heard from your own lips that your brother was indeed the only true son of the great hero Achan. I have also told him I made a mistake when I said you were from Xori. You are actually from a little village called Shorni, rather close to my own, which makes it seem reasonable that Achan might have shared your sister's bed. Don't worry about ever running into anyone else from Shorni. No such place ever existed."

She rose to her feet and motioned for Marrah to stand too. "I'm now about to lie to these two with such beauty and artistry that you would weep with joy if you could understand. It's my only talent, really. Perhaps if I'd grown up among my own people, I'd have been a great composer of songs." She smiled wistfully. "So Marrah of Shorni, draw that linen towel over your face and bow your head. They like a woman humble. It brings out what little good there is in them."

She looked over at Akoah, who was still sitting where she had fallen. "As for your friend, I can't stop them from forcing sex on her, but I'll do what I can to persuade them to make her a concubine instead of a slave; that way she'll go to one man instead of the whole pack. As a concubine, she should live a good while, perhaps long enough to curse me for saving her."

"We'll escape before they can touch her again," Marrah said fiercely. "I swear we will."

Dalish kept on smiling but there were tears in her eyes. "My dear sister, don't you think I'd have escaped long ago if escape were possible? You don't know them yet. You can't imagine how far from home they're going to take you or how much you'll suffer. You're a woman and proud of it, but in their land women are worth less than horses, and girl children are worth nothing at all. Pray to the sweet Goddess they marry you to a man who's a little less brutal than the rest. It's the best you can hope for."

"What about you? You seem independent enough."

"Do I?" She shook her head sadly. "I'm not. At night I lie down with Slehan the scar-faced and do whatever he orders, and when he gives me to one of his friends, as he often does, I pretend to be honored. I'm just his concubine, and if I weren't so useful his wives would have poisoned me long ago."

Rising to her feet, she gathered her shawl around her and went to tell the warriors the story of Arang, son of Achan, and his humble aunt, Marrah.


Not long after that, Marrah and Arang were holding each other and crying, partly with fear and partly with joy.

"I thought you were dead," Arang whispered, as he kissed Marrah's cheeks and touched her face. The scar-faced warrior seemed disgusted at the sight of Arang's tears. He shook his head and walked off with a snort of contempt.

Lathak, he muttered, and the brown-bearded man nodded. The word had an ugly sound.

Arang turned to Dalish. "What did he say?"

Dalish translated. The word meant "coward," she told him, and if he didn't want to hear it every day of his life, he should never cry again—at least not where any of the men could see him. "You're lucky they think you're just a boy." She pointed to Slehan's horse. "A man who cries sometimes ends up like that. Once that horse was a stallion, but now you'll notice it's lacking something rather important." She shot an anxious glance at the two warriors, who were sitting on a log, staring at Arang and talking to each other in low voices. "Slehan gelded it himself with his own dagger, and I think he rather enjoyed the process."

The
Year
the
Horses
Came

273

For weeks Marrah and Arang were forced to travel east on horseback as Akoah and the unfortunate women of Shambah plodded along next to them. The slave girls—for that was what the women were called now—had once been priestesses and farmers, potters and metalworkers, mothers, traders, carpenters, and hunters, but the nomads treated them with no more care than the cattle they were also driving east, and like the cattle, many died. The lucky ones died of fever; others, particularly mothers who had lost their children, died of grief; but most died of exhaustion. At night, the warriors took the survivors from campfire to campfire, forcing sex on them until they were sick with shame and lack of sleep. At dawn, the march began again, matched to the pace of horses and cattle, not human beings. The slaves were forced to keep up, and if one faltered she was beaten.

Even those who started out with good sandals and sturdy clothing were soon left with rags that offered little protection from the sun. The warriors rode from sunrise to sunset, rarely stopping until they pitched camp. When they were thirsty, they would wet their lips with a few drops from their water skins or make a small slit in the neck of one of the cows and put their lips to it, but the slaves

275

had no water skins, and the smell of fresh blood made most of them sick.

"For the love of the Goddess Earth, sister, give us a drink," they begged Marrah, but when she tried to lean down and offer them a sip from her water skin, the armed warrior who always rode next to her would reach out and knock it aside before it reached their lips. Dalish warned that if she went on trying to help the slaves, she might end up marching with them, but Marrah stubbornly continued and it was a tribute to how persuasive Dalish had been that she wasn't stripped and thrown down to die with the rest.

Thanks to Dalish's lies, Marrah was the aunt of the son of a hero, and so, while the women of Shambah suffered, she was forced to sit high above them and watch. The best she could do was keep Akoah alive by making sure she was fed, clothed, and not taken around to the campfires at night, but other than that she was powerless. Imprisoned in her hot robes, she saw the world through a narrow slit in her shawl, but what she saw made her ashamed, and sometimes when the women were crying for water, she found herself wishing she too had died of fever or been killed outright like the captain of the *raspa*. Then she would remember how much Arang needed her, and she would force herself to sit up straight. She would grab the reins with a firm hand and try to think of some way to use the charms the priestesses of Nar had given her. She couldn't save the women of Shambah by dying with them. It was her duty to survive long enough to help them escape.

If listening to the women's pleas for water was the worst torture, the horses themselves were a close second. Riding was an uncomfortable, bone-jarring experience that made both her and Arang seasick at first. Although the nomads sometimes used a sort of saddle made of leather, they usually clung to the bare backs of the beasts, directing them by long thongs attached to antler cheekpieces and a two-piece wooden contraption called a bit that they jammed in the animal's mouth. In theory, you were supposed to guide a horse by lightly tugging on the reins or giving it a jab in the side with your heel, but the beasts seemed to sense that Marrah and Arang had no idea what they were doing and they delighted in trying to throw them off.

Soon Marrah got the knack of pulling hers to a stop before it could do any damage, but Arang's legs were too short to grip a horse properly, and he fell off again and again. Every time this happened, the warriors stopped and an ominous silence filled the air as they waited for him to climb back on. The look of disgust on their faces made Marrah anxious. She never forgot what Dalish had said about how Slehan had enjoyed gelding his stallion, and she was constantly afraid Arang might provoke the men to violence. There were seventy of them, all heavily armed, and Arang was too often the center of their attention. But he was young and stubborn and angry about having been called a coward, and his anger made him defiant.

"I hate riding," he cried the second or third time he fell. "In the name of the Goddess, Marrah, let me at least get up behind you and hang on to your waist. This cursed beast they gave me is trying to kill me." He glared at his horse, which was quietly cropping grass. The nomads began to gather around him, but none dismounted.

Dalish rode up and reined in her mare. "Get back on that horse," she said quietly. "A boy who can't ride is worthless, and one who refuses is so dishonored there's no telling what they'll do to you." She pointed to his clothes. They were luxurious by nomad standards, although any temple weaver in Shara could have turned out better: a white tunic and a pair of matted white wool leggings, soft boots, and a small gold pendant shaped like a sun. "They've dressed you like a little chief, and if you want to win their respect you have to act like one. Remember you're the son of Achan."

"Screw Achan," Arang said. He seemed to be learning Hansi swearwords first, and it was remarkable how many of them were sexual. Dalish's eyes narrowed.

"You're just lucky your accent is so bad they didn't understand that. Now get back on that horse, you stubborn little fool, or I'll translate what you just said. If you're going to kill yourself and your sister, I'm not going to get myself impaled along with you." Frightened by her threat, Arang pulled himself back up on his horse, and from then on, every time he fell off he kept his mouth shut.

He always hated riding, but in time Marrah's bones stopped aching and she began to enjoy it. To her surprise, she even developed an affection for her horse, a brown mare that carried her patiently once Marrah learned to control her. Soon she was scratching the animal behind the ears and talking to her, because the beast seemed to enjoy the sound of her voice; she even gave her a name: Tarka. The word meant "freedom" in the language of the Shore People, and every time she said it, she thought of Xori, Sabalah, and the Sea of Gray Waves.

She also thought of Stavan. The only consolation she had besides Arang's company and Dalish's kindness was the thought that she was drawing closer to him. Perhaps she might see him, but then again

The
Year
the
Horses
Came

277

perhaps not. The Sea of Grass was huge, and she had no reason to think Slehan's warriors would take her anywhere near the tents of their Great Chief. Still, at night as she lay on the ground beside Arang, she imagined Stavan walking toward her through the tall grass, and sometimes when she finally got to sleep she dreamed of making love with him. But it might have been better not to dream at all; on mornings after she'd spent the night with him in her imagination, she woke feeling more lonely and discouraged than ever.

They rode on, and as the sun grew hotter, the land seemed to surrender to it. By the end of the second week, the cool green forests were only a memory. As they passed from scattered islands of trees into the tall grass, the oaks shrunk into stunted bushes, the bushes themselves shriveled, and the Earth Herself lay down and became a featureless plain without so much as a hill to break the monotony. Actually the plain was broken by ravines and riverbeds, but you couldn't see them until you almost fell into them, and the few willows and black alders that struggled up through the sandy soil near the water were like visitors from another world. On the plain itself there were no trees at all, only tall feathered grasses that dipped and rose in green waves with every passing breeze.

As the land leveled, the sky expanded. At midday it was a vast sheet of incandescent blue, filled with immense clouds that raced before the wind, taking on strange spiritlike shapes. At dawn and at sunset, the white hot light broke into savage reds and purples, and at night, as Marrah and Arang lay on the ground, thousands of cold, brilliant stars glittered over their heads like crystal teeth.

It was a violent land that had spawned a violent people, and as Marrah rode under the implacable sun with a mouth as dry as straw, she began to understand how the nomads had come to worship Han. Then she would remember that this place too was part of the Goddess Earth, and no matter how harsh it seemed, it must have a purpose.

There were even times when she was forced to admit that the steppes were every bit as beautiful as Stavan had said. During the first weeks, the colors were unsurpassed. Mixed in with the tall, drying grasses of late summer, the last flowers of the season bloomed like bits of a broken rainbow. When the wind blew and the feathered stems swayed, they danced in and out between the golden blades in a dizzying, sweet-scented swirl.

"That one's called pheasant's eye," Dalish told her one morning, bending down from her horse to pluck a bright orange blossom, "and that yellow one over there is named sunbutter. The little pink blooms are morning stars, and the blue ones are baby's eyes." When Marrah expressed surprise, Dalish explained that among the Hansi flowers were considered women's things, which no doubt accounted for the poetry of their names.

Another week passed, the plain grew drier, and the flowers disappeared. Soon there was no shade anywhere, not even in the ravines: only grass, dust, and flies. Sometimes rain fell in blinding sheets that left them half drowned, and once it hailed so hard they had to take refuge under the horses. By now there was no wood to build fires so they ate cold food, some of it so repulsive that even though Marrah was hungry she often turned away in disgust. She particularly disliked raw cow's liver, but the nomads chewed on the bloody bits as if they were a great treat. Raw mice and skinned voles also nauseated her, but sometimes she could manage to choke down a bit of uncooked bird that had been plucked and well cleaned.

"When they're in their own camps, they cook over fires of dried dung and eat decent things like roasted mutton and cheese, plus the bulbs we women dig up and the wild grains and greens we gather," Dalish said. "But war parties like this one pride themselves on living like a wolf pack. They eat whatever's at hand, most of it raw and much of it rotten."

Arang held his nose and made a retching noise, and Dalish chuckled. Insects were another nomad favorite, she warned him, and if one of the warriors handed him a grasshopper, he'd better not puke. "It's a great honor, and if you don't eat it, legs and all, like it was the best honey cake ever to come out of your mother's oven, you're going to be in big trouble. Besides, grasshoppers aren't so bad if they're toasted. The nomads eat them like we eat nuts. You may even get a taste for them after a while."

They learned a lot of things from Dalish. She rode beside them day after day, teaching them Hansi, explaining the strange customs of the nomads, and warning them when they were about to do something dangerous. From Dalish they learned that in the spring the nomad women plucked wool from the molting sheep and pounded it into cloth rather than weaving it. They did have a few small looms, and sometimes they braided a little hemp or vegetable fiber to make bridles and belts, but pounded wool was what they wore year round. They had all sorts of ingenious ways of decorating this material, which they called "felt," but no matter what they did to it, felt was never as comfortable as linen.

The
Year
the
Horses
Came

279

"It's not only heavy, it itches," Dalish complained as she scratched at her elbow by way of illustration.

Metal refining was another skill the nomads lacked. According to Dalish, most of copper adornments they wore had been stolen from the border villages and reworked into sun signs by slave women. There was a permanent camp of these women somewhere on the steppes, but its location was a secret.

"Sometimes I've imagined what it would be like to rescue the coppersmiths and set them free, but since I can't even free myself, it's only a dream." Dalish frowned and looked down at the copper bracelets that jangled on her wrists, and Marrah and Arang fell silent. They knew she had to wear them; she was Slehan's concubine, after all, and no chief's concubine went bare-armed. Still, it was terrible to think of the poor slaves who had been forced to pound them out of temple adornments.

But their conversations weren't always so grim. Sometimes Dalish told them odd things that made them smile. One morning she explained that menstruating women were forbidden to touch milk because the nomads believed it would go sour. On another occasion, she claimed that warriors always urinated in the direction of the setting sun—an idea so silly that Marrah and Arang laughed and shook their heads, but later they realized she had been telling the truth.

But it was her stories of the Hansi gods that interested them the most. They already knew the nomads worshiped a sun god called Han, but Dalish explained that Han was also known as the God of the Shining Sky. The Hansi thought of Him as a fierce warrior chief who fed on the blood of His enemies at sunrise and sunset. The stars were His horses and cattle, and He drove them into the heavenly pastures each night and out each morning. The Hansi believed they were Han's special people, His "wolves," and Han had granted them the right to rule over everything on earth. After Han, their most important gods were Choatk, god of the underworld, and Aitnok, the storm god. When Marrah asked if the nomads had any goddesses, Dalish said they did, but all of them were wives and concubines with no power except through their divine masters.

"The most important thing you have to understand about the nomads is that they don't value women and children. They're warriors, and everything female fills them with contempt. We think of the Earth as the living body of the Goddess, but to them it's dead. The steppes are a prison Han exiled them to hundreds of generations ago when their first ancestors tried to steal the star cattle. Everything good and wonderful is male, and it's up there in the sky, invisible and out of reach."

When she'd finished explaining the gods to them, she tried to explain how the nomad tribes were organized, but there were so many chiefs and subchiefs that Marrah and Arang got hopelessly lost. It seemed the nomads spent most of their time stealing each other's cattle and fighting over water rights. Many of the feuds went back generations, and it didn't seem at all uncommon for one chief to pledge loyalty to another and then turn around and slaughter him.

"Let me try to make it simple for you," Dalish said one morning as they ambled through the endless grass. "You haven't been taken captive by the Hansi themselves but by a smaller group of tribes called the Chanki. Slehan is chief of the Chanki, and he and his boys are poor relations who owe the Hansi Great Chief loyalty because of some battle they lost, who knows how many generations ago." She smiled as if the thought of the Chanki losing a battle was pleasant.

"Zuhan always sends the Chanki to do his dirty work. Slehan may look like a big man among his own people, but just watch what happens to him when we get to Zuhan's camp. He'll crawl." Her smile faded, and she grew serious. "Or maybe he won't crawl this time. After all, he's bringing back the son of Achan and his aunt, not to mention new slave girls, so he's sure of a warm reception. True, most of the cattle he stole died or were eaten on the way, but anyone could have seen they weren't fit for the steppes. Slehan will have no trouble explaining that away, especially when he tells Zuhan what he's been longing to hear."

She stopped and gave Marrah and Arang a long, measured glance as if trying to decide whether or not to go on. Then she shrugged. "I suppose it's just a matter of time before you two figure out what's happening, so I might as well tell you now. Remember how you told me you took a warning to Shara?" They nodded. "Well, now you're taking something else to the Great Chief, something you'd probably give your lives not to take, but you don't have any choice. You see, when Zuhan's youngest son came back from the West"— she lowered her voice and looked around nervously—"he told the Great Chief that everything in the forest lands was shit. 'Not worth the trouble of raiding,' he said. 'Ugly women, stupid men, no gold,' and so forth. But unfortunately for him, Zuhan had already heard otherwise, so he ordered Slehan and his crew to head in that direction and find out who was telling the truth. Chanki war parties have been harassing the northern border villages for years, so at first Slehan just raided some villages farther south, but then he stumbled on Shambah, and you know the rest."

She took a deep breath and looked back at the slaves plodding wearily through the grass, urged on by mounted warriors, who prodded them every time they stumbled. "Slehan's taking captives and loot back to Zuhan to prove it's worthwhile to ride west, and I'm afraid when Zuhan sees it, it's going to put his youngest son in an awkward situation. Evidently Stavan lied to his father. Ordinarily, Zuhan would give him a traitor's death—cut off his hands and feet, put him on a sledge, pile brush around him, set it on fire, and let the horses drag him until he stopped screaming—but fortunately the Great Chief already thinks he was bewitched, so maybe he'll be spared."

Marrah had grown very pale at the mention of Stavan's name. This was the first time she'd been told they were actually heading toward the Great Chief's camp, but what joy was there in the knowledge when in the same breath she learned that Stavan might already have been murdered in ways too horrible to imagine? Arang was biting his lips, perhaps thinking the same thing.

Dalish looked at them sharply. "Whatever happens, there are a few things both of you have to remember. First, you can't stop Slehan from laying those gold temple adornments at Zuhan's feet and telling him there's more gold to be had in the forest lands. The gate to the West is open now, and it's going to take more than a woman and a boy to close it. Second, when you ride into the Great Chief's camp, neither of you should acknowledge his youngest son by so much as the flicker of an eyelash—unless, of course, you want to make sure Zuhan ties him on a burning sledge and puts one of you on either side to keep him company." She looked from Arang to Marrah, and a cruel grin spread over her face. "Now that would make a pretty fire."

Marrah frowned and Arang looked startled. Both of them were upset to see their friend smiling like a nomad and mocking death, but later they realized she had been brutal on purpose. She wanted to shock them and make them mad enough to remember, and she succeeded. Now when Marrah dreamed of Stavan, she often dreamed of walking toward him and then turning away. She would break into a run and he would run after her, calling her name. Suddenly an armed warrior would appear, ride her down, and grab her by the hair. Pulling her up on his horse, he would point to Stavan and demand to know how Stavan knew her.

"I don't have any idea," she'd cry. "I've never seen him before!" Sometimes the warrior would believe her and let her go; more often, he wouldn't. Fortunately, she was never able to remember what happened next.

Another week passed, and as they rode farther and farther east, Marrah began to understand why Dalish had never been able to escape. One day was so much like another it was hard to tell them apart. The flat land rolled on and on until you were lost without a river to follow or a single landmark worth remembering. Dalish insisted that the nomads were following ancient trails. "Only warriors are trained to see them," she said. She pointed to a labyrinth of small animal runs that snaked in and out of the tall grass. "You and I only see confusion, but they take their direction from the sun and stars and claim they can tell different bits of flatness apart. I think they have some extra sense that people born in kinder lands lack."

She must have been right, because one day near the end of summer they suddenly came upon a dozen leather tents pitched in a haphazard fashion along a stream so small it looked as if it would barely fill a cup. A herd of hobbled mares, long-haired sheep, and fat cattle was grazing nearby, guarded by small boys and dogs. Old men slept in the afternoon sun, and silent, brown-shawled women were bent over cooking fires.

"Slehan's camp," Dalish said, waving at the tents. "My home for the last seven years. How do you like it? How does it compare to the temples of Shara and the cities of the River of Smoke?" She spat in the direction of the cooking fires. "In my own village, I served the Bird Goddess. Here I gather dried cow shit for the fires, carry water, and fuck Slehan, making his four wives so jealous that they once actually stopped fighting with one another long enough to put a poison adder in my bed." She looked at Marrah's empty water skin. "You're going to have a hard time of it here. Women are pitted against each other, and you're not that kind. You and your brother are both too softhearted. I don't think you'll make it." And with that, she kicked her horse and rode away, leaving Marrah behind.

Feeling betrayed and insulted by the one person she'd come to trust, Marrah rode into the camp fuming with anger; she glared at everyone and got down off her horse like a woman who had never been afraid a day in her life, which, once again, was just what Dalish had intended.

The
Year
the
Horses
Came

283

They stayed in Slehan's camp one night, not long enough to learn much except that when their wives were present the nomads ate their food cooked instead of raw. The slaves were herded into a corral fenced with thorns, and the nightly forced sex stopped for the first time in weeks, presumably because the warriors were busy with the women they'd left behind. Marrah and Arang were given a small tent of their own, carpeted with soft rugs that were surprisingly comfortable, but whenever they looked through the flap they saw an armed warrior standing guard over them as usual.

At dusk two old women brought them a spit of mutton, some strange-tasting milk, and a pile of toasted bulbs that reminded Marrah of lilies. Everything was carried in baskets or laid out on pieces of leather as if they had no pottery, which, she later learned, was not the case. Despite what she had seen of the nomads, she was so used to honoring her elders that she tried to address the old women as if they were village mothers, but even her sign language alarmed them and when she made a stumbling attempt to say thank you in Hansi, they pulled their shawls over their faces and scurried away like frightened mice.

Disappointed, she and Arang turned to the food, which was the best they'd had since they left Shambah. Unfortunately, they drank all the milk before they realized it was like wine, and both of them spent the rest of the night alternating between foolish laughter and bouts of nausea that made them run for the tent flap. In the morning they woke up with fierce headaches. Later they learned that as the guests of honor they'd been given kersek, fermented mare's milk.

Dalish, who nearly laughed herself sick at the sight of them, explained that kersek was one of the three things Hansi warriors took before battle to make them fierce. The other two were bdash, a kind of cake made from the sticky gum of hemp flowers, and patiak, a mushroom that gave men the power to walk for days without eating or sleeping, provided they kept drinking their own urine. Of the three sacred foods, kersek was the only one women were permitted to consume, but as Marrah climbed unsteadily back on Tarka with a stomach that felt as if a host of nomads had already ridden through it, she found herself wishing the tribe had chosen to honor her and Arang in some other way.

Of the fifty or so women who had been taken captive when Shambah was burned, the nomads had intentionally weeded out the weak. Only thirty had lived to see the end of summer, and from these thirty, Slehan had chosen ten of the strongest. After bathing the chosen ones and dressing them in leggings and long tunics, the nomad women slipped hempen cords around their necks and tied them together in a line. Jeering and mocking and even spitting on them, they pushed the slaves toward the waiting warriors, who untied them, forced them to mount horses, and then tied them together again. Most of the women were terrified of the horses, and when one fell off they all fell. The warriors and their women seemed to find this very amusing. Finally the men stopped laughing and retied the women so they couldn't fall. Akoah was put at the head of the line, and as she rode past Marrah, she gave her a quick, desperate look, but as always they had no chance to speak. The nomad women had draped a string of copper adornments around Akoah's neck, tossed a shawl over her head, and painted her eyelids with black grease and her lips with ocher, and Marrah was relieved to see she'd been given a pair of boots.

"She's a special present for Zuhan," Dalish said. "The others are presents too, but not quite as special. You'll notice that while she has a shawl, they ride bareheaded and unadorned. That means they're just common slave girls. The nomads are very particular about dividing women up into different sorts."

"I don't understand the differences. It seems to me all their women are forced to have sex with men they don't want."

Dalish laughed. "You'll understand soon enough. You're a wife—or you will be, once they find you a suitable husband. Thanks to you, your friend's a concubine even though she was taken in battle. I used to be a slave, but in a weak moment Slehan made me his concubine, and believe me, I appreciate the difference. I have to wear paint so everyone knows I'm not a wife, but at least no one can fuck me without Slehan's permission."

Just then Slehan rode by and motioned for Marrah and Dalish to stop talking to each other. He was an impressive sight, mounted on a fine black gelding and dressed in richly embroidered leggings and some of the gold adornments he'd stolen from Shambah.

"Look at him," Dalish said contemptuously as soon as he was out of earshot. "His pride's long, but his dagger's short." And making an obscene gesture with her smallest finger, she kicked her mare into a fast trot.

The
Year
the
Horses
Came

285

Once again they rode east through the tall grasses. There were fewer warriors now. Most of Slehan's men had returned to their own camps, but those who were left were young and strong and they set a quick pace. Still, this was no war party. Every night just after sunset they stopped, built small fires, and cooked strips of meat on the hot rocks. The result was gritty but edible, and Marrah no longer had to look away when she put food in her mouth.

If she had been searching for Zuhan's camp on that endless, flat plain, she could have wandered until she was an old woman without finding so much as a burned-out campfire, but it was less than a week before Slehan's scouts came back with the news that they'd found the tracks of the Great Chief's herd. The season of snows was coming, and Zuhan had turned south, as expected. The scouts speculated that he was headed for the same place he'd camped last winter.

"He used never to camp twice in the same place," Dalish told Marrah. "But they say he's grown so old and powerful he no longer fears anyone. The spring before last he called up his warriors, and they wiped out the last of the Tcvali. Since then, Zuhan sits in his tent, smoking hemp, drinking kersek, and complaining he's run out of enemies."

The next morning they came to a great swath of flattened grass. Turning south, they followed it, and within a few days they saw the smoke of Zuhan's campfires smudging the horizon.

lthough the campfires looked close at hand, they rode for most of the morning before Zuhan's sentries intercepted them. The first two came riding up bareback, bows drawn and ready to shoot. They were hardly more than boys, but they challenged Slehan as if they had a whole war party behind them.

"If you come in peace, disarm yourselves," they commanded, and to Marrah's astonishment, Slehan and his warriors threw their spears to the ground and unbuckled their swords. The sentries rode closer and inspected the pile of weapons. Then they inspected the unarmed warriors. They seemed suspicious, as well they might since Slehan and his men still wore daggers long enough to slit their throats, but evidently some kind of custom had been satisfied. The tallest wheeled around and rode off to tell Zuhan he had visitors. As soon as he was out of sight, the one who remained positioned his horse so any man trying to retrieve a weapon would have to fight his way to it.

All in all, it was as unfriendly a welcome as Marrah had ever seen, but it must have been the way the Hansi usually greeted guests because no one seemed offended or surprised. When a dozen more warriors charged up on horseback and surrounded them, Slehan's men took it in stride. As for Slehan, he turned his back on the armed guards as if they were some minor annoyance, and if he was at all intimidated by the number of arrows aimed at his heart, he didn't show it.

The same could not be said of Marrah. Zuhan's warriors radiated violence the way a fire radiated heat, and she could easily imagine them turning on Slehan. Perhaps Arang was thinking the same thing, because when she looked over at him he was staring straight ahead with a grim expression on his face. Dalish seemed at ease, which was encouraging, but when Marrah looked more closely she saw Dalish was gripping the reins of her horse so hard her knuckles were white.

They rode on. The grass around the camp was taller than it had been in other parts of the steppes, and it grew thickly: brown, green, and lush as hair, topped with heavy heads that brushed against their wool leggings, leaving chaff and seeds behind. Soon they came to a wide, flat area where the animals had cropped it short, and then to the herd itself. The horses came first, standing in small groups, head to tail, swatting flies off one another. Each stallion was surrounded by a dozen or more mares and lanky-legged colts; they were wild-looking, short-maned, stocky beasts, and if they'd ever been broken it didn't show. Beyond the horses was a great herd of cattle, stretching out in all directions as far as the eye could see, all busy grazing. They were lean, hornless, and stubborn-looking like the horses, and some of the larger bulls looked quite dangerous, but the warriors rode past them without a second glance. Closer to the camp, within easy walking distance of the tents, the nomads had pastured their long-haired sheep, their goats, some riding horses, and a herd of hobbled milk mares.

In many ways, the animals were a beautiful sight; if Marrah hadn't been so worried, she would probably have enjoyed seeing so many different kinds peacefully grazing together. No two were the same color: the horses alone came in browns and chestnuts, tans and grays, blacks and whites and everything in between; the cattle were as different as a pile of unglazed potsherds; and the fat long-haired sheep looked wonderfully comic as they waddled from place to place like big overstuffed pillows. But she had no heart for either humor or beauty. The Hansi tents were coming closer by the minute; just ahead, love and trouble were waiting for her, so mixed together she felt only confusion and fear every time she looked up and saw the camp.

Long ago, when she was a little girl, Sabalah had warned her to be careful what she wished for or the Goddess might give it to her. At the time, that advice had seemed like another piece of grown-up nonsense, but now she understood what her mother had meant. For over two years she'd been wishing to see Stavan again: she'd gone into the Dreaming Cave to look for some sign of him, stood on the cliffs of Shara and watched the boats come in, begged the Goddess for a vision or a word. Now her wish had been granted. She was being taken to the very place where she was most likely to meet him, but what a reunion! If she so much as spoke to him, he might be killed; if she got off her horse and ran to him and hugged him and asked him to tell her what he'd been doing since they last saw each other, they'd probably both be killed. Even if she rode past him as if she'd never seen him before, something terrible could happen. The nomads might be savage and unpredictable, but they weren't stupid. Arang looked nothing like Achan. He was small and dark, while Stavan's brother had been tall and yellow-haired. Perhaps Zuhan would fly into a rage as soon as he caught sight of her brother, denounce him as an imposter, and execute them both. Or if Arang survived, perhaps Zuhan would take one look at her, realize she was the witch who had enchanted Stavan, and order one of his warriors to put a spear through her before she could cause any more trouble. In either case, Stavan could easily die trying to defend them.

The thought of the three of them going back to the Mother with Hansi spears in their chests was disturbing. She rode with her head down, lost in thought, trying to puzzle it all out. The short mane of her horse stretched out beneath her eyes like a raised path, rippling a little with each stride the animal took. When she looked up again, she found that time had run out: they were on the outskirts of Zuhan's camp, and the first tent was only a few hundred paces away.

The camp was much smaller than she'd thought it would be—so much smaller that she blinked and took a second look. She had expected to see hundreds of tents, but there were only forty or so, pitched along the banks of a small river that curled like a slender thread over copper-colored stones. As always the sky overhead was spectacular—as blue as a bolt of dyed Shamban linen, shot through with small white clouds that seemed to have been raked into furrows—but the camp itself was nothing to brag about. A few of the largest tents were finely made, and one big white one had been elaborately decorated with sun signs, but most had been mended more

The
Year
the
Horses
Came

289

times than not, stitched together with bits of hide that gave them a shabby, exhausted look. Because of the shortage of good wood for tent poles, they were all lopsided and clung close to the ground like a heap of withered brown mushrooms. Later, she learned there was plenty of room inside, but her first impression was that Stavan's people lived in a place as poor as any fishing village and not nearly as comfortable.

As they entered the camp, children came running, dogs barked, and women stood up with spits of meat in their hands to watch them pass. There were a dozen men who could have been Stavan and weren't: a dozen or more just his age, with yellow hair and blue eyes, who didn't have his face or his smile. Marrah didn't know whether to be disappointed or relieved.

They rode on a little farther. Suddenly, without warning, they were surrounded by still another band of tall fierce-looking warriors, who reined in their horses in a cloud of dust, scattering women, dogs, and children in all directions. The leader of the new welcoming committee was a tall man with a sun tattooed on his left cheek and a missing left ear. Glaring at Slehan, the man with the missing ear began to yell various questions in a harsh, crowlike voice. Although Marrah's Hansi wasn't very good, she had no trouble understanding what he was saying. He was the leader of Zuhan's bodyguards. Did they come in peace and did they come unarmed, or were they prepared to die?

Slehan gave the man a cool, arrogant smile. Did Zuhan's warriors think he was fool enough to ride into the Great Chief's camp looking for trouble? Let them put away their spears. He brought great treasure from the West: slave girls, gold, cattle, Achan's son.

When the warriors heard Achan's name, they lowered their spears and stared at Arang in awe. Even the man with the missing ear looked impressed. Would Slehan be so good as to come to Zuhan's tent at once to tell him the joyful news? the leader asked politely. Slehan would. The leader thanked him. He even bowed to him. The change in his attitude was amazing. He and his warriors were all humbled now. Marrah thought some of them still looked suspicious, but perhaps that was only her own fear getting in the way. The leader put away his weapons and said something she couldn't follow. It was probably an apology or a welcome, because when he was finished he rode up to Arang and kissed him on both cheeks and everyone cheered.

After that, things happened much too quickly. Before she quite realized what was going on, the leader and his men had hurried Arang, Slehan, and the Chanki warriors off in the direction of Zuhan's tent, leaving the women and sentries behind. Once Arang was out of sight, there were no more polite exchanges. The sentries forced the slaves to dismount by poking at them with the butts of their spears and bellowing orders that Dalish translated. Rounding them up as if they were a small herd of cattle, they marched the women off. Dalish and Marrah were then ordered to dismount. Their feet had hardly touched the earth before Dalish was ordered to go to Zuhan's tent and Marrah was handed over to three sturdy middle-aged women who indicated by gestures that she was to follow them.

The women were big, and Marrah wasn't sure she liked the way they were inspecting her. She'd seen that look on the nomads' faces before, and it always meant trouble. She turned to Dalish. "What do you think they're up to?"

"I'll ask them." She said something to the women in Hansi, and one of them replied. "She says they want to offer you something to eat and drink."

Marrah was somewhat reassured. Even though the women didn't look exactly friendly, they didn't look altogether hostile, so she followed them, hoping for the best. She didn't like being separated from Arang and Dalish, but after the dusty ride through the herd, she could use a drink of water. Besides, she didn't have any choice—not with armed warriors watching her every move.

As she and the women walked through the camp, people came out of their tents to stare, but no one said anything and no one followed. Once again, she saw several young men who resembled Stavan, but he was nowhere in sight.

Soon they came to a tent that hardly looked tall enough to accommodate a child. When Marrah stepped inside, she nearly fell flat on her face. The tent had been pitched over a hole some ten or twelve hands deep, lined snugly with wool rugs. She had to admit this wasn't a bad idea when you lived in a place where the wind blew hard enough to stop birds in mid-flight, but it would have been nice if someone had warned her. She steadied herself on one of the tent poles and looked around, curious to see how ordinary families lived, but except for a rack of meat drying by the fire pit, there was nothing in sight but some baskets, a few pillows, and two or three of the large leather bags the nomads carried all their worldly

The
Year
the
Horses
Came

291

goods in. As far as she could tell, whoever lived in this tent had no pottery except a few sunbaked jars and griddles of the most primitive kind, no metal, and no loom. Everything had obviously been designed to be picked up, tossed on the back of a packhorse, and carried off at a moment's notice.

As her eyes adjusted, she began to see other things—weapons mostly: a long dagger in a leather case, two singing bows, a sheaf of spears, a quiver of arrows, a horsehide shield painted with suns, a blunt battle-ax heavy enough to crush a skull with one blow, and a strange, wicked-looking thing that looked like a cross between a spear and an ax. She shuddered and turned away. The Hansi might be poor potters, but when it came to making things that killed, no people could match them. It wasn't reassuring to see so many weapons, but undoubtedly every family owned dozens.

The rugs under her feet were more welcoming. She was standing on a large mat of brown felt decorated with a border of horses and stars appliquéd in white wool. If the tent hadn't smelled of dogs, horses, and sour milk, it would have been a rather pleasant place to live.

She suddenly realized that the three women had stopped talking and were staring at her. Something was about to happen, but what? Where was the water they'd promised, and where was the food? The fire pit was full of cold ashes. The leather buckets were empty. I don't like this at all, she thought, but I can't let them suspect I'm frightened. She straightened up to her full height (which wasn't much compared to theirs) and gave them her bravest smile. It was a smile that said You don't scare me, and she hoped they believed it.

"Your home . . . beautiful," she observed in stumbling Hansi, but the women just went on staring. "How many children you have?" The youngest woman held up six fingers, but the others said something to her and she lowered them. Marrah remembered that Dalish said Hansi women started bearing children as soon as they came of age and often had as many as fifteen before they stopped. Of those fifteen, usually only two or three lived long enough to have children of their own. It sounded like a horrible life, and she knew if she hadn't been so anxious she would have felt sorry for them. On the other hand, maybe asking them how many children they had hadn't been such a good idea. She decided to try again.

"My name Marrah. What your names?"

They said nothing. Suddenly it dawned on her that they were moving closer. She tried to back away, but there was nowhere to go.

As soon as they saw her flinch, the oldest woman yelled something, and all three jumped her.

Marrah yelled back; she kicked and slugged and even tried to claw her way out of their grip, but she was hopelessly outnumbered. One grabbed her, one held her, and one caught her arm and twisted it behind her back, forcing her to the floor. When she was completely immobilized, the largest gave a grunt of satisfaction and settled down on her chest, pinning her to the rug. Seizing Marrah by the neck, the woman looked straight into her eyes and grinned. She had a square face, reddish hair, and blue tattoo marks on her cheeks. Her eyeteeth had been filed to points, and despite her embroidered robes and many adornments she smelled like a horse.

She said something in Hansi, and the others laughed. Encouraged, she let fly a whole string of words, and they laughed some more. By now Marrah was thoroughly terrified. She tried to bite the arm that held her down and got a hard slap in the face. "Cagk," the woman ordered, making it clear she'd like nothing better than to hit Marrah again.

Marrah stopped fighting and lay there frightened half out of her wits. What in the name of the Goddess were they going to do to her? Was she about to be raped like Akoah or killed outright like Cyen? She'd been a fool to think the nomad women were any less dangerous than their men. Perhaps Zuhan had already found out about Stavan, and these women had been ordered to hold her prisoner while the warriors prepared the sledge that would drag her to her death.

But if they were preparing to kill her, the women were certainly behaving strangely. Now they had her down, they were ignoring her. One pulled out a small clay pipe, stuffed some dried leaves in the bowl, and went outside to borrow a few live coals from a neighbor. When she came back, the pipe was lit. She passed it around, and the women began to talk and laugh, pausing sometimes to cough and slap each other on the back. Whatever was in the pipe seemed to be making them cheerful, and Marrah hoped they smoked a lot more of it. She knew by now that they weren't priestesses inhaling sacred smoke. According to Dalish, the Hansi had no priestesses or village mothers or women of power of any kind.

She tried to turn her head, and the woman who was holding her bent down and inspected her closely. "Cagk?" she repeated. Marrah nodded, and the woman relaxed her grip a little, but Marrah's relief was short-lived. She was just trying to think of some way to convince them to let her sit up when the tent flap opened with a rush of cool air and four older women entered. One was very tall and richly dressed with a small band of copper around her throat and another in her hair. She looked a little like a priestess queen dressed in ritual adornments, except that no priestess would have had such a cruel mouth and arrogant eyes.

The women who had wrestled Marrah to the floor seemed intimidated. They put away their pipe and bowed, and one of them led the queen—or whatever she was—to a large, soft pillow. The woman sat down in a billow of fine robes and a jangle of adornments. Her arms were covered with bracelets from shoulder to wrist, and she had several nose rings, one of which was gold. Her three attendants squatted down at a respectful distance, and there was a brief silence. Everyone looked at Marrah expectantly. Marrah started to get frightened again. Now what?

She didn't have long to wonder. The queen smiled and waved her hand as if she were swatting a fly. Suddenly, the woman who had been sitting on Marrah's chest grabbed her by the throat again, and at the same moment the other two pinned down her arms and legs so she was even more helpless than she'd been before. Two of the attendants rose to their feet, came over to where she was lying, and began to tug off her leggings. She yelled and fought, but if she had been outnumbered before, she was doubly outnumbered now. Soon they had her stripped from the waist down.

She lay there, feeling ridiculous and terrified. A kind of cold dread washed over her. What in the name of the Goddess were they going to do next?

All at once one of the women grabbed the lips of her vagina and spread them. At this Marrah screamed with all her might, but once again no one paid any attention. The next thing she knew, the queen and all the other women were gathered around peering at her—peering up her actually—and making satisfied clucking noises. One of them even pulled back the tent flap so the others could get a better look.

Crimson with rage and embarrassment and half petrified with fear, she lay there helpless while they poked about. Finally, they seemed satisfied. The queen motioned for the women to release her and allowed her to pull down her tunic and put her leggings back on. It took her a few moments to realize they were done with her, but when she finally understood that they didn't intend to do her any more harm she had to fight back tears of relief.

Then the strangest thing of all happened. As she sat there with her arms wrapped around her legs, glaring at them and wishing she knew enough Hansi to curse them as they deserved to be cursed, they started to congratulate her. There was no doubt that was what they were doing, because each one in turn smiled, patted her on the back, said something in Hansi, and then kissed her formally on both cheeks. Even the queen kissed her like she was a long-lost daughter.

Wonderful. What a relief to know they approved of her private parts. If this was the way they welcomed strangers when they were feeling friendly, what did they do when they were feeling hostile?

The kissing and patting continued. When everyone had taken a turn, the queen and her attendants left the tent. Time passed and soon they returned, wreathed in smiles. The queen pointed to Marrah and said something to the others that seemed to excite them. The next thing Marrah knew, she was being led out into the sunshine, where a large crowd of women and girls was waiting expectantly. There must have been nearly a hundred, all dressed in leggings, long tunics, and brown shawls. As soon as they caught sight of Marrah, they began to cheer, clap their hands, and make a weird, high-pitched warbling noise. It took her a moment or two to realize they were singing.

They were being friendly so there was no need to panic, but what was going on and where was Dalish? If she had ever needed a translator, she needed one now, but Dalish was nowhere to be seen and neither was Arang. She looked past the singing women and saw that everything in the camp had come to a standstill. Meat was cooking untended on the fires, little children were running around unsupervised, and the men had all gone somewhere—presumably to Zuhan's tent to hear Slehan's account of the raid on Shambah. Perhaps they were celebrating his victory, because as the women broke into another chorus of warbles, drums began to beat. The sound of the drumming excited the women even more. The singing rose to fever pitch, and some of the younger ones linked arms and began to dance around Marrah, calling out things to her that she would have given anything to be able to understand. As the women danced, they kept moving in on her so she had to move away to keep from colliding with them. It took her a while to realize they were slowly herding her toward the river, but even when she understood they intended to drive her into the water, there was nothing she could do but keep moving.

When the dancers got her down to the river, the three women who had sat on her grabbed her by the hands and dragged her in. Fortunately, the river was shallow, because as soon as she was waist deep they started trying to push her under. She fought back, but they laughed and pushed some more. When they started to scrub her with handfuls of fine sand, she saw they were just trying to give her a bath, so she stopped fighting and let them.

The water was cold, but not all that cold for someone who had been raised on the shore of the Sea of Gray Waves, and once she stopped struggling, the women were surprisingly gentle. Pulling off her tunic, they unbraided her hair, wet it, lathered it with some kind of plant juice that smelled vaguely like mint, and rinsed it until it squeaked. Then they led her to shore, rubbed her dry with a clean blanket, and seated her on a rock, and one began to comb out her hair while the rest stood around singing and clapping their hands.

Up to that point, the bath had been a more or less pleasant experience, but soon things got strange again. When her hair was combed and fairly dry, a women came forward with a bag of something that proved to be rancid butter. Marrah protested and made frantic motions to convey the fact that she thought it smelled awful, but either they didn't understand or they didn't care. Ignoring her, they proceeded to butter her from head to foot, smiling all the while as if they were doing her a great favor. When her curls had been reduced to a single, slick thing that looked like a long, greasy snake, they braided her hair again, wound the braid around her head, and stuck feathers and ornaments in it.

When she stood up, she felt as if she were balancing a pudding on her head, but the women must have thought she looked lovely because there were smiles everywhere. In place of her old leggings and the linen tunic she had worn all the way from Shambah, she was given new clothes made of matted white wool and white calfskin boots that tied at the ankles. When she insisted on keeping her old belt and her medicine bag, they let her—although not without a long discussion and many frowns. The final thing they did before they led her back to the tent was to muffle her in a long white shawl so only her eyes showed.

And that was it. She expected to be taken to Zuhan or at least brought to the queen's tent, but instead she sat alone all afternoon, well buttered and looking like a lumpy white bag. Outside, the women went on singing and dancing and the drums went on thumping, but whatever the party was in honor of, she didn't seem to be invited. Perhaps that was just as well. She no longer feared they were going to kill her, but she suspected she wasn't going to be happy when she learned why they'd dressed her up.

The day grew warmer, and the air in the tent heated up. By the time the shadows were long, she had begun to feel like someone who had tripped and fallen into a trough of itching ointment, but every time she tried to throw off the shawl or pull up the ends of her leggings to enjoy a good scratch, some woman would poke her head through the tent flap and cluck at her disapprovingly.

Late in the afternoon Dalish finally appeared. One look at her face and Marrah knew she didn't bring good news. She leapt to her feet and seized Dalish's hands. "What have they done to Arang?" she cried. "Have they hurt him?"

Dalish squeezed her hands reassuringly. "Don't worry. Arang's fine. They're feeding him honey and toasted grasshoppers this very minute."

"Grasshoppers? Oh, poor Arang. He hates them so!" It wasn't a sensible thing to say, and she knew it. What did grasshoppers matter when Arang's life was at stake.

Dalish smiled a little, and the red tassels on her forehead swung like a row of silent bells. "Arang may hate grasshoppers, but he's very brave. He's sitting beside Zuhan right this minute, munching away like a little Hansi chief. Every once in a while, they honor him with something else disgusting, and he eats that too and says thank you."

"They're honoring him?" Marrah was so relieved she could hardly speak. She sat down and put her face in her hands. When she looked up, Dalish was looking back with a sympathetic expression. "Then they must believe he's really Achan's son."

"Yes, luckily for us they do." Dalish settled down beside her. "Zuhan's not only swallowed the whole story, he's decided to adopt your brother into the tribe." She mopped her face with the hem of her shawl and sighed. "Personally, I think it's something of a miracle. Arang looks no more like Zuhan's grandson than I do, but the old man's frantic for an heir. He knows the subchiefs will never follow Vlahan the Bastard, and as for your former lover"—she lowered her voice and looked around cautiously—"the less said the better."

Marrah longed to ask her if she'd seen Stavan, but the look on her face indicated the question wouldn't be welcome. There was a strained silence.

The
Year
the
Horses
Came

297

"So when does this adoption ceremony take place?"

"Right away." Dalish mopped her face again.

"Do I get to go to it?"

"Everyone gets to go. That's the whole point: Zuhan's old, and rumor has it he's not in the best of health. He has no intention of dying before he's makes every last man, woman, and child in this tribe accept your brother as his legitimate grandson."

Suddenly Marrah understood why she'd been bathed and buttered. She pulled up the cuffs of her leggings and gave herself the luxury of a thorough scratch. Evidently she'd worried herself nearly sick for no reason. "So that's why they greased my hair and dressed me in this fancy outfit."

There was an unpleasant silence. Dalish didn't smile as Marrah had expected her to do. Instead, she looked down at her hands. "Not exactly." She looked up again, and a pained expression crossed her face. "I should have told you right away, but it isn't easy to bring you such a message."

Something cold and unpleasant filled the tent. "What are you talking about? What message?"

Dalish mopped her forehead again. There was a guilty look in her eyes, one Marrah didn't like. It was a look of complicity and betrayal. "They dressed you in white wool because—" She paused and began again, and Marrah had the distinct impression she was stalling for time. "Did you know that old Zulike, Zuhan's peace-weaving wife, has publicly declared that you're a virgin?" She smiled a little, but it wasn't a real smile. "Zulike said she was very surprised to see that you had a maidenhead, especially since you're so old, but I told her you'd begged your father to refuse all offers of marriage so you could devote your life to your nephew, and she seemed impressed. Of course she doesn't know anything about how our people share joy. Around here men never wait to enter a woman. I don't imagine the nomads have ever seen anyone over twelve with a maidenhead intact."

Marrah had no idea what she was talking about and said so. She was impatient and worried, and she was starting to feel angry as well. She wished Dalish would stop looking at her that way. She needed to know the truth, but Dalish was hedging.

"A maidenhead." Dalish mopped her forehead again. "You know: that little piece of skin a woman usually has over her birth place, the one that breaks the first time she lets a man enter her. By all accounts yours is a little the worse for wear, but it's still there, which is the important thing. The nomads worship a woman's maidenhead, and every man wants to be the first to break it."

Marrah was too amazed to speak. Finally she found her tongue. "That's the single most disgusting thing I've ever heard! No wonder you didn't want to tell me."

Dalish bit her lip and looked away. Her face suddenly turned stony, and when she lifted her eyes to Marrah's they were hard. "I wish that was all, but the fact is, you've only heard half the news." She paused. "Zuhan sent me here to tell you that he's giving you to his son, Vlahan." She spoke quickly. "You're in luck: you're going to be Vlahan's wife, not his concubine. The wedding ceremony takes place this afternoon, and there's no use your falling apart, or screaming, or making any objections, because there's not a thing you or I or anyone else can do about it."

Marrah felt as if she'd been hit. She rose to her feet. "You can't mean it. This is terrible." She paced across the tent. "I can't do it."

Dalish rose and stood with her hands folded across her chest. When she spoke her voice was like ice. "Be quiet, I tell you. What do you expect me to do, go back to Zuhan and tell him you've refused his son? Count your blessings. They could have slit your throat by now, but instead Zuhan's honoring you."

"Honoring me!"

"Yes, honoring you." Dalish's voice broke, and she began to cry. "Marrah, I can't help you. I want to, but I can't. If I tell Zuhan you won't do it, he'll probably kill both of us. Vlahan's no prize, but you'll just have to marry him." She seized Marrah by the shoulders as if she was going to shake her, but instead she drew her close. "Dear friend, I'm sorry. I'm so sorry. I—" Perhaps she was going to say she was sorry a third time, but if so, she never got the word out. Her voice broke in mid-sentence. Putting her hands on Marrah's cheeks, she drew her still closer and kissed her on the forehead. "They'll come get you just before sunset. Be brave, dear." Then she turned and fled from the tent.

# CHAPTER SIXTEEN

J ust before sunset a dry wind began to blow. It came from the west, scattering seeds and leaching the last bits of green from the summer grasses. The swifts rode it, diving for small insects; the gray partridges and black-bibbed quail hid from it; the horses and cattle turned their backs on it; and even the sheep had enough sense to close their eyes against the dust. It wasn't one of the great winds of midsummer that swept up from the south, baking the steppes and making life intolerable, but it was strong enough to flap tents and chap lips, and as Marrah stood among the Hansi women watching her brother being adopted into the tribe, the wind burned in her throat like hot ashes and her eyes wept of their own accord.

It seemed right that she should be crying that evening, even if the tears were only wind tears and her heart was cold with despair. It was an incredible piece of luck that Zuhan was adopting Arang, but no matter how hard she tried to tell herself this, everything about the ceremony made her feel as if she were losing him forever.

301

The drums were the worst part. As she stood there, guarded on all sides by the women, the drums hammered and hammered at her until she felt as if they were pushing her heart out of shape and beating her into submission. There weren't just a few drums; there were dozens. Wild men played them, bare-chested and crazed-looking men with teeth filed to points and white skeletons painted on their bodies. As they struck the drums, they howled like wolves and screamed like wildcats, and their eyes rolled back in their heads.

The nomads moved to the drums, not in any kind of orderly dance but in an ominous shuffling rhythm, back and forth, side to side, pushing against Marrah and carrying her with them. She felt lost in the smell and heat of their bodies. They were so much taller she couldn't see over them, so much heavier she couldn't hold her ground, so she was forced to dance, and while she danced she cried her wind tears and thought of Arang and her coming marriage.

Sometimes when she collided with a wool shawl or stepped on someone's foot, a face looked down at her, but otherwise she was ignored. Still, they must have noticed her because after a while the women shoved her up front where she could see. But it was an evening when it would have been better not to have eyes or ears. All her life she remembered her first sight of old Zuhan, the Great Chief. He sat cross-legged on a low platform covered with white rugs. Behind him, the tall grasses swayed like a wave about to break, and overhead the sky was turning a sullen red, shot through with gold and a purple color that reminded her of crushed grapes.

He was an old man, gray-haired and lean with a face that looked disturbingly like Stavan's. He had the same strong jaw that Stavan had, the same slender nose and high cheekbones, but there was no trace of Stavan's gentleness or good-nature there, and Marrah could see at once that only a fool would expect mercy from him. His face was the face of a man who loved power: intelligent, hard, vindictive. The coldness of the steppes had gotten into his eyes, and she could see the darkness of long winters in the way he held his mouth and the violence and heat of summer in the set of his jaw. He stared out at the crowd—and perhaps at her—with cold blue eyes that never blinked. On his head he wore a sun crown of gold and copper, and in his right hand he held a horse-headed scepter heavy enough to crush a man's skull.

Arang sat beside him, looking like a small, frightened child. At the sight of him she felt pity and love fill her heart—and anger too. They'd done things to Arang that were cruel and stupid; things only outlaws would do to a twelve-year-old: stripped him down to a leather loincloth and painted him to make him look fierce, drawn a white wolf mask on his face, marked him with red ocher, hung a string of wolf paws around his neck, punched holes in his ears and stuck hawk feathers in them, and cut off most of his hair. But they hadn't been able to erase the frightened expression from his face. He sat coiled up around himself, clutching his knees in his hands, and every time he looked at Zuhan or the drummers or, worse yet, at the terrible leather-lined cup at his feet, he trembled like a rabbit about to bolt. The cup was obviously made from a human skull and the Goddess only knew what Zuhan intended to do with it, but Marrah couldn't call to Arang over the drums and tell him to be brave. She couldn't offer him anything, not even the sight of her face, because in the dust and the dancing she was only another shawled figure swaying in front of him, one of hundreds, and it was clear he didn't recognize her. And all the while the drums were saying: *He is taken into the tribe. He is taken. He is a Hansi.*

Time passed, the drums went on beating, and the women went on shoving Marrah from side to side until her feet were sore and she was exhausted. At last, just when she had given up hope of ever hearing anything else, the drumming stopped and Slehan came forward to present Zuhan with the loot he had taken from Shambah. He walked proudly through the crowd looking every inch the conqueror, but the truth was, he didn't have much to offer: only some gold temple adornments, some bolts of cloth, the slaves, and Akoah. Akoah was so muffled in her shawl that Marrah couldn't see her face, but she could tell she was terrified by the way she shrank from Zuhan.

Zuhan hardly seemed to notice Akoah and the slaves. He inspected the bolts of cloth and the temple adornments, testing the weight of the linen and scratching at the gold as if he thought Slehan might be trying to trick him by offering copper. As he sifted through the loot, his eyes narrowed and he frowned. It was clear he was seriously displeased. Shambah hadn't been a rich city, and there were only a few ceremonial chains, some earrings, and half a dozen bracelets carved with triangles and other goddess signs. Zuhan fished out one of the earrings—a small gold butterfly about the size of Marrah's thumbnail—crushed it, and threw it at Slehan contemptuously. Then he made a short speech. Marrah couldn't understand the words, but she didn't need to. The meaning was clear. "Is that all?" he was asking Slehan. "Is this what you've brought me? Where's the rest?"

She expected Slehan to try to defend himself or at least apologize, because anyone with any sense could see that the next thing Zuhan

The
Year
the
Horses
Came

303

would do was order his warriors to seize Slehan and shake the rest of the nonexistent loot out of him, but instead of begging Zuhan's pardon, Slehan smiled a long, cold smile, reached into his leather pouch, pulled out a necklace, and presented it to Zuhan with an arrogant bow. It was hard to see what Slehan had to smile about. The necklace was ugly, very long but crudely made. Still, there must have been something in the gift because a murmur of approval ran through the crowd, and the women next to Marrah made little hissing noises of pleasure. How odd the nomads were. Here was this primitive ornament—which on second glance didn't even look like a necklace—not made of gold or even copper, yet everyone was admiring it as if it had been crafted by the best goldsmiths in Shara. The truth was, it looked like a string of dried figs. But odd figs: they came . . . in pairs. . . .

Suddenly she realized what she was looking at. She closed her eyes and shoved her shawl in her mouth to keep from screaming. A wave of revulsion passed through her. When she recovered enough to open her eyes again, Zuhan was holding the necklace and inspecting it from all angles. He seemed pleased. Perhaps he was thinking it would be easy to get more treasures in a place where so many men could be conquered by so few.

At last Zuhan grew tired of admiring Slehan's string of horrors. He waved his hand, assigning the slaves: five to Slehan, no doubt to reward him for such a great victory; four to various warriors who must have served him in some special way. The women went off weeping. When the slaves had been disposed of, Zuhan indicated that Akoah should stand behind him. Later Marrah learned this meant he had taken her as a concubine.

Again the drummers began to drum, but this time the rhythm was slower: very regular and almost hypnotic. The beats rose and fell like waves slapping against the shore, and the women around Marrah moved more languorously. It was clear by now that many of them were in a trance state, but not the trance state priestesses experienced. When Marrah looked to either side, she saw their lips were parted slightly and their eyes had a faraway, dreamy look, as if they were waiting for an imaginary lover who would never arrive.

But she was wrong about that. The Hansi women knew exactly who they were waiting for, and he wasn't imaginary at all. Suddenly the drums stopped again, the crowd parted, and she saw a small herd of horses being led through the throng by five of the oddest-looking men she had ever seen. They had been painted blood red from the tops of their heads to the tips of their toes, and their long hair stuck straight out from their heads for three handspans or more, like haloes of fire. They must have been costumed to represent the sun, because the man who followed them definitely represented lightning. His face was painted with white rain signs, and his body was black except for a jagged white bolt of lightning that ran from the top of his left shoulder down his left side. As he came closer, she saw the lightning bolt had been painted over a long, ugly scar.

Although the man was scarred, he was in no way crippled, and he walked proudly, strutting past the nomads, who bowed to him as if he were the Goddess incarnate. His odd wedge-shaped face, greenish eyes, and small nose gave him a wolfish look and made it impossible to tell how old he was. He could have been thirty or fifty or even seventy, but if he was an old man, he had the body of a young one: muscles like rocks and long, cruel-looking hands.

As he drew near to Marrah, she heard the women around her whisper "Changar."

The Hansi diviner stopped in front of Zuhan and made the smallest possible bow. It wasn't really a bow at all, just a nod of the head, but Zuhan seemed satisfied. He nodded back as if to say, This man is almost—but not quite—my equal, and lifted his horse-headed scepter. As soon as the crowd saw the scepter lifted, the men cheered and the women began to warble. The drummers started drumming furiously, moving their hands so fast that from where Marrah was standing they seemed to have two complete sets of fingers. If she had known what was coming next, she might have tried to push her way to the back of the crowd again, but instead she just stood there, half deafened by the noise.

When the cheering had died down a little, Changar turned and motioned for the horses to be brought to him. Even Marrah could tell they were exceptionally fine: five mares and five young stallions, all strong and fit and clear-eyed, with glossy coats and manes plaited with bits of red thread. They had been hobbled so they wouldn't bolt through the crowd, but there was still something wild and beautiful about them. They had the look of animals that had never been tamed.

When the horses were in place, Changar stood absolutely still for a few moments. Perhaps he was admiring the animals, or perhaps he was talking to one of his gods. In any case, it was clear by now that he was about to perform some kind of important religious ceremony.

The
Year
the
Horses
Came

305

After a while, he approached the horses and began to speak to them in their own language, whinnying softly and stroking their heaving sides. The horses' eyes were wide with fright and several of them had their ears laid back against their heads, but at the touch of his hand they relaxed. Marrah was surprised to see how gentle he was with the beasts. He cooed to them like a lover and sang to them like a mother.

But his gentleness was all pretense. When the horses had stopped struggling, he said something in a low voice, and two of the sun warriors stepped forward and handed him their daggers. They were wicked-looking weapons with hilts worked in copper and bone blades edged with flint. Changar stuck one dagger in the earth—the sign of Han, Marrah recalled. The other he held by the hilt, close to his side where the horses couldn't see it.

After that there were some prayers, some songs, even some chanting done in a low drone that raised the hair on her arms, but for a long time nothing else happened. Then suddenly Changar walked over to the nearest horse and slit its throat. Before the poor animal had fallen—before Marrah had time to scream or the crowd had time to cheer—he had passed to the next horse and killed it too. On he went down the line, moving so swiftly he seemed to fly, and every time his dagger touched horsehide, blood gushed onto the ground. The poor beasts bucked and screamed and tried to kick, but they had been well hobbled and not one escaped. When all ten lay in the dust bleeding to death, Changar seized the skull drinking cup and filled it from their throats like a man filling a jar from a fountain.

She wanted to turn away from the sight of that bloody cup, but she couldn't. The only animal she had ever seen sacrificed was the she-goat Stavan had killed over his brother's grave, but that had been nothing compared to this. This was a massacre; it was like Shambah all over again, only this time defenseless horses had died instead of defenseless people.

She had the feeling that she was being given a look into the hearts of the nomads, and what she saw made her sick with fear. There hadn't been any need to kill those horses. No one was hungry; no one needed their hides to patch a tent. Ten beautiful animals had died, screaming and terrified, because the Hansi thought their god liked to see his creatures suffer. Because of some terrible sin they had committed in the past, the nomads had forgotten that the Earth was their Mother and the animals were their brothers and sisters. They believed they were all alone in the world, and their loneliness had made them insane.

The insanity of that loneliness glowed in Zuhan's eyes as he took the skull cup from Changar. It was in his face as he pulled out his own dagger, made two shallow cuts in his upper arm, and mixed his blood with the blood of the horses. It was even in his hands as he lifted the cup to his lips, took a long drink, and then passed the cup on to Arang.

Arang stared at the bloody skull with fear and disgust. He looked as if he might vomit, but somehow he managed to raise it to his lips. Marrah couldn't bear to watch him drink. This time she closed her eyes, and when she opened them again, he had a smear of red around his mouth and Changar was striding toward him looking displeased. With a grunt of disapproval he seized Arang's arm, pushed up his sleeve, and cut him just below the elbow so that Arang too bled into the cup. Arang flinched but didn't cry out. His eyes grew round and his lips turned pale, but he held his ground, and Marrah was proud of him.

Changar passed the cup to Zuhan again, and Zuhan drank and passed it back to Arang. Once again, Arang was forced to take a sip of blood, and as he did so, the crowd cheered.

"Achan! Zuhan!"

"Zuhan! Achan!"

"Han, Han, Han!"

The drums took up the beat; the cheer became a chant. Zuhan rose to his feet, embraced Arang, and kissed him formally on both cheeks.

"Hansi!" the crowd chanted. "Hansi! Hansi!"

Arang looked close to tears. He faced the crowd and tried to smile, but his lips trembled. The nomads didn't seem to notice, or if they noticed they didn't care. They just went on yelling the word "Hansi" until Marrah wanted to stuff her fingers in her ears. Arang was theirs—whether he wanted to be or not.

After that she expected more horrors, but to her unspeakable relief nothing terrible happened. Perhaps Zuhan had changed his mind about marrying her to Vlahan, or perhaps she'd simply been forgotten in all the excitement, but in any event no one paid any attention to her. The adoption ceremony went on for a little while longer, and then suddenly the drumming stopped and everyone began to mill around. Arang was surrounded by a crowd of well-wishers, men

The
Year
the
Horses
Came

307

mostly, but a few older women who kissed him on the cheeks just as Zuhan had done. For some reason they wouldn't let her anywhere near him, but since he didn't seem to be in any immediate danger, she relaxed. After a while, women appeared with skins of chilled *kersek*, and the warriors helped themselves. It looked as if they had a long night of drinking ahead of them.

She waited patiently, trying to make herself as inconspicuous as possible, and when the sky had turned the color of bleached bone, she walked back toward the camp with a crowd of dancing, singing women. It was still light enough to see, but some of them carried small tallow candles that flickered in the dusk. The wind had died down and the dust had settled, but the dancers soon stirred it up again.

Now that the adoption was over, Marrah felt more hopeful. The sacrifice of the horses had been horrible and Arang had been forced to do disgusting things, but he had come through in one piece, as had she. Neither of them was dead or married to a stranger. In the land of the nomads that was about as much as a person could ask for.

She looked at the tall grasses and the pale sky. There was a peace to the steppes, especially just after sunset. Everything seemed to be holding its breath, waiting for the stars to appear. To her left, a small flock of sheep huddled together in a woolly ball.

All at once, she realized why it was so quiet. The women had stopped singing. Now that's strange, she thought, but before she had a chance to understand, there was a sudden clatter of hooves, and the women on each side of her scattered. There was no other warning. She simply looked up and saw a warrior swooping down on her, and before she could yell or run he grabbed her and pulled her up on his horse. He was a big man in his late twenties, red-bearded, with long brown hair, a flat nose, fleshy cheeks, and a cruel, sensual mouth.

She yelled and fought as he pulled her toward him, but he only looked amused. He was strong, and his fingers bit into her shoulders like stone. "*Cagk*," he ordered, and at the sound of that word, which she knew by now meant "give up" and "give in," she went half crazy.

"Let go of me!" she screamed. "I'm Arang's aunt! Zuhan will punish you for touching me!" But what did he care what she said? He couldn't understand a word, and besides Zuhan himself had given her to him. He was Vlahan; she could see it in his eyes and in the way he held her as if he owned her. Mare, cow, ewe, those eyes said. She-goat, pretty little colt, *cagk*.

She kept on struggling, but it was an unequal match. He held her off until he grew bored with watching her flail about. Then he pulled her to him and covered her mouth with his. His lips were slippery and his breath smelled disgusting, but she couldn't shake him. When he finished kissing her, he threw her roughly over the front of his horse and began to ride away with her. As they passed through the crowd of women, the older ones laughed and the younger ones began to sing. She felt completely humiliated and helpless, but she was too proud to cry in front of them so she began to curse instead. The man didn't know what she was saying, but he could guess. All at once he reined in his horse, grabbed her hair, jerked her head back, and slapped her so hard she saw stars.

As she reeled back, sick and dizzy from the blow, she heard a familiar voice. Somehow she managed to turn her head. There, not more than fifteen paces away, was Stavan! He was much thinner than he'd been when she last saw him, and he was dressed in rags with straw in his hair and no boots on his feet, but it was Stavan for sure.

"Help me!" she cried. Did he hear her? She never knew. Two warriors were pursuing him, and as she yelled for help they leapt on him and started to wrestle him to the ground.

Stavan gave a cry of rage. He balled up his fist and hit one of the men, knocking him down, but two more ran up and grabbed his arms. The five men scrambled in the dust, with Stavan getting the worst of it.

Vlahan looked at the struggle thoughtfully for a moment before he gave Marrah another blow that knocked her flat against the side of the horse. Numish, he said, and the women all laughed.

Later she learned that numish was the Hansi word for "bewitched."

CHAPTER SEVENTEEN

S tavan had once told Marrah that Hansi brides
passed their wedding nights in a special white
tent decorated with clan signs, but all Vlahan
did was ride back to his own tent, drag her in-
side, and order his wife and concubine to clear out. The concubine
was a small, frightened-looking girl who couldn't have been older
than twelve: a Tcvali chief's daughter with pale skin, pale gray eyes,
and hair the color of wet straw. The wife was the square-faced, redheaded woman who had sat on Marrah, and when she saw her struggling in Vlahan's arms she gave her a look of pure hatred. Her name
was Timak, and the concubine's name was Hiknak. Later, Marrah
came to know both of them well, especially redheaded Timak, who
did everything she could to make her life unbearable, but on that
first night she was too terrified to see how much Timak hated her. As
Vlahan pulled her into the tent, she begged both women to help her,
but at a single word from him they ran like rabbits and left her to
face him alone.

After they were gone, Vlahan threw her on a pile of rugs and
stood over her, laughing and kicking her down every time she tried
to sit up. When he tired of that game, he stripped off his leggings
and, without even removing his boots, fell on her, tore her thighs

apart, and thrust himself in her. She was so dry and unwilling that his penis burned like a hot stick. Screaming and beating on his back, she tried to throw him off, but he weighed twice as much as she did and his arms were like ropes. He seemed to find her cries of pain quite natural, even exciting. He ignored her and shoved himself in and out of her with a strange, distant expression on his face. As soon as he came, he rolled off, grabbed her by the chin, pried her mouth open, shoved his penis in it, and forced her to bring him to climax a second time. By then she knew that if she bit him he'd break her neck, so she did what he wanted, gagging at the smell of him.

The same horror was repeated several times. When he was finally satisfied, Vlahan fell asleep, and she lay beside him sobbing and humiliated. She hated him so much that if she could have reached his dagger she would have stuck it into his heart, but he had put it well out of reach, and every time she so much as moved, he woke and made more demands on her.

She spent a sleepless night, half smothered by the heat and smell of the enemy who lay next to her. For the first time in her life she felt shamed by sex, and she cried—very quietly—for Stavan, who might be dead, and for love, which would never be quite the same again.

The final humiliation came the next morning when Vlahan jerked her to her feet and indicated by gestures that she was to go get him a drink of water. Sore and sick with lack of sleep, she staggered to the other side of the tent, picked up a collapsible leather bucket, and limped toward the open flap, hoping that at last she might be able to escape. Instead, she found a whole group of old women waiting outside.

As soon as they saw her, the women pounced on her, laughing and making obscene gestures. Zulike, Zuhan's wife, was among them, and when she had finished pinching Marrah's cheeks and parading her around for the others to inspect, she went into Vlahan's tent and came out with one of the rugs Vlahan and Marrah had slept on the night before. There was a spot of blood on the rug no bigger than a half a palm, but the women seemed delighted by this proof of Vlahan's brutality. Holding the rug so the blood was clearly visible, they went from tent to tent, displaying it proudly. They sang and laughed and drove Marrah before them so she could be seen by everyone in the camp.

Marrah was too proud to cry in public. She walked behind her own blood with a face of stone, not looking to the left or right as Vlahan's rape of her was proclaimed as a happy event. Later she learned that displaying the bloody rug was an ancient Hansi custom. If a bride didn't bleed, she could be sent back to her father, demoted to a slave, or even murdered by her own husband. Instead of taking revenge, the dead woman's family was obliged to give the bride price back, and the bride's mother was so shamed she sometimes committed suicide.

After Marrah was paraded around the camp, she was taken back to Vlahan's tent. Vlahan's wife, Timak, met her on the threshold with her brawny arms folded across her chest and a grim, cold look in her eyes. Motioning for Marrah to come closer, she suddenly lifted her foot and kicked her hard in the stomach. Then she fell on her, slapping her, scratching her, and biting her. As the two women rolled in the dust, the others cheered them on, but once again, it was an unequal match. Marrah was younger, but Timak was taller and strong as a horse. Soon she had Marrah down and was beating her head on the ground. When Marrah, knocked half senseless, gave up fighting, Timak climbed off her with a grunt of satisfaction, went into the tent, came out with a basket, and threw it at her. Picking up a handful of fresh horse dung, she spread it on Marrah's white tunic and indicated by gestures that she was to go gather a basket full of the stuff and spread it out to dry beside the tent so it could be used for the cooking fire.

Happy to do anything to get away, Marrah picked up the basket and went off in search of dung, but she was not allowed any privacy. Wherever she went, someone always followed her, ready to raise the alarm if she so much as lifted her eyes toward the freedom of the steppes. She worked until she was numb with exhaustion, and each time she brought back a full basket of dung, Timak greeted her with a grim smile, a harsh word, and a slap. Later she learned that it was traditional for the first wife to abuse any new woman her husband brought into the tent and that by Hansi standards Timak was being almost pleasant.

Time passed. As Marrah busied herself laying out the dung to dry as Timak had ordered, she worried about Arang. She hadn't seen him since yesterday, and as the sun dipped lower and lower toward the great, flat horizon, she began to be afraid that Changar had slit his neck the way he had slit the necks of the horses. It was a horrible image and she did her best to put it out of her mind, but she had suffered too much violence to think peaceful thoughts.

"Sweet Goddess," she prayed, "let Arang come back safe." But it grew later and Arang didn't come, and her anxiety increased until not even Timak's threats and loudly barked commands could keep her from stopping to listen every time she heard the sound of an approaching horse.

Finally, just before sunset, Arang appeared, walking slowly between the long shadows cast by the tents. He was dressed in Hansi leggings and a short belted tunic, all very finely embroidered with suns and stars, but at the sight of his face, Marrah screamed and ran to take him in her arms.

"Don't hug me while the nomads are watching," he begged, pushing her away with trembling hands. He sat down beside the dung basket and looked at her as if he were about to cry. Both his cheeks were covered with bloody scars and the rest of his hair had been cut off. He looked wounded, bewildered, and very young.

They sat silently for a while. Finally she spoke. "What did they do to your face?" She reached out to caress him and stopped herself just in time. He was right. Nomads never showed any tenderness to each other in public. For all she knew, one hug could get them both beaten senseless.

Arang touched his left cheek, winced, and looked around apprehensively. "They put Achan's clan marks on me." His voice trembled. "Changar pounded the tattoos into me with the point of a dagger and I think he promised I'd get more when I came of age, but I'm not sure. Dalish wasn't there to translate."

"Oh, Arang, that's terrible!"

"It was. But I didn't cry. I couldn't." He lowered his voice to a whisper. "If I'd cried, I think they would have killed me." He drew himself up into a ball, arms around knees, like a little turtle pulling into its shell.

She felt so sorry for him she forgot her own troubles for a moment. "You poor thing. It must have hurt a lot. Just look at you—cuts all over and none of them clean. I think they used charcoal!" She reached for her medicine bag. "We have to get a barberry leaf poultice on those sores right away before they fester."

He shook his head.

"What do you mean no? Don't be silly. Do you want your face to drop off?"

"It's not just my face."

"What do you mean?"

"They did something else to me."

"What?"

To her surprise he wouldn't tell her.

"Please, talk to me. I'm your big sister. I love you. Whatever they did wasn't your fault."

He ducked his head, looked away, was ashamed. Little by little, she brought him around and he haltingly explained that Changar had given him some kind of drink that made him lose all feeling in his body, and when he was too numb and dizzy to fight them off the men had pulled down his leggings and cut off part of his penis.

"They did *what?*" Marrah leapt to her feet, almost knocking over the dung basket. By rights her cries should have brought Timak out in full force, but as soon as Arang appeared, Timak went away, so for the first time since Vlahan had carried her off, she was able to rave and curse to her heart's content. "They mutilated you!"

Arang stared at her wide-eyed, impressed by the level of her anger. "I think they do it to all boys."

"That's insane!"

"But they do. I know because Zuhan pulled down his leggings to show me his penis, and then the other men did the same. They even brought in a little boy for me to look at."

"That does it! You're coming with me right now!" She took him by the hand and pulled him to his feet. "I'm going to put something soothing on all your wounds, and I do mean *all* of them." She led him toward the tall grass at the edge of the camp, and to her relief no one stopped them. Trampling down a space big enough to accommodate them both, she told him to sit down so he couldn't be seen and to warn her if he heard anyone coming. Then she opened her medicine bag, took out a packet of barberry leaves, and began to chew them until they were soft. She would much rather have pounded them with water since they were terribly bitter, but until she somehow managed to make herself a mortar and pestle, she was going to have to rely on her own teeth. When the leaves were a soft mush, she smeared a thumbful on Arang's cheeks. The rest she laid out carefully on a thin strip of clean linen.

"Off with your leggings," she ordered. Like anyone raised among the Shore People, Arang felt as comfortable naked as clothed. He pulled down his leggings.

"Oh, Arang, that looks terrible!" She knelt to wrap the poultice around his wound, but before she could touch him he gave a cry of warning and backed away. At the same instant a hand grabbed her wrist and jerked her sideways. She fell, dropping the poultice. When she looked up, she found herself staring straight into a pair of cold, green eyes. The eyes belonged to Changar, and he was furious.

*The
Year
the
Horses
Came*

315

He motioned for Arang to pull up his leggings. Then he turned on Marrah and gave her a hard slap across the face. She had already learned that it was useless to fight back, and evidently Arang had learned the same thing. He didn't make a sound. He just sat there looking terrified as Changar reached down and jerked her medicine bag off her belt.

Changar opened the bag, inspected the contents, and gave a grunt of displeasure. He dumped everything on the ground, knelt, and began to paw through it, ripping open packets of precious herbs and powdered roots. As Marrah looked on helplessly, the bittersweet smell of dozens of irreplaceable medicines filled the air. Changar opened the dried thunder, inspected the small clay balls, and bit into one of them. Whatever was inside must have tasted bad because he made a terrible face and spit out a wad of black phlegm. He closed the pouch and shoved it in his pocket. The powder of invisibility made him sneeze, but he kept that too, looking at Marrah suspiciously as he stowed it in his own medicine bag.

When he had finished taking what he wanted and destroying the rest, he stood up with a rattle of wolf tooth necklaces. Holding the empty medicine bag in front of Marrah's face, he said one of the few words of Hansi she knew in a low, ominous voice that sent chills up her spine. The word was *nech*; it meant "never." The diviner pointed in the direction of Vlahan's tent, indicating that they should return at once. Then he turned and left as silently as he had come, taking Marrah's empty bag with him.

"You're lucky you only got slapped," Dalish said the next morning when she came to Vlahan's tent to console Marrah. "And you're doubly lucky they think Arang's only a boy. Otherwise if Changar had found him with his pants down and you kneeling over him, you'd be dead."

"But the charms the priestesses of Nar gave me are gone, and all my medicines with them. What will I do if someone gets sick? I can't gather new ones; I've hardly been able to recognize a single plant since we left the forest."

Dalish frowned and looked around to make sure Timak was nowhere in sight. Even though they were talking in Shambah, she always acted as if they might be overheard. "Instead of worrying about charms and sickness, you should thank the Goddess that Changar had enough sense to see you were trying to heal Arang and enough generosity—if you can call it that—to make some allowances for the fact that you couldn't possibly know that he's the only one around here allowed to cure anything. If you'd been a Hansi woman he wouldn't have just slapped you; he would have kicked out your teeth or maybe even had you strangled."

She patted Marrah's knee sympathetically. "I know you've been through all sorts of horrors in the last two days, but try to look on the bright side. I came to tell you some good news. Zuhan wants Arang to have a translator until he learns Hansi, so Slehan's given me to him." She smiled. "I like the idea of being Zuhan's concubine. He's so old I doubt he can do much more than gum my breasts. Zulike could make my life unpleasant, but under the circumstances I don't think she'll bother. So I'm here to stay."

She took Marrah's hand, hiding it carefully under the edge of her shawl. "Now tell me what's happened since the last time I saw you. I know what Hansi wedding nights are like. Did Vlahan hurt you? You may have lost your medicines, but I have a few things that can soothe the worst of it. There's a special plant called 'bridesheal' that all the Hansi women use. It's strictly forbidden, of course, but Changar hates to have anything to do with women's illnesses so he pretends not to notice."

Encouraged by her sympathy, Marrah began to describe how Vlahan had grabbed her after the ceremony, but when she came to the part about Stavan, Dalish silenced her by putting a finger over her lips, and when she spoke there was no sympathy in her voice. "If you ever say that name out loud again, I'm going to get up, walk away, and only speak to you when Zuhan forces me to translate. Are you out of your mind? You said you saw this lover of yours, but how much did you see of him? I've been talking to the other concubines, and they've told me all about Zuhan's crazy son. He wanders around barefoot with straw in his hair, he won't mount a horse or look at a woman, and whenever Zuhan takes pity on him and invites him to some public ceremony, he spends the whole time babbling to himself."

She smiled bitterly. "I know you've been secretly hoping he'll save you, but the poor fool can't even save himself. He sleeps with the horses, and sometimes when the women come out to milk the mares they find him trying to eat dry grass. Give up on him. I'm telling you this as a friend. He's the last person you can rely on."

A week passed and then another. Every night Vlahan forced Marrah to have sex with him, but the tent was no longer empty. Now Timak and Hiknak lay nearby, listening to her protests and his orders. Although Marrah had hoped Arang would come to live with her, she was grateful Zuhan had insisted on taking him into his own tent. Arang didn't get along well with Zulike—who could?—but she wasn't allowed to torment him the way Timak tormented Marrah, and besides Arang was only there at night. During the day, Zuhan's warriors took him out to the steppes to teach him how to ride and hunt like a man.

Sometimes several days would pass before he could find time to visit her. When he did show up, it was a holiday of sorts. Timak and Hiknak would make themselves scarce, and Marrah would have time to sit down and hear what Arang had been doing. Mostly he was learning to throw a spear and shoot arrows from a galloping horse, which was, he told her, his idea of what the Hansi hell must be like.

"I like shooting a bow when I have both feet on the ground, but when I'm on the back of one of those cursed beasts, I can't aim straight and I nearly fall off every time. What I'm really afraid of is that Vlahan and the others are going to take me on a raid some day and I'll be expected to kill someone."

Sometimes, they would walk out to the edge of the camp into the tall grass, and if they were sure that neither Changar nor anyone else was around, Arang would lay his head in her lap and she would stroke his hair. Once or twice they even sang Sabalah's song together in low voices, and when they were finished their eyes were wet with tears.

But as the days passed, Arang seemed to grow more distant. Once he showed up with a bruise on his forehead, and when Marrah asked how he got it, he refused to tell her. When she persisted, he snapped at her. "I thought it might be a nice idea to dance for Zuhan, but Zuhan didn't like my style. My best backflips and most graceful steps horrified him, and when I was done, he had one of his warriors beat me. Now are you satisfied?"

Another time she asked him if he ever saw Stavan, and he gave her a bitter smile. "Oh, yes, I see my dear *aita* all the time, and if Timak ever let you walk out to where they keep the horses you'd see him too. He lives with the herds. He doesn't seem to recognize me or anyone else. I don't know what happened to him, but I think he's lost his mind. The warriors are all afraid of him; they say he's *votok*." And when Marrah asked what that meant, he explained the men feared Stavan was possessed by demons.

He was learning Hansi fast—much faster than Marrah—and he was learning other things too. One morning Timak pushed back the tent flap and stuck her head out to shout at Marrah just as Arang was walking up. Breaking into a run, he yelled something at her in Hansi, and Timak froze in mid-sentence and ducked back inside. When he came up to Marrah, he had a big grin on his face.

"I guess that took care of her." He settled down comfortably on an overturned basket. "I doubt she'll bother us anymore this morning."

"What did you say?"

"I told her if she didn't go inside and leave you alone, I'd beat her."

"Arang, you didn't! Why she's old enough to be a village mother. How could you be so disrespectful?"

"She's just a mean old woman." Arang shrugged. "And not pretty either. Zuhan told me I can order any woman I want around, even Zulike." He looked at her thoughtfully. "Even you."

"You just try and see how far it gets you, you little brat." She had to get him out of here before Zuhan made him into a Hansi warrior. His gentle nature was being twisted. He was fighting it, but he was only twelve. How long could she expect him to resist?


After Arang yelled at Timak, she treated Marrah with more respect. Now, instead of slapping her and pushing her out the door to collect dung, she handed the basket to her, grumbling in a low voice. Sometimes she sent her for water or to gather wild greens and roots. On one or two occasions she even let her help Hiknak milk the cows and mares or cook Vlahan's dinner, which was no easy process. Since the nomads rarely used pottery, they either roasted meat directly over the fire or boiled up a kind of stew by tossing hot rocks in a lined basket or skin bag. If the rocks were too hot, they were apt to split when they hit the liquid, scalding the cook and burning through the basket; on the other hand, if they were too cold, they sunk to the bottom without warming the stew. Marrah's first attempt was almost solid rocks, but instead of slapping her, Timak merely muttered a curse, emptied the broth into a new basket, and began all over again.

Vlahan was particularly fond of the fat, micelike voles that fed on the wild grasses, and after she failed so miserably at boiling stew, Marrah was assigned the task of gutting the little animals, singeing

The
Year
the
Horses
Came

319

off their hair in the flames, and putting them in a small pit to bake. The Hansi ate other strange things: grubs, snakes, lizards, and—as Dalish had promised—grasshoppers. But mostly they ate beef, horse meat, cheese, wild-grass-seed porridge, and a kind of pudding made from milk and blood.

She was so busy that sometimes she forgot to worry, but all she had to do was look up and read the hatred in Timak's eyes to know she was bound to a lifetime of drudgery and abuse unless she managed to escape. Still, as time passed, her life improved a little. She suspected Arang had threatened Timak again, because suddenly, after days of watching her, Timak let her go out alone to gather dung. It was a relief to walk into the tall grass and sit where no prying eyes could follow. On the steppes she was free to dream of home and forget, at least for a while, the horrors of Vlahan's bed.

The only bad thing about her new freedom was that as she passed through the camp she often saw Stavan. The first time this happened, she was so excited she started to speak to him, but he kept on walking and looked right through her as if he'd never seen her before. The next time their paths crossed, he was sitting in the shade playing with a bit of horsehair and babbling to himself like an idiot. It grieved her terribly to think he had actually lost his mind, but it seemed to be true. After a few more unpleasant encounters, she hurried in the opposite direction whenever she saw him coming. Dalish was right. Whatever there had been between them was over, and it was both foolish and dangerous to try to get him to recognize her.

Then, on a day in early autumn when the steppes had turned gold and the night had been cold enough to leave a rim of frost on the ground, she was sitting among the tall grasses thinking of home when suddenly the stalks parted and Stavan himself stood before her. He was barefoot, with straw in his hair, wearing a torn tunic and a necklace of thorns, but his eyes were as clear and sane as any she'd ever seen.

Falling to his knees, he clasped his hand over her mouth to keep her from crying out in surprise. "Hush," he whispered. "We don't have much time. I have to tell you something. I'm—" He stopped in mid-sentence, and Marrah heard the sound of Hiknak and another woman approaching. Before she had time to be frightened, he had disappeared, sliding off into the dry grass so swiftly and quietly that by the time the two women were in sight there wasn't so much as a moving blade to give him away.

She snatched up her basket, rose to her feet, yelled out a greeting in broken Hansi, and pretended to be busy looking for dung, but she was so excited she couldn't do much more than wander in circles, stopping every once in a while to crouch down and wait in case Stavan wanted to find her again. But he must have thought it was too dangerous, because there was no further sign of him.

She got a good scolding from Timak when she came back to the tent with a half empty basket, but for once she didn't care. Stavan had only said a few words to her, but she knew beyond a doubt that he was no more crazy than she was.

That evening Arang came to visit her. The warriors had had him out on the steppes all day, riding and shooting at targets until he could hardly stand up. His fingers were bruised and he was covered with gray dust, but when she told him about Stavan he threw back his head and laughed.

"He's not crazy?"

"No."

"Then he'll help us escape! Hurrah!" He pounced on her and gave her a hug. "No more nomads, no more spears, no more horses! How I've detested being trained as a warrior! How I've hated it!" They danced around, laughing so hard Timak glared at them suspiciously, but what did they care? Soon she'd be nothing but a bad memory.

That night not even Vlahan could make Marrah cry. As he lay on top of her, she watched him coldly from a great distance. He might own her body, but her soul was out on the steppes with Stavan, riding west toward Shara.

The
Year
the
Horses
Came

321

CHAPTER EIGHTEEN

S he woke the next morning, sure Stavan would
come to her as soon as she walked into the
safety of the tall grass, but she never had an opportunity to stray more than fifty paces away
from Vlahan's tent. Timak was as ill-tempered as a sick goat. The
moment she rose from her pallet, she began barking orders, shoving
poor Hiknak when she didn't move fast enough and following
Marrah outside to make sure she didn't waste any more time peeing
than was absolutely necessary. Handing both younger women a cold
breakfast of leftovers, she ordered them to eat it quickly and start
folding up the blankets and packing the leather saddlebags. They
were breaking camp, she informed them, and she had no intention
of ending up at the end of the line eating everyone else's dust just
because they were a pair of lazy sluts.

In less time than Marrah could have believed possible, the stakes
were pulled up, the tent was down, and the poles and hides had
been converted into a sledge. Soon everything Vlahan owned was
neatly packed away, the cooking fire was doused, and Timak was
standing with her hands on her hips looking impatiently in the direction of the herds. If Vlahan didn't come back with the horses
soon, they were going to be one of the last households to leave. He

323

was an unreliable, lazy bastard, but if either Marrah or Hiknak ever told Vlahan she'd said any such thing, she'd tear out both their livers.

Hiknak grinned shyly at Marrah behind Timak's back, and for the first time Marrah felt a bond of sympathy with the little concubine. Obviously Hiknak was pleased to hear Timak curse Vlahan. Timak was right; they were going to be late. All over the camp women and children were feverishly taking down tents and packing bundles. Some of the sledges were already hitched to horses, and Zuhan had mounted a white gelding and was about to give the marching command. Arang sat beside him on a smaller horse, not the gray one he'd ridden from Shambah but a fine, glossy-coated beast the color of honey. Marrah waved when she saw him and he waved back, but they didn't have a chance to speak to each other, which was a pity. She wanted to talk to him some more about Stavan, but Zuhan was keeping Arang very close these days. Unless Arang came to her, she couldn't get anywhere near him, since women were forbidden to approach members of the Great Chief's household without their husband's permission.

Changar sat next to Arang, mounted on a black stallion, looking at everything with a cold, imperious gaze. Stavan was nowhere in sight, which was just as well as far as Marrah was concerned, since she wasn't sure she could have so much as looked in his direction without Timak—or, worse yet, Changar—suspecting something.

Timak continued to fume and sputter until Vlahan appeared with four horses. He handed them over to her without a word of apology and galloped back toward the herd to help round up the cattle. Timak hitched one horse to the sledge and ordered Marrah and Hiknak to bridle the others. She had a nasty temper, but she was a fast, competent worker, and as Marrah tried to follow her directions, she felt a grudging admiration for her. These nomad women might scurry around like frightened mice when their men gave an order, but they were strong as bulls, and when it came to getting a bit into the mouth of a nervous horse without getting kicked, no one could match them.

When the horses were bridled, the three women mounted and formed a line with Timak at the head and Hiknak and the sledge horse bringing up the rear. Just in time, too, because as they settled into place Zuhan motioned to Changar. Bowing to the Great Chief, the diviner lifted a white flute-shaped instrument to his lips and blew a single high-pitched blast. Later, Marrah learned that the marching trumpet was made from a human thigh bone, but even when she was mercifully ignorant of that, the sound sent a chill through her. The mare must not have liked it either; she laid her ears back and pawed the ground, and it was all Marrah could do to keep her from bolting out of line.

At the sound of the trumpet, the whole camp began to move: first Zuhan and his bodyguards, then Changar and Arang, then the women and children of each family on a first-come-first-serve basis, with the late ones straggling to catch up. As the women and pack-horses lurched into motion, the men out on the steppes began to drive the horses and cattle forward with high-pitched yips. Slowly, like a great river, the herds began to stir, sending up clouds of pale dust that stained the sky. Soon the place where they had camped for so many days was nothing more than a long line of flattened grass, with holes where the tents had been and small humps of bones and other garbage. Already crows and buzzards were circling overhead, ready to swoop in and clean up the scraps.

Their progress through the tall grass reminded Marrah of the ride from Shambah to Slehan's camp, only it was slower and much less brutal. No one went thirsty, and around midday the whole tribe stopped to feed the children, water the horses, and eat a cold meal. That evening they pitched camp before dark, lit small cooking fires, and unpacked enough blankets and baskets to make themselves comfortable. The next morning, just after sunrise, Changar blew the marching trumpet, and they took to the trail again.

This went on for several days. Marrah saw Arang all the time, sometimes with Zuhan and sometimes with Dalish, who appeared to be giving him lessons in Hansi. As they rode along side by side, Dalish would point at a bird or a plant and her lips would move, and Arang would nod and look as if he was trying to repeat what she'd just said, but the two of them were always too far away for Marrah to hear. She tried not to feel left out, but it was hard. The best she could do was wave to Arang and give him knowing glances. It was all very frustrating, especially on the third day when she was sure she saw Stavan walking in the dust beside the cattle. It might only have been one of the older herdboys, but even the chance that it was him excited her so much she thought of nothing else.

The warriors rode behind and beside the great herd, pushing the animals forward slowly and cutting off any strays who tried to wander in the wrong direction. The women were ordered to keep their horses in check, and the children were cautioned not to yell or make sudden movements. If the herd stampeded, it could take days to round the animals up. In the morning everyone checked the sky. Violent thunderstorms could sweep across the steppes, coming out of nowhere. Many of the horses were so wild a single bolt of lightning could set them running, and when the horses ran the cattle often ran with them. At night, people sat around the campfires telling stories of tribes that had been wiped out by their own herds.

But this was a fall march, not a summer one. Except for one afternoon of drizzle, the sky stayed as clear and blue as a string of clay beads, and even the wildest horses spent most of their time cropping grass. Only one thing of real interest happened as they moved south. One morning Hiknak rode up beside Marrah and began in a hesitant way to talk.

"Why don't you order me around?" she asked, pushing a string of dirty blond hair off her thin forehead and looking at Marrah shyly.

Marrah smiled at Hiknak, thinking how childlike she looked under the paint that rimmed her eyes. It was always hard to remember she was a woman, even though the Goddess knew Vlahan and Timak had beaten the childish joy out of her long ago. "Why should I order you? Doesn't Timak give enough orders for any ten people?" She was glad she finally spoke enough Hansi to carry on a conversation.

"But you're Vlahan's wife, and I'm just his concubine. You're supposed to curse at me and kick me every once in a while, or people will think you don't care that he takes me into his bed."

Marrah laughed. "Little sister, I'm never going to kick you or curse you or even raise my voice to you if I can help it, and as for Vlahan I suspect that both of us would just as soon the clumsy brute screwed his horse as either of us."

Hiknak turned bright pink and giggled. "Don't let Timak hear you say that," she warned, looking nervously in Timak's direction. She lowered her voice. "She thinks he's a stud from heaven."

Marrah was intrigued. "But you know different?"

Hiknak nodded. "Oh, yes. I came to Vlahan a virgin just like you; if I hadn't still had my maidenhead, Zuhan's warriors would have raped me to death or made me a slave. But I had a friend in my father's camp."

"What was his name?"

"Her name was Iriknak," Hiknak said softly. "And a sweet, good woman she was too. She was my uncle's youngest concubine, just my age, with the kindest voice and the brightest smile you'd ever want to see. Vlahan killed her, and someday I'm going to return the favor.

I'm telling you this because I've been listening to what goes on between you and him at night, and I know you must hate him too." And with that, Hiknak gave her horse a kick and rode off, leaving Marrah speechless.

Well, well, she thought, let that be a lesson to me never to underestimate anyone.

At last, for reasons Marrah never quite understood, the tribe arrived at a more permanent camping place. As far as she could see, the water was no better and the grass no taller than it had been where they'd camped the night before, but everyone seemed delighted by the choice, and as the women and children unpacked the tents and delved to the bottom of the leather bags, a rumor ran through the camp: this was where they were going to spend the winter unless Han sent Changar a sign to tell them to move on.

Marrah liked working with Hiknak a lot better now that she knew how the girl felt about Vlahan, and as the two of them set up the tent under Timak's disapproving glare, they gave each other little secret signals of reassurance and rebellion. The site Vlahan had selected was at the edge of camp, and as Marrah pounded in the tent stakes she looked longingly at the tall grass. If she could find a free moment to slip away, perhaps Stavan would notice and follow her. But it was all idle speculation. The tent was set up, the bags unpacked, the fire lit, fresh dung spread out to dry, and supper cooked, and it was nightfall without her being able meet Stavan anywhere but in her imagination. Meanwhile, Vlahan was off at the Great Chief's tent, drinking kersek with the warriors to celebrate the tribe's arrival at their winter campground, and no doubt he would come home drunk and demanding, and the night would end in the usual miserable way.

Unfortunately, she was right. They waited up for Vlahan until even Timak looked as if she could hardly keep her eyes open. The fire died down, was fed, and died a second time. Finally they heard him coming. He was singing something, a Hansi war song perhaps. Marrah caught the word "wolf" and the word "enemy" before he stumbled through the tent flap. When Timak tried to help him take off his boots, he cursed and pushed her aside. Grabbing Marrah by the arm, he pulled her into his bed, but the kersek must have been particularly strong or he must have drunk more of it than usual because instead of climbing onto her he fell asleep almost at once.

The
Year
the
Horses
Came

327

Well, that's a mercy, she thought as she lay next to him, listening to his thunderous snores. Not only is he unconscious, he looks as if he's going to stay that way. Relieved, she turned her back, closed her eyes, and drifted off into the first real sleep she'd had in weeks.

She woke sometime later with a start. Vlahan had clasped his hand over her mouth. Curse him to a thousand Hansi hells! Why did he always have to want her night after night? She started to struggle even though she knew it wouldn't do any good. If he was going to wake her, let him wake Timak too. Why should anyone get any sleep around here if the master was drunk and demanding? But before she could make a sound, Vlahan moved closer. It was very dark, but not so dark that she couldn't see it wasn't Vlahan at all. It was a blond-bearded man with white-blond hair. It was Stavan!

Great Goddess! What was Stavan doing in Vlahan's tent? Had he lost his mind? Behind her, only a palm's breadth away, she could hear Vlahan snoring softly. Timak and Hiknak lay nearby.

Impulsively, she reached up, threw her arms around him, drew him down, and kissed him. He kissed her back quickly and silently as a shadow. His lips were sweet, and he smelled warm and familiar. It had been so long since they last kissed. Perhaps he was only a dream. Perhaps in a few seconds he would disappear and she would wake to find the sun up and Timak yelling at her to go out and gather dung. But Stavan didn't feel like a dream or taste like one. It was incredibly exciting to be lying next to Vlahan kissing him—incredibly exciting and incredibly dangerous.

Stavan clearly had no intention of dying at Vlahan's hands if he could help it. Releasing her, he pointed to the bottom edge of the tent, indicating that he had come in by pulling up a stake. Follow me—he gestured, and she nodded—but be careful. He pointed to Vlahan, and she nodded again. As soon as he was sure she understood, he kissed her hands and waved goodbye. Then, so quickly that he seemed to disappear, he rolled under the bottom of the tent.

Marrah inched away from Vlahan, holding her breath, terrified he might wake up, but he went on snoring. She slid across the rugs without a sound and crawled under the loose edge of the tent. An instant later she was kneeling on the cold ground under a sky full of stars looking at Stavan. She felt like a bird that had escaped from a cage. She wanted to kiss him and hold him and run with him and never look back, but she had too much sense to do any of these things. Instead, she only looked at him and breathed so quietly her breath was less than a whisper.

Stavan put a finger over her lips and cautioned her to be absolutely silent, but she wouldn't have made a sound at that moment if the Goddess Herself had commanded her to. The camp was still, but as usual not everyone was asleep. Here and there among the leather tents, fires burned. Sometimes the shadow of a sentry passed in front of the flames. Marrah knew there would be more armed sentries at the perimeter, in addition to the boys who always slept with the horses and cattle. Even though Zuhan had wiped out the Tcvali, no Hansi camp was ever left unguarded. She crouched lower and tried to stay calm. They were in a very dangerous situation.

Motioning for her to follow him, Stavan dropped on his belly and began to snake his way toward the tall grass. She crawled after him, filled with a happiness that just barely overcame the terror of moving through the darkness past the dogs and sentries. The ground smelled like dust and dung, and once she almost sneezed but caught herself in time. Fortunately they only had to crawl a short distance before they reached the grass. Once it had closed around them, they rose to a crouching position and ran as quickly and quietly as they could.

Marrah was never sure exactly how Stavan knew where he was going or how they managed to elude the boys who guarded the herds. All she could see was grass and a patch of night sky that moved as they moved. As they trampled the grass, their feet made a cracking sound that seemed terribly loud, but evidently it wasn't. Perhaps the wind made such sounds at night, or perhaps the sentries couldn't tell them from the horses and cows. They ran on and on until she felt she might drop from exhaustion, and then they ran some more. The backs of her legs ached and she longed to stand up, but she knew if she did she'd be taller than the grass.

Finally they did stand, and then they ran faster than ever. There was no moon, only the dim glow of starlight and the swaying stalks. At last, when she was about to reach out and beg him to stop, he stopped without being asked. For a long time he froze, listening intently. Somewhere in the distance, she heard the hoot of an owl, but otherwise there wasn't a sound. The sky to the east was dark without a trace of Zuhan's campfires.

"We can talk now," he whispered, but instead of talking they fell on each other and kissed. Breathless, she pulled away.

"You crazy man," she cried, returning to kiss him on the eyelids, the cheeks, the chin. "You dear, brave, crazy man! You wait all this

The
Year
the
Horses
Came

329

time to speak to me and then you come to me in Vlahan's very tent! What if Vlahan had wakened?"

Stavan laughed. "I may be crazy but I'm not stupid. I drugged the bastard's kersek. A herd of wild stallions could stampede through his tent tonight, and he'd go on snoring." He took her hand. "But come. We can't stand here talking. There'll be time for that later." He led her through the tall, sweet-smelling grass again, moving so quickly she didn't have enough breath to ask for a more complete explanation. Before long she heard a horse whinny softly and smelled the warm musk of its body. A few moments later they came on a gray mare bridled and ready to ride and, hobbled next to her, a black gelding.

"Mount up," he commanded. He offered her his cupped hands. "I want to talk to you, but I want to do it somewhere the sentries won't stumble on us." She mounted the mare and he mounted the gelding and they rode quickly through the darkness along a narrow trail that looked like some kind of animal track. Finally he motioned for her to rein in the mare. Getting off, they led both horses through waves of tossing black grass, down into a gully sheltered from the wind. They hobbled them next to a small thicket of stunted bushes and sat down on the sand.

He took her hand and held it for a moment, and she suddenly felt shy. It had been over three years since they'd been together like this. On the banks above them, the wind rustled the dry grass. A lock of hair blew across his forehead, and he pushed it away with his free hand.

"We have to talk quickly. There's not much time. Someone might wake up and miss you. We're going to escape."

"Yes!" she cried, and as she spoke she felt the wind blow up and under her, lifting them both into the dark, free sky. She drew him to her and gave him another quick kiss. The blood beat in her temples

Mary
Mackey

330

like horses' hooves, and she imagined herself riding west with him and Arang and nothing between them and Shara but a wide, windswept plain. "Tell me everything. Tell me what I can do. I'll do whatever needs to be done."

And so he told her, stopping often to kiss her and hold her, and as he talked she began to feel like her old self. Every word he said gave her hope. Soon she wasn't Marrah the slave wife any more; she was the girl who had jumped off the cliffs of Xori into a tossing sea, the woman who had walked across half the world; she was Marrah, daughter of Sabalah, Marrah who could hold her own against any man.

First, he said, she had to understand that she was watched more than she realized. Changar had set the eyes of the Hansi on her, which was why he hadn't been able to come to her sooner. But last week and again tonight he'd taken the chance because something was about to happen that would change everything: Zuhan was going to make Arang his heir—not in four years or so, as everyone had always assumed, but in five days, maybe less. Right now Arang was already surrounded by Zuhan's bodyguards most of the time, but once he was designated the heir, he would be surrounded by guards of his own every minute of every day just like Zuhan was. They had to make a run for it as soon as possible: tomorrow if they could, or the next day at the very latest, while Arang still had some freedom.

It was a bad time to go, he wouldn't lie to her. Winter was coming, and Zuhan was bound to send armed warriors after them; the Hansi trackers were the best on the steppes. He'd wanted to wait until early spring when they'd have a better chance of surviving, but they had to go now, so here was his plan: Arang still had a little freedom—more than she did—since no one actually thought a ten-year-old would try to escape with winter in the offing. He couldn't risk talking to Arang, but she could. She should make some excuse to see him—almost anything would do since she was known as his aunt—and when they were alone together, she should tell Arang to ask Zuhan to let him spend a night with the herdboys. Arang should complain that he hadn't been allowed to play with other boys and speak very respectfully of a desire to look after his grandfather's cattle. With a little luck, Zuhan would be flattered and consent.

That night when everyone was asleep, Stavan would come for her, lead her out of the camp, and bring her here, where he'd have fresh horses and supplies waiting. Then he'd go back and get Arang. With a little luck, they should be well on their way before anyone realized they were missing. They'd ride north and east, not south and west, and when they were sure they'd lost the trackers, they'd double back. If everything went well, they'd reach the forest lands before the big snowstorms hit. If not, they'd winter over in one of the western river valleys. There were caves where they could take shelter, and they wouldn't starve as long as he had a bow.

As Marrah listened, she grew more and more excited. It wasn't a perfect plan; it was dangerous and she knew she should be thinking of everything that could go wrong, but instead she thought of how sweet it would be to go back to Shara. She thought of her grandmother and her friends; of the fresh, salty smell of the Sweetwater Sea;

The
Year
the
Horses
Came

331

of olives, and figs, and wine, and bread, real trees, and honey-colored cliffs; but most of all, she thought of how much she hated Vlahan. If she escaped, she would never again have to feel his sweaty body grinding against hers or smell the sour odor of kersek on his breath. She would lie next to Stavan at night, making love only when she felt like it, and every breath she took would be a breath of freedom.

Suddenly she realized what was wrong with the whole plan.

"But what about Dalish and Akoah, and the five Shamban women Slehan has, and the four that went to Zuhan? What about them?"

The look on his face told her everything. "Fourteen people?" he said softly. "Fourteen, Marrah, and ten of them women who can barely stay on a horse—how far do you think we'd get before the warriors caught up with us and killed us all?"

"But to leave them here in slavery! How can we? Stavan, every night of my life I'd think of them." She got up and walked away from him, out into the dry streambed where the pale rocks gleamed in the starlight like white bones, and she looked up at that alien star-filled sky, so bright and close it looked as if she could reach up and touch it. And yet it was so far away, so immense. Close and far and impossible, she thought. And she knew then that no matter how hard she tried to make it otherwise, only she and Arang and Stavan were riding west. She returned to Stavan, sober-faced and pale. Taking his hand in hers, she held it, and when she spoke her voice was steady.

"Only the three of us then," she agreed, and as she spoke she felt like a traitor, but what choice did she have? Dalish, she thought; Dalish, perhaps. She couldn't quite give up on Dalish, but the rest, yes, she could. She had to.

Stavan drew her to him and held her, but when she closed her eyes all she could see was Dalish, Akoah, and the women of Shambah. Go away! she ordered, but they just stayed there, looking at her. She found herself wishing that she had a pipe of hemp or a cup of kersek. Wasn't that how the Hansi warriors forgot the people they'd killed? How could she live with this without being drunk on something?

She opened her eyes and found Stavan looking at her. "Kiss me," she commanded, and he did. It was a long kiss, and somewhere in the middle of it, she found the forgetfulness she was looking for. They kissed some more, and after a while they lay down. She took off her heavy wool tunic and leggings and Stavan took off his, and they stretched out on his cloak under her shawl, breast to chest and knee to knee in all the sweet nakedness of love. Soon he was dragging the tips of his fingers over her nipples, spreading her lips, caressing her with his tongue, and drinking the salt and sweetness of her, and she was smelling the musk and animal scent of his body. He was hard and eager, but he never once did anything she didn't invite, and his respect was at the same time so familiar and so long-lost that she shivered and wept and cried out to him that she'd been afraid that the joy of love had left her forever but now she'd found it again.

When she cried, he comforted her and kissed her and made love to her in the old way, like a man of her own people. They lay head to foot, and after what seemed like a long time, he brought her to an orgasm that made her moan.

They did foolish things that night when they should have been riding back to camp; the specter of death hovered over them, and knowing this might be the last time, they made the most of it. Sometimes they were tender and sometimes they rolled around, kissing so hard it seemed as if they might swallow each other's tongues.

There came a moment when she reached out and tapped him on the thigh, and he entered her, and for the first time they rocked back and forth together, and he came inside her, not once but several times. Then they rolled over and she rode him, high and hard, bringing herself to a slow, steady climax.

Afterward they lay in each other's arms looking up at the sky. Overhead, the stars had changed and the night was passing, but neither of them could bear to get up, put on clothes, and ride back to the camp. Marrah curled up and Stavan held her. They felt like two people in a boat, drifting on a great dark sea.

"Do you think we started a child?" Stavan whispered.

"I hope so," she said and moved closer.

They didn't mention Vlahan, but both of them knew Marrah soon would be sleeping beside him again. Better our child than his, they could have said to each other, but they didn't need to. They understood each other perfectly.

Later, as they rode back toward camp through the tall grass, they were silent. The wind had stopped, and a motionless peace seemed to have descended on the steppes. It wasn't dawn yet, but Marrah could feel the light hovering somewhere just over the edge of the horizon. Stavan sat straight on his horse, moving with it in an easy way she'd never mastered. He looked at home in his wool leggings and hooded tunic; his eyes were as pale as the stars, and even his hair was the color of the dried grasses. He was part of this world, he fit in, and no matter how close they got or how long they lived together there would always be this difference between them. And yet she loved him. She didn't love his people or their way of life or anything about them, but she loved Stavan. I've chosen him over my own, she thought guiltily. Again she thought of Dalish and Akoah and the women of Shambah, and she prayed that a miracle would happen. Let the earth shake or the sky fall; let us wake up one morning and find the Hansi have all disappeared. Let me take them back to the Sweetwater Sea.

While she prayed for the impossible, Stavan's thoughts were taking a more practical turn. He rode up beside her, reached out, and patted her horse on the neck. "We're going to need a signal. If Zuhan lets Arang sleep with the herdboys, I'll hear about it, but you won't." He frowned and thought it over. "Let's agree that if you see me playing with a ball of brown wool you'll know I'll be coming for you that same night. And if you see me with a ball of white wool, it means you're to come into the tall grass as quickly as you can because something's gone wrong and I have to talk to you right away."

"Why wool?"

"Because it's easy to get; besides, it's just the sort of thing a crazy man would do." He smiled, a little bitterly, she thought. "Becoming a fool hasn't been easy, you know; it's taken thought. But it's been easier than being sane. If I'd been sane when my father rode against the Tcvali, I'd have been expected to kill and rape like a sane man."

"And tomorrow when I see you, you'll be a fool again?"

He nodded.

"You'll walk right past me?"

"Right past."

That was a sobering thought. Not knowing what to say, she reached out and took his hand, but it was hard to make much progress that way, so she dropped it, and they rode on.

*Mary*
*Mackey*

When they got to the spot where they had to leave the horses, he pressed two small objects into her palm. She tried to look at them, but the sky had begun to cloud over and it was too dark to see. "One's a pack of sleeping powder," he explained. "When I give you the signal, see it gets into Vlahan's stew. I want everyone in that tent asleep except you."

She felt the other thing he'd handed her. It was wrapped in a piece of leather, tied with hemp. "What's this?"

"A present, a bit of good luck. But don't take time to open it now; we have to hurry."

They ran back through the grass, past the sentries and the dogs. When they came to Vlahan's tent there was no time to say goodbye. Stavan lifted the bottom edge and Marrah rolled inside, and just in time too, for not long after she'd stretched out next to Vlahan, Timak woke up and shuffled outside and Marrah heard the sound of her piss hitting the dirt. Soon the breakfast fire was smoking and Vlahan was sitting up, demanding food and complaining of a terrible headache.

All morning she walked around in a state of excitement, hardly hearing Timak's nagging commands. She folded the bedding, went down to the river with Hiknak to get water, swept out the tent with a handful of dry grass, peeled roots, and skinned a rabbit, spitted it, and put it on the fire so Vlahan could have something fresh to eat. He was in a horrible mood, as irritable as a sick hog, and she took care to stay away from him until after he'd eaten. She'd noticed that when he was hungry he was often unpredictable, and she had no desire to cross him, even by accident. When he'd stuffed himself with rabbit and had a pipe of hemp, then she'd go to him and ask for permission to visit Arang, but until then the more space between them, the better.

As she worked, she thought about last night. Sometimes she furtively ran her fingers along her arms, thinking of how Stavan had touched her, and sometimes she licked her lips, remembering how hungrily they had kissed, but when she went down to the river, she took care to wash carefully. Vlahan had a nose like a dog, and she didn't want any trace of Stavan's scent on her.

She did take one chance, however. When Timak was occupied with Vlahan and Hiknak was busy basting the rabbit, she found some excuse to go into the tent. Kneeling in the circle of light that came through the smoke hole, she pulled out the present Stavan had given her, unwrapped it, and found herself holding the Tear of Compassion. Suppressing a cry of surprise, she looked at the little butterfly for a moment, floating in the clear yellow rock as peacefully as if it had never been dragged across half the world. Then quickly, before anyone could come in and catch her, she tied it around her neck and hid it under her tunic. This wouldn't do for long. She'd have to put it in her pouch so Vlahan wouldn't see it, but today she'd give herself the pleasure of wearing it. Reaching down, she touched Earth for luck.

After that, she had no more time to think. She ran to the store baskets, found the hunk of cheese Timak had sent her for, and made it outside just in time to get a cuff on the ear from Vlahan, but she didn't care. Instead of glaring at him, she knelt at his feet with the most exquisite patience while he heaped insults on her for her slowness, laziness, and general lack of worth. What did it matter what this fool said to her?

Vlahan seemed impressed with her new docility. "She's learning," he said to Timak. Timak, however, was not pleased. She looked at Marrah with narrowed eyes and when the time came to spread out the fresh dung, she made sure to hand her the largest basket.

By midday, Vlahan seemed to have recovered from his hangover. He was nasty, but it was only the usual nastiness. Waiting until Timak was safely out of earshot, Marrah quickly washed the dung off her hands, came up to him, and knelt at his feet again. "I want to ask you a favor, husband," she said, casting down her eyes demurely as a modest nomad wife should. Her Hansi might have been better, but it was good enough, and Vlahan looked pleasantly surprised. This was definitely the longest sentence she'd ever said to him, and he had no way of knowing how the word "husband" stuck in her throat.

He lifted his pipe to his lips, took a long stream of smoke into his lungs, and looked her over. "What?" he said. He was a man not given to long or complicated conversations.

"I want your permission to go see my nephew." She came within a hair of saying "brother" instead of "nephew." The thought that she'd come so close to spoiling everything made her shudder, but Vlahan, as usual, hardly paid any attention to her except when he wanted her in his bed, so her sudden expression of alarm passed unnoticed.

"When?"

"This afternoon." She knew she should say something else. He was looking at her expectantly. "Please, husband."

"Hmm," he said, and his eyes narrowed the way Timak's had earlier. "I think not."

It was all she could do not to yell at him that she was going to go whether he gave her permission or not, but she knew by now that if she did so, she wouldn't be able to see Arang for days, so she kept her temper and even managed a humble smile. "May your wife ask why?"

"No," Vlahan said, and with a wave of his hand, he dismissed her.

Stunned by the failure of her request, she went back to spreading out dung. What was going on? True, she'd never asked to go to Arang before because Arang came to her almost every other day, but Vlahan had let her walk freely around the camp. She had to have his permission to approach Zuhan's tent—no woman could come near it without her husband's consent—but why should he object? Did he know something? Had he awakened last night, found her gone, and figured out where she was?

She shuddered at the thought of what he might do to her if he suspected she had been unfaithful. She had heard a number of stories about how the Hansi treated women who betrayed their husbands. The lucky ones were pelted with rocks until every bone in their bodies was broken, but most died in much slower, more horrible ways. She felt sick with anxiety, but there was no way to warn Stavan. He'd be out with the herdboys by now, playing the fool with straw in his hair. If she couldn't get to Arang, there was certainly no way she could get to him, and they hadn't had the foresight to arrange a signal that could be seen from a distance.

But as it turned out, she worried for nothing; or, rather, she worried about the wrong thing. Vlahan had not wakened, and he had no idea she'd been with Stavan. His reason for denying her permission to go to Zuhan's tent had nothing to do with her. That afternoon, the ceremonial drums began to beat, and a runner came through the camp calling all the warriors to the Great Chief.

The drums continued beating all day as the women went about their work, and sounds of singing could be heard coming from behind the leather curtain that separated the men's secret rituals from profane eyes. Near dusk, Changar himself appeared, leading a string of fine horses through the camp. He was dressed in his wolf robes, and the terrible necklace of Shambah hung around his neck.

"There'll be blood in the cup today," Timak said as he passed, and as usual she was right. By the time night fell, everyone including Marrah knew that seven horses had been sacrificed to Han and that Zuhan, the Great Chief, had declared Arang son of Achan his one and only heir and appointed Vlahan, the bastard, to be his guardian until he came of age.

When she heard the news, she went inside the tent, lay down on a pile of blankets, and turned her face to the wall. The plan she and Stavan had made wouldn't work now. They'd missed their chance by only a few days. She thought of Arang, of how he would be surrounded by guards, his food tasted, his every movement watched. Their bad luck made her sick with disappointment.

"Get up," Timak ordered, coming in to kick her. "There's a fire to be tended and water to be fetched." But Marrah stubbornly refused to move.

"Leave me alone," she said. She needed time to think. Of a new plan, of some way to get to Arang; of a hundred things that couldn't be said out loud. Timak was so stunned she forgot to go on kicking. "Leave me alone," Marrah repeated, "or I'll tell my nephew you abuse me." She didn't expect the threat to have any effect, but to her astonishment, Timak gathered up her shawl and hurried out of the tent.

Well, well, she thought. It looks like being the aunt of a future Great Chief is going to have some advantages. She felt triumphant, but her triumph was short-lived. Not long after Timak had beat a hasty exit, Vlahan came back from the ceremony, strutting like a chief in a fine new robe and a necklace of wolf teeth. Pulling Marrah to her feet, he shoved her in the direction of the fire.

"Help Timak cook my dinner," he ordered, and then, just to make sure she understood who was talking, he slapped her so hard her ears rang. Stumbling outside, she did what he'd told her to do, but that night, when he dragged her into his bed, her patience snapped and she fought him with all her strength.

"I hate you!" she screamed. "Don't touch me!" Every time he laid a hand on her she shuddered with repulsion and struck out at him, but he was stronger than she was and ultimately he managed to wrestle her to the ground. Tying her hands behind her back with one of his bowstrings, he raped her and then tossed her out of bed to lie all night half smothered in the cold ashes of the fire.

In the morning, Timak came up with a nasty grin and cut her loose. "You'd better behave," she warned, "or you'll get plenty worse than that." Bruised and humiliated, Marrah staggered to her feet and started toward the river to scrub herself clean, but Timak stopped her.

"You're too vain," she said. "Always washing and primping when there's work to be done." Thrusting a leather bucket in Marrah's hands, she led her out to milk the mares and watched her with cold, suspicious eyes until the chore was done. Then she set her to digging out the tent pit, a hard job since the turf had to be cut with a stone knife and pried up in blocks.

That afternoon, as Marrah was bending over the fire picking out roasted roots with a forked stick, Hiknak came up and began to throw on more dried dung.

"The fire's already hot enough," Marrah snapped. It wasn't fair of her to take her disappointment out on Hiknak, but she was so miserable at the prospect of spending a whole winter in the same tent with

Vlahan that she probably would have snapped at the laughing priest-esses of Nar if they had been anywhere in sight.

"Hush," Hiknak whispered. "I want to talk to you. I have some advice. Don't fight him."

"What?" Marrah stopped, one hand poised over the coals.

"Don't fight Vlahan. He likes it." Hiknak raised her head. Her thin pale face looked moonlike and girlish, but her eyes were hard. "I should know. I fought him too at first, but now I not only give in, I even act like I want to do it. As soon as he found out I was willing, he stopped wanting me. He specializes in breaking things—horses, women, they're all the same to him. So I repeat, don't fight him."

It was good advice, but it proved useless.


All day the drums had been beating and the warriors had been cele-brating, but having heard the worst of the bad news yesterday, Marrah no longer paid attention to the sound. Out on the steppes the men were playing war games, and sometimes if she shaded her eyes with her hand, she could see little figures riding full tilt at each other or the silhouette of a warrior rising in his saddle to take aim at some-thing with a singing bow, but it was all happening very far away. There would be no chance to talk to Arang until the games were over.

As she cut through the tight-rooted turf and dug into the earth, she worried about him. She hoped they weren't forcing him to drink more horse blood or, worse yet, tattooing him.

By the time it was almost dark, her hands were scraped and bleeding but she had made a hole in the turf roughly the size of the tent. Timak inspected her work and turned away with a grudging grunt of approval. "Tomorrow you make it deeper," she said, but when it came time to hand around the food, she gave Marrah a big-ger portion than usual.

After the evening meal, they began to wait for Vlahan. As usual, Timak busied herself with sewing, Hiknak braided hemp, and Marrah picked thorns out of balls of unwashed wool. It was cold outside so they put more dried dung on the fire, and a pleasant dried-grass scent filled the tent. If Marrah hadn't known that Vlahan would be coming home drunk, she would have felt almost cozy sitting there probing the greasy wool while Timak droned on about people she didn't know and gossip she hardly understood.

It grew later and later and still Vlahan didn't appear. Over on the other side of camp, the drums went on beating. Hiknak began to nod over her rope, Timak took a furtive nap, and Marrah could hardly keep her eyes open. Just when they had all resigned themselves to another endless wait, Vlahan suddenly pushed aside the tent flap, letting in a gust of cold air. His face was as red as his beard, but as soon as he spoke Marrah could tell he wasn't drunk.

"Go to bed," he commanded, waving impatiently at the three women. Marrah scrambled to her feet and headed for Hiknak's pallet, sure he'd come after her and force her into his bed, but instead he sat down by the fire. Hiknak made room for her and they lay back to back under the blankets, waiting, but nothing happened. Vlahan just kept sitting by the fire. From time to time a strange expression crossed his face. He looked deeply satisfied about something, but perhaps that was only an illusion created by the flickering shadows.

When Marrah finally realized that he wasn't going to drag her out of bed and force her to have sex with him, she went to sleep. Later, just before dawn, she woke. The fire had gone out, but he was still sitting in the same place.

## CHAPTER NINETEEN

W hen Marrah woke a second time, Vlahan was lying on his own pallet with his face turned toward the wall, Timak was snoring, and Hiknak was sound asleep, curled in a warm circle. She got up carefully so as not to wake them, draped her shawl around her head, and went outside to find the ground sprinkled with snow. The eastern sky was red, and the tall grass looked cold and heavy. The great herd was only a collection of dark shadows, but she could hear the cows and milk mares making the low, rumbling noises that meant their udders were full and would soon need tending to.

She knelt beside the fire pit, blew on the banked coals, and fed them with bits of straw until they sprang to life. Carefully she piled little chips of dung on the flames and then larger ones. Around her, other women were doing the same thing; the crisp air of the steppes was beginning to fill with the smell of smoke and roasted meat. The flames licked at the dry fuel, and a small line of sparks rose straight up like a thread of dyed wool. Marrah sat back on her heels and wondered how long it would be before Timak woke up and came out to set her at digging the tent hole again. The ground didn't look frozen, but it was clear that yesterday had been none too early to begin. Winter had definitely arrived.

She stared at the melting snow and thought of the big storms that would soon sweep down from the north. Where would she be when the drifts began to pile up? She'd better be back in Shara, sitting beside the charcoal brazier in the Temple of Children's Dreams, telling the story of her adventures to her grandmother, because if she was trapped in the same tent with Vlahan all winter, she'd do something desperate. Perhaps today she'd be able to talk to Arang or get a message to Stavan. All they needed was a plan that would give them a head start before they were missed.

She was trying to put such a plan together when she heard a terrible shriek. She jumped to her feet and looked around for the source of the noise, but all she could see were lopsided brown tents. There was another shriek, followed by still another. Suddenly, the whole camp exploded into life around her: people threw open the flaps of their tents and staggered out half asleep; the women who were already up dropped their milk buckets, threw their food baskets to the ground, grabbed their children, and began to wail. Babies howled, dogs barked, warriors swarmed around half dressed, clutching spears and daggers. Thinking the camp was under attack, she looked around for something to defend herself with, but there was nothing in sight except a collapsible leather water bucket and a bit of frayed rope.

"Ai! ai! ai!" a familiar voice cried. Marrah spun around and saw Timak standing outside the tent with her hair unbraided and flying in all directions. In one hand Timak held her best shawl, and as Marrah watched in disbelief, she began to bite and rip it into shreds. Behind her, Vlahan stood with his arms folded across his chest, watching the whole performance impassively, while Hiknak peeked cautiously around the edge of the tent flap as if she knew what was going on but didn't want to be part of it.

"What's that terrible noise?" Marrah cried, pointing in the direction of the shrieking, but Timak just went on ripping up her shawl and Vlahan went on staring. By now, Hiknak had disappeared entirely, and as for their near neighbors, every last man, woman, and child appeared to have gone crazy. She could see other women tearing their clothing; some were smearing themselves with ashes and mud, and several of the older ones had fallen to the ground and were rolling about in what looked like convulsions. Most of the men were no longer running. They'd frozen in place expectantly, spears in hand, as if they were waiting for something.

The wailing of the women grew louder, but over it all the horrible noise Marrah had first heard rippled back and forth like the call of a strangled bird, coming closer and closer. Suddenly she saw an incredible sight: Zulike, Zuhan's wife, was running from tent to tent. She was barefoot and wore a torn shift. Every time she came to a new group of people, she would fall to her knees, stretch out her arms, and beg for something, but whatever it was, the people always refused her. A man—but if no man was present, a woman or even a child—would walk up to her and kick her, knocking her over. When that happened, Zulike would pick herself up, make the horrible sound, and run on to the next tent, where the same thing would happen all over again.

Marrah watched her progress with an equal mixture of repulsion and fascination. What kind of grotesque ritual was this? It looked as if Zulike was pleading for her life, but what could she have possibly done to get herself in so much trouble? Had she betrayed Zuhan? Not very likely at her age, but still you never knew. Had she taken some young warrior for a partner? If she had, more power to her. Marrah didn't like Zulike much, but she liked Zuhan even less. Give old Zulike another chance, she thought. Spare her life. But the Hansi just went on kicking her, knocking her over, and listening to her scream.

The bizarre ceremony was repeated time and time again. Finally Zulike arrived at Vlahan's tent, the last in the camp. Her knees were scraped, and her hair was full of straw and mud. Her nose ring and earrings had been jerked out, leaving bloody holes, and there were only pale bands of flesh where all her bracelets had been. Throwing herself to her knees, she groveled in front of Vlahan. "Take pity on me!" she cried. "I always thought of you as my son, always loved you the best." She crawled forward. "Vlahan the wise, Vlahan the merciful, take pity on old Zulike. I never cared that you were Zuhan's bastard or that your mother was a slave. I always thought you should be the one to rule the Hansi. Be merciful and spare me this disgrace."

Marrah felt slightly sick. It was horrible to see anyone—especially an older woman—so humiliated. She remembered how she too had pleaded with Vlahan and what it had gotten her. For the first time, she felt a sympathy for Zulike. May the Goddess spare her life, she prayed, and she thought of what Zulike might have been like if she'd lived in Shara: a grandmother, respected by everyone, and sitting on the city council instead of crawling in the mud.

Vlahan was silent for a long time. He just stood there, looking down at the old woman in a cold, thoughtful way. "Get up," he commanded at last.

The
Year
the
Horses
Came

343

Zulike rose to her feet and stood upright, swaying slightly from side to side with a dazed look on her face. Her gray hair hung in strings around her cheeks, and her eyes were bloodshot. She looked pathetic and a little frail, despite her hard, square chin and the muscles in her arms.

"Why aren't you dead yet?" Vlahan asked.

It was such a cruel, unexpected question that Marrah gasped, but everyone else, including Zulike, seemed to take it as perfectly normal.

"I've been a good wife," Zulike moaned in a small voice.

"Speak up."

"I said I've been a good wife."

Vlahan nodded. "Yes," he agreed. "That's true. Everyone knows your virtue has never been questioned. So why aren't you dead yet?"

Zulike began to tremble and bite her lips. "Because nobody would give me a blade."

"Why not?"

"They say I didn't watch Zuhan well enough, but what could I do? He was well last night—you saw him yourself. But this morning when I got up he was dead." She began to shriek again. "Give me my rights! I'm his first wife. I have a right to follow him to paradise! I'm the grandmother of the Heir! I won't be dragged to the Great Chief's grave like a common concubine! The law says I have the right to lie by his side. I know you poisoned Zuhan; everyone knows it! You couldn't be Great Chief because you're a bastard, so you decided to rule through that dark-skinned boy who doesn't look any more like Achan than a toad. Well, rule and be damned! All I want is my death, and the law says you owe it to me!"

Vlahan's face had become absolutely impassive at the mention of poison, but his eyes narrowed. There was something yellow in the depths of them, something flamelike and ugly. He motioned to two young warriors who were standing nearby. "Send the wife of Zuhan after her lord," he ordered.

"Wait!" Zulike screamed. "I want to kill myself. I demand the right to die by my own hand like a faithful wife! You can't strangle me like a slave!"

Paying no attention to her, the taller of the two warriors stepped forward and unstrung his bow so quickly that the string was still vibrating when he wrapped it around her neck. Zulike's eyes bulged and her mouth opened, but nothing came out. For a second the old woman and the warrior stood face to face like two lovers locked in some horrible embrace. Then he released her and she fell to the ground.

Marrah screamed, but no one heard her. The instant Zulike fell, a cry of joy and approval went up from the nomad women. Singing and clapping their hands, dozens of wives rushed forward in a flurry of brown shawls and long tunics. Some bent down and picked up Zulike's body while others danced around it making high-pitched warbling sounds. Their ash-smeared faces were crazed-looking and their heads were uncovered, but no one seemed to care.

> The Great Chief is dead
> and gone to paradise,

they chanted,

> and his good wife's gone after him.
> Send his slaves and his concubines,
> send a hundred horses.
> Let Zuhan ride in glory
> to the Palace of Han
> where the God Himself sits
> on His burning throne!

Passing Zulike's body from hand to hand, the singing women carried the dirty brown bundle away as Marrah stood looking after them in horror. She understood everything now: Zuhan was dead, and the nomads were about to send all his women after him. Vlahan ruled the Hansi, and Arang was in his power.

For a second she was so terrified she couldn't move. She saw the bowstring again, and Zulike's staring eyes, and heard the sound her body had made when it hit the ground, and she imagined what Dalish and Akoah would look like after the warriors finished with them. Fear crept up her legs and along her spine, turning her bones to water and her heart to ice. Putting her hands over her eyes, she turned away from the muddy spot where Zulike's body had lain.

Give in, the fear whispered. You'll never win against them. They have brute strength, and all you have are your wits. What good are wits against this wolf pack? Give in to Vlahan before he kills you too. Be a "good" Hansi woman; be an obedient wife.

At the thought of being a "good" Hansi woman, something snapped inside her. It was an odd sensation, like a wooden peg slipping into a hole, and where it came from was a mystery. I'd rather die! she thought. I'd rather go down fighting! I'm getting out of

The
Year
the
Horses
Came

345

here, and I'm taking Dalish and Akoah and the women of Shambah with me. Better we all die out on the steppes than leave even one woman behind!

For a moment she just stood there, amazed, wondering where this crazy, stubborn courage had come from. Gradually it dawned on her that it was her own. Goddess born and Goddess bred, she thought, and not about to give up.

She took her hands away from her eyes and looked at Vlahan, who was standing with his arms folded across his chest, staring at a large crowd of men who had gathered in a semicircle around him. She saw a number of familiar faces in the crowd, including Slehan's, but Stavan was nowhere in sight. Behind Vlahan, a dozen heavily armed warriors had taken up position, spears held menacingly. Marrah recognized most of them as Zuhan's former bodyguards. They were young and fierce-looking, all scarred veterans of a dozen battles, and all clearly loyal to Vlahan. There was no doubt who now held power in the camp.

Several moments of uneasy silence passed, broken only by an occasional low muttering from some warrior at the back of the throng. Then a trumpet sounded in the distance, and Changar appeared, leading two horses. One was Vlahan's black stallion, and the other was Zuhan's pale gelding. Arang sat on the back of the gelding, looking frightened. He was dressed in a white wool tunic, white leggings, and an embroidered cape with a tasseled hood. A small gold crown encircled his forehead, and a chain of wolf teeth and gold suns hung around his neck. In one hand he held Zuhan's horse-headed scepter and in the other a small ceremonial dagger.

But Arang and Changar didn't come alone. Around them, enclosing them in a sort of armed box, rode six more bodyguards, all stripped to the waist as if they were about to go to war. They bristled with spears and knives, and three of them had their bows strung and trained on the crowd.

When Arang saw Marrah, his face brightened a little and he started to say something to her, but Changar stopped him with a glance and he sunk back terrified. The bodyguards parted, making an armed aisle from Changar to Vlahan. Without so much as a nod at the crowd, Changar walked up the aisle and handed Vlahan the reins of the two horses. Then he bowed stiffly and stepped aside.

Vlahan put one hand on the stallion's back, leapt up, and sat for a moment looking out at the crowd. There was a silence thick enough to cut. Beneath it, somewhere out of sight, the threat of violence rumbled like distant thunder. "Behold your new Great Chief," Vlahan said, pointing to Arang. "Behold the son of the hero Achan, grandson of the great Zuhan, whom I have promised to guard faithfully until he comes of age. Let any man who disputes this boy's right to rule the Hansi fight me now in fair battle or hold his peace."

No one came forward to risk the wrath of Vlahan and the armed men who stood around him. Satisfied, he tossed the reins of Arang's horse back to Changar. "Lead the little chief back to his tent," he said.

Changar bowed and took Arang away, and the six mounted bodyguards went with them, bows still ready.

Vlahan turned back to the crowd. "Today we'll mourn the hero Zuhan in the customary way." He spoke in a low, level voice, saying more than Marrah had heard him say in all the time she'd lived in his tent. "All fires will be extinguished, and everyone will eat cold meat; we will dig the Great Chief's grave, gather his treasures, and round up his horses. Today and tonight Zuhan's body will lie in front of his tent for everyone to see, and Zulike, his peace-weaving wife, will lie in honor beside him. Tomorrow we will have the funeral games and the sacrifices, but this is the time of darkness when Zuhan's soul is wandering through hell on its way to paradise, and we must lament and pray to Choatk the Terrible, Great Chief of the Underworld."

The crowd began to stir, and Marrah saw Slehan and several other warriors exchange angry glances. Vlahan began to describe the funeral games, but she didn't wait to hear any more. Grabbing a handful of ashes from the fire, she smeared them on her face. Then she simply walked into the crowd and began to push the men aside. On any other day, she would have probably gotten a good box on the ear or worse, but today the warriors paid no attention to her. Thinking she was off to join the other women, they made way for her, grumbling a little but never taking their eyes off Vlahan.

As soon as she was clear of them, she began to run. No one called after her. No one ordered her back.

She'd never been to Zuhan's tent before, but she had no trouble finding it. Most Hansi tents had four poles but his had eight, and its white sides were covered with sun signs and stars. Zuhan himself welcomed her. They had laid him out on a pile of rugs with a spear in one hand and a dagger in the other. The dead man was wearing nothing but a leather loincloth and a white cape, but his body was decorated with war paint and chains of wolf teeth; gold suns and other adornments hung around his neck. He made a strange sight lying there dressed like a young warrior. They had put bundles of fresh-smelling herbs around him, but a strange bitter odor rose from his body. His arms were thin and muscular, but his chest was hollow, covered with grizzled tufts of hair, clan marks, and old, ugly scars. As for his face, it was like a mask—chalky white with blue sunken hollows where his eyes had been. But it was his lips that interested Marrah the most. Someone had obviously tried to compose his features and failed. Half his mouth was twisted in a death agony, and the tip of his tongue protruded slightly. He had clearly died a terrible death and had just as clearly been poisoned.

Behind him, six bodyguards stood with spears in their hands blocking the entrance to the tent. Marrah was relieved when she saw the armed men, because that meant Arang was probably inside. The guards looked at her without curiosity, but it was obvious they had no intention of letting her pass. One of them pointed his spear at her in a halfhearted fashion while the others passed around a water skin, which, from the look on their faces, might have contained something more than water.

She cupped her hands to her mouth. "Arang!" she called. "It's me, Marrah. Tell the guards to let me through."

At the sound of her voice, Arang immediately pulled aside the tent flap and stuck his head out. "Marrah, am I glad to see you! You can't imagine what's been going on!" He turned to the guards and ordered them to let her pass, and when they hesitated he ducked back inside, got the horse scepter, and pointed it at them with so much dignity that even she was impressed. His Hansi was perfect; he sounded like he'd been speaking it all his life, and it had the desired effect. Perhaps yesterday the guards would have taken orders only from Zuhan, but Zuhan was dead and Arang was the new Great Chief, at least in name. The moment they caught sight of the horse scepter, they waved her through with respectful bows.

As she passed them, she smelled the sweet-sour scent of *kersek*. So the drinking had begun already. What kind of shape would they and the other warriors be in by the time Zuhan was buried? She wondered if it would do any good to have Arang order the guards to saddle horses so they could escape, but no doubt if that had been possible he would have done it long ago. He might only be twelve, but he was nobody's fool.

To her surprise, Arang was the only person in the tent. Motioning for her to sit down on a pile of embroidered pillows, he sat beside her and tossed the horse scepter on the ground. He made a small, compact package with his legs drawn up under him, but he had grown a lot over the past few months. The boyishness was beginning to leave his face, and the tattoo scars gave him the battered look of a much older person. The constant practice with bows and spears had made him muscular and lean and the Great Chief's crown lent him dignity, but in the end he was still her little brother.

"What are we going to do!" he asked as soon as they were settled, as if, as always, she had all the answers.

"We're going to escape," she told him, and as she said the words she knew they were true. She started to tell him everything, beginning with the moment she woke to find Stavan bending over her and ending with Zulike's death, but something in his face stopped her. Again she looked around the tent, taking in the piles of rich blankets, the overflowing food baskets, the long tunics and shawls tossed carelessly on the floor, the horse masks and clay jars and bags of treasure, and again it struck her as strange that all of Zuhan's possessions were here except the most important ones: there were no weapons and no women.

"Where's Dalish? I thought she'd be here with you even if the others were somewhere else, but no doubt there are other tents where—"

"She's gone," Arang said quietly. There was no longer anything childish in his voice. "Vlahan's warriors came to take her and Akoah and the others away as soon as Zulike started screaming that Zuhan was dead. I think they're holding them prisoner in a tent somewhere near the place where they plan to dig his grave." He paused. "When Vlahan told me they'd all be strangled and I'd be given new women, I went after the bastard with my dagger. It was a crazy thing to do; he nearly broke my wrist tearing it out of my hand, but I don't care. It was well worth it, and at least I know he doesn't dare kill me. But he wanted to; I could see it in his eyes."

Stunned, Marrah stared at the discarded tunics and overturned baskets and wondered if their bad luck was ever going to stop. But Arang wasn't finished. He went right on talking as if everything he

The
Year
the
Horses
Came

349

was saying was all part of the same thought. "Have you ever made *kersek*, Marrah?"

She was so surprised by the banality of the question that it took her a moment to answer. "Why, of course." She looked distractedly at the deserted tent. "Keeping the warriors supplied with *kersek* is one of the main reasons women exist. But what's that got to do with Dalish and Akoah?"

"I'll explain later. Just tell me how it's done."

She could tell he was trying to get at something, but she didn't know what. Still, if he had any kind of plan at all, it was better than nothing, so she described how the women chewed the wild grains and spit them into leather bags filled with a little warm water and honey; how fresh mare's milk was poured in and the mixture allowed to sit by the fire or in the sun until it fermented. She was about to explain how the whole mess curdled into a kind of wet cheese if you left it too long, when Arang stopped her.

"Don't you put some kind of spice in it?"

Oh, yes. She'd forgotten that part. The women sometimes added things to the milk—fresh hemp buds or finely chopped mushrooms or even a strange green lily-like plant that made the *kersek* smell like soup, but that was never done until the last minute because the herbs turned black and slimy if they stayed in the milk too long. When there was a big festival, all the bags of *kersek* were put into the river to cool and then, just before they were needed, the women opened them and put in the herbs.

"That's all I needed to know." He settled back with a satisfied smile on his face. "My plan will work."

"What plan?" She looked at him, hoping against hope that he'd thought of something she'd overlooked.

"It's simple: we put the powder of invisibility in the *kersek*. The warriors drink it, and when they can't see us anymore, we all escape."

"Oh, Arang!" She was so disappointed that she could hardly speak. "Have you forgotten? Changar took the dried thunder and the powder of invisibility when he took my medicine bag. All I have left is the yellow stone the priestesses gave me, and what can that do against—" She stopped in mid-sentence. Arang had pulled two small leather pouches out from under one of the pillows and was dangling them in front of her nose.

"The charms!" She grabbed for them. "How in the name of the Goddess did you get them back from Changar!"

"I stole them," he said, and then he laughed the way he'd always laughed when he was up to no good. It was a proud little-boy honeycake-stealing sort of laugh. "You should see the expression on your face, Marrah. You look like a sheep who just ran into a tree. It wasn't so hard. The old fake dragged me into his tent to dress me and paint me up for that little scene with Vlahan, and I saw both bags lying in a corner on a pile of junk—which is probably what he thought they were. I took them when he wasn't looking. He'll never miss them." And he would have said more only Marrah grabbed him and gave him such a hug he pleaded for mercy instead. "Let go," he grumbled, "you're going to break my ribs." But he was laughing and she was laughing, and for a moment it seemed like the priestesses of Nar themselves were standing in Zuhan's tent.

"Help me find a ball of white wool," she cried, "so I can tell Stavan to get the horses ready. We won't just take Akoah and Dalish, we'll take the women of Shambah and all the slaves. We'll ride through Vlahan's warriors like the wind rides through the grass. We'll be invisible!"

"But for how long?" Arang asked.

That was a sobering thought. They stopped laughing and hunted around for a ball of white wool. Soon they found a whole basketful, which wasn't surprising since everything Zuhan wore had been white. Picking up a good-sized one, Marrah hurried out of the tent, but not before she and Arang both knelt and touched Earth for luck.

Her luck held. No one bothered her or asked her why she had strayed so far from Vlahan's tent. She passed through the camp as if she were already invisible, past the men who were sharpening their wooden hoes to dig Zuhan's grave and the women who were washing Zulike's body; past children who were playing at funeral by rubbing ashes on one another and babies who slept in the sun as calmly as if no Great Chief had ever been born or ever died. She even walked by Slehan, who was so absorbed in talking to another warrior he didn't look up. The dogs didn't bark, and the horses didn't whinny. There was too much going on for a woman to be noticed.

She thought she might have to go all the way to the herdboys' fires to find Stavan, but she should have known he would be trying to come to her. She found him sitting in the mud not more than five

The
Year
the
Horses
Came

351

hundred paces from Zuhan's tent. He was playing with a bit of horse-hair, and he didn't even look up when she dropped the ball of white wool at his feet as if by accident. Instead he giggled, picked up a handful of dust, and threw it into the air, and when it came down on him he sneezed. She had to admit he made a pretty impressive fool. Picking up the ball of wool, he smelled it, plucked off a bit, and began to wrap it around his finger. His tunic was in rags, and his face was black with ashes and tears.

Marrah looked at the tall grass, and he gave an almost invisible nod. There was no need to say anything.

Retrieving the wool, she continued to walk through the camp, staying where Stavan could see her. There had never been a better day for moving around unnoticed. Timak was laying out Zulike's body, Vlahan was consolidating his power, and no one else cared. When she was absolutely sure nobody was watching her, she simply walked into the tall grass without a backward glance.

A few minutes later she and Stavan were sitting on the ground behind a screen of high golden blades like two people marooned together in a basket. He had his arm around her, their foreheads were touching, and they were whispering furiously in Shambah, pausing every once in a while to listen. But there was nothing to alarm them: only the sound of chanting coming from the direction of Zulike's body and the steady thump of the funeral drums.

"*Kersek*," Marrah was saying, "powder of invisibility . . . Arang . . . stolen from Changar . . . funeral games . . . the warriors . . . all together in one place."

Stavan was nodding. Yes, he thought it just might work. Yes, he'd have the horses ready. But he didn't like the part about her putting the powder in the *kersek*. They argued a little more in quick, low voices, and finally he gave in. He'd let her put the powder in the *kersek*, and when the invisibility came, she'd give a great cry, and he'd ride the horses into the middle of the ceremony and they'd all escape.

The time had come to part. "I'll go first," he whispered, "and if anyone spots me, I'll lead them away from you. Wait awhile, my love; then keep low so no one can see you."

She crouched down and made herself small while he stood up until his head broke through to the sky. The sun flashed in his hair. Suddenly he started back and gave a loud cry.

"Be quiet!" she called to him in a low voice. "Are you crazy?" But there was a spear at his throat and three more at his chest, and before she could spring to her own feet, a second face was looking down at her.

"Good afternoon, wife of Vlahan," Changar said. He smiled a slow, wolflike smile. "Perhaps you'd like to explain to these warriors what you're doing in the tall grass with Zuhan's fool of a son?"

The
Year
the
Horses
Came

353

## CHAPTER TWENTY

Hail to the happy brides
who breathe the air of paradise.

TRADITIONAL HANSI SONG

Zuhan the Brave, Great Chief of the Hansi, Son of Han and Ruler of the Steppes, was dead, and his warriors and women were digging his grave in the cold mud with wooden hoes and antler picks. The sky had turned a sodden gray, and a cold wind was blowing from the north, howling like a wolf as it swept across the plain. The tall grasses bowed before the coming storm just as Zuhan's subjects had once bowed before him, but after tomorrow no one would ever bow to Zuhan again. He would lie for thousands of years under the grass, surrounded by the bones of his horses and the skeletons of his wife and slaves; his fine woolen garments would rot, his copper necklaces would turn green, the flesh would fall from his face, and the worms would eat his proud heart.

But the Hansi warriors had no sense of how short their Great Chief's eternity was going to be. They thought he was as immortal as the stars, so despite the snow flurries and biting wind, they worked furiously to prepare a worthy resting place for him. Some of the younger ones even got so hot digging they threw back their hoods or took off their woolen tunics altogether and worked bare-chested. They knelt or stood, scrabbling in the muddy earth, and as they worked, their women followed behind them, filling baskets with the soil and

355

dumping it in a big pile that would later be mounded over the finished grave. It was hard work, because every basket that was emptied had to be brought back filled with stones to line the floor and walls. Otherwise the mud would cave in on Zuhan, Han would refuse to accept him into paradise, and the Hansi would be shamed for all eternity.

Despite their labors, Zuhan's grave looked like a muddy hole as the day drew to a close, but when it was done it would be a symbol of royalty and power. Fifty horses would be killed, stuffed with straw, and staked out around the rim. One end of the huge rectangular chamber would be filled with Zuhan's treasures, since a Great Chief could not arrive in paradise empty-handed: weapons mostly—spears and daggers, singing bows, arrows, quivers, axes, and shields—but there would be baskets of bracelets and necklaces as well, some made of copper but most strung with animal teeth—wolf being the most highly prized—fine rugs too, and soft wool blankets, and even jars emblazoned with sun signs and filled with the jerked meat and dried fruit Zuhan and his household would need to sustain them on the long journey to the Heavenly Pastures.

When the treasures were all safely stowed in their proper places, Zuhan himself would be brought to his eternal resting place on a fur-covered sledge pulled by three black horses. Zulike would follow on a smaller sledge, and the two bodies would be lowered into the grave on ropes woven from white horsehair and dipped in blood. The warriors who had guarded Zuhan during his lifetime would lay him out on a white calfskin pallet stuffed with sweet-smelling straw and put his dagger in his right hand and his horse scepter in his left. Then Zulike would be laid at his feet, face down, so she wouldn't see paradise before him.

When the bodies were in place, the most devoted warriors would cut off their hair and throw it into the grave until Zuhan was covered in a blanket of devotion made of every color from gold to black. But before that, the grave would be filled with another offering. Changar and his assistants would stand on the rim, strangle Zuhan's concubines and slaves, and throw them into the tomb to share eternity with their master. That was quite usual, so usual that as the warriors dug into the cold ground they hardly thought about it. But there was to be an additional sacrifice at this funeral—actually, two additional sacrifices. One was Vlahan's younger wife, the pretty little savage from the forest lands who had been caught in the tall grass with Zuhan's idiot son. Since she was the aunt of the new Great Chief, not everyone approved of the fact that Vlahan had handed her over to

Changar. Vlahan had been angry, of course. What man wouldn't be? But most thought he should have killed her on the spot like a wronged husband was bound to do instead of making her part of the ceremony. Others said Vlahan could do anything he wanted to with this wife, who'd borne him no sons and wasn't even his first; while still others whispered that this was Vlahan's way of showing that he ruled the Hansi and not the little dark-haired boy who sat in Zuhan's tent claiming to be the son of Achan.

The sacrifice of Vlahan's wife was unusual enough, but it was the second extra sacrifice that caused the most whispering as the wooden hoes and antler picks bit into the dirt. Changar had proclaimed that Stavan the Fool was to share his father's grave as if he were a small child instead of a grown man, not because he'd gone into the tall grass with Vlahan's wife—a fool couldn't be punished for anything since he didn't know what he was doing—but for a much less acceptable reason. Changar claimed he had heard Lord Han Himself calling Stavan to paradise along with his father. Now girl babies were often sacrificed at a funeral, and sometimes even small boys if the dead man had many male children, but the grown son of a chief? Never, not in all the history of the Twenty Tribes. Crazy or not, a chief's son had certain rights.

When Slehan had seen Vlahan hand Stavan over to Changar, he had called his warriors and women together and ridden out of camp. Several Hansi warriors who had been particularly loyal to Zuhan left with him, and there was already talk of war. Worse yet, as the news spread, other subchiefs might join Slehan in rebellion. Slehan had reportedly said he would be ruled by the son of Achan but not by a bastard.

The coming sacrifice of Zuhan's idiot son had already set loose bad spirits. The horses were restless, as if they could smell violence and betrayal in the air. The cows and mares were hard to milk, and the sheep had all huddled together in a frightened flock. As the wind blew and the sky darkened, the warriors talked of war, the women whispered anxiously among themselves, and Zuhan's muddy grave grew deeper.

In the prison tent, Dalish, Akoah, and Marrah sat on a pile of rugs listening to the sound of the wind and the murmur of voices. Sometimes they could hear a pick scrape against a rock or the thud of stones being dumped into the pit, but except when the women came to bring them more food, they could see nothing of the outside world except the circle of gray sky that hung above the smoke hole.

"Will they strangle us?" Akoah whispered. Her eyes had the crazy, frightened look of a small animal caught in a trap. Marrah put her arm around her and tried to comfort her, but Akoah was trembling so hard her fear was contagious. Marrah felt Akoah's fear enter her mouth and lodge in her throat. She saw a bowstring vibrating in a warrior's hand, Zulike's fingers clawing at empty air, her body turning face down as it fell to the ground. Closing her eyes, she took a deep breath and forced herself to think of miracles instead: a storm that would scatter all the warriors and give them a chance to escape, a bolt of lightning that would burn Changar to a cinder, a stampede or a whirlwind or an enemy attack. If she gave in to the fear of death, it would overpower her and she'd go to the stake like a frightened sheep.

No matter how frightened I get, I have to keep acting as if there's something I can do, she thought. She drew Akoah closer. "No one's going to strangle you," she promised.

"But what if they do?" Akoah bit her lip, and tears formed in the corners of her eyes like two crystal pebbles. Outside, the wind was making a moaning sound, and sometimes a little chaff blew in under the bottom of the tent. Akoah shuddered and touched her neck with the tips of her fingers. "Will it hurt terribly?"

"No," Dalish said. "It's very quick." Marrah knew Dalish was lying. Being strangled wasn't painless at all. You'd have plenty of time to feel everything. What did you see at that last moment? Did the Goddess grant you a vision of some kind or did you die as blindly as you'd lived? She wanted to ask Dalish if anyone had ever survived strangling and come back to tell what the moment of death was like, but she didn't want to frighten Akoah any more than she was already frightened.

The red tassels were still swinging defiantly across Dalish's forehead, and her gaze was level. Dalish was brave—perhaps braver than she was. Again Marrah thought how easy it would be to give up and sit with her arms wrapped around her knees like Akoah, but there was Arang to think of, and Stavan. Arang was probably sitting in a warm tent eating a hot meal because Vlahan couldn't run the risk of hurting him in any way, but Stavan could have been severely beaten for all she knew. She thought of Changar's face looking down at her through the grass. She should have pulled Stavan's dagger out of its sheath and plunged it into his heart. She never should have let them take him alive. On the other hand, where there was life, there was the possibility of escape.

She held Akoah until she stopped shaking and wiped the tears from her eyes with the edge of her shawl. When she had calmed down, Marrah let go of her and turned to Dalish. It was time for the two of them to make a plan—not because a plan might work but because without one they would be as lost as Akoah. "Do you think Arang has enough power to stop the sacrifices?"

Dalish shrugged. "I'm not sure; I doubt it, but on the other hand maybe some of the more rebellious warriors would side with him if he tried. From what I've seen, Vlahan's universally disliked."

The two of them talked for a long time. After a while Akoah dozed, resting her head against the tent pole, but they stayed awake, creating impossible escapes and last-minute rescues. When they finally ran out of possibilities, they simply sat quietly, holding hands and looking at the fire. A sense of calm settled over Marrah. None of their plans had the remotest chance of working. Unless a miracle happened, they were going to die, but instead of frightening her as it had before, the thought of death brought her peace. She and Akoah and Dalish didn't believe in an afterlife like the nomads did, but they didn't believe in hell either. They might suffer a few moments of terrible pain as Changar strangled them, but then they would go back to the Mother. They would sleep in Her womb again, as peacefully as seeds or unborn children, and when their souls returned to earth, they'd be free of any memory of suffering.

She watched the shadows flickering across the walls of the tent. They reminded her of the dancing animals in the Caves of Nar. How long ago that day seemed! Perhaps next time I'll be reborn as a deer or a flower or a bird, she thought, and she imagined herself hovering above the Sea of Gray Waves looking down at Xori. Goodbye, Mother. Goodbye, dear friends. Goodbye, Uncle Seme. Goodbye, Great-Grandmother Ama. I'd always meant to come back to you, but now it looks as if I won't.

The shadows went on dancing, and Marrah went on watching them. Gradually her hand loosened and fell out of Dalish's, but Dalish, who had fallen asleep, didn't notice.

Outside on the steppes the nomad warriors were killing and gutting the fifty horses that would be stuffed and staked out around Zuhan's grave. Piles of bloody entrails lay steaming in the cold. Half a dozen women knelt in the mud, cutting the livers free and trimming the fat from the hearts. The horse guts would make a rich stew, one that would give the warriors strength to mourn Zuhan properly.

Not far away, the tomb builders were working by torchlight. It was snowing harder now, so several tents had been taken down and stretched over the hole to form a roof. Beneath the leather canopy, the stone walls of the grave were more than half finished. Women were already scrubbing out the burial chamber with ashes and cold water, while just over their heads young men were pounding stakes into the half-frozen ground. Each stake was a tent pole, donated at great sacrifice since oak was nearly as precious as gold. When the men were finished, the stakes would ring the tomb. There were thirteen in all: nine for Zuhan's Hansi slave girls; two for his concubines; one for Vlahan's unfaithful wife, and one—the strongest—for Stavan.

The young men thought a long time before they pounded in each stake. They had to leave enough room so Changar could stand between the sacrifice victim and the edge of the grave, but not so much that the body would have to be carried. When Stavan and the women were cut loose, they should fall gracefully into the Great Chief's tomb, not flop on the ground like cows butchered by some clumsy herdboy. The men inspected the possible sites from all angles. Changar was very particular, and no one wanted to offend him.


Marrah opened her eyes with a start to discover that light was pouring in through the smoke hole. Dalish and Akoah lay sleeping on either side of her, Akoah curled into a tight frightened ball, Dalish spread out comfortably with her head pillowed on her shawl. A thin layer of dry snow had blown in under one edge of the tent, and the fire had died down to nothing.

She sat up cautiously. Let Dalish and Akoah sleep. Today was no day to wake them early. She took a deep breath of cold air and exhaled. The smoke of her breath spiraled like a snake. Today I die, she thought, and she looked around the tent memorizing everything: the sun patterns on the rugs, the crudely thrown pots, the leather water skin that rested against one of the tent poles like an old dog. Life had never seemed so sweet before, or so precious. Even the stones in the fire pit looked beautiful. They lay at odd angles, each with a particular texture of its own. Some were cracked and some were streaked with soot and some lay pillowed in the soft gray ashes like islands. Why hadn't she taken more time to appreciate the beauty of ordinary things? She had let so much of life slip past unnoticed.

She was thinking of all the things she had always meant to do someday when she heard the familiar high-pitched warbling of the Hansi women. The singing seemed far away, but as she listened it drew closer.

"Dalish," she whispered.

Dalish sat up so quickly it was hard to believe she'd been asleep. "What is it?"

"Listen."

They listened as the singing grew louder. There were flutes, some small drums, copper finger cymbals, and something that sounded like a sort of tambourine. By now Akoah was awake too. She clutched Marrah's hand and stared at the tent flap.

"Are they coming for us?"

Dalish nodded.

"What are they singing?"

"A wedding song."

Akoah and Marrah were surprised. "A wedding song?" Akoah pulled her shawl around her shoulders and gripped Marrah's hand more tightly. "What wedding? What are you talking about?" But Dalish must have been right because the music wasn't funeral music at all. It was loud and joyful, and Marrah could easily imagine the women joining hands and dancing in circles the way they'd danced on the day they married her to Vlahan.

"Translate for us, Dalish."

Dalish was reluctant, but finally she did. "It's a traditional song the nomads sing only when a Great Chief dies. There are a lot of verses, but the chorus is always the same:

> "Hail to the happy brides
> who breathe the air of paradise.
> Rejoice, rejoice,
> soon you'll be with the gods.
>
> "Today is Han's day.
> Today is Zuhan's day.
> Today is the best day to die."

The
Year
the
Horses
Came

361

When Dalish came to the word "die," Akoah cried out and put her hands over her face, and Marrah felt the cold terror grip her again. The peace she had found earlier disappeared. It wasn't going to be easy to face death with any kind of dignity. Would she plead and scream like Zulike when she saw the bowstring? Would the last thing she saw be Changar's satisfied smile? She dug her fingernails into the palm of her hands and tried to push the fear somewhere where it wouldn't overwhelm her, but the voices kept coming closer.

"No day is a good day to die," she said defiantly, but there was no reply, and when she looked up, she saw Dalish looking back at her with wide, frightened eyes.

For a few seconds they stared, each looking for reassurance and neither finding it. Then all at once the singing stopped, the tent flap was jerked open, and five women stepped across the threshold carrying buckets of warm water and baskets heaped with white wedding garments. One was redheaded Timak, who looked particularly satisfied when she caught sight of Marrah. Hiknak walked a few paces behind her, looking down at the ground as an obedient concubine should. Marrah didn't know the other three, although she had seen them around the camp, but they were all big, chosen no doubt for their ability to handle terrified victims.

"Good morning," Timak said. She smiled, showing her filed teeth. It was only the second time Marrah had ever seen her smile, and the expression didn't become her. It gave her a leering air like a hungry wolf. "We've come to dress you for the ceremony." She gestured to the women to put down their baskets.

The sight of Timak made Marrah feel defiant again. "What if we don't cooperate?" She folded her arms across her chest and glared.

Timak shrugged. "Suit yourselves. There are armed guards outside who will be happy to strip you and dress you if you fight us." Since it was clear she was telling the truth, Marrah gave in. As Hiknak and one of the younger women stripped her and began to sponge her down, she stood in stony silence, glaring at Timak. Timak wasn't going to lay a hand on her. That was the price of her cooperation. Dalish also submitted silently, but Akoah screamed and shook so hard that two of the women sat on her, pinning her to the floor.

For a while everything was in an uproar as they wrestled Akoah out of one set of clothes and into another, and in that brief moment Marrah made one last attempt to save their lives. Hiknak hadn't once so much as looked her in the face, and for all Marrah knew she had sided with Timak against her, but she remembered how much the little concubine hated Vlahan, and that gave her an idea. Grabbing for her belt, she pulled off the pouch that contained the powder of invisibility and pressed it into Hiknak's hand so swiftly that not even Dalish saw her do it.

"Put this in the warriors' *kersek*!" she whispered.

She had no time to explain, no time to be sure Hiknak had understood. Akoah stopped screaming, and Timak rose to her feet. She looked at Hiknak suspiciously. "What's taking you so long? Get that slut dressed, or we'll miss the start of the ceremony."

"Yes, mistress." Hiknak knelt at Marrah's feet and began to tie on her white leather boots. Not a word or a look of acknowledgment passed between them. Once Marrah caught Hiknak's eye, but Hiknak only looked at her blankly as if she'd never seen her before. The packet was nowhere in sight, so presumably she'd slipped it into her robe, but there was no way to know if Hiknak had the slightest intention of doing what she'd begged her to do. Why should she? She wasn't in danger of being strangled for many years yet, and now that Vlahan was Great Chief in all but name perhaps her life would improve.

Bitterly disappointed, Marrah let Hiknak finish dressing her. It had been a stupid idea. She was lucky Hiknak hadn't raised an alarm. On the other hand, it really wouldn't have mattered. Even Timak couldn't do much to her at this point.

When the three "brides" were washed and dressed, the women picked up their old garments and tossed them into the fire pit. The fire was out, but no doubt they intended to come back later and burn them. Gathering up the buckets and baskets, they left as quickly as they'd come. Even Timak didn't take time to gloat. She just turned her back and walked away as if the three of them were already dead.

As soon as the tent flap closed, Marrah knelt down, pulled her old belt out of the fire pit, and wrapped it around her waist. It was the only thing that had come all the way from Shara with her, and she wanted to die with it on. She opened the drawstrings of her pocket, took out the Tear of Compassion, and tied it around her neck where it belonged. The butterfly looked pale in the dim light, but the stone was as golden as ever.

"Is that magic?" Akoah cried.

"Yes," Marrah said, "but it won't—"

She had no time to tell Akoah that the charm wouldn't save them, because at that very instant the armed guards came into the tent to tell them to prepare themselves for death. There were seven, all young warriors stripped to the waist despite the cold, and when Akoah saw the skulls painted on their chests and the black spears in their hands she went crazy with fear. Falling to her knees, she began to scream and cry and beg for her life. It was terribly unnerving, but Marrah couldn't blame her. She wanted to scream and cry herself, but pride held her back.

The guards pulled Akoah to her feet, tied her hands, and dragged her out of the tent. Then they came back for Dalish, who went like a queen with her head held high. When they returned for Marrah, they found her standing quietly in the empty tent with her eyes closed and her fingertips pressed together in the sign of the Goddess. They pried her hands apart roughly and tied them behind her back. She could have resisted, but she didn't.

If I have to die, let me die like a priestess, she thought. Let me die doing harm to no one.

One of the warriors shoved a spear tip between her shoulder blades and prodded her toward the open tent flap, and Marrah stepped out into the sunlight. It had snowed heavily overnight, and the whole world was white. Snow lay on the tall grass, bending it into strange shapes. The mound of earth that would be piled over Zuhan's grave was as smooth as a loaf of uncooked bread, and the flat horizon behind it glittered like the edge of a knife. In the pale blue sky a few long clouds curled before the wind, taking on scarflike shapes.

Marrah blinked and stopped for a moment, almost blinded by the brilliance, but the warrior prodded her forward. The snow made a faint squeaking sound under her boots. To her left a dead horse had been stuffed with grass and stuck on a stick like a child's treat. Its short black mane was gaily braided with brightly dyed bits of wool and its mouth was open as if it were about to whinny, but the beast's eyes were glassy and dead. To the left of the horse was another dead horse and beyond it still another and another, set in a great circle around Zuhan's grave. Inside the circle, the whole tribe had gathered, men on one side, women on the other. The warriors' brown tunics and leggings were ripped and smeared with ashes, but they seemed to be in a good mood. Skins of kersek were passing from hand to hand, and whole families of women were busy bringing more. Somewhere out of sight drums were beating, but Marrah was too short to see who was doing the drumming.

As she approached, the crowd opened up and made way for her. Curious faces stared at her. A young man with a wolf on his forehead smiled at her encouragingly, and an old woman in dangling earrings patted her on the shoulder. It wasn't that they were being cruel, at least not by their standards. They knew she was on her way to die, but as far as they were concerned her death was a public matter, so they crowded around her and pushed their faces into hers until she could hardly breathe. She was so close she could smell the cheese on their breath and see the chapped places where the wind of the steppes had burned their cheeks. A young woman held up a red-faced, squalling baby, and she realized she was being asked to bless the child. Somehow she'd become an object of veneration. It was unnerving.

"Take the child away," she pleaded, but she was so upset she spoke in Shambah. The young mother smiled, thinking no doubt that Marrah had given a blessing to the baby, poor thing.

More curious faces, more pats on the head and shoulder. Now she could see the drummers, sitting on a blanket with their drums between their knees. Their faces had been painted red and black, and their fingers were striped with yellow. As they drummed their hands flew like birds and they leaned back with half-closed eyes, already hypnotized by their own music. Sometimes one of them would reach out and shake a string of shells or small copper bells, and the crowd would break into song. Mostly it seemed to be about Zuhan and how great a chief he had been, but once Marrah was positive she heard Arang's name.

Every time she took a step, the drums got louder. Suddenly the crowd parted, and she saw Zuhan's grave gaping in the mud like an open mouth. The hole was twenty paces long, twelve paces wide, and four times as deep as a man was tall, lined with white stones. Around the rim, stakes stood at regular intervals like the posts of a half-finished fence, each carved from stout oak and topped by bunches of eagle feathers and bright red banners. The banners snapped gaily in the wind, but there was only horror beneath them. Two of the stakes held Dalish and Akoah, tied hand and foot like pigs trussed for slaughter. A third held Stavan.

The nomads had stripped him down to his loincloth, painted sun designs on him, and gagged him so he couldn't cry out, but they'd left on his boots and draped a cloak of fox pelts around him so he wouldn't freeze. He must have put up a struggle because his left cheek was badly bruised, his lip was split, and his hair was matted with dried blood.

For a moment Marrah just stood there letting the horror of the sight sink in; then she started screaming. In the end, that was how they took her to her own stake, screaming and fighting them every step of the way.

"You can't kill him!" she shouted. "He's Zuhan's son! Let him go, you murdering scum! Let all of us go! This is Vlahan's work! Vlahan killed Zuhan! I'm speaking the truth! This is a plot; this is—"

They silenced her by jamming a wad of wool in her mouth, but she went on struggling, bruising her wrists on the leather thongs as she fought to free herself even though she knew it was hopeless. To her right, Dalish was staring straight ahead, her face twisted with grief. She too wore a gag. They hadn't gagged Akoah, but then they hadn't needed to. The little sailor had fainted; in fact, if she hadn't been tied to her stake, she would already have fallen forward into the grave. As for Stavan, Marrah couldn't see much of his face, but the look he was giving her made her wild with hatred for the men who had tied him to the stake. She looked at the nomad warriors and thought she would die hating them, and the Goddess would understand and forgive her.

She was just imagining how much satisfaction their deaths would give her when she heard a high-pitched wailing and Changar appeared, leading nine women tied together at the necks like a string of horses. The diviner was an impressive sight, cloaked from head to foot in wolf pelts, his face dusted with ocher, his eyes outlined in white, his hands painted blood red. As he twitched the rope, urging the frightened women forward, he sang a fierce song about the beautiful death Zuhan's slave girls were about to die, and the warriors all answered in a chorus, banging the butts of their spears on the ground.

The singing and pounding seemed to terrify the poor women even more. Clutching at each other, they wept and begged for mercy, but no one paid any attention to them. The youngest was a Tcvali girl of about twelve, the oldest a Hansi woman well into middle age, but neither age nor beauty was going to save them and the crowd knew it.

Marrah felt sorry for them. They were all going to die, she and Dalish and Akoah and Stavan and the slaves, but to die without courage, to die trembling and screaming like a trapped rabbit, was particularly horrible. She wished she had some way of telling them that the Goddess was merciful and they wouldn't suffer long, but there was nothing she could do but stand by in silence and watch them go crazy with fear.

At the sight of the waiting stakes, the youngest slave—a plump, dark-haired Tcvali—fell to her knees, dragging the others down with her. For a few moments, the women clung together in the dirty snow in a clumsy heap, calling on Zulike to help them, but—as Marrah well knew—Zulike was long beyond helping anyone.

At the sound of Zulike's name, Changar stopped and turned around. For a moment he stood with his hands on his hips, looking down at the women with a slightly disgusted expression on his face, as if to say, Why are you females making so much trouble? Then he tossed the rope to the guards and indicated with a wave of his hand that they should pull the slaves to their feet and tie them to the stakes. Soon the nine women were bound and gagged and had taken their places around Zuhan's tomb.

As soon as Changar was satisfied that they weren't going to cause any more trouble, he pointed to the drummers, who took up the beat twice as fast as before. Again the crowd parted, forming a long aisle, men on one side, women on the other. In the distance, Marrah saw three black horses plodding slowly through the tall grasses. At first they were only formless blotches on the horizon, coming from a great distance like the dark clouds of an approaching storm, but as they drew closer, she could see they were pulling Zuhan's funeral sledge. Behind Zuhan, Zulike rode in lesser state, dragged toward the grave by two brown mares.

Even in death, the Great Chief had bodyguards. There were more than a dozen, all strong young warriors with painted faces, filed teeth, and clanking copper ornaments. They rode in single file on the best horses the tribe possessed, wearing splendid red hoods that stood out against the pale sky like tongues of flame. Each held a long spear or a dagger ready, as if death itself might stage a surprise attack at the last minute.

But they were nothing compared to Vlahan. Dressed all in white, he rode Zuhan's pale gelding with the air of a man who had triumphed over everything worth triumphing over. His head was bare and his face smeared with ashes, but his eyes were so cold and arrogant that even the drummers paused and stared in awe as he passed. Marrah expected to see Arang riding behind him, but there was no one else, only an aisle of crushed grass to show where the horses had passed. She looked down the aisle and saw the lopsided Hansi tents strewn along the edge of the river. Pale gray smoke rose from one or two cooking fires. Arang had been left behind.

Even she had to admit it was a stroke of genius. The new Great Chief of the Hansi was back in camp with the old people and the

The
Year
the
Horses
Came

367

newborn babies. Vlahan wouldn't have to worry about him screaming when he saw his sister tied to the stake or doing something desperate when he saw Changar slipping the bowstring around her neck.
It was the new chief's guardian who was bringing the old chief to his
grave, and not just any guardian but the illegitimate son of Zuhan
himself, dressed like a god and as proud as one. Anyone could see at
a glance who really ruled the Twenty Tribes.

When Vlahan reached the tomb, he dismounted and handed the
white gelding over to Changar, who killed and bled it with one quick
swipe of his dagger, but from the moment Marrah saw that Arang
wasn't going to be present she lost all hope and stopped caring. Let
Vlahan strut and Changar chant; let the warriors lower Zuhan and
Zulike into the tomb; let them kill half a dozen more horses and
drink blood from the skull cup; let them smoke hemp, drink kersek,
shoot at targets, throw their daggers, sing until they were hoarse,
drum until they were numb, and beat their spears on the ground
until the shafts split. She didn't belong to their world anymore. She
belonged to the Mother.

The day passed. The nomads sang, drank kersek, and sang some
more. The drums went on beating as the funeral games were played
out and the victors crowned. Changar recited an endless ballad about
Zuhan, and every man in the tribe added a verse. At midday there
was a feast of roasted mutton, and later bowls of horse-gut stew were
passed around by the women. As the warriors ate, the sky above
Zuhan's tomb clouded over and turned the color of curdled milk. All
the while, Marrah stood proudly. Sometimes she looked at Dalish,
sometimes at Stavan, sometimes at Akoah, and sometimes at the
slaves, but she no longer struggled. At first she felt brave but gradually the fear of death rose in her again, crushing her chest and making her mouth drier than the wool gag. The moment when the
sacrifices would be made was drawing closer. Would it come now as
Changar stepped forward and draped a long string of wolf teeth
around Vlahan's neck? Would it come as the drummers began to
pound out a different beat?

Suddenly, she knew *exactly* when she and the others would be sacrificed: not while the drums beat or the men danced but at sunset.
The nomads believed that at sunset Han went back to paradise to
round up the stars and drive them out into the night sky. When Han
went, she and Stavan and Dalish and Akoah and the slaves would go
with him.

As if mocking her fear, a breeze sprang up, blowing the clouds south. The hems of the nomad's capes trembled, and the tails of the dead horses staked around Zuhan's grave fluttered. The wind was so strong it picked up dry snow from the top of the mound and scattered it like sand. Marrah closed her eyes as the snow blew into her face, stinging her cheeks. When she opened them again, the sky overhead was clearing fast. Soon the sun appeared, low and heavy, hanging just above the western horizon.

At the sight of the setting sun, the drummers suddenly stopped, and for a few moments everyone froze in place. Then Changar turned and bowed to the sun. "Great Han," he cried, "we salute you!"

"Great Han," the warriors responded, "we praise you!"

"God of our fathers . . ."

"And of our grandfathers . . ."

"Confounder of our enemies, who bathes the world in His blood . . ."

"At sunrise and sunset . . ."

Sure enough, the sky was turning blood red even as they spoke. Marrah watched in horrified fascination as the sun sank lower and lower. Above the glowing ball, two long narrow clouds lay pointed at one another like dagger blades. Behind them, streaks of vermilion shot into the vast heavens above the steppes, fading to the color of molten gold as they traveled east.

Changar had lifted his ocher-stained hands over his head so the red light of the setting sun turned his palms redder still. "Take your servant Zuhan to paradise," he cried. Suddenly he threw back his head and howled like a wolf, and the nomads howled with him. The cry of the Hansi wolf pack rose above Zuhan's grave, as lonely and terrible as death itself. The sound turned Marrah's bones to ice, but she had only a few seconds to stand there shuddering at the unearthly noise. Before the last yelp was out of the warriors' mouths, Changar grabbed the nearest bow, bent it, and loosened the string in one easy motion. Wrapping the ends around his hands, he strode over to the little dark-haired Tcvali slave and strangled her as quickly and matter-of-factly as a cook wringing a bird's neck.

If Marrah could have screamed, she would have, but the gag choked her into silence. The crowd cheered, and Changar stepped aside and motioned for someone to cut the body loose. A warrior came forward, a tall man with black hair and a horse tattooed on his

The
Year
the
Horses
Came

369

right cheek. Marrah recognized him as the tribe's best tracker, a man named Iktahan. Iktahan drew out his dagger and cut the cords that bound the Tcvali slave to the stake. For an instant the dead woman stood upright, swaying a little. Then her body pitched forward and she fell into the grave, hitting the stone floor with a dull thud. She landed just to the right of Zulike and lay there in a heap with one arm draped across her face as if she were still begging for mercy.

"Happy bride!" Changar cried.

The drummers drummed, the crowd broke into the wedding song, and someone struck a pair of copper finger cymbals together. The nomad women linked arms and began to dance the circle dance they had performed at Marrah's wedding. Soon several small children were dancing with them.

As Changar moved on to the next victim, Marrah shut her eyes. She had seen enough. She felt sickened and completely powerless. They were all helpless; they could do nothing to defend themselves. They would all die, one by one, with Changar's bowstring around their necks.

But if her eyes had lids, her ears didn't. No matter how hard she tried, she couldn't shut out the sounds. The horrible wolf howls were repeated, and more bodies hit the stone floor of Zuhan's tomb. When she looked again, seven of the stakes that had held the slaves were empty. Stavan must have witnessed the murders because there were bloody marks on his chest where he had strained against the ropes. Dalish stood like a statue—perhaps she had put herself into some kind of trance—but poor Akoah was coming to.

Her eyelids fluttered. Slowly, she opened her eyes and lifted her head. Seven slaves were already down there with Zuhan, and Changar was about to send an eighth. As the diviner approached the next victim, Akoah realized what was happening and began to scream. The noise she made wasn't like anything Marrah had ever heard before: it was inhuman and terrible, and all the fear in the world was in it.

Changar stopped with his hands poised in midair and turned toward Akoah. He had clearly intended to strangle all nine slaves before he sacrificed the concubines, but her wailing annoyed him. Sparing the eighth slave for the moment, he made his way to the other side of the tomb. As he walked, the wind blew at his wolf pelts and tossed his gray hair back like a horse's mane. His white-rimmed eyes and blood-red face made him look like a predatory beast, but the expression on his face was a human one. He was irritated.

As soon as the crowd saw Changar move in Akoah's direction, they knew he had decided to sacrifice her early. The drummers took up a new rhythm, and the women stopped dancing and began to sing.

> Happy bride, happy bride,
> you'll breathe the air of paradise.
> Rejoice, rejoice!

But something was wrong. The song had a ragged edge; some of the women were off key, others seemed to have forgotten the words, and still others suddenly stopped singing. Perhaps it was the sight of Changar that made them stop. As he walked toward Akoah, he began to do strange things. First he hesitated; then, for no obvious reason, he stumbled. He steadied himself by catching hold of one of the empty stakes and stood for a moment looking puzzled. He passed his hand over his face and rubbed his eyes. Then Akoah screamed again, and he turned on her as a man might turn on a barking dog.

"Quiet!" he shouted, but poor Akoah was past taking orders from him or anyone else. At the sound of his voice she began to throw herself from side to side like a woman possessed, wailing and pleading at the top of her lungs. Her black hair swung in a snarl; her eyes were white and half rolled back in her head; her lips were bloody where she had bitten them in panic. Marrah had once seen a rabbit cornered by a fox; the rabbit had screamed like Akoah was screaming, only Akoah's screams were worse because they made sense.

"Don't let him kill me!" she begged. "Please, don't let him kill me! I don't want to die! Help me! Marrah, help me!"

When she heard Akoah calling to her, Marrah went half crazy. She pulled at the leather thongs until they cut her wrists, but the thongs held and her cries were lost in the wool gag. There was nothing she could do except watch.

In the end, Akoah's death was mercifully fast. Changar strode over to her, slipped the bowstring around her throat, and yanked his hands quickly in opposite directions. Akoah's head jerked back, and she made one last sound, small and high like a wounded bird. Then she quivered all over and slumped forward, and for a moment there was silence.

Marrah closed her eyes. She was crying, but she hardly noticed her own tears. The sickness and grief inside her were so great that

The
Year
the
Horses
Came

371

they swallowed everything, even her fear. May her soul find peace, she thought. May Akoah sleep with the Mother. She thought of Hoza and the Womb of Silence, the bones of her ancestors, and Mother Asha's blessing. Then she thought of Zuhan's muddy grave, and the terror took hold of her again. Soon she would hear the sound of Akoah's body falling on the stones, and shortly after that it would be her turn.

Determined at least to face her death straight on, she opened her eyes and discovered to her surprise that Changar had still not given the signal to cut Akoah loose. He was standing beside the corpse, looking at it in a strange way as if perhaps he had regrets. He scowled and blinked like some night animal that had ventured out in the daylight. A warrior was standing at a respectful distance, dagger in hand, waiting for the signal to send Akoah after the others, but the signal wasn't coming. A few moments passed and Changar continued to stand next to Akoah.

Something strange was going on.

The nomads began to whisper to one another. The drummers stopped drumming, the women stopped singing, the warriors stopped pounding their spears, and everyone waited for Changar to get on with the ceremony. Finally when it was clear that he wasn't going to give the signal, Vlahan rose to his feet. As he did so, his white cloak caught the wind and billowed out behind him like a sail. He looked fierce and commanding, every inch a Great Chief from the end of his red beard to the tips of his leather boots, but there was an odd expression in his eyes, one Marrah had never seen in all the weeks she had been forced to share his bed. It wasn't fear exactly, it was uncertainty. Vlahan blinked a few times and squinted like a man who had an irritating bit of sand under his eyelid. Possibly he was going to say something, but Marrah never learned what it was, because just as he opened his mouth, Changar bellowed like a gored bull. "Help!" he yelled.

At the sound of the word, the drummers threw aside their drums and leapt to their feet. For a few moments everything was chaos as warriors went for their daggers, women screamed, and children shrieked in terror. But before anyone could rush to Changar's aid, something amazing happened. The diviner turned his face toward the setting sun. For less time than it took a heart to beat, he stood there blinking up at the blood-red clouds. All at once, he threw his hands over his face.

"I can't see!" he howled. Taking a step backward, he stumbled. He grabbed for the stake to steady himself and caught the sleeve of Akoah's tunic. The material held; then there was a ripping sound, the sleeve slowly parted from the tunic, and he was left with a handful of white felt. He made another desperate grab for Akoah and missed. For a moment he tottered on the slippery edge of Zuhan's grave, his arms flailing in the air. Then he lost his footing and fell in.

After that everything happened at once. As Changar fell, other people started screaming that they too were blind and the whole crowd went mad. Women wailed, fell to their knees, and covered their faces with their shawls. Warriors shouted that the sun had gone out. When they tried to run, they stumbled into each other. In their panic they trampled their own wives and children and pushed one another into Zuhan's grave.

If Marrah hadn't been tied to the stake, she would have gone into the grave with them, but the leather thongs were strong and the knots held. She stood like a woman lashed to the mast of a small boat as the storm of violence raged around her, and as she watched the sightless nomads trampling one another, she understood: Hiknak had put the powder of invisibility into the *kersek*!

But that wasn't all Hiknak had done, for as Marrah stood there, unable to move, Hiknak herself appeared. Her blond hair was braided back out of her face, and she had thrown away her shawl and hiked up her tunic so she could run like a man. There was a look of triumph in her pale gray eyes—no, not triumph, ecstasy. Hiknak was a woman filled with the ecstasy of revenge. In her right hand, she held one of Vlahan's daggers. If Vlahan could have seen her, he might have screamed even louder than he was already screaming, for if ever a woman looked ready to send a man back to the Mother, it was Hiknak. The only thing that saved him was Zuhan's tomb. He was on one side of the pit, caught up in the panicked crowd, while Hiknak was on the other. If she could have got to him, he would have been a dead man, but she couldn't, so she used his dagger to cut Marrah free instead, and then she freed Stavan and Dalish.

As soon as they could move, they ran for their lives with Hiknak leading the way. By then the crowd on their side of the grave had thinned out, so it was possible to avoid the stumbling warriors. Later, Marrah was to marvel at how invisible they were at that moment. No one raised an alarm; no one came after them; not a head so much as turned in their direction as they fled into the tall grass.

The
Year
the
Horses
Came

373

Stavan grabbed a bow and a quiver from one of the fallen warriors, she picked up a dagger, and Dalish made off with a bow and a spear.

Hiknak had seen to everything. There were horses waiting for them, saddled and ready to ride; fast lean horses, some of the best in the herd. Stavan waited for Marrah, Hiknak, and Dalish to mount. Then he was up too, kicking his stallion in the ribs, and they were riding around the great herd with the cold wind biting their faces and the pounding of the hooves in their ears.

"Arang!" Marrah cried, and they turned toward the camp, scattering horses and cattle.

The sentries had been given *kersek* too. When they heard the sound of five riders coming up fast, they ran for safety, tripping over their own feet and bumping into the beasts they'd been set to guard. Only one had enough presence of mind to throw a spear in their direction, but it fell harmlessly, and they left him behind, screaming of betrayal and stabbing at thin air.

As the Hansi tents drew closer, Marrah saw that the camp was practically deserted. Only a few very old women milled around in panic, their brown shawls flapping in the wind. A few of the guards who had been left to watch over Arang were stumbling from tent to tent, trying to raise an alarm, but everyone of fighting age was blind. On the edge of camp, half a dozen fierce-looking warriors were riding in wild circles screaming threats and yelling war cries that would have frozen Marrah's blood if they'd been able to see her. As she and the others galloped past, two of the armed men collided with each other, and their horses reared, throwing them to the ground. Marrah thought of how hard the priestesses of Nar would have laughed at the sight.

Into the camp they rode, scattering fires and sending the old women scurrying for cover. Zuhan's tent was still pitched in the same place, and Arang was standing outside. He had on a warm cape, stout boots, and a pair of winter leggings. There were two bundles on the ground beside him, several bows, and three water skins neatly filled and tapped shut. Marrah couldn't help thinking he looked like a traveler waiting for a boat.

She pulled her horse to a stop, sprang off, and ran to him. Arang grabbed her, picked her up off the ground, and whirled her around. He might have the body of a dancer, but his arms were the arms of a warrior. As for his heart, it was still hers.

"You took long enough," he said.

Marrah laughed and cried, thinking of Akoah and how close she had come to escaping, thinking of her own joy at the sight of Arang and the prospect of freedom, and as she cried and laughed, Arang laughed and cried with her.

Stavan as usual was more practical. "What do you have in those bags?" he demanded.

"Food, flints, some warm clothes," Arang said.

"Good work. Come, mount up. We have some hard riding to do. Those warriors won't stay blind forever, and we have to get a good start on the trackers."

Hiknak had caught one of the guard's horses, a big roan with a broad rump and a dark mane. She led it forward, and Arang climbed on. He sat comfortably, holding the reins in one hand. Marrah saw that her brother was becoming a man, and she felt his strength being added to her own.

"The Goddess help me," Arang said, "but I've come to love these beasts."

"Then let's take them back to Shara with us!" she cried, and with that they wheeled around and rode out of the camp.


They rode all night. A little before dawn, it began to snow. By mid-morning the flakes were coming down hard and fast, filling in their tracks almost as fast as they made them. The snow drifted and blew; it rose on the wind and filled the great white sky; it transformed the steppes into an endless roll of soft linen; it erased every trace of their passing. When they finally stopped to rest, Stavan built them a snow cave, and they slept together as warm as if they'd been in one of the longhouses of Xori.


That night Marrah had a dream. She was walking in the woods. Suddenly she saw a white owl sitting on a dead branch. The owl blinked; her eyes were as yellow as gold. In their dark centers Marrah saw the whole world reflected: every rock and stone, every tree, every city, every person, every animal, everything, even the tiny birds that nested in the tall grasses and the insects that lived for only a day. Realizing the owl must be the Goddess, she knelt before Her.

"Where are you going?" the owl said.

"Home, dearest Mother."

The
Year
the
Horses
Came

375

"Then go with my blessing." The owl rose into the air. In Her talons She held a feathered cape like the one Marrah had worn on her coming-of-age day. The cape was woven of feathers of every color of the rainbow—colors no one had ever seen before, colors no one had even dreamed of.

The owl let the cape fall and Marrah caught it. As she touched the feathers, she felt a great sense of joy and well-being. All the pain of her captivity vanished like melting snow, and she knew they would reach Shara safely.

"Come," the owl called. "Hurry up, Marrah; there's no time to waste. Dinner's ready and your mother's waiting for you."

The great bird spread Her wings and flew west.

Marrah wrapped herself in the feathered cape and set out after Her.

*Historical Note*

The Goddess-worshiping cultures of Old Europe persisted for another two thousand years. By 2500 B.C. the conquest of the matristic, earth-centered societies was complete, at least on the surface, but the God of the Shining Sky never triumphed entirely. Even today both currents run through European culture.